The honor of your presence is requested
at the events of a lifetime....

KING'S RANSOM
by Diana Palmer

A PRINCE OF A GUY
by Kathleen Korbel

EVERY NIGHT AT EIGHT
by Marion Smith Collins

They're fit for a king....

DIANA PALMER

got her start in writing as a newspaper reporter and published her first romance novel for Silhouette Books in 1982. In 1993 she celebrated the publication of her fiftieth novel for Silhouette Books.

Affaire de Coeur lists her as one of the top ten romance authors in the country. Beloved by fans worldwide, Diana Palmer is the winner of five national Waldenbooks Romance Bestseller awards and two national B. Dalton Books Bestseller awards.

KATHLEEN KORBEL

is a four-time winner of the Romance Writers of America's RITA Award. She has also garnered *Romantic Times* Career Achievement awards in Category Romance and Suspense. Aside from romantic fiction, she has also written medical suspense thrillers as Eileen Dreyer.

Kathleen lives in St. Louis with her husband and two children. She devotes her time to enjoying her family, avoiding anyone who tries to explain the intricacies of the computer and searching for the fabled housecleaning fairies. She has had her best luck with her writing and with her family, without whom she couldn't have managed to achieve her career. She hasn't given up on those fairies, though.

MARION SMITH COLLINS

has written nonfiction for years and is the author of many contemporary romance novels, as well as one book of general fiction. She's a devoted traveler and has been to places as far-flung as Rome and Tahiti. Her favorite country for exploring, however, is the United States because, she says, it has everything. She has been a public relations director, and her love of art inspired her to run a combination gallery and restaurant for several years. In addition, she is a wife, mother and grandmother. She lives with her husband in Georgia.

Royal Weddings

Diana Palmer
Kathleen Korbel
Marion Smith Collins

Published by Silhouette Books
America's Publisher of Contemporary Romance

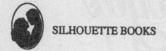 SILHOUETTE BOOKS

by Request

ROYAL WEDDINGS

Copyright © 1996 by Harlequin Books S.A.

ISBN 0-373-20129-X

The publisher acknowledges the copyright holders of the individual works as follows:
KING'S RANSOM
Copyright © 1993 by Diana Palmer
A PRINCE OF A GUY
Copyright © 1987 by Eileen Dreyer
EVERY NIGHT AT EIGHT
Copyright © 1992 by Marion Smith Collins

Printed in U.S.A.

CONTENTS

A Note from Diana Palmer

Dear Reader,

One of the first novels I ever read as a girl was *The Sheik* by E.M. Hull. I loved sheik (or sheikh, as it is sometimes spelled) books, and after I discovered romance novels, I wanted nothing more than to write a sheik book of my own.

Well, the way it turned out, my hero is definitely Arabic, but he doesn't have a desert tent to his name and he hasn't kidnapped the heroine. She is forced to live with him because he is being protected from potential assassins by government agents.

The government agent in this one is with the CIA. I used a little poetic license here, because actually it's the Secret Service that usually protects foreign dignitaries. But I already had Lang Patterson in place and I had established him as a CIA agent when I wrote this sequel to *Night of Love*. I have the greatest admiration for the CIA and the FBI. I always did, long before I became addicted to watching the exploits of fictional agents like Mulder, Scully and Skinner (my favorite!) in "The X-Files" on TV.

So in this book I got to do two of my favorite things—write a sheik book and root for the intelligence community. I hope I accomplished both without undue embarrassment to either. (Note to the CIA: I spent four years on a college campus waiting for you to recruit me, and you never showed up. Come on, guys, I'm only forty-nine, and I could lose weight, honest!)

Love,

Diana Palmer

KING'S RANSOM

Diana Palmer

Chapter One

It had been the longest three weeks of Brianna Scott's life. She had enough trouble as it was, with her twelve-year-old brother in a coma. Tad had been in the unconscious state for three years, since the tragic death of his and Brianna's parents in an automobile wreck.

Brianna's fingers stilled on the computer keys as she fed a letter into the machine's memory. She didn't like thinking about how much longer Tad might remain in the coma. His full name was Timothy Edward, but he'd been Tad since he was born. She was ten years his senior, and she'd taken to giving bottles and changing diapers immediately after he was born.

Their mother had never been in very good health, and Tad's birth had been a major setback for her. Brianna had been handy around the house, thank goodness, or the advent of a new child into the family might have been a disaster. With Brianna's help, her mother was able to regain her health and take proper care of the little boy.

"You look thoughtful," Meg Shannon Ryker mused, pausing beside Brianna's desk with Daphne, her husband's secretary.

"I was just thinking about something," Brianna said. She smiled up at the lovely blond woman who'd married the top executive of Ryker Air only two days ago. It had been a stormy courtship, and a long-standing one, but the marriage hadn't really surprised anyone. The way Steven Ryker and Meg looked at each other was enough to set off major fireworks.

"I'm taking Daphne out for lunch," Meg said. "Can you cope?"

"As long as *he* isn't around," the younger woman said grimly.

"Steven took *him* out for lunch," Meg assured her. "He'll probably go right back to his hotel afterward. After the shoot-out he endured a while ago, it's a miracle that he's still alive. Steve and I can't even take a honeymoon until we get this mess straightened out."

"Aha," Brianna said merrily. "You hate him, too, don't you?"

"Not really." Meg chuckled. "He's very nice."

"Not to me, he isn't," Brianna said shortly. "He looks at me."

"You're very pretty, you know," Meg said, noting Brianna's exquisite complexion and big blue eyes in their frame of short, straight black hair.

"That isn't what I meant," Brianna corrected. "He...glowers at me. Glares at me. Stares daggers at me. *That* sort of looking."

"I see. Well, you did throw a paperweight at him," Meg pointed out.

"He insulted me," the younger woman muttered. "It wasn't my fault! I love barbecue. Everybody I know loves barbecue. How was I supposed to know that all his colleagues who were also cabinet ministers from Saudi Mahara were Moslems and they can't eat pork?''

"We didn't tell you, so we get to share the blame," Daphne offered, smiling. "I'm sorry. I meant to, but we got busy."

"We've never been so busy before," Meg agreed. "This new contract for Saudi Mahara's jets has been one long headache, although I certainly don't blame Ahmed for it. I'm glad we got the job. It means a stable budget for the company for years to come."

"I know that," Brianna said silently. "But..." Her eyes bulged. "Isn't that Lang?" she asked.

"Oh, Lord, don't let Steven see him," Meg squeaked, because she'd spotted the tall, husky government agent, too. Lang was well built, in his early thirties and handsome enough to turn heads. He was a wild man, though, and Steven Ryker didn't appreciate his devil-may-care attitude.

"What is he doing here?" Daphne wondered.

Lang noticed the three women staring at him. He moved toward them with a grin on his face that was reflected in his dark eyes. He was impeccably dressed in a dark suit, white shirt and conservative tie. The conservative look was a bald-faced lie. Lang was a law unto himself.

"I know, you can't resist me," Lang said, nodding. "But you're a married woman, now, Meg. Control those urges. Your husband already offered my boss a bribe to send me to Antarctica on a fact-finding mission."

"Inside a whale, if I remember correctly," Meg mused.

"Why are you here?" Brianna asked worriedly.

He evaded her searching gaze. "You'll find out soon enough," he promised. "I'm waiting for your husband," he added to Meg.

"Steven didn't mention that you were expected," Daphne said curiously.

"I asked him not to. We're very cloak-and-dagger about this," he explained. "No leaks. No loose lips."

"It's something to do with Ahmed, isn't it?" Brianna asked coolly. "Go ahead, tell me it isn't."

"He's trying to avoid being assassinated," Lang reminded her. "He's a foreign dignitary and we're sworn to protect him. We can't let somebody take him out here in Wichita. Bad for our image," he added.

"Can't you send him home and let his own people protect him?" she asked plaintively.

"Not really. Two of the ringleaders of a terrorist squad that we captured before they did him harm got loose on the way back to Saudi Mahara. Their colleagues have organized a second coup attempt in as many weeks. This is going to be one touchy issue until we resolve it."

"But I thought Ahmed was being sent home, too," Meg began.

Lang shook his head. "Too risky now. We've come up with a way to keep his identity secret and to protect him and his king. We're installing a man impersonating the king in the Hilton with armed guards on the whole floor. He won't leave his room, and if they make a try for anybody, he'll be first. He's one of our men, of course," Lang added with a grimace. "Getting the royal treatment. Lobster tails every night. Full breakfast served in bed every morning. I volunteered, God knows I did, I'd never have minded the risk. But they thought I was too eager," he said with disgust.

The women tried not to laugh. He flexed his broad shoulders. "Anyway, I'm going to have my hands full. Speaking of full hands, guess who just walked in?"

Steven Ryker and Ahmed ben Rashid were about the same height, both dark haired and dark skinned, but Steven's eyes were a light silvery color and Ahmed's face showed his Arab heritage. He had a mustache, too, unlike Steven. He smiled at Meg and Daphne, but the look he gave Brianna could have fried an egg.

She gave it back with interest.

"Daphne and I were going to lunch," Meg began.

"Go ahead, darling," Steven said gently, pulling her close to kiss her. "I can't turn loose yet. We have some business to discuss."

"You aren't leaving?" Lang asked Brianna suddenly.

She hesitated a minute, startled by the question. "Well, no, not yet...."

"Good." He turned to Steven. "We'd better get to it."

"All right. See you tonight, sweet thing," Steven told Meg, and the smile they shared made Brianna faintly envious.

She turned her attention back to her work, while Daphne and Meg called their goodbyes and Lang went with Steven on into the executive office.

"Yes?" Brianna asked Ahmed with a glare. "Did you want something?"

"You are obnoxious even before you speak," he said curtly. "In my country, you would live on bread and water forever with such an attitude."

"I'd rather live on bread and water than sit at an elegant table eating lobster with *you*," she said with smiling malice.

"As if you would ever receive such an invitation from me," he returned with faint contempt. "I have my pick of women, you see."

"The Sheik of Araby," she said under her breath.

"I beg your pardon?"

She lifted her eyes to his. "I do hope you enjoy your trip back home when you go, and the sooner the better."

He gave her an indifferent appraisal. "A woman with a tongue such as yours should welcome even the most casual conversation from a man. I am certain that you are unmarried."

"Yes, I am," she agreed happily. "Did my happy expression give me away?"

He frowned. "Give you...away?"

"Did it betray my state of unbridled bliss?" She corrected.

He didn't seem to find her comment amusing. "Women in my country delight in marrying and producing children."

"Women in mine don't have to get married and have children if they don't want to, or wear a veil, or join a harem, or become the property of their husbands," she replied sweetly.

He glared at her. "You are insulting. Such an undisciplined tongue will one day cost you any possibility of making a good marriage."

"One can only hope," she agreed with a sigh.

He said something in his own language. It sounded musical and insulting, and Brianna glared at him.

"Uh, Ahmed, could we see you for a moment?" Lang called, trying to avert a disaster.

Ahmed glanced at him and back at Brianna. He was standing stiffly beside her desk and reluctant to leave the field. The woman made him angrier than anyone in this country ever had. The death threats, the assassination attempts were all insignificant beside making this woman treat him with the respect that was his due. Women usually fell over themselves trying to catch his eye, get his attention. This one only insulted him, making a joke of his status. He couldn't remember feeling such rage.

"Ahmed?" Lang called again, more insistently.

"Oh, very well," the Arab said irritably.

Chapter Two

Brianna didn't see Ahmed again that day. But the next morning, he walked past her desk and gave her a look so icy that it made her shiver. She returned it with cold dislike as he passed through the office where she did her secretarial duties. If she disliked him, the reverse was also patently obvious.

Brianna found the tall Arab something of a puzzle, as many of the other employees also did. He'd been introduced as Ahmed ben Rashid, a cabinet official of the Arab republic of Saudi Mahara. But he had the arrogance of an emperor and a temper to match. She wondered if Lang was somewhere close by. The CIA was much involved in his protection, and there was something going on. Ahmed had been in the office just yesterday. Why was he back today? Wasn't it a risk for him to be seen in public?

If the bodyguard he carried around with him was any indication of the esteem in which his country held him, the

United States government would do well to keep him safe, Brianna thought. But for her part, they could guard him on Alcatraz. She tried to imagine his regal presence sitting in a damp cell and her blue eyes twinkled with mischief.

"Nothing to do, Brianna?" Steven Ryker asked dryly from behind her.

She turned to face the president and CEO of Ryker Air, red faced. "Oh. Certainly, Mr. Ryker," she stammered. "I was just, uh, just, uh..."

"He doesn't like you any more than you like him," Steven pointed out. "The difference is that he hides it better."

"He doesn't, you know," she returned stiffly. "He called me names, he insulted me, he had me in tears...."

"You got even," he reminded her, smiling reflectively. "Do you have any idea how close you came to causing an international incident?"

"One can only dream, sir." She sighed, and smiled, pushing back her short black hair.

"You're hopeless," he murmured, laughing. "Stop glaring at him. He's one of our best customers."

"He's buying jet fighters to kill people with," she began.

He held up his hand. Since his marriage to pretty Meg, he'd mellowed just a little. "His government is," he countered.

"Same difference." She glared after the Arab's retreating back. "Why is he here again today?" she moaned.

"It's a secret," he said with an odd look. "But it has something to do with the fact that somebody blew up his jet last night."

Her eyes widened. "Who?"

"We don't know. Fortunately it was deserted at the time. The pilot was just on his way across the tarmac. But the government has decided to conceal him here until his people back home catch the two conspirators who escaped from custody. They think he may still be a target."

"Oh, brother," she said heavily, remembering all too well that Ahmed had almost been killed, and Steven and Meg and his private secretary along with him.

"The only good thing is that they don't know exactly what Ahmed looks like. The men who could have recognized him are in tight custody in Saudi Mahara."

"Are they going to take him to Washington to protect him?" she asked hopefully.

"Why would they want to do that?" a deep, amused voice asked.

Brianna and Steven turned to face the newcomer. It was dark, handsome Lang. The CIA man had saved Steven's new wife from would-be kidnappers a short while ago, but Steven was still irritated at him because of the manner in which he'd saved Meg. Steven thought Lang was reckless.

"If it isn't the secret pain-in-the-neck agent," he muttered. "Hello, Lang."

"We meet again," the other man said with a grin. "Hi, Brianna, how about lunch? Or would you rather skip all the picky stuff and just get married now?"

She laughed. "You'd run a mile if I said yes."

"Probably. You could try and see."

"No, thanks. I have work to do."

"Indeed you do," Lang said, taking her arm. "Come along, Ryker. You're in on this, too."

"I am, but I don't like it."

"We've found the perfect place to hide Ahmed," he said, hurrying them toward Steven's office. "It's great.

It's safe. It's the last place in the country they'd ever look for him."

"Where? Can I ask?" Brianna queried.

Lang paused at the closed door with his hand on the knob. "Why, in the bosom of his deadliest enemy, of course. Figuratively speaking," he added, and arched his eyebrows several times at Brianna.

She felt her jaw drop. He couldn't be thinking...meaning...

"Come in, and I'll explain."

Lang opened the door. Ahmed was standing at the window, his hands neatly folded behind him, his profile sharp and aristocratic as he gazed down on the parking lot below. He turned as Steven and Brianna came in with Lang, and his liquid black eyes made threatening flashes at her.

"Ahmed," Lang said brightly, "look who I've brought with me. It's your cousin by marriage, with whom you'll be living in your guise of a poor migrant cowboy."

Brianna pinched herself, but it didn't do any good. Ahmed glared viciously at the government man. Steven Ryker had to smother laughter.

"Stay with that she-cobra?" Ahmed asked haughtily. "I have told you already, I should rather live in the zoo!"

"That would suit me, too. You can stick him in the cage with the snakes!" Brianna said. She glared at Lang. "I live alone. I'm a single woman. I don't live with men. I don't like *him*. I especially would not live with him." She pointed at Ahmed.

"Everybody knows that. Which is why nobody will look for him at your apartment. And to make it even better, we're going to give him the credentials of a Mexican itinerant laborer, a cousin of yours from Chihuahua who just lost his job in Texas and needs a place to rest up and look for more work. Where better than with his favorite cousin?''

"I don't have any cousins from Chihuahua!"

"Now you do. Lucky girl," Lang added.

Brianna's fists clenched beside her neat gray skirt. She glared hotly at Ahmed's stiff face. "I don't even have male visitors. My reputation would be shot!"

"A relative can hardly be considered a blight on your reputation," Lang told her. "You'll be under constant surveillance, and you'll be safe. More important, so will he."

"No." She dared Lang to argue.

He moved closer, looking apologetic. "You have a twelve-year-old brother in a coma," he said quietly. "He's in intensive care in the local hospital and your insurance is about to run out. If the insurance stops, he'll have to be moved, and the specialized treatment he's been getting will also stop."

Brianna's heart climbed into her throat. "How did you find that out?"

"I'm a secret agent," Lang said calmly. "No secret is safe from me."

She drew in a rough breath, aware of Ahmed's curious stare. "What point are you trying to make?"

"If you help us, we help you. Ahmed's government is prepared to incur the expense of your brother's treatment, hospitalization and eventual rehabilitation if and when necessary."

It was almost too much to believe. Brianna moved to a chair and sat down heavily. All her worst fears were being brought into the light and vanquished. Tad was all she had left of her family. She adored him. It was like a miracle. Almost. Having to have Ahmed in her apartment was not going to be pleasant.

"Think about it," Lang advised. "Take a day or so to deliberate. Then we'll get back in touch. But we can't waste much time, you understand. If you refuse, we'll have to take other measures. That will negate our agreement to look after your brother."

Brianna winced. She couldn't refuse. Her brother's well-being was everything.

"If he moves in with me," she began, glancing uneasily at Ahmed, whose dark face was totally without expression, "how long will he have to stay?"

"Until we catch the two escaped assassins," Lang said. "We're pretty sure that they'll come here to Wichita and make a try for him. We'll be waiting if and when they do."

"What if they don't?"

"You'll have had the opportunity to learn a lot of Arab customs and your brother's bills will have been paid."

She lowered her eyes to the floor. She was going to regret this. Living with a man like Ahmed would be terrible!

"I'll be back in touch," Lang said when she was silent.

"I don't need to think about it," she said, raising her eyes. "I can't refuse. You knew it, too."

"I like to think I've planned well," he said, nodding.

"I won't be his personal slave," she added shortly, and her eyes shifted to Ahmed.

His dark eyebrows lifted. "God forbid," he said fervently. "I have very high standards for servants."

Her eyes narrowed. "And I have high ones for houseguests. I won't be imposed upon. You won't interrupt my routine."

He shrugged. "My requirements are few."

She didn't know why, but the way he said it made her uneasy. She had a suspicion that behind that tranquil expression, he was already plotting ways to upset her.

* * *

She was right. Ahmed moved in that very day, arriving with a virtual entourage of people carrying furniture, suitcases, trunks and other items.

Lang was with Ahmed, and two men accompanied him.

"This is great," Brianna said, glaring at all of them as she stood aside to let them into her apartment. Down the hall, doors had opened and two curious faces peered at the excitement. "Just great. Why didn't you hire one of those lighted signs to put outside the building and announce that you were moving him in here?"

Lang grinned. "Because we all look like poor working cowboys, don't you think?"

She stared at them intently. Well, they did rather look like working people. None of them was wearing a suit, including Lang, who was dressed in a pair of the most disreputable-looking, faded, tattered jeans she'd ever seen, with boots and a denim shirt. He didn't look like a secret agent at all.

Lang intercepted that curious look and grinned. "It's the latest thing in spy disguises. In this sleeve is a TV camera," he said, holding out a big, long arm, "and in the other is a miniature guided missile."

She glared at him. "What amazes me is that you still have a job at all!"

"Oh, they can't fire me," he said confidently. "I have an aunt in Congress and an uncle in the President's cabinet."

"I'm impressed," she said.

"So am I," he assured her. "I tell people about them all the time—especially my bosses in D.C."

"Why does that not surprise me?" she murmured.

He chuckled. Ahmed came in behind the rest of the load carriers and looked around disdainfully, with his lean hands palm down on his hips and a disgusted look on his mustachioed face.

"To think that I should come to this," he muttered haughtily. "By Allah, a tent would suit me better!"

"Not half as well as a narrow box would," Brianna began.

Lang dragged her off to one side. "Now, now," he soothed. "He's just not used to American apartments. You'll have to give him time to adjust. He'll get used to it."

"I won't," she assured him darkly. "Having to spend even a week with this man is going to require every thread of patience in my entire body!"

"There will be compensations," Lang promised. "Your brother's medical bills will all be paid, and you have to admit that it would be worth most any sacrifice to have that."

"It would," she had to agree. "You can't imagine how worried I've been—" She stopped and took a deep breath. "Tad's very special to me."

"Is that his name, Tad?"

"You know it's Timothy Edward," she mused, smiling knowingly at him. There wasn't much that got past Lang. "But I've always called him Tad for short."

"He's twelve, right?"

She nodded, averting her eyes. "He was so young when—" she paused "—when we lost our parents."

"Never give up hope," he said quietly. "I've seen miracles. Even the doctors admit that they still happen."

"I guess so. But after three years, hope dwindles."

He patted her on the shoulder awkwardly. "You might enjoy having our friend here for a while," he said. "He's not bad company."

She stared at him without blinking.

"Give it a chance, anyway," he coaxed. He glanced up at one of the men with him, who'd gone over the place with some sort of electronic equipment. "Anything?" he asked the man.

His colleague grinned and shook his head. "Clean as ice."

It was a small electronic instrument. Brianna glanced at Lang's sleeve with real curiosity.

"I was kidding about the TV camera." He chuckled. "And maybe exaggerating a little about the missile launcher."

"I saw a movie with one of those fiber-optic camera things," she remarked. "I was impressed."

"I'll wear one the very next time I come to visit," he promised with a wicked grin.

"What do I call him?" she asked with resignation.

"Ahmed?" He pulled out a brand-new ID card and a driver's license and passport and green card, all of which were intended to grace the pockets of her houseguest. "Pedro Rivera," he said. "Age thirty-four, native of Chihuahua, Mexico, occupation, farm laborer."

"Is he really going to work on a farm?" she asked hopefully. Her smile was evil.

"Ahmed?" Lang found that hilarious. "No, he's sort of between jobs, and he's depending on you to support him while he looks for work. He'll look very hard, we'll see to that. Applications in all major local businesses, and so forth."

"You could get him a job translating," she said.

"That would be tricky."

"Oh?" Her blue eyes were curious. "Why?"

"Well, he, uh, doesn't speak any Spanish."

Her face widened into a gleeful look of triumph. "None? None at all? How interesting! And he's supposed to be a Mexican laborer?"

"He said Spanish tastes terrible in his mouth and he refuses to learn it," Lang admitted with a grimace. "He speaks French quite well."

"Then why not let him pose as a Frenchman?"

"It would take too long to explain. Trust me," he added. "This will work. It's almost foolproof."

"Like the Titanic was almost unsinkable."

"Pessimist," he accused. "Think of the service you're doing your country!"

"By harboring a Middle Eastern cabinet official? How in the world does that help my country? I'm not Arabic," she added coldly, glaring toward Ahmed, who was still muttering about his inferior surroundings.

"His country's strategic location makes it of great value to us," Lang explained. "The Middle East is a lighted stick of dynamite right now, with all sorts of factions fighting for control. We depend on oil from that part of the world."

"We shouldn't," she pointed out.

"I realize that," he said. "But the fact remains that we depend on foreign oil and we have to have it or our technology goes down the drain. We have to keep a lot of people happy overseas to ensure our continued supply. Ahmed is one of the people we have to keep happy."

"I thought his country had a king. Why don't we have to worry about keeping *him* happy?"

"If we keep Ahmed happy, it will keep *him* happy," Lang assured her.

She shrugged. "Okay by me. But for my money," she added, "they could boil him in oil and serve him on a bed of lettuce."

"What a mind. And you look so sweet," Lang commented dryly.

"I was sweet, until you and the Valentino clone over there invaded my life!"

Lang had to bite back laughter. He didn't dare show amusement, especially since Ahmed had overheard her and was joining them, spoiling for trouble.

"I beg your pardon?" he asked Brianna, and his liquid black eyes made her feel intimidated.

"I said, I hope you'll be comfortable here," she lied. "I'm going to cook my specialty for supper tonight."

"Not barbecue, please," Lang said out of the side of his mouth.

She gave him a speaking look. "Actually, I thought something Spanish might be in order. Chili, for example," she added, smiling at Ahmed, "with jalapeño peppers and refried beans."

"Ah, spicy fare," Ahmed said, smiling back.

She hesitated. "You . . . like . . . spicy food?"

"Indeed," he agreed readily. "I have no taste for bland meat."

She'd have to remember to cook him some unsalted spaghetti.

"Are we through?" Lang called to his cohorts.

"You bet!" One tall man came lumbering up. "Everything's in place—bugs, surveillance equipment, the works."

"You're going to spy on us?" Brianna choked.

"They might as well," Ahmed said haughtily, giving her an appraisal that spoke volumes. "Or were you hoping they might have something to look at?"

She clenched her small fists at her sides and forced thoughts of paid medical bills to the front of her mind.

"I'd rather eat nails," she assured him.

"No doubt you could, with a mouth like that," he agreed politely.

Lang got between them. "He's your adored cousin," he told her. "You love him. You're going to take wonderful care of him because your country wants you to."

"Then why can't my country live with him?"

Lang shook his head. "Believe me, I'd like nothing better," he said with a diplomatic smile in Ahmed's direction. "But I have some leave coming and I thought I'd go down to Texas and visit my brother and his family."

"Why can't he—" she pointed at Ahmed "—go down there with you? There are plenty more Mexicans in Texas than you're likely to find in Wichita."

"Oh, I'd hate to deprive you two of the opportunity to get to know each other," he said, tongue-in-cheek. "Think what it will do for international relations. Besides, my plans may change."

They stared at each other coldly. Lang moved out of the line of fire, motioning to his colleagues.

"Well, here you are, then," he said. "Nice and comfy, make yourself right at home. I'm sure Brianna will take excellent care of you."

"Are you?" Ahmed asked. "And what of my bodyguards?"

"They'll be around. So will our people," Lang said somberly. "Just don't take any unnecessary risks or deliberately make yourself a target. Mostly we'd like you to stay in the apartment while Brianna's at work. If you go out, mention out loud that you're going, and where. We'll have you trailed."

"This is outrageous," Ahmed said curtly. "I see no reason why my own bodyguard could not..."

"Because you're on American soil," Lang reminded him. "In this country, we're responsible for the welfare of foreign nationals. So be kind to government workers and let us do our jobs. Okay?"

Ahmed shrugged. He moved toward the window and stood there, looking out as if he felt too confined already.

"And don't spend a lot of time in front of the window," Lang pleaded. "You make an excellent target. We can't possibly watch every window in every building in Wichita twenty-four hours a day."

Ahmed moved back into the room, nodding his consent.

Lang was the last of the group out the door. "Well, I'll leave you to it."

"One moment," Ahmed called. "Who is going to unpack for me? I have no servants here."

Lang hesitated. He glanced at Brianna, who took up a belligerent stance that no one with normal perception could mistake. "Uh, well, we'll see about that later. Good day."

"I've been stabbed in the back by my own government," Brianna muttered once he was gone, her blue eyes spitting at her houseguest. "Don't expect me to help you push the knife in farther. I am not a servant. I do not unpack for my guests. You have two perfectly good hands. You can unpack for yourself."

He linked his hands behind him and stared at her. The intensity of the look made her very nervous, and she retreated to the kitchen. "I'll start working on something to eat."

He lifted the edge of a hand-crocheted doily and examined it. "I prefer shrimp cocktail for an appetizer," he remarked absently. "And with Mexican fare, I should think an aged Bordeaux would suffice."

She came out of the kitchen and looked at him. "Now listen," she said. "I do not have a wine cellar. I drink an occasional glass of sweet sherry or white wine, but I know nothing about vintages or which color wine goes with which food."

"A minor impediment," he said with a careless wave of his hand. "You can learn."

"I have no wish to learn, much less do I want a staggering Arab to put to bed at night," she added, pleased at the shocked lift of his eyebrows. "Furthermore, my budget doesn't run to shrimp cocktail. I make a good salary, but after I pay the bills, there isn't a lot left over for fancy food. You'll have to make do with what I can provide."

He sighed wistfully. "From caviar and Brie to this," he said in a long-suffering tone. "*Mon Dieu,* how are the mighty fallen."

She went back into the kitchen, muttering under her breath about how she'd like to fell him herself.

Chapter Three

Brianna went to the hospital to see her brother that night, leaving Ahmed complaining about the meager channels she had on her cable TV. He didn't ask where she was going and she didn't volunteer any information.

She sat by Tad's bedside, as she did most nights, watching the face that was so much like her own. His eyes were closed. But when they had been open, they were as blue as hers. It seemed so long ago now that Tad had laughed and played like a normal boy his age. She missed his mischievous personality. He'd been such a happy child. Why, oh, why had this to happen?

Sometimes she felt old when she sat with him. He hadn't wasted too badly. They fed him intravenously, and the nurses turned him and checked his vital signs to make sure he was getting what he needed to support his young life. Once the doctor had talked to her about shutting off the life support, but Brianna couldn't do it. She couldn't give up hope, not after they told her that his brain seemed to be functioning with some normalcy. She refused to quit. The last thing her mother had said to her, in the wrecked car, bleeding and gasping for air, was, "Don't let Tad die." It had been an odd thing for her to say, but Brianna hadn't forgotten. Tad was in no pain, and Brianna had hope. She couldn't give up.

She talked to him. She held his frail hand and told him all about her life, about her job, about what she was doing. She didn't tell him about Ahmed. It was the first secret she'd kept, but it would do him no good to know. She talked about the apartment instead and how she was going to redecorate the guest room for him when he could come home.

By the time she got home, tired and dispirited, Ahmed was in bed. She went into her bedroom and, on an impulse, locked the door. She was too tired to worry about having a man in her apartment and soon fell asleep.

When she got home the next afternoon, after a particularly long day, she was totally unprepared for the fierce thudding sounds coming from her bedroom. It sounded as if the whole place were coming down around her ears.

She got a bigger surprise when she made it to the door and discovered that he was supervising four dark men in business suits, who were putting away his clothes. In the process, they had unearthed half of Brianna's possessions and had deposited them in chairs, on dressers, and in the hall.

She dropped her purse in the middle of the floor and gasped, "What are you doing?"

"Making room for my things," he said from his lounging position in her best easy chair. "These quarters are hopelessly inadequate. That closet in the guest room barely holds all my suits. The other things must go in here."

"This is my room!" she wailed. "You can't move my things out!"

"I am your tenant," he said comfortably. "You must accommodate me." He stopped and called out something in curt Arabic. The men stopped what they were doing. One spoke for the rest in what sounded like an apology. Ahmed rattled off some more Arabic and made a dismissing sign with his elegant hand. The men went back to work.

"Tell them to stop," she said. "They can't do this. I have to have clothes to wear to work. I can't wear them all rumpled...!"

"Your clothes are hardly of any concern to me," Ahmed said, surprised. "It is my own appearance which is of prime importance."

She counted a long way past ten. It didn't help. "You get those men out of my bedroom!" she shouted. "And you follow them right out the front door!"

He ignored her. So did the men.

"You can't take over my bedroom!" she tried again.

"The guest room is inadequate. The bed is lumpy. I have no intention of sleeping on a lumpy bed."

"Then why don't you call the President and ask if you can stay with him at the White House?" she raged.

He considered that for a moment. Then he shook his head. "It is a bad time," he said simply.

She glared at him. She glared at the men. Everybody ignored her. She picked up her purse and went into the living room. At least he hadn't tried rearranging that yet!

The men left and he came sauntering out in a white-and-gold caftan with silver threads. He looked more foreign than she'd ever seen him look in the princely regalia.

She hadn't considered before how alone the two of them were. The night before, she'd been to visit Tad and the sight of him had affected her much more deeply than before. She'd arrived late, and she hadn't seen Ahmed at breakfast. She'd gone straight in to work, thinking, silly her, that it was working out very well. Ha!

"You must do something about the television," he began. "There are too few channels. I want the French stations. Another thing, there is no fax machine here." He gestured impatiently. "How am I expected to attend to matters of state without a facsimile machine? I need a telephone line upon which these juvenile neighbors of yours are not always discussing—what do you call them?—arcade computer games!"

She just looked at him. He still didn't understand her budget. He made it more obvious by the day.

"And these... plants," he muttered, fingering the leaf of a philodendron with distaste and glaring at a trailing ivy plant, "they make the room feel like a rain forest. I prefer desert plants. They make me feel at home."

"I'll send right out for some stinging nettles and cactus," she assured him.

His black eyes narrowed. He had an arrogance of carriage that sometimes made him look dangerous. He was using it now. "You mock me. Few have dared that over the years."

"What will you do, cut off my head?" she challenged.

"I believe I... we... outlawed beheading some years ago." He waved his hand. "It was becoming politically incorrect with our allies. They found it offensive."

She couldn't believe he wasn't kidding. She moved toward the kitchen. "I'll fix something to eat." She turned. "No shrimp," she said. "And no wine. I had in mind some hot dogs."

"Hot . . . dogs?" His eyes bulged. "Hot dogs!"

"I like hot dogs with chili," she said.

"You served chili last night," he began.

"And I'm using up what was left tonight, on hot dogs." She sighed, exasperated, and frowned. "Don't you understand? I don't throw away food, ever! I stretch it. If I have leftover bread, I make bread pudding. I waste nothing! I can't afford to!"

It didn't register. "You have credit cards, surely."

"I owe up to the limit right now," she explained. "I just bought a new bed, for *my* bedroom," she emphasized, "because the mattress I was sleeping on was so lumpy. Until then, there wasn't a bed in the guest bedroom. Lucky you, not to have to sleep on the floor or the sofa!" she added sarcastically.

"I would never do such a thing," he said absently. "It would be unseemly. What is this limit? I have no limit."

"Why does that not surprise me?" she asked the ceiling.

He looked up to see who she was talking to, and she walked off and left him.

"I will have vichyssoise instead of hot dogs," he said. "I prefer cream and churned butter," he added with a smile.

She took down a boiler, filled it with water and put two hot dogs in it. She turned on the burner. Then she took a whole potato from the bin, walked into the living room and handed it to Ahmed.

"There you go. Instant vichyssoise. Just peel it and add cream and churned butter and a little water and simmer it for half an hour or so. Should be just delicious," she added, and walked right into her bedroom and closed the door with a snap.

* * *

When she came back, he was nowhere in sight. The potato was lying on the counter in the kitchen and the guest room door was closed. Her telephone had been unplugged and removed from the table by the sofa. She frowned, wondering what he could be up to.

Minutes later, he came back, carrying the telephone. He set it on the table and sprawled on the sofa.

"You might plug it back in," she suggested.

"Why?" he asked. "I unplugged it, after all, and plugged it into the bedroom wall. I am fatigued." He laid his head back on the sofa. "And very hungry. I had a hamburger from the corner diner for lunch."

He made it sound as if she should feel guilty about that. "With fries?" she asked cheerfully. "They make good fries."

"I loathe french fries," he informed her.

She'd mark that down mentally and soon she'd serve him some, she decided irritably.

She dished up her hot dog and added mustard and catsup to the bun she'd placed it in. "There's one left if you want it," she offered.

He glared at her.

She shrugged. "Starve yourself, then." She sat down at the table. Just as she lifted the hot dog to her mouth, the door buzzer sounded.

Ahmed got up and pressed the button beside the door. "Yes?" he asked haughtily.

There was a spate of Arabic, which he answered in kind, and pushed the door release.

"You can't do that! What if it's the people who are after you? They'll kill us all!" she raged.

He gave her a look. "It is my men," he told her. "Do you not think I know them by now?"

She started to argue, decided against it and went back to eating her hot dog.

Her peace didn't last long. An entourage of men in suits carrying boxes marched in, displaced her from the table with intimidating looks, and spread out a feast fit for a king for Ahmed. Then they left, without receiving a word of thanks.

He rubbed his hands together. "Ah," he said, inhaling the aromas of lobster and fresh sautéed vegetables and fresh-baked breads. He went into the kitchen, got a plate and utensils and proceeded to fill the plate. "You may join me if you wish," he added carelessly.

She glared at him and deliberately took a bite of the hot dog.

He hid a smile. Proud, he thought. It was an emotion of which he was not ignorant. She was no beauty, but she had spirit and compassion. Perhaps he would buy her a car when this charade was finished.

"You didn't thank your men for bringing all that to you," she remarked when she was washing up.

His face registered surprise. "Why should I? It is my fate to be served, and theirs to be my servants."

"You sound like a prophet quoting the Koran," she said. "I understood you to say that you were raised a Christian."

"I was," he agreed. "But I understand and respect the religion of my people," he added.

He turned his attention back to the exquisite cheese cake he was just finishing. "A most adequate meal," he said finally, getting up from the table to sprawl back on the sofa. The remains of his meal were strewn all over the table and the cabinet. Brianna, already tired, eyed the mess with distaste.

"You may clear away now," he said offhandedly.

"*I* may clear— *You* may clear!" she raged. "This is my home. Nobody orders me around in my own home! I'm not a servant!"

"You are my landlady," he said imperturbably. "And you can hardly say that I am not paying for my stay here."

That brought Tad back to mind. No, she thought, she couldn't say that. He wasn't paying, but his government was. She had to adapt to him. Perhaps it wouldn't be for much longer. The thought cheered her. She packed away the trash and washed up the few remaining dishes.

"I should like a cup of cappuccino," he murmured as he changed the channels on the television. "Sweet, but not too sweet."

"I don't know how to make cappuccino."

He turned, his expression one of amazement. "You cannot make cappuccino?"

He made it sound like a mortal sin. She shifted. "No." She hesitated. "What is it?"

"Cappuccino?"

"Yes."

"You are joking."

She shook her head. "Is it some sort of after-dinner drink?"

His expression softened as he realized just how unworldly she was. He got up from the sofa and approached her, noticing how nervous she became when he paused very close to her. "It is a coffee with frothed cream and cinnamon, very sweet. I am fond of it." He caught her arm, ever so gently, and held her in place.

"Oh. Well, I can't make it. I'm sorry," she added. His touch bothered her. How odd that it should disturb her so. She tested his hold and found him willing to let her break it. She stepped back and then looked up to see his reaction.

He was amazingly patient, almost contemplative, as he looked down at her. His black eyes mirrored his introspective mood, sweeping slowly over her exquisite bone structure, over her straight nose and down to her soft bow of a mouth.

"Women are property in your country, aren't they?" she asked, feeling chilled at the memory of what she'd read about some Arab nations.

"Not in mine, no," he replied. "We are a modern nation. There are those of our women who are not deeply religious, who consider the veil archaic and refuse to wear it. Our women work in public jobs and hold responsible positions in government." He smiled ruefully. "Needless to say, I am labeled an infidel by some disgusted neighbors."

"I expect your king is, too," she replied.

He cleared his throat. "Of course."

"Arabic is pretty," she said after an uncomfortable silence. "I have a friend who can speak a few words of it. It's musical."

"So they say."

"But it is," she argued, smiling nicely. "When you speak English, your voice has a lilt. It sounds very...intriguing," she said after a careful choice of words.

He lifted one dark brow. "Intriguing? Not sexy?"

She flushed, and he smiled again.

"*Vous êtes un enfant,* Brianna," he said quietly. "*Une très belle fleur avec les yeux comme la mer.*"

She frowned. "I don't understand French," she said hesitantly, registering the depth and sensual tone of his deep voice as he stared at her much too intently for a mere acquaintance.

"It is just as well," he said wistfully. "Come and watch television with me."

"What are you going to watch?" she asked, because she knew already that it would do no good to demand access to her own television. He was being generous right now, but it wouldn't last. He didn't have it in him to be considerate for long.

"A special program on the connection between stress and the immune system," he said, surprising her. "It is a new study, one which has been challenged by many scientists. But I find the premise an interesting one."

She did, too. Her doctor often worried about her obsession with being at the hospital four out of every five days to sit with Tad. She never missed, even if it meant freezing or getting soaked, or waiting half an hour for a ride. He said that one day she was going to fall victim to some debilitating illness because of the strain. She never had, though. Not yet. There was a minor cold and a bout with the flu, but nothing more serious than that.

However, as she watched the program with Ahmed, she began to understand the connection they were trying to present. It was a little disturbing. Tad might be in a coma for the rest of her life. What then? She felt a surge of panic as she realized what she hadn't in three years—that she might never see the light at the end of the tunnel. It was the first time she'd considered that hope might one day be lost forever.

"This is not what I expected to see," he said suddenly. He changed the channel. "Illness depresses me. I had hoped for something scientific. Ah. This is much more pleasant." He left it on the public-television station, where a new Sherlock Holmes adventure was just beginning.

She was taken aback by his abrupt action. She couldn't find the right words to express what she felt. Illness depressed her, too, but she had no choice at all except to deal with it. She couldn't change the channel of her life to something more pleasant.

She watched the program with him, absently rubbing the edge of her blouse between her fingers. The blouse was getting frayed. She would have to scrap it before too much longer. That was disturbing. She didn't have much money for clothes.

After a few minutes, she realized just how tired she was. She got up from the sofa. "There's a bottle of cola in the fridge, if you get thirsty," she said.

"No Perrier?" he asked without looking away from the screen.

"Dream on." She sighed.

He didn't reply. She moved toward her bedroom, glancing back as she went down the hall. He obviously hadn't realized yet that he was going to sleep on that lumpy mattress in the guest room. He'd probably get the idea very soon. She wasn't giving up her brand-new bed.

She went into the bedroom and closed the door. Then she locked it and placed a chair under the doorknob. She nodded. *There you go,* she thought. *Get through that!*

Mindful of any hidden cameras, she turned out the lights before she disrobed. She was blissfully unaware that the agency had infrared cameras and film, and also that they were discreet enough not to bug her bedroom. Well, not with a camera, anyway.

Having donned her long gown and brushed her hair, she got into bed and pulled the covers up with a sigh. She was almost asleep when she heard the soft whine of the television cut off and footfalls coming down the hall.

There was a sudden stop, an exclamation, and then several loud words in Arabic at the door to her bedroom.

"You might as well calm down," she called through it. "I've double locked the door and there's a chair under the doorknob. It will take a battering ram to get in here. This is my bed, and I'm sleeping in it. If you don't like it, you can call somebody and complain!"

"You think that I will not?" came the haughty reply. "You will be surprised!"

"No, you will," she mused aloud. "Because no red-blooded American gentleman is going to try to force a woman to give up her bed."

She lay back down with a smile and closed her eyes. She didn't even feel guilty. He had no idea how hard and long she'd worked to afford this moderately priced new bed and mattress and box spring. He seemed to have no idea at all what things cost. Presumably his government fulfilled his every whim. It must be nice, she decided, to be in the diplomatic service.

If she'd thought she was home free, she was in for a surprise the next morning. He still wasn't up when she left, and she didn't leave him any breakfast. After his threats of the night before, she didn't think he deserved any. But her conscience plagued her all the way to work.

Once she got there, Mr. Ryker called her into his office. Lang was sitting cross-legged in a chair. He smiled as she came in.

"Oh, no," she pleaded. "Not you again."

"You'll break my heart if you keep talking like that," he complained. "And here I am to compliment you on the way you're taking care of your sweet cousin."

"He isn't sweet," she muttered. "He's a barracuda in a mustache. He commandeered all the closets and all my drawer space, and he even tried to get into my bed last night!"

Lang gasped. "Why, Brianna, I'm shocked!"

"Not while I was in it," she said impatiently. "I mean he tried to take over the master bedroom!"

"Yes, I know. He telephoned my boss this morning, early. He also telephoned the Pentagon, the Joint Chiefs of Staff and the Secretary of State. Not to mention," he added, "the Secretary of Defense." He shook his head. "You have no idea how much trouble you've caused."

"He didn't call all those people. He couldn't... wouldn't!"

"He did." He smiled ruefully, pushing back a stray lock of dark hair that fell onto his broad forehead when he leaned forward. He rested his forearms over his knees. "In fact, I've been chewed out since daylight this morning. If you don't let him have the master bedroom, I'm afraid his government may declare war!"

She sat back in her chair, her face almost the color of the soft red turtleneck sweater she was wearing with her gray skirt. "I don't believe this."

"You'd better. I'm not even joking," he added solemnly. "This is a man who's quite used to getting everything he wants. He's never been refused in his life. He's rich and powerful and he isn't used to being denied—least of all by a young lady of your age and position."

"He's only a cabinet minister," she protested. "How can he have that much influence?"

"He has relatives in power in Saudi Mahara," he explained.

"Oh."

"We'll furnish you with a new bed for the guest room," he offered. "And a new vanity and a chifforobe. How about that?"

She hesitated. "Why not just let him bring a bed of his own to the apartment and sleep on that?"

"Great idea. We'll suggest it to him."

"Could you do it before I have to go home?" she asked. "I'm beginning to recognize several words in Arabic, and I don't think they're very nice."

"I can guarantee it." He grinned sheepishly at her start of surprise. "The bugs . . . ?"

"Yes. The bugs." She turned her head a little. "You, uh, you don't have any cameras in the bathroom or anything?"

He chuckled, noticing that Steven Ryker had put his hand strategically over his mouth.

"No, we don't. I promise you. We don't have cameras anyplace where they'd embarrass you."

She let out a long, audible breath. "Oh, thank God. I've been dressing and undressing in the closet."

"No need for that. None at all." He hesitated. "There's just one little thing. How did he get you to cook him vichyssoise and lobster?"

"But I didn't," she said. "I have no idea how to make those things. He had his men bring them in last night."

Lang was suddenly, starkly serious. "He what?"

"He had his men bring all that stuff in."

"Well, I'll be. You take five minutes to go to the men's room and look what you miss!"

"I thought you had the telephone bugged," Brianna said.

"I did. But Collins tripped over the wire and broke it. We were trying to make a splice. . . . Oh, never mind. Calling out for lobster, was he? Well, we'll see about that!"

Lang stood up, and he looked very angry. Brianna brightened. She wished she could go home and watch him give Ahmed hell.

She couldn't. But just the thought of it got her through the whole day, smiling.

Chapter Four

But when Brianna got to the apartment that night there was absolutely nothing out of the ordinary. Nothing very visible, at least.

Ahmed was sitting on her sofa glaring at the television, where a soap opera was playing. Two people were in bed, making passionate love. The sounds of it were embarrassing to Brianna, who sideskirted the sofa and went straight down the hall to her bedroom.

She took off her jacket and stretched, stiff from hours of sitting. As she turned, she noticed Ahmed in the doorway, watching her with eyes whose expression she couldn't define. She didn't know that the stretching motion had outlined her young body in the most sensuous, arousing kind of way. Or that Ahmed, a connoisseur of women, had stopped dead just to look at her.

"What is it?" she asked.

"They have removed the telephone directory and the

information service does not function," he muttered. "This is your doing."

She grinned. "Yes, it is. Didn't I do good? Furthermore, I am sleeping in this very bed tonight and you are going to have a nice, new bed in the guest room. I did that, too."

"You did no such thing," he denied. "I have spoken to your friend Lang. He is sending over a bed. But it is you who will sleep on it. I am occupying this room as of tonight."

"You are not! This is my apartment, buster, and nobody kicks me out of my own bedroom!"

"If you do not vacate it, there will be an international incident of proportions which you cannot imagine," he countered smugly.

"You spoiled old brat!"

He gaped at her. "I beg your pardon!"

"Lang told me that nobody ever said no to you in your life. Well, it's time somebody did! You can't just walk in and take over. You have no right!"

"I have more rights than you," he countered. He folded his arms across his chest. The blue silk shirt he was wearing made his eyes look even darker. "Call Lang. Lodge a protest. He will not take your side against me. He will not dare."

"I don't give a frog hair who you are or what you do, this is where I live and I'm not budging!" she raged, her Southern drawl emphasized in anger.

He was frowning. "Frog hair?" He shook his head and muttered something in Arabic. "These frogs, they have no hair. Are you demented?"

"Yes," she answered him, "I am demented. That's why I allowed them to talk me into letting you stay here!"

His dark eyes sketched her angry face and lowered to the smooth, sleek lines of her body before they returned to capture her startled eyes. "How old are you?" he asked.

"That is none of your business," she said uncomfortably.

"I can find out."

"Go right ahead." She felt a little shaky. "Now, if you don't mind, I'd like to change before I have to start cooking again."

"Had you not complained, we could both be served with lobster thermidor," he reminded her.

"I don't like lobster," she muttered. "At least, I don't think I do. I could never afford any, even to taste."

He scowled. "You are paid a good salary."

"Of course I am," she agreed. "But it doesn't stretch to foods like lobster. I have a little brother in a coma, don't you understand?" she asked softly. "Every spare penny has gone toward his comfort, until now."

He seemed surprised. He moved a little awkwardly. "Yes, yes, I have heard about the boy."

"Well, he's more than gossip to me," she replied. "I took care of him after he was born, played with him, fed him, diapered him.... I had to, because Mother wasn't well for a long time. But he was a joy, not a burden. He's a smart boy," she added, hanging on to the good times for all she was worth, fighting the hopelessness and fear. "He'll get up out of that bed one day, and play baseball again...."

Ahmed was touched by her reluctant show of emotion. He found himself wondering about the boy, about her. He hadn't been curious before, but now he was.

"What do the doctors say of his chances for recovery?"

"They say as little as possible," she replied, having regained her almost-lost composure. "Medical science can't do any more than it already has. The brain is still very much an unexplored territory, you know. Comas are unpredictable."

"His has lasted long?"

"Three years." She moved toward the door and held the doorknob impatiently. "If you don't mind?"

He moved back into the hall and she closed the door. It hurt to think how long Tad had lain in the hospital bed, knowing no one. She was going to see him tonight, but like all the other nights, it would be an exercise in futility, in loss of hope. She was growing more depressed as time passed.

She changed into jeans and a loose, long-sleeved white knit shirt and socks. She didn't bother with her hair or her face. After all, Ahmed was not an invited guest whom she wanted to impress. He was, at best, a positive irritant.

When she reached the living room, he had the television blaring on the news channel. She ignored him and went into the kitchen to cook. It was going to be meat loaf tonight, she thought heavily. She was so tired of meat loaf, but it would stretch to two days. She glanced at Ahmed and wondered how he was going to like something that unglamorous.

"What culinary delight are you planning for this evening?" he asked with resignation.

"Meat loaf, mashed potatoes and green beans."

He made a terrible face.

"There's always soup," she continued.

He made a worse face and turned away from her to glare at the television screen.

"Why don't you call the CIA and tell them you're starving here? Maybe they'll find you a nice new place to live."

He didn't reply. He looked even more unapproachable than he usually did.

She went on with her chores, humming softly to herself. If he wanted to starve himself rather than eat what normal people did, that was just too bad.

"Think of it as an exploration of ethnic fare," she told him when she'd put everything on to cook and she was sitting in the big armchair by the sofa. "This is what Americans eat every week."

"No wonder your country is so uncultured."

"Uncultured?" she asked, affronted. "And what are you, Mr. Camels-in-the-desert-under-a-tent?"

He gaped at her. "I have no camels in a desert tent!"

"You know very well what I mean," she returned. "You live in a country full of camels and tents and deserts."

"We have cities," he said. "Opera, symphony orchestras, theaters. We have libraries and great universities."

"And sand and desert and camels."

He glared at her. "You know nothing of my country."

"You know nothing of mine," she returned. "Most of us have never experienced that rarified air you breathe when you're over here. Steak and lobster, five-star hotels, chauffeured limousines.... Do you think the majority of the people in this country know what any of that is?"

He scowled at her. "You do not understand. These things are my right."

"You have it too easy," she said curtly. "You should have to work for minimum wage and live on leftovers and drive a car that always sounds like it's got half a potato shoved up its tail pipe! Then you'd know how the rest of the world lives.''

''All that concerns me is how I live,'' he said simply. ''The rest of the world must cope as it can.''

''What a selfish attitude!''

''There will always be people who are poor,'' he said philosophically. ''Why should I deny myself because there are people less fortunate in the world?''

''You might consider doing something to help the less fortunate, like taking a cut in your salary and giving up some of the trappings of your luxurious life-style.''

He drew up one long leg. He was wearing jeans, very tight ones, and she found the sight of him lounging on the sofa very disturbing. ''My life-style, as you call it, is my heritage. I intend giving up nothing. However, I have done what I can for my own people,'' he said, ignoring her glare. ''And your definition of poverty might find some resistance in my country. Our native nomadic tribesmen find their life-style satisfying and superior to the spiritual poverty which exists in our cities. They do not consider themselves poor, despite the fact that industrialized Westerners look down on them.''

She frowned. ''I don't understand.''

''That is obvious.'' His dark eyes smiled faintly. ''You think that because you have great machines and factories that you are superior to less developed peoples.''

She hadn't considered the question before. ''Well...we are. Aren't we?''

''Have you been to college, Brianna?''

She felt something flower inside her at the way he spoke her name. He made it sound musical, somehow. She had to stop and think to remember the question. ''No,'' she replied. ''I took some business courses to improve my typing and shorthand.''

"When you have the time, and your circumstances are improved, you might benefit by a few courses in sociology and racial diversity."

"I suppose you have a college degree," she said.

"Indeed. I am an Oxford graduate."

"In . . . ?"

He smiled. "Science, with a major in chemistry and physics. My father greatly approved my choice. Our people were the founders of science."

"In that case, with such a background," she said impishly, "perhaps you could chemically create a lobster for yourself in the kitchen."

He frowned. Then the words made sense and he chuckled. The sound was very pleasant to Brianna's ears, deep and rich.

"Perhaps I could, given the right ingredients," he mused.

An item on the news caught his attention. He turned back to listen and Brianna escaped back into the kitchen.

After a few muttered comments about the lack of proper silverware and china and linen napkins, which made her glower at him, he settled down to the meal with surprised pleasure.

"I have not tasted such food before," he said. "It is good."

"You needn't sound so surprised. I'm not exactly hopeless in the kitchen. My mother was a wonderful cook. She taught me how." She lifted her eyes. "Does your mother cook?"

He laughed uproariously. "No. Her hands were never allowed to do anything so menial."

She felt reprimanded and flushed a little. "Yes, well, in America it isn't considered menial."

"I beg your pardon, I did not mean to insult you," he said surprisingly. "You are a good cook."

"Thank you."

He took a last bite of the meat loaf and sipped sweetened, creamed coffee with obvious pleasure.

"You said her hands *were* never allowed," she asked. "Is your mother no longer alive?"

"What a soft way you have with words, Brianna," he said with a curious smile. "Always the passive, not the active voice, when you ask something that might be hurtful." He put down his fork. "Yes, she is dead. So is my father. They were murdered."

She dropped her fork. It clattered against the inexpensive ceramic plate, the noise loud in the sudden silence. "Oh, I am sorry," she stammered.

"It was a long time ago," he said. "The sting is still there, but their murderers were caught and executed."

All that reminded her that Ahmed was himself a target of would-be executioners. She grimaced as she looked at his impassive face. "Aren't you afraid?"

"Why waste energy in such futility?" he asked. "I will die when my time comes." He shrugged. "It is our destiny to die, is it not, one day?"

"Well, if assassins were gunning for me, I wouldn't be quite so casual about it!"

He smiled. "You are a curious girl."

"Woman," she corrected.

He lifted an eyebrow, and his eyes were old and wise. "Girl," he replied softly.

She got up a little jerkily and collected the plates. "I made a cherry pie for dessert," she said.

"Ah. My favorite."

"Is it?" She was sheepish. "Mine, too."

"A thing we have in common. Shall we find more, I wonder?"

She didn't answer him. He was getting under her skin, and he frightened her in emotional ways. She wasn't eager to let him turn her life upside down.

They finished the pie in silence. He went back to the television while she cleared the table, washed up the few dishes and went to get her coat and purse.

"Where are you going?" he asked, looking at her over his shoulder.

"To see Tad."

He got up and turned off the television. "I shall accompany you."

"Now, wait a minute," she said. "They said you shouldn't leave the apartment."

He was putting on his coat, ignoring her. "They will know that I am accompanying you. They will be watching."

She threw up her hands. "I never saw a man so enchanted with his own demise!"

He joined her at the door, ignoring her cry. "Shall we go?"

She gave up. She could hardly restrain him. He was very tall, close up, and she imagined he was very fit, too, if those muscles she'd seen in his legs and arms were any indication.

"Do you work out?" she asked suddenly.

"In a gym, you mean? Not really. I ride my horses and work with them."

"You have horses?" She was impressed. "I love horses. What sort are they?"

"Lippizaner stallions," he said.

"Those huge Austrian ones? But aren't they terribly expensive?"

"Astronomical." He noticed her suspicion and chuckled. "They are the king's," he explained. "But he allows me to train them for him, during my spare hours."

"Oh, I see. How nice of him."

He looked very smug, and lights danced in his black eyes. "Indeed."

It wasn't going to be such a bad evening, she thought. He was in a good mood.

And it lasted just until they reached her little car. He stopped and gaped at its bruised front fender, its rust spots covered with Bondo in preparation for the paint job she was having done on the installment plan. It was going to be red one day. Right now it was orange and rust and gray. Its tires were good, though, and its seats were hardly ragged at all. There was the small crack in the dash....

"You expect me to ride in that!" he exclaimed, bug-eyed.

"It's the only car I own," she informed him.

"It is... pitiful."

She put her hands on her hips and glared up at him. "It is not! It's a diamond in the rough. Just because it isn't cosmetically perfect...!"

"It is a piece of junk!" he said harshly. "Why do you not buy something new, instead of riding around in this death trap?"

"Because it's all I can afford!" she countered proudly. "Do you think everybody can just walk into a car dealership and buy a new one whenever they feel like it? This is the best I can do, and you have no right to make me feel ashamed of my car!"

He started to speak just as a car pulled slowly up to the curb, a sinister-looking black one, and stopped in front of Brianna's car. She saw it and without even thinking, she suddenly pushed Ahmed against her car and tugged his head down, so that he was between the car and her body.

"What are you doing?" he exclaimed, fighting her hold.

"Will you be still?" she squeaked. "What if it's *them?*"

"The CIA?"

"The assassins!"

"Oh. Oh, I see." He chuckled. "How very flattering, Brianna."

"Will you keep your head down?"

His lean hands found her waist and gently pushed her away from him. "Brianna, look, *chérie.*"

He turned her face toward the black car, where Lang was lounging by the back fender. He seemed lazily amused.

Brianna flushed. She quickly stepped back from Ahmed and pushed at her disheveled hair.

Lang walked toward them. "Hello, little lady," he drawled. "I was just passing and saw you and your cousin here and figured you might like a lift. Having car trouble?"

"Yes, indeed," Ahmed agreed.

"Then I'll be glad to drive you two wherever you want to go."

Ahmed put Brianna in back and himself in the passenger seat beside Lang. She was still seething about Ahmed's insults. She loved her little car, dents and all. Arrogant jerk, she thought, glaring at the back of his head.

"Would you mind telling me how it is that I have a Mexican cousin when I'm very obviously of Irish ancestry?" she asked Lang irritably.

"By marriage, of course," he said, chuckling. He glanced at her in the rearview mirror. She looked flushed and Ahmed was unusually silent. "Did you think I was going to shoot him?" he asked, gesturing toward his companion.

"I didn't know it was you," she protested. "I just saw a big black limousine. Next time, I'll push him out in the street," she muttered under her breath. "He insulted my car."

"That is not a car!" Ahmed joined in the conversation. "It is a piece of tin with spots."

"How dare you!"

"Excuse me," Lang interrupted. "But where are we going?"

"To the hospital," Brianna said.

"I should have remembered. You go almost every night." Lang's eyes met hers in the rearview mirror. "How long do you think you can keep it up before you collapse?"

"I've managed for almost three years," she said tautly. "I'll manage for as long as it takes."

He didn't say another word, but his expression was stark. Ahmed sat quietly pondering what he'd learned of Brianna all the way to the hospital. It surprised him to discover that she intrigued him. It must not be. They were worlds apart. She was an innocent, as well. He must marry one day for the sake of heirs, but they would of necessity have to be by an Arab woman. These flights of fancy must be suppressed. They were unrealistic.

Brianna left Lang and Ahmed in the waiting room. She was allowed into the intensive care unit alone, where she sat holding Tad's frail hand and talking to him about the weather and her day, as she always did. His dark lashes lay on his pale cheek, his unruly dark hair falling onto his forehead as he slept in his oblivion.

"Oh, Tad, I'd give anything if you'd wake up," she whispered huskily. "I'd give anything I owned!"

But he didn't, couldn't, answer her.

Lang leaned back against the wall, watching her through the glass, with an uncommunicative Ahmed at his side.

"Torture," Lang said heavily. "That's what it must be for her to go through this every day."

"Is there no other family, someone who might share her burden and lighten it?" Ahmed asked.

"There's no one...just her and the boy."

He let out a long breath. "Nurses could be arranged, you know," he said. "Around the clock. The best in the country."

"Ahmed, nurses can't cure a coma," Lang said. "You know that."

"They might spare her," he returned, nodding toward Brianna.

"Do you really think she'd stop going to see him, even if you could put round-the-clock doctors in there with the boy?" Lang mused.

"No. You are right, of course, I was not thinking." His eyes lingered on the young woman. "She is fragile to look at. But underneath, there is great strength." He turned his attention to Lang. "Do you know something of how that came about?" he added, indicating Tad.

"There was a wreck," Lang said. "They were going on vacation. A speeding car took a curve too fast and hit them head-on. The car rolled. Brianna's father and the driver of the other car were killed instantly. Brianna's brother was knocked unconscious. Her mother was..." He hesitated. "Her mother was fatally injured," he said, sparing the other man the details. "She lived until the next morning. She died just before help came. If anyone had spotted the car even an hour sooner, she might have lived, but it went down an embankment and was hidden from the highway.''

Ahmed moved closer. ''Brianna was in the car all night?''

''Yes. Trapped. She had two cracked ribs and a broken hip. You may have noticed that at times she moves a little awkwardly.''

''No. I had not.''

''She was in terrible pain, and she'd lost some blood. But Tad was the worst. It took Brianna over a year, and therapy, to get past the nightmares.''

Ahmed studied her in silence. ''She has great courage.''

''Yes. She's an extraordinary young lady.''

''How old?'' He stared at Lang. ''How old is she?''

''She's twenty-two, I think.'' His eyes narrowed. ''If you seduce her,'' he warned quietly, ''I'll come after you. I don't give a damn about your status or company orders, I'll make you pay if you hurt her in any way.''

Ahmed's eyebrows lifted. ''You are smitten with her?''

''I am protective of her,'' Lang corrected. ''She's my friend.''

Ahmed smiled quietly. ''She is a rosebud, waiting for the sun. I would be a frost to deny her the hope of blossoming,'' he said. ''I am much more aware than you think of the consequences. I have no evil intentions toward her. In between battles, I find her charming company.'' He glowered at Lang. ''You will not tell her this, of course. One cannot afford to parade one's weaknesses before an enemy.''

Lang's rigid stance relaxed. He even smiled. ''No, one can't.''

Ahmed clapped Lang on the back. "Despite her en-
mity toward me, did you see how quickly she jumped to
my aid when she thought you were an assassin?" he
mused. "She delights me."

"As if that tin can would have stopped a bullet from
even a small-caliber weapon." Lang chuckled.

"She knows nothing of guns or wars or assassina-
tions," Ahmed said. "Nor shall she. I must make certain
that she takes no chances on my behalf again. There could
have been tragic consequences had it been a true attempt
on my life."

The other man sounded resigned and somehow sad.
Lang found his response to Brianna curious. Ahmed was
a rake, in his own fashion, although he was curiously
protective of Brianna.

"We're keeping a close eye on both of you," Lang assured him. "She'll come to no harm."

"She had better not," Ahmed returned grimly, and his
dark eyes made a threat of their own as they sought
Lang's. "I consider her welfare no less important than my
own. You understand?"

"I do," Lang said with a slow smile. "But I wonder if
you do?"

Ahmed scowled with curiosity, but before he could take
Lang up on the odd statement, Brianna came out of the
ICU, had a brief word with the nurse and joined the men
at the door.

"Any change?" Lang asked.

She only shook her head, her eyes lowered. "Can we
go?" she asked dully. "I'm very tired."

Chapter Five

Brianna didn't sleep well that night. The black limo, the hopelessness of Tad's condition, the arguments with Ahmed were all combining to make her emotions a wreck.

At least the nightmares hadn't come back. She got up the next morning feeling drained. For once, Ahmed was awake. She found him in the kitchen in that long, foreign-looking caftan he lounged in, trying to discover how her coffeepot worked.

"I'll do that," she said, and moved uncomfortably when his dark eyes slid over her slender figure in her nightgown and pink robe. She was perfectly decent, except for her bare feet. She wondered why he should be staring at her so.

"You should dress first," he told her quietly. "It is unseemly for a maiden to appear before a man in her night clothing."

"Oh, I can't do it, but it's all right for you?" she challenged, indicating his caftan.

He smiled slowly. "Yes."

"I can wear my nightclothes in my own apartment if I want to," she informed him.

He moved closer. It was a sort of movement that Brianna had never experienced before, sensual and predatory and faintly threatening. His eyes didn't move from her face, didn't blink, and all the expression left his features. The only thing alive there was the growing dark glitter of his eyes.

"I'll, uh, just get dressed, why don't I?" she stammered, and ran for it.

When she came back, he was dressed, too. She made breakfast and he ate it without complaint. He gave no indication that anything out of the ordinary had happened. But Brianna tingled all day remembering the look in his eyes.

When she came home that afternoon, it was to find Ahmed sitting on the top step in her apartment house. He was playing with a Slinky, a small, dark-haired little boy sitting beside him.

"Again," the child pleaded.

"Oh, my aching back," Ahmed groaned comically. "You mean I must do it still again and chase this coil of wire down the steps?"

"Yes!" The child laughed.

Ahmed chuckled. "Very well, then. But this is the last time.'"

"Okay."

The Slinky came slowly down the steps, picked up speed and toppled right at Brianna's feet.

Ahmed came down behind it, spotted her and smiled as he retrieved it. "We were having a bit of fun," he explained.

"So I see. Lang won't like it."

"What he doesn't know won't bother him," Ahmed informed her. He handed her the Slinky. "My friend Nick will let you play, if you like. Won't you, Nick?" he asked the little boy.

"Sure!"

Brianna smiled at the child. "And you know I'd love to. But I have to feed my cousin."

"Aww, Pedro isn't hungry, are you, Pedro?"

"Pedro" grimaced. "Well, my boy, actually I am, a bit. Do you mind? We can do this again sometime."

"No, we can't," Nick wailed. "I have to go stay with my grandma for a week. We're leaving as soon as my dad gets home."

"I am truly sorry," Ahmed told him. "I have enjoyed our games."

"Me, too. Will you come back and see me again sometime?" Nick asked, his big eyes pleading.

Ahmed smiled, smoothing over the dark hair. "Sometime," he agreed.

"Okay, then." He ran back up the stairs, making plenty of noise.

Ahmed led the way up the stairs to Brianna's apartment and held the door open for her.

"You like children," he observed.

"Very much."

"You should marry, and have some of your own," he told her.

"I have Tad to look after," she said evasively. "I need to change."

He stopped her, without touching her at all, just standing in front of her so that she couldn't get past him. "There is something more, something deep," he said, searching her evasive eyes. "You have no desire to marry. I can see it in your face."

"We're not all cut out for marriage." Her face was flushed. "Please. I have to change."

His lean hands gently closed on her thin shoulders. "Tell me."

She closed her eyes. He was impossible this way, so tender and compassionate that he seemed almost another man entirely. "I can't," she whispered. Her big blue eyes opened straight up into his. "Please let me go!"

He accommodated her, standing back. "As you wish," he said quietly.

She went quickly into the bedroom and closed the door. She leaned back against it, her face twisted in anguish, her lip very nearly bitten through. Why did he have to ask questions that hurt her? she wondered. Why couldn't he just mind his own business!

She started to go into the kitchen, as she did every day, when he stopped her.

"Lang has reconnected the telephone," he murmured dryly. "And I have taken advantage of the situation. Wait."

"You haven't ordered out again?" she said nervously. "It's taking too big a chance, even I can see that!"

"My own men are attending to my needs," he said simply. "There is no risk of infiltrators."

"The neighbors here are not blind," she said, exasperated. "How is a poor Mexican laborer affording all that expensive food? People will wonder!"

He scowled. "Poor Mexican laborer?" He echoed her words.

"You!"

He shifted, as if he found the description distasteful. "I cannot live on hot dogs," he said curtly. "I did enjoy the meat loaf and vegetables, but I am accustomed to richer fare."

"You'll die of high cholesterol and gout," she accused.

His eyebrows arched. "This from a woman who is contemplating a meal of hot dogs, which ooze cholesterol?"

"I like hot dogs!"

"And I like quenelles of sole and sautéed asparagus with crepes flambé for dessert," he replied.

"Your poor starving people," she muttered. "Do they know that you're eating like a king while they chew on cold mutton in their desert tents?"

He pursed his lips. "Most of them eat couscous and lamb curry," he replied. "And semolina. Cold mutton is hardly appealing."

"I was making a point."

The knock at the door spared him an answer. He let his men enter the apartment, laden as they were with cardboard boxes of uncertain origin.

None of that looked like expensive food. It looked like the contents of a yard sale.

Ahmed grinned at her. "Disguised cuisine," he said. "Don't you approve?" He threw orders at the Arabs, who dispersed the contents of the boxes onto the table and left the apartment minutes later.

"Lobster tails," Ahmed indicated. He obtained a fork, speared a morsel and held it to Brianna's startled lips. "Taste," he said gently.

She took the bit of lobster into her mouth, disconcerted by the way Ahmed's attention suddenly fell on her lips as she savored it.

"It's . . . very nice," she said uncertainly.

"You have a flake of it on your chin. Be still." He took it on the tip of his finger and offered it at her lips. Holding her eyes, he eased it onto her bottom lip, but the movement of his fingertip was suddenly very sensual. He nudged it past her teeth and into her mouth and watched with pleasure the way her cheeks flushed and her breathing changed.

The tip of her tongue encountered his finger. She jerked back, and she saw the expression in his eyes darken and threaten. With her last instinct for self-preservation, she stepped away from him, shaken.

"Thank you for the taste," she whispered. "But I think I still prefer hot dogs."

"As you wish."

He was finding it hard to breathe and act normally. He should not have touched her. It would make things worse.

She fixed herself a hot dog and opened a small bag of potato chips.

"Even more cholesterol," he said, pointing at the potato chips with a forkful of chive-and-butter-and-sour-cream-choked potato.

"Look who's talking," she returned.

He chuckled. "You have spirit."

"Around you, I need to have it," she muttered.

He finished the potato and pushed the plate containing it and the remains of his lobster away. He retrieved the crepe with its exquisite fruit filling and nibbled at it. "Would you care to sample this?" he asked.

She flushed, remembering her earlier weakness. "I don't like sweets, thanks," she lied.

He didn't reply. She was suddenly very transparent and he felt a weakening in himself that he didn't like. Lang was right. Involvement with Brianna would be tragic.

The nightmare she'd staved off for two days came that night. She hadn't gone to see Tad, because there was such a terrible rainstorm. The thunder and lightning frightened her, but she pulled the covers over her head and tried not to notice them. Clad in her silky green gown, because it was an unusually warm night for autumn, she lay stiffly until the worst of the lightning abated and she fell into an uneasy sleep.

But the nightmare came to replace the storm. She was trapped in the car. Her father was dead. She could see his face. Her mother's pain was vocal, almost visible. She begged Tad to wake up and talk to her. She begged Brianna not to let him die, not to let them kill him. Her voice went on and on, while Brianna struggled with pain that racked her in agony. She had to get out, to save her mother. She had to get out, but her mother cried out and the light went out of her eyes. . . .

"No!" she screamed, fighting the hands that were trying to lift her, to save her. "No, no, no! I won't let her die . . . !"

"Brianna!"

She felt the whiplike movement of steely hands on her upper arms and her eyes opened by reflex. Ahmed was sitting on her bed, his face solemn in the light of the lamp by the bed. He was wearing some sort of silky dark pajama bottoms, but his broad, hair-covered chest was bare. He looked out of place in her frilly bedroom.

"Brianna, talk to me," he said, unconvinced that she was completely awake even now.

"I'm . . . all right. It was the nightmare," she whispered, shivering.

"You screamed. I thought the nightmares were a thing of the past," he added.

She didn't know that Lang had told him about the wreck. She sought his dark eyes. "They were," she said dully.

His gaze drifted over her face and down to the deep cleft of her breasts under the opaque lacy bodice of her gown. She hadn't realized before that the lace left her dark nipples quite visible. But then, nobody had ever seen her in the gown before.

Her hands began to lift, because his rapt gaze was disturbing. Her nipples went suddenly hard, tingling with unknown sensations, and she blushed at the blatant evidence that would tell him how much he affected her.

"Beautiful," he said gently, watching them change. "They are as the blush of dusk on the rose."

Her hands paused in midair. She watched him, puzzled, curious.

He looked into her soft, puzzled eyes. "Has no man ever described your body to you before?" he asked quietly.

"No one . . . has seen it," she began huskily.

His brows jerked. His eyes went over her again, appreciating the creamy satin of her skin above the gown, at the pulse in her throat, at the soft swell of her lips. He hadn't touched her. He only looked.

That was enough. He made her afraid. She didn't understand the feelings he engendered. She wasn't sure that she liked them.

"You must go," she whispered shakily.

"In a moment," he agreed. "First, though, *chérie,* I want to be certain that the nightmares are gone."

"They are. . . ."

"Let us make sure of it." He looked somber, very adult and mature. "The best way to stem a nightmare is to create an experience to supplant it. Do you not agree?"

"That depends . . . on the experience . . . you have in mind," she managed breathlessly.

"Something very innocent. Like you, *ma chérie*," he added with a tender smile. "There is nothing to be afraid of, only a contact which will prove to you that innocence can be as arid as my desert."

As he spoke, he lifted her from the pillow and smoothed the spaghetti straps of her gown down her arms.

"You mustn't!" she protested when she realized what he meant to do.

But he pulled her face into his throat and continued, pushing the gown to her waist. Then he slid his lean, warm hands around her bare back and began to move her bare, hard-tipped breasts against his hair-roughened chest. She gasped. The sensation was beyond her understanding. It made her breasts swell, her body swell. There was a sudden uncomfortable tautness in her lower body, a rush of heat. Her hands stiffened where they rested on his bare shoulders, feeling his strength.

"*Relax,*" he whispered at her ear, his voice lazily sensual, amused. She was like a tightly coiled spring, but her breasts were exquisite. He liked their softness, their hard little points digging into his muscles as he teased her body with his. "Do you like it?" he breathed, letting his hands slide under her arms now, to brush her from side to side with damning sensuality.

Her nails were biting into him unconsciously. "You must...stop," she stammered, shivering as his thumbs worked onto the soft swell of her breasts and began to caress them.

"Only this, I promise," he whispered. His teeth nibbled gently at her earlobe. "Nothing to compromise you, nothing to shame you. Let me touch you, Brianna."

Her voice broke. His touch was maddening. He made her want shameful things. She shivered, and despite her reluctant mind, her body drew away to give him complete access to her breasts, while her face burrowed, ashamed, closer against his warm throat.

"No, no," he coaxed, lowering his mouth to her tightly closed eyes. "Do not be ashamed to enjoy what I can give you. I mean you no harm." His mouth pressed hungrily at her temple while his fingers trespassed onto the fullness of her breasts and traced patterns that made her writhe before they came to rest over the hard tips of her breasts.

She clung to him, biting her lower lip almost through, letting his hands caress her while his thumbs and forefingers molded her nipples until her whole body ached.

"You delight me," he whispered roughly. He moved, sliding his exploring hands up and down her silky back in lazy sweeps while he held her nakedness against him once more. She could feel the thunder of his heartbeat shaking them both, and she hadn't the will to ask him to stop. She wanted it to go on and on, to never end. She hadn't known that there could be such joy in a man's touch.

She didn't know that her hands were in his hair until she felt him gently remove them. He lifted her away from him and laid her down against the pillow firmly, his hands on her wrists while his glittering eyes dropped to her bare breasts. The next step, she knew, would be to let him peel the rest of the gown away. She would feel his eyes on her, and then his hands, and . . .

"No!" she gasped. If he did that, he would see her hip. She couldn't bear for him to see it!

He was incredibly perceptive. He knew that she wasn't protesting the thought of his eyes on her body. He had a good idea, from what Lang had said, why she was so reluctant.

"Which hip is it, *chérie?*" he asked softly.

She stopped moving and stared up at him, red-faced. "Which hip?"

She hesitated. "The . . . the left."

He smiled apologetically, and with slow, gentle hands, moved the fabric of her gown down over her hips and discarded it.

She lay frozen while he moved the elastic of her briefs to give him a full view of the damage that had been done in the wreck. There were scars against the smooth flesh, from the injury as well as the surgery that was needed to repair it. She held her breath, almost afraid to look at him.

But when she did, his eyes were gentle, patient. "Ah," he said softly. "Is that all?"

She shivered, in relief mingled with uncertainty.

"Brianna, such a body is a gift of the gods," he said very quietly. "A few small scars are of no consequence, except as marks of bravery and sacrifice. You are exquisite."

She felt odd. Embarrassment should have overcome her, but she didn't feel it. She searched his eyes with curiosity, wonder.

"And now there will be no more nightmares, yes?" he asked softly, smiling. "You will sleep and dream of my eyes upon you."

Heat burned into her cheeks. He smiled. "This is shyness," he said, tracing the redness across her cheekbones. "It delights me."

Without awkwardness, he pulled her gown back up and replaced the small straps on her shoulders. He bent and brushed his lips gently across her closed eyelids. "You have given me a gift of which you are truly ignorant, are you not?" he whispered. "You have invited me to be your first lover."

"I ... didn't mean to," she replied uncertainly.

He lifted his head, and his eyes were tender. "Nothing would give me greater pleasure," he said with sincerity. "But we are fated for different roles in life than to be together. I would take your innocence only if I could offer you the future. I cannot."

He was closing a door. She felt sad, but it was nothing she hadn't known already. She had Tad, and Ahmed was from another country, another culture.

Her hand lifted to his face, hesitant, until he carried it the rest of the way. She traced his wide, firm mouth, his mustache, his high cheekbones and the thick ridge where his dark eyebrows lay. His hair was thick and black and cool to the touch. She found him devastating, as dozens of women before her must have.

He took her palm to his lips and savored it. His heartbeat was still visible. *"Bonne nuit, ma chère,"* he whispered.

"I don't understand," she began shyly.

"You don't understand what?" he teased. "French, or why you permitted me such a liberty?"

"Both, perhaps."

"You are very young," he said. "Curious and shy. I find it a disturbing combination. One day, a man will carry you to bed in his arms and you will learn that a scar means nothing to a man in love."

He put her hand back down and pulled the covers over her. "Sleep well."

"You, too."

He turned out the lamp and rose from the bed, tall and suddenly dear. He paused before he closed the door to look back at her with an inscrutable expression.

Brianna slept. And there were no more nightmares.

There was a new familiarity and an equally new tension between Brianna and Ahmed after that night. He made certain that he never touched her, nor did he refer to what had happened. Brianna could have believed from his behavior that it had never happened at all. For her own peace of mind, she supposed that she should try.

But he was tense and he became more so as the days passed. Lang discovered that he was still having food imported, and a confrontation rapidly ensued.

"I cannot live on oblong orange containers of meat of mysterious origin wrapped in buns!" Ahmed raged, waving his hands expressively. "I have a palate, which is unaccustomed to common fare!"

"Hot dogs are no worse for you than that high-priced cream-covered slop you eat!" Brianna shot back.

Lang looked heavenward for guidance. "Look," he said, stepping between them to face Ahmed, "you have to cooperate with us or we can't protect you."

"It is my own men who have been importing food for me," Ahmed informed him. He was as tall as Lang, although not quite as husky. He was formidable looking, just the same. "They have brought it in plain brown boxes, and not in their suits or native dress."

"Yes, but the restaurant where they're getting the food is a public place," Lang argued. "They've been seen coming around to the back laden with cardboard boxes. The police are watching them. They think they've stumbled onto a smuggling operation!"

Brianna hid her face in her hands and choked on laughter.

Ahmed was unamused. "You might enlighten them," he advised Lang.

"I have," he said irritably. "At considerable expense to my skin. They didn't take kindly to being left in the dark about the circumstances of your stay with Brianna."

"That is hardly my concern," the Arab said with cold hauteur.

"It should be," Lang countered. He paused, rubbing his hand over his chin, the other hand jammed into his pocket. "You're one major headache."

"If I were in charge," he informed Lang, "I should draw the assassins into the open and deal with them myself."

"We'd love to," Lang returned curtly. "But we have no idea where they are right now. We've searched the city, but we can't unearth them. We're fairly certain that they haven't made it into the country yet, although they were spotted on the Yucatán coast earlier this week. Meanwhile, it would be of great benefit to you, and to us, if you could be a little more discreet!"

Ahmed shrugged. "I have been discreet."

"Stop importing exotic food!"

"Tell her—" he pointed at Brianna "—to stop shoving oblong orange containers of suspicious meat wrapped in buns at me!"

"Hot dogs," Brianna corrected. "They're hot dogs!"

"Brianna, if we bring you some groceries, can you cook him something else?" Lang asked, trying to compromise.

"Bring me some mushrooms," she said with a venomous smile, "and hemlock and beef steak. I'll fix him a meal he'll never forget!"

"You can't poison foreign dignitaries," Lang explained patiently. "They have to be carefully handled."

"Spoilsport!"

"We'll get something right over," Lang promised Ahmed. "Now, will you please leave the catering bit alone?"

Ahmed was reluctant. "I suppose that I could. She is a passable cook," he added without looking at Brianna.

"I'm a good cook," she retorted.

"Make an apple pie with whipped cream, and I'll join you for supper," Lang said.

She smiled at him. "Would you, really? Bring me some apples and whipping cream, then."

He chuckled. "I'd be delighted."

Ahmed moved between them. "A bad idea, I'm afraid," he told Lang. "You have been seen by most of the terrorist group. It would hardly be politic for you to be seen here."

Lang grimaced. "He's right," he told Brianna sadly.

"I can save you a piece of apple pie," she said with a defiant look at Ahmed.

"That's a deal. Well, I'll say so long."

She walked him to the door, aware that Ahmed was watching every move she made. She felt a new tension and wondered why.

"Watch out for him," Lang said, nodding toward the man in the distance. "He's a ladies' man, and you'd be a whole new experience for him."

She smiled at him. "Thanks, Lang. But I'm not totally stupid. I'll be fine."

"Okay. Take care."

"You, too."

She closed the door behind him, grateful that she was able to keep her expression blank. It wouldn't do to let Lang see that Ahmed had already discovered her for himself. She felt shaky inside remembering the feel of him against her. She couldn't afford to feel like that, either. This was just a passing experience. She had to remember.

She went back into the apartment and forced a smile. "How about a cup of coffee?" she offered brightly.

"Lang is attracted to you," he said shortly. "He leads a dangerous life, and he will not easily give it up."

"I know that." She was shocked. "I have no interest in Lang, except that he's very sweet and I like him."

He stared at her for a moment. Then he relaxed and turned back to drop onto the sofa. "I would enjoy a cup of coffee."

"Thank you," she prompted.

He frowned.

"Thank you," she repeated. "It's courteous to thank people when they offer to do things for you."

Ahmed continued to frown.

"A little courtesy makes people feel of value," she continued. "You might try it."

He hesitated until she went into the kitchen and started the coffee. But when she put it on the table, he looked up.

"Thank you," he said stiffly.

Brianna smiled. "You're welcome!"

Chapter Six

Lang didn't show up that night when Brianna went to see Tad, and Ahmed insisted on accompanying her. That meant he had to be crammed into the passenger seat of her tiny vehicle, and he complained all the way to the hospital parking lot.

"If you hate my poor little car so much, why insist on coming with me?" she asked angrily.

"Because it is dangerous for a woman to be outside after dark alone," he said, "in any city."

He was concerned for her. The realization made her feel warm inside, protected. She stared at him, entranced.

He touched her face lightly, aware that she was creating a sort of weakness in him. She pleasured him.

He withdrew his hand with reluctance, noticing that she had leaned closer involuntarily, trying to maintain the light touch.

"You disturb me, Brianna," he said huskily. "It is a weakness which I can ill afford. Come."

He unwound himself from the seat and waited for her to get out. He escorted her to the hospital with a firm hand under her elbow. But before they got to the front door, his hand had begun to slide down until his long fingers could intertwine sensuously with hers.

She stopped, aware of explosive sensations caused by his touch. He looked down at her, his jaw taut as the same feelings worked on him. His fingers contracted around hers, pressing his palm hard against hers, and for long minutes they stood on the sidewalk under a streetlight and simply stared at each other.

"This is unwise," he said, his voice deep and husky. But he moved closer, so that his body was right up against hers.

"Yes." She laid her cheek slowly on his chest, over the trench coat, and listened to the hard, heavy beat of his heart.

His hand freed hers. His arms came up, slowly, and around her. He drew her close and bent his dark head over hers. He rocked her gently against him in the damp darkness and wondered at the peace he felt.

When he let her go, she was hard-pressed not to wobble on her feet. She clung to his hand as they went up in the elevator. She left him reluctantly to go see Tad.

He waited, his eyes unseeing as he stared at the carpeted floor. Brianna was becoming too important in his life. He wasn't sure he could let her go when it became necessary. How odd that she'd managed to instill feelings in him that all the experienced women of his acquaintance couldn't. He felt tenderness with her. It was a new feeling entirely, for him to feel tender toward a woman.

When she came back, he was more disturbed than ever. He took her hand and led her back to the car, gently helping her into the driver's side before he got in beside her.

"How is he?" he asked.

She shook her head. "There's no change."

She started the car and drove back to her apartment. This time when they got out, he kept a distance between them. When they entered her apartment, he excused himself with a plea of fatigue and closeted himself in the guest bedroom.

Brianna was surprised by his sudden change of attitude. She hadn't known what to expect from him, but this certainly wasn't it. He seemed suddenly distant and unwilling to let her near him.

The next morning, when she dressed and went to fix breakfast, she overheard him speaking to Lang on the telephone. What he was saying stopped her in her tracks, out of sight in the hall.

"I tell you, I cannot stay here!" he raged. "The situation is becoming unbearable. You must make other arrangements." There was a short pause while he listened. "Talk to them, then, but I expect solutions, not excuses!"

He slammed the telephone down and Brianna retreated to her room, almost in tears. So it was like that, was it? He couldn't bear to be around her anymore. Was he afraid that she was going to embarrass him by falling to her knees and confessing undying love or something? She flushed. She must have given away something of her tumultuous feelings the night before, when she'd laid her head so trustingly against his chest at the hospital. How could she have been so weak? He attracted her, made her aware of longings she'd never experienced. She wanted him. But there was more to it than even that. She...cared for him.

She stared at her white face in the mirror. This wouldn't do. She had to get a grip on herself. She must fix breakfast and go to work and not let this upset her. She had Tad to think of, and no hope of a normal life as long as he was comatose. She had to think about Tad, not herself.

With that firmly in mind, she pinched some color into her cheeks and went back down the hall again. Ahmed was sitting on the sofa.

"I'll fix something for you to eat before I leave," she began.

"That is not necessary. I am not hungry."

She picked up her coat and purse. "Suit yourself. Goodbye."

"Are you not going to have your toast and coffee?" he asked suddenly.

"I'm not hungry, either," she said without looking at him.

She opened the door and went out. She felt sick all over. It had been bad enough before, when they argued. Now it was worse. He couldn't bear even to be in the apartment with her.

She'd only just made it to the steps when he opened the apartment door and called to her.

"What?" she asked stiffly.

"It is not healthy to go without breakfast when you are accustomed to it," he replied formally.

She looked back at him with glaring blue eyes. "I can take care of myself, thank you."

His face closed up. "Eat something at work, then," he said shortly. "Presumably you have a coffee shop nearby."

"I'll eat when I feel like it!"

His dark eyes slid over her like seeking hands. She flushed and he made an annoyed sound. He went back into the apartment and closed the door with an audible snap.

Lang came by her office at lunchtime. He perched himself on the desk and studied her with too much interest for a casual observer.

"You've been crying," he remarked. "And I don't need three guesses."

"He wants to get rid of me," she said furiously. "And I want to get rid of him, too! I hate having my cooking insulted!"

He smiled wistfully. "He's protecting you," he said.

She scowled. "What?"

"He's protecting you," he repeated. "I don't think he realizes it, but he's trying to get you out of the line of fire. He thinks you're in danger as long as he's around. You are, but we're Johnny-on-the-spot. You're both as safe as you can get. And moving him out of the apartment won't solve any problems, it will only create more. I told him that."

"What did he say?" she asked, trying to sound disinterested.

"That you mustn't be hurt, whatever the cost," he said, smiling.

She flushed. "How very nice of him. That wasn't how he sounded on the phone this morning."

"He's got a lot on his mind."

"I suppose he does," she agreed reluctantly, "with spies and assassins following him around everywhere."

"And his own bodyguard," he reminded her.

"That, too."

"You don't believe me, do you?" he mused. "You think I'm making up excuses for Ahmed, to keep you in our good graces."

"You spies are all alike," she said. "You do the job, whatever it takes."

"Well, I might have exaggerated a little," he confessed, "but not much. I still think Ahmed's main concern is that you might get hurt."

"That's not what he said."

He studied the fabric of his slacks. "Not exactly."

"What did he say, exactly?"

"That he'd be climbing the walls in another two days if I didn't get him out of there," he confessed.

"He won't be the only one," she shot back, infuriated. "He's driving me batty!"

He studied her flushed face, seeing far more than she wanted him to. He pursed his lips and smiled a little and she went scarlet.

"I'll see what I can do," he promised, rising from the desk.

"Thanks, Lang."

"Meanwhile, wear pajamas at night, will you?"

She gasped, horrified.

"He only said that you had a nightmare. And you were wearing a gown designed to undermine all a man's good resolutions and moral character."

"It was not!" she exclaimed. "It's just a common, ordinary, run-of-the-mill gown, and I never asked him to take it off me!"

Lang whistled and averted his eyes. She looked even more horrified. Her face went from scarlet to stark white and her hands covered her mouth.

"No wonder he's climbing walls," Lang said wickedly.

"You get him out of my apartment!" she snapped.

"With all haste, I promise," he said comfortingly. "Meanwhile—" he leaned closer "—wear pajamas!"

"I'll wear armor," she muttered.

He chuckled and left her sitting there, dreaming up ways and means of strangling her apartment dweller. How could he! How dared he!

She fumed all day long. When she got back to the apartment that night, she'd reached flash point.

"How dare you!" She exploded the minute she closed the door behind her.

Ahmed raised both eyebrows and pushed the Off button on the television remote control. "How dare I what?" he challenged.

"How dare you tell that Peeping Tom that I had on a gown!"

He looked stunned. "I said no such thing to him," he began slowly. "Nor would I have. The memory of it is a deeply personal thing, for the two of us alone to share. It would offend my sense of honor to divulge it to anyone else."

She stopped, touched by the way he expressed the memory. "But he said..."

"Yes?"

He looked dangerous. She hesitated. "Well, he said you wanted to leave here because I was driving you up the walls."

He smiled. "You are."

She was confused, and looked it.

He got up from the sofa and took away her purse and coat, depositing them on a chair. "Sit down and have some coffee. I made it. It is surprisingly good, for a first attempt."

She couldn't have imagined Ahmed making coffee. But he was right. It was good.

He sat near her and leaned forward, his dark eyes intent. "I told Lang nothing except that I dislike the risk of remaining here."

"Because of all that catered food?" she prompted.

"Because I find you much too desirable," he said solemnly. "You have no knowledge of men, or of the deceit even an honorable man can employ when desire rides him hard. It was dangerous, the way we were together last night at the hospital. You are vulnerable to me, and I to you. I have explained already how I feel about the situation."

"Yes, I know." She sipped her coffee. "Then if you didn't tell Lang, how did he know?" The coffee cup hung in midair. "Cameras...!"

"No," he assured her. "There are no cameras in the bedroom. I had my own men sweep it, to make certain. It disturbed me that you might be spied upon as you slept."

"Thank you."

"Where is the gown you wore?"

"I washed it and hung it in the window to dry." She caught her breath. "So that's how...!"

"A telescope, no doubt," he mused. "And there are microphones which can pick up a heartbeat from a great distance."

"Oh, dear," she groaned.

"Lang would not permit such a blatant violation of your privacy," he said, "and my men would not dare eavesdrop on me."

"I hope you're right. It nauseates me to think that someone might have watched, listened...."

His dark brows drew together slightly. "You know very little of the world," he said gently. "There are men who think nothing of..." He laughed. "Never mind. It is not fit talk for your ears. Drink your coffee."

"I suppose you have your pick of women," she murmured without looking at him. "In your position, I mean.

Diplomats travel in high social circles, and you're not bad looking."

"You flatter me."

Her eyes lifted, searching his impassive face. "I've never had much time for dating. I went out a time or two, but Mama was unwell a lot after Tad was born, and I had to help her look after the house, and after him. Most boys weren't interested in me anyway. I was always thin." She fingered the coffee cup. "After the wreck, I thought my hip looked horrible."

He laughed gently, without malice. "And now?" he teased. "What do you think of it now?"

She smiled back. "I think that you were very kind."

"I had a great deal more than 'kindness' in mind, Brianna," he said softly. "You are very desirable. I find myself lusting after you, and that is why I wish to leave here. An affair between us would be a tragic thing."

"There must be many women in your life who would gladly give you what you want," she said demurely.

He looked very introspective. "Perhaps. But it will be best if Lang can find other accommodations for me. This enforced togetherness will lead to disaster eventually."

"I haven't any plans to drape myself nude across your bed," she remarked.

He looked at her with lazy appreciation. "Even the prospect makes my head swim," he murmured. "You realize that I would find it impossible to resist you?"

"I would find it impossible to behave in such a way," she confessed. "I want to explain . . ."

The ringing of the telephone, an unusual event, stopped her in midsentence. She dived for it, listened for a minute and went deathly pale. She hung up.

"Brianna, what is it?" he asked softly.

"It's Tad," she said numbly, her eyes tragic and shocked. "He's gotten worse. I have to go to him...."

"You are in no condition to drive. Get your coat."

He phoned for a cab, certain that the agency had bugged the telephone.

Sure enough, when they got to the curb, there was Lang with the limo. He packed them inside grimly and sped toward City General without a word.

Tad's frail body convulsed over and over again. Brianna watched until she began to cry. Ahmed drew her into his arms and comforted her all through it. He refused to leave her, even when the doctor came and gave her a sedative.

"How is she?" Lang asked when Ahmed reappeared from the room they'd given her.

"She is not well," he replied. "She has spirit, but even so much will eventually give way. The boy's condition is dangerous. He may very well die."

"And if he doesn't?" Lang asked.

Ahmed pursed his lips. "Then he may come out of it," he said with a smile. "This is what the doctor hopes. It is evidence of frenetic brain activity, which can go either way. For Brianna's sake, I hope the boy recovers."

"When will they know?" Lang asked.

"Soon, I hope."

And it was. Minutes later, Ahmed was called in by Dr. Brown, who was laughing with tears running down his cheeks. "Come and look," he said. "Then I'll let you wake Brianna and tell her."

He drew the tall Arab to the ICU, where a young boy's eyes were open and he was being examined by another doctor. He looked at Ahmed with fuzzy curiosity.

"He will recover?" Ahmed asked.

"With treatment and time, of course!"

Ahmed paused long enough to tell Lang before he burst into the room where Brianna was sleeping restlessly.

"Wake up, darling," he whispered, unaware that he'd even used the word. "Wake up, let me tell you."

She opened her eyes heavily, peering at him through a fog of tranquilizers. "What is it? He's gone?" she asked suddenly, choking on the word.

"No! He's awake. He's come out of the coma, Brianna. He's going to be all right!"

She sat up, clinging to Ahmed's strength while she fought to be lucid. "Tad's all right," she echoed. "Oh, thank God!"

He held her while she cried, then helped her as she struggled to get to her feet.

"Steady, darling," he said gently. "You'll keel over." He helped her into her shoes, unaware of the endearments he was whispering to her.

She leaned on his arm and walked into the ICU, dazed and stunned and deliriously happy when she saw Tad's blue eyes sparkle with sudden recognition.

"Sis . . . ter?" he whispered.

His voice sounded strange. It was the long period of disuse, Dr. Brown assured her.

"Tad," Brianna whispered back, smoothing his dark hair. "I love you, Tad."

"Love you," he managed to say. "Mom? Dad?"

She looked, anguished, at the doctor. He nodded solemnly. She looked back at Tad, forming words she didn't want to speak. "We lost them both. I'm so sorry."

He began to cry. The sound was haunting. Brianna had had three years to cope with the loss, but to Tad, they were only minutes beyond the terrible wreck. He sobbed, shaking all over, and Brianna gathered him up as best she could with all the tubes and wires, and held him, murmuring comforting words.

When he was calm again, she laid him back down and dried his tears.

"We still have each other," she told him. "You can come home and live with me. We'll be fine, Tad. Really we will."

"Head hurts," he murmured.

"We can give you something for that," Dr. Brown said.

"No!" Tad grabbed the doctor's hand. "Mustn't!"

"Don't worry," Dr. Brown said gently. "You won't go under again. You have to trust me."

He looked at Brianna, terrified. She nodded. "It's all right. None of us wants to lose you now. It's been such a long time, Tad. I've come every other day to see you. I've hardly missed a day at all."

"I know." He frowned. "Remember . . . your voice."

She laughed, delighted. "I told you," she said to Dr. Brown.

"Who is he?" Tad asked, looking at Ahmed. "Saw him . . . through the glass."

"This is, uh, Pedro," she stammered. "He's a cousin of ours. From Chihuahua," she added helpfully.

"No cousins . . . in Chihuahua," he murmured.

"Oh, now, Tad, you remember Uncle Gonzales, don't you, who married Aunt Margie?" She bit her lower lip.

"Don't remember . . . much," he confessed.

She relaxed. "You will," she promised. "For now, you need to get some rest. Tad, it's so good to have you back!"

"Good . . . to be back." He smiled and closed his eyes.

She looked quickly at Dr. Brown.

"He'll be all right," he assured her. "Don't look like that. He'll be fine!"

"You're sure?"

"I'm sure." He looked at Ahmed. "Take her home, young man, and give her two of these. She'll sleep. She needs to," He handed Ahmed the tablets.

"I shall see that she does," Ahmed assured him. He drew Brianna to his side and along the wall to the elevator.

She let him take her down to the car, where Lang was waiting, beaming. He'd already talked to the doctor. Brianna listened to the conversation, but she was too muzzy and exhausted to register much of it.

When they got to the apartment, Lang left them at the door. Ahmed herded her inside and gave her the tablets, making sure she swallowed them down with a glass of water.

"Thank you," she whispered.

He smiled at her. "For what?"

"For all you did."

"I did nothing."

"That's what you think." She knew the tablets would take several minutes to take effect, but she was already drowsy. "I'll see you tomorrow."

"Certainly. Sleep well."

She nodded, wandering down the hall to her room. She closed the door and walked to the bed, and passed out on it.

Ahmed found her sprawled there minutes later when he looked in on her.

He chuckled. It seemed to be his role in life to play valet to her. He removed her clothes and put her into her gown. He almost removed her briefs as well, but that would probably send her into hysterics, he decided, when she woke. He slid her under the covers and pulled them up over her.

Her sleeping face was very vulnerable. He studied her in silence, watching her lips part as she breathed. She looked so fragile like this, and he felt guilty for being a burden to her during his occupancy. He'd have to be more patient.

There was, of course, no hope of leaving the apartment now. She would need someone with her, and Tad would be coming home soon. He would be needed.

That was a new, and strange feeling. No one had ever really needed him before on a personal level. He found himself feeling protective of not only Brianna, but of her young brother, as well. Odd feelings for a man in his position.

Well, he could sort them out tomorrow. He started to rise, but Brianna caught his arm and pulled it to her breasts, murmuring something in her sleep.

"What is it?" he whispered.

"Don't...go," she said drowsily, her eyes closed. "Stay."

He chuckled softly. She was in for more than a few shocks when she woke, it seemed. He pulled loose long enough to divest himself of everything except his own briefs. Then he climbed in beside Brianna and curled her into his body. She flinched a little at first, at the unfamiliar contact with a man's nearly nude body. But after a minute, she relaxed and curled trustingly back against him.

It wasn't going to be the most comfortable night of his life, he mused dryly, but he couldn't remember a time when he'd felt more at peace. He closed his eyes. Tomorrow was soon enough to face the implications of what he'd just done.

Chapter Seven

Brianna felt a weight on her arm. She moved and fell even closer to a warm, muscular sort of pillow. She must be dreaming. Her hand moved over what felt like a furry animal. It paused and moved again.

"Careful, *chérie*," a voice whispered drowsily near her ear. "Such caresses are much too dangerous early in the morning."

She opened her eyes. A pair of liquid black ones smiled into them. She jerked up, shocked to find herself in bed with Ahmed. The sheet covered his waist, and his chest was bare.

So was hers, she discovered as the cover fell and she realized that she was nude.

She jerked the cover closer, flushing violently.

"It was your idea," he pointed out. "You felt that the gown was too hot, so you removed it. And, uh, apparently everything else. Then you curled into my body and went immediately back to sleep. I confess, I was unable to. I feel like a man who has been through the rigors of hell.''

"The tranquilizers," she stammered apologetically. "I'm not used to drugs. They...sometimes make me behave...strangely."

"I did notice. You made a rather blatant request."

She groaned and pulled the cover over her head.

"There, there. I understand."

"I'm ruined!"

"Not yet," he mused. "However, if you are still of the same mind you were in last night, I find myself more than capable of accommodating you."

She groaned again. "Oh, don't!"

He chuckled, stretching. "It was a revelation, to feel you like that against all of me." He groaned softly. "I confess that I removed the rest of my own clothing, so that I could enjoy the silky warmth of you even more. It took all my willpower not to carry through. You were deliciously soft and sensuous."

She was staring at his face. "You mean...you have nothing on?" she gasped.

He rolled over onto his side and propped himself upon an elbow. "Not a stitch."

She chewed her lower lip almost through. "I have to get up."

He swept his arm toward the side of the bed invitingly.

"I can't...with you looking."

"How could I not look at something so captivatingly beautiful?" he asked simply. "You are a work of art."

She flushed. "Well...you mustn't look at me, all the same."

"Then you wish to have me get out of bed first, *n'est-ce pas?*"

"Please."

He searched her eyes with a deep laugh. "Delightful little wretch. Will you hide your eyes in your hands, I wonder, and then peek through them to see what a man looks like when he is aroused and needful of a woman?"

She flushed. "You stop that! I won't look!"

"As you wish." He threw back the covers and got up, stretching so that his body was taut and the muscles rippled all the way up and down. And Brianna, with her hands over her eyes, parted her fingers just enough to get a shocking, blatant view of him. Surprisingly, she couldn't manage to cover her face back up. She took her hands away, her heart pounding, her throat dry, and he turned completely toward her, letting her look.

"It is not something of which you need be ashamed," he said softly.

"Oh, my," she said on a shaky breath.

He smiled. "You flatter me with those big eyes, *chérie,* but they make it all the more difficult for me to practice restraint." He turned away from her and found his silk briefs and pajama bottoms. He slid them up over his slim hips and snapped them in place before he turned to look at her. The cover had dipped, so that only the tips of her breasts remained covered.

"Still so shy," he accused. "You slept with me."

She flushed. "Not . . . like that."

"We slept nude, in each other's arms," he said. "Like lovers."

"But we aren't!"

He smiled gently. "We will be," he said softly. "The prospect of it makes me dizzy with pleasure. You're silk and satin. Innocent and sweet and brave. What more could a man ask of life than such a woman?"

"I won't be your mistress," she managed.

"Oh, Brianna," he said tenderly, "never could I ask you to be so small a part of my life as that."

She was puzzled. Her eyes sought his and found only dancing mischief in them. "Well, then, what do you want?"

"What you whispered in my ear last night as you slept," he said.

"But I don't remember."

"You will, at the appropriate time. Get dressed while I make coffee. Tad will be awake and impatient to see you!"

"Tad!" She laughed. "It wasn't a dream, then!"

"No. Not at all. Get up."

He went out, closing the door behind him. She jumped out of bed and rushed toward the bathroom just as the door suddenly opened again and Ahmed stared at her with rapt delight.

"Stop that," she said.

He shook his head and smiled apologetically. "I couldn't resist. Hurry, now." He closed the door again.

She darted into the bathroom, embarrassed and excited. She had a new lease on life, it seemed, and Ahmed was part of it.

Tad's eyes lit up when Brianna walked into the new private room he'd been given. He looked much better, with some color in his cheeks, and his speech had improved, too.

"I feel like Rip Van Winkle." He chuckled, his voice a little rusty but much more animated than it had been the day before. "Hi, cousin!" he added, smiling at Ahmed.

"Good morning, young cousin," Ahmed said indulgently. "I trust you feel more yourself?"

"I feel much better. I was worried about Bri, though," he confessed, falling naturally back into his old familiar way of addressing her. "They told me she had to be sedated."

"I'm fine now," she assured him. "I had a good night's sleep and I'm all right."

"I'm sorry I gave you a fright," he said, wondering at her faint color.

"You can give me all the frights you want," she told him warmly. "It's so wonderful to have you awake and alert and talking to me. Tad, you're all I've got in the whole world," she added huskily.

"Not quite, *chérie*," Ahmed said from behind her, his hand gently smoothing her hair.

She flushed, looking up into dark, possessive eyes.

"When can I get out of here and come home?" Tad asked eagerly, changing the subject.

"I'll ask your doctor. I'll pester him five times a day until he's desperate to let you leave," she promised dryly.

"Thanks, sis!"

But it wasn't that easy to persuade Dr. Brown to dismiss the boy. He insisted that Tad stay long enough for more tests to be conducted, and until they were certain that his body could manage on its own. However, he added with a grin, if Tad's appetite was any indication, keeping him fed was going to be the biggest headache Brianna would have.

Since the night Brianna had spent in his arms, Ahmed was convinced that marriage to her would solve some of his most pressing problems. The major one would be his hunger for her, which grew by the day. He wanted not only her perfect body but her warm heart and brave spirit. The minor problem would be his country's relations with the United States. Surely it would pave the way for better ones in future if he had an American wife. The more he thought about it, the more convinced he became that it would be a wise move. The details could come later. Now it was enough that the decision had been made.

He drew Lang to one side while Brianna was with her brother.

"You must make haste to solve this thing," he told Lang. "I can waste no more time waiting for assassins to do their deadly business."

Lang's eyebrows rose. "Are you and Brianna at each other's throat again?"

"It is not that at all," he said. "I wish to go home and be married."

Lang was shocked and trying not to show it. "Isn't this a bit sudden?" he asked.

Ahmed waved his hand expressively. "I have waited most of my life. Now this assassination plot has made me aware of my own vulnerability, of the risk to my people if I die without issue. I tell you, I believe my brother-in-law is mixed up in this," he added solemnly, his dark eyes unblinking on the other man's face. "He is the only one who could move against me with such ease and with co-operation from bribed officials. No doubt he has made many promises."

"You mentioned that once before. We've acted on it. We have operatives making every effort to wrap it up quickly."

Ahmed nodded. "I hope that it will not take much longer. Now that I have made the decision, I wish to implement it as soon as possible."

"I suppose congratulations are in order, then," Lang said, thinking how hard this was going to hit poor

Brianna, who was so obviously infatuated with Ahmed. The man didn't even seem to notice that!

"Yes. Another thing, we must have a larger apartment for the duration of this charade," he said. "If Tad comes home with us, and I assume that he will, the apartment she now occupies will not be large enough for the three of us."

"We have a safe house nearby...."

"Unwise," Ahmed said at once. "Even if Brianna did not find it suspicious, the boy might."

"You're right. An apartment, then, in a building where we have a floor under surveillance. Will that do?"

Ahmed smiled. "Yes. Thank you."

"Where do you plan to be married, in Saudi Mahara?" Lang asked.

"It must be there, obviously," the other replied impatiently. "The duties of state," he added sadly. "I myself would prefer something quiet and simple, but it would be unthinkable not to have all the trappings."

"I understand. Well, I'll get the ball rolling," Lang replied.

Ahmed's dark eyes twinkled. "You look sad. You are a bachelor, too. One day, perhaps you will find a woman who can make you happy."

"I already did," Lang said ruefully. "But being the brilliant fellow I am, I kicked her out of my life and sent her running." He laughed curtly at the joke he made and went in search of a telephone.

Brianna was so excited about Tad that she hardly noticed the passing of time. But Ahmed's curiously tense attitude disturbed her and when she could manage it, she maneuvered Lang into an alcove to question him.

"Ahmed is very quiet," she told him. "Has something happened that I should know about?"

He ground his teeth together. "Sure you want to hear it?" he asked.

"I've got Tad back," she replied simply. "I think I can take anything now."

"I hope so. He—" he nodded toward Ahmed, who was reading a magazine in the waiting room beyond the hall "—is impatient to go home and get married."

Get married. *Get married.* Brianna heard the words with every heartbeat. She hadn't realized until that moment how much Ahmed meant to her. Now it dawned on her that he would certainly need to marry a woman from his own country. He was a high cabinet official. Of course! How would it look if he married a foreigner? How could she have been so stupidly blind!

"I see," she managed to say through a tight throat. She even smiled at a concerned Lang. "I've been living in dreams, haven't I, Lang?"

He grimaced. "Brianna, I wish . . ."

"It's all right," she assured him numbly. "I've been expecting it. Good heavens—" she laughed "—he couldn't very well get involved with an American woman, could he?"

Lang's eyes were sympathetic. "I didn't want to tell you."

She took another steadying breath. *Fate has given me a trade,* she thought. *It's traded me Tad for what I might have had with Ahmed.* She wanted to laugh hysterically, but it would not change the situation. She'd been a minor amusement for Ahmed. She'd been falling in love, but he'd been teasing, playing, while he planned all along to marry some woman back home. She felt like a fool.

"I need to go and see about Tad."

"Time does heal things, somewhat," he remarked, his hands deep in his pockets and a sudden, pained look in his eyes.

"I know." She touched his arm gently and then walked back toward the intensive care unit. She didn't look in Ahmed's direction at all.

She didn't change her attitude toward Ahmed noticeably. She was polite and courteous. But the distance between them grew, and he noticed her reticence without understanding what was wrong.

Lang hadn't told him that he'd mentioned Ahmed's upcoming marriage. But Lang had told him that they had an agent pretending to be Ahmed installed in a classy downtown hotel being very obviously guarded in his hotel suite. And there had just been an attempt on the man's life. Ahmed was concerned now for Brianna's safety, and Tad's. If he was discovered, all the red herrings in the world weren't going to stop the terrorists from striking at him; nor would they care if they happened to kill some innocent person who simply got in the way.

Ahmed, and Lang, went with Brianna every time she went to the hospital now. But Ahmed, sensing her withdrawal, didn't come any closer. He was protective and tender, but not amorous. Not at all. She wasn't sure if she should be hurt or grateful. After all, he had somebody else, and he hadn't even been honest enough to tell her.

Tad's animated presence almost made up for Ahmed's reticence. She delighted in his company, spent every available minute with him. And when the doctor said she could, finally, take him back to the apartment, she all but danced around the room with joy.

"I have already told Lang that we must have a larger apartment so that we each have a bedroom."

That wasn't all he'd told Lang, but she didn't say any more. "It might be wise" was the only comment she made.

He scowled. "You are withdrawn," he said quietly. "Since the night I slept with you in my arms, you have hardly had three words to say to me."

"I've decided that it was a mistake," she said without looking at him. "I don't want to get involved in a relationship that has no future."

His brows jerked together. "What do you mean, no future?"

She turned her head. "I think you understand me. I'm not going to be your plaything. Not when you've got a woman back home already."

He averted his eyes. "I am a man, full grown. I feel the occasional need for a woman in my bed. I will not apologize for being human."

"I didn't ask you for an apology," she returned. "I simply said that I'm not standing in for another woman."

"There would be no question of that."

"Good. I'm glad we understand each other." She put the car into gear and drove home, with Ahmed quiet and contemplative beside her. He'd already started planning a state wedding, and here was Brianna all upset about his mistress and refusing him. He'd already telephoned to tell the woman back home that he was marrying. He'd given her a handsome compensation and provided for her old age, and they parted friends. But apparently Brianna couldn't accept that he had a past. It made him sad. He'd thought her more forgiving than that.

And she still didn't know it all. Inwardly he was remembering just how great a deception he and Lang had worked on Brianna. There was a truth she hadn't yet discovered, one that would certainly have changed their relationship or even killed it once she knew. He hadn't wanted to tell her. He'd planned to wait, to find the right words, the right time. But she seemed unwilling to even speak of a future with him now. He'd waited too long.

He looked at her sadly. She was very young, of course. Perhaps he expected too much, too soon. He would have to bide his time and hope that she wasn't as unaffected as she seemed.

By the next day, Lang had found them a new apartment. It took all of a day to have everything moved into it by Ahmed's friends. Brianna was shocked at the way he did things, literally snapping his fingers to get people to do what he wanted. She'd never been exposed to anyone with such a sense of power and confidence. She stood in awe of him, but she was determined not to let it show. The woman back home was welcome to him, she told herself. She didn't want him!

While she unpacked, Ahmed spoke privately with Lang. "The boy will be safe here with us?" he asked worriedly. "I would not have him hurt now for all the world."

"He won't be," Lang said. "You'll all be as safe here as you would be in a bomb shelter twenty stories down. You're completely surrounded. There are bugs and cameras everywhere," he added meaningfully. "For your own protection. Remember them."

"Do you think I might need to remember them?" Ahmed laughed heavily. "She has no interest in me now that her brother is conscious. I have become the forgotten man."

Lang couldn't help but feel that it was the best thing to happen, since Ahmed was making marriage plans.

"I'm sorry. I know how you feel," Lang replied, and his eyes were distant. "I've had years of being the forgotten man."

Ahmed scowled, curious. Lang looked very different when he spoke that way.

"There was a girl back home," he told the Arab wryly. "I made a mistake. I tried to apologize, but it was too late. Now I can't get near her. She hates me."

"I am truly sorry."

"Me, too," Lang replied. He got to his feet. "Life goes on. I'll leave you to it. We'll be somewhere close when you bring the boy here. No more catered meals," he added.

Ahmed raised both hands. "Very well. I suppose that in an emergency I can learn to eat cursed hot dogs." He glowered at Lang. "My counterpart enjoys filet mignon and cherry crepes jubilee nightly, I suppose?"

Lang chuckled. "One of the perks of his 'position.'"

"Yes. Well, tell him not to enjoy it too much," came the haughty reply. "His position is very temporary indeed."

"He certainly hopes so," Lang informed him. "We're very close to a solution. I can't tell you any more than that. And I'm sorry to add that you were right to suspect your brother-in-law."

"And what of my sister?" he asked solemnly.

"I don't know yet."

Ahmed was preoccupied as he rode with Brianna to the hospital to get an exhilarated Tad that very afternoon. Brianna was apparently in high spirits. Her boss had given her the day off, and the women in the office had gone in together to get a special present for Tad. They hadn't told her what it was. They'd wrapped it up, and it was very big. She was as curious as Tad about the contents.

"I would have brought it with me," she told Tad, "but the box wouldn't fit in here with the three of us."

"Unsurprising," Ahmed said with disgust, looking around him. "I do not fit in here."

"You'll have to ask your boss for a raise, Bri, so we can get a better car," Tad said.

"I like this one, thank you," she returned. "Once it's painted, it's going to be beautiful."

Tad made a sound in his throat and she smiled, but the smile never reached her eyes. Ahmed thought that he'd never seen her look so helpless. It infuriated him that she was willing to throw away what they felt for each other out of misplaced jealousy.

They unloaded Tad and his things and got him upstairs to the tenth-floor apartment. This one had three bedrooms and a living room, with a spacious kitchen. Brianna hummed as she worked, putting together a special meal.

Meanwhile, Tad had opened the suspicious box and let out a whoop.

Brianna stuck her head around the doorway to see what he had. She burst out laughing.

It was a collection of everything from a football helmet to a baseball and bat, all that a young man needed to join the human race again, including a Walkman tape player and several tapes to play in it.

"I've never heard of any of these people," he murmured as he looked at the tapes.

"You'll probably love them," Brianna said. "Marjorie bought the tapes, I'm sure. She has a son your age. She'll know what's popular." She frowned. "My goodness, Tad, we'll have to see about getting a tutor for you, so that you can catch up to your age level in school."

"That is easily arranged," Ahmed said gently. "Later, though. Not today."

She didn't look at him. "Of course not today," she replied. She went back into the kitchen and fixed a balanced meal worthy of Tad's first night home, with all his old favorites.

"This is great." He sighed when he'd cleaned up the very last of the chicken-and-rice casserole and the canned apricots and homemade rolls. "Bri, that was the best food I've ever had."

"You flatterer," she said, smiling at him warmly. "I'm glad you liked it. Your appetite is certainly going to please Dr. Brown."

He leaned back in his chair, studying Ahmed. "How did you wind up here, Cousin Pedro?" he asked curiously. "Did our aunt and uncle send you up here from Chihuahua?"

"Why, yes," Ahmed lied easily, and his eyes smiled. "To look for work. And I have," he continued. Lang had placed all sorts of applications from "Pedro" in strategic locations. But no one had called him about work.

"Sure." Tad smiled with some puzzlement. "But that Spanish accent of yours is the oddest I've ever heard."

"It's been years since you've heard one," Brianna reminded him.

"Well, yes, I guess so." He flexed his legs. "It's so good to be able to get up and walk. I don't guess any of my old friends are still around?" he added.

"Todd Brock is," she said, smiling at his surprise. "He calls every month or so to check on you. He has ever since the wreck."

"Wow! Do you have his telephone number? Can I call him?"

"Of course, I'll get it for you." She hesitated. This was going to present many complications. She couldn't let him tell Todd where he was, or who was living with them. She grimaced.

"You're worried," Tad said, suddenly curious. "You don't want me to call him. Why? What's going on?"

Chapter Eight

Brianna stood in the middle of the floor with a mind that refused to work. She couldn't think up a good reason to satisfy that suspicious look in her young brother's eyes.

"She has only just managed to reacquire you from the hospital after three long years," Ahmed said softly, smiling at the boy. "Is it not natural that she should jealously guard your company for at least the first few days you are back at her side?"

Tad colored and laughed roughly. "My gosh, yes. I'm sorry, sis. That was thoughtless of me, really!"

She walked over and hugged him warmly, her eyes mirroring her gratitude to Ahmed over Tad's shoulder. "I'm sorry," she said. "It's just that we've only just become reacquainted and I don't want to share you for a few days. So, do you mind?"

"I don't mind at all." His blue eyes twinkled. "Todd can wait."

"Thanks, Tad."

He shrugged. "What are brothers for?" he mused, and then laughed.

One disaster was averted. Brianna found it difficult to avoid the questions that kept coming, though. Inevitably Tad noticed how careful Brianna and Ahmed were about what they said, about going out, about letting anyone in. He was a sharp boy. He didn't voice any of his curiosity, but it was there in his eyes just the same. He had his own television in his room, and he was quickly and eagerly catching up on three years of news and new developments in his favorite subject, science. But he was giving his two companions looks that became more perceptive by the day.

"Tad is suspicious of us," Ahmed told Brianna one evening when they were alone in the kitchen after Tad had gone to bed.

"Yes, I know. It's a strain for all of us," she replied. "But it won't be for much longer, will it?"

"I hope not," he replied quietly. His dark eyes narrowed in impatience. "I long to be free of the necessity for this stealth and deception."

"So do I."

"You do not look at me anymore, Brianna," he said suddenly, lounging in the doorway with eyes she found difficult to meet. "You look beyond me or you talk to my chin. You avoid eye contact. Why?"

She deliberately dried a dish. There was a nice dishwasher in the apartment, but there were too few dishes for a load. She liked the feel of the warm soapy water on her hands.

"I hadn't noticed doing any such thing," she said defensively.

"Talk to me!" he said curtly. "Explain this violent change of attitude. Is it because you learned that I once had a mistress?"

She dropped the plate in the soapy water and fished it back out quickly, with trembling hands. "Your private life is no concern of mine," she said through numb lips. "You'll be going home soon, won't you?"

He shifted irritably. "Yes, I must, once this situation is resolved. I have responsibilities which I cannot shirk."

"We all have those, I guess," she said sadly. She washed the last of the dishes and let the water out of both sinks.

He jerked away from the door facing and came to stand directly behind her, so close that she could feel the heat and strength of his tall body.

"Have you traveled at all?" he asked. His warm breath stirred her hair.

She really should move away, she told herself. And she would, in just a minute. "Not really," she replied. "I've been to Mexico, but that was just a quick trip over the border from El Paso while on vacation with my parents and Tad, when I was in my early teens."

"Have you never longed to see other places, other countries?" he continued.

She could hear the soft whisper of his breath. Her body tingled at his nearness. She had to concentrate. What had he asked?

"Yes, I'd love to travel," she said huskily. "It's a big world, and I know very little about it. Tad would like it, too. But it will be a long time before that can happen. He isn't fit for long vacations just yet."

"He is young. He will recover swiftly now."

"He likes you," she remarked.

"And I like him, Brianna. He has character, that one. Like his sister."

His hands had gone to her waist, strong hands that tugged her back into the curve of his body. His cheek was against her hair, and he was breathing more heavily now. She couldn't move. She closed her eyes and savored the sweetness of the contact.

"What has gone wrong between us, *chérie?*" he asked quietly. "Why have you turned away from me?"

She bit through the skin on her lower lip and winced at the self-inflicted pain. "We're very different," she began.

"Different." His hands contracted roughly. "And yet, so alike in many ways. I am a Christian, did you know? I never accepted the Moslem faith."

"Yes, I remember." Her fingers rested lightly over his strong hands, feeling the roughness of skin and hair and the steely strength of them as they held her.

"I enjoy classical music, as you do," he continued quietly. "I would live a simple life if I could."

Odd phrasing, she thought curiously. "Why can't you?"

"Because of those duties and responsibilities I told you about," he replied. "Many people depend on me."

Her fingers had become involuntarily caressing over his. Her body throbbed with insistent pulses. She moved back toward him, a little stir of motion that aroused him viciously.

His lean fingers dug in at her waist and his mouth dropped to press hotly into the side of her neck. He nipped her with his teeth and, feeling her jump, slid his mouth to her ear.

"They have cameras and microphones in every room, even in this one," he said harshly. "Whether you realize it or not, that small movement which you have just made was a blatant invitation, one which I madly wish I could accept. But do you really fancy making love for the amusement of our hosts?''

She gasped and tore out of his grasp, facing him from several feet away with wide, shocked eyes. "You started it!" she accused.

He was rigid with desire and temper, his black eyes flashing, his fists clenched by his sides. "And you were an innocent bystander, led into sin?" he chided icily.

"You could lead a stone boulder into sin with a voice like that!" she snapped back. "I'll bet you didn't stop with one mistress, I'll bet you had twenty-five!"

His eyebrows arched. "Why should that matter to you? You have already stated, emphatically, that you have no interest whatsoever in my personal life."

"And I don't!" she assured him. Her blue eyes sparkled like sapphires in a face gone white with pain and hurt.

He said something she didn't understand. "What do you want of me?"

"I want you to go home," she said through her teeth, "and get out of my life!"

"Gladly," he agreed. "As soon as they catch the men who are trying to kill me!"

"Someone's trying to kill you, Cousin Pedro?" came a shocked voice from behind him.

He turned, and there was Tad, clad in pajamas and looking as if he'd been struck.

"Why are you awake?" he asked gently. "Could you not sleep?"

"Not with all the noise," he murmured dryly, glancing at his sister. "She never used to raise her voice at all, you know."

"Truly?" He looked at her, and there was something very speculative in his bold stare. "She raises it to me constantly."

"You should try to get along," Tad told him. "She's a nice girl, really."

"I know that, to my cost," Ahmed said with a speaking look in Brianna's direction that made her turn scarlet.

"Who's trying to kill you?" Tad persisted.

Ahmed grimaced. "It was a figure of speech," he began.

"No, it wasn't, really," Tad said, grinning. "We've got men watching the apartment from across the way with high-powered telescopes, and I've spotted two video camera fiber-optic connections. And the telephone's bugged, because I opened up the mouthpiece and looked."

The two adults wore equally shocked looks. "How do you know what a bug looks like?" Ahmed asked him.

"There's these old spy movies I've been watching on television," Tad explained. "And there's been an ongoing documentary on the CIA that showed about bugs and stuff. Gosh, it's so exciting! I hope you don't get shot, of course. But if you do, I know what to do for a gunshot wound," he continued, while Ahmed buried his face in his hand and chuckled helplessly. "I watched a show about the medical corps, and they showed real gory pictures of how they treat wounds. It was great!"

"Oh, Tad!" Brianna groaned. "You shouldn't be watching that sort of thing!"

"I'm not squeamish," he muttered. "I want to be in law enforcement when I grow up. Forensics, maybe. Did you know how much you can learn about a body from examining the skull?" he continued excitedly.

"I think you should go back to bed," Brianna said gently.

"I guess I should," he said with a sigh of resignation. He glanced from one of them to the other. "Are you going to start yelling at each other again the minute I leave the room?" he asked politely.

"Not really," Brianna assured him. "I'm tired, too. I plan to go to bed very shortly."

"Okay." Tad stood in front of Ahmed, who towered over him again. "You don't have a Spanish accent," he said bluntly. "You speak English like Omar Sharif did in *Lawrence of Arabia.*"

Ahmed's chin rose proudly. "You are intelligent," he told the boy. "And not easily fooled."

Tad smiled. "Thanks. Does that mean I get to hear what's really going on here?"

Ahmed smiled back. "No."

Tad shrugged. "You win some, you lose some. Good night."

He went away without another argument. Ahmed watched his retreat thoughtfully.

"He would make a fine diplomat," he remarked. "He is both intuitive and observant."

"What a delightful occupation to wish on him," she said curtly. "Look at what it's done for you!"

He cocked an eyebrow, turning to stare at her. "You have a very sharp tongue," he remarked. "It has been many years since anyone, much less a woman, dared speak to me as you have."

"They were probably afraid you'd chop their heads off," she muttered.

"In the distant past, that might have been a possibility," he told her. His eyes grew intent on her flushed face.

"You have no idea what my culture is like, even today, have you?"

"You've got lots of oil in your country and everybody wants it," she replied.

He smiled. "True."

"You have a king and a parliament, your country was created out of Arabia just after World War I, you import high-tech items from the United States and Western Germany, your universities are some of the oldest in the Middle East, and the majority of your people are Moslem."

He nodded. "Very good."

"We have a new set of encyclopedia that I'm still paying off. Why isn't there a photograph of your king in it?" she asked suddenly.

"Because of the increased risk such publicity would afford him," he said simply. "Our king has been the target of assassins before this."

The slip didn't get past her. "You mean they're after your king as well as you?"

He hesitated. "Well, yes."

"Oh, my. I hope he's well guarded."

"He is," Ahmed returned dryly. "*Too* well guarded," he added loudly.

In a nearby room, several dark-suited men with earphones almost rolled on the floor laughing.

"What do you mean?" Brianna asked with a frown.

"They have him in a hotel surrounded by bodyguards and security people, being fed very well. I expect when they let him out, he will be like your Old King Cole of fantasy."

She laughed. It was the first time she had, in several days. "Roly-poly? Is he short and stocky?"

"The man in the hotel is, yes," he returned truthfully.

"I don't suppose there are many handsome kings around." She nodded and turned away.

He quickly composed himself. "I have a chessboard, if you play."

"I'm sorry," she replied. "I never learned."

"I could teach you."

She shook her head. "I'm very tired. This has been a difficult week. For all of us," she added, lifting her eyes to his. "You look very tired."

"I am. Tired and a little disappointed."

"Why?"

He searched her face with eyes that adored it. "I had certain hopes, Brianna. They have come to nothing."

She stared back at him with curiosity. "This woman back home..."

"She is my *ex*-mistress," he said curtly. "There is nothing between us now."

"I didn't mean that one. The other one," she prompted.

He was very quiet. "Which...other one?"

"The one you're going to marry!" she said, exasperated.

His lips parted on a spent breath. He searched for words, but he couldn't find any appropriate ones. "Am I getting married, then?"

"You told Lang you were," she said quietly. She lowered her eyes. "He told me."

Ahmed's expression was briefly murderous. He looked around the room. "I hope he has no plans to visit the Middle East when this situation is over. I think he might look very interesting at the end of a scimitar!"

"Why are you angry with him? He only mentioned it."

"Only!" His eyes came back to her and calmed a little. She'd been jealous. Hurt, too, perhaps. Her recent behavior began to make sense. It would be all right. She wanted him. His heart felt suddenly light and carefree. He would have some very difficult arrangements to make. And then a quick trip to the altar was certainly in store, before anyone else could throw more spikes into his wheel.

He didn't stop to think if his plotting was fair to Brianna. He'd always done things to suit himself. He was doing it now. She would be well provided for, and so would her brother. She would adjust to life in another country if he could make her care for him enough. He was certain that he could.

"My marriage plans are hardly finalized yet," he said. "And the lady in question is unaware of my intentions."

"Does she love you?" she asked involuntarily, her sad eyes searching over his beloved dark face.

He saw for the first time what she couldn't hide, that she adored him. He smiled slowly. "Do you know, *petite,* I think she does."

She made a faint smile. "I wish you happiness, then."

He couldn't drag his eyes away from her. She was so pretty. He moved toward her, lifting her chin with his fingertips to study her sad blue eyes.

"Will you miss me when I go back to my own country?"

"Tad and I both will," she said hesitatingly.

"And I shall miss you." He searched her face with faint misgivings. She cared for him. But could she love him? He bent slowly toward her mouth. Incredibly, as intimate as they'd been together, he'd never kissed her. He wanted to.

But she pulled back. "The, uh, the cameras," she said discreetly.

He muttered something in Arabic and took her by the hand, pulling her with him down the hall.

"Where are we going...not in here!"

"It is the only place Lang is unlikely to put a camera," he returned, closing them up in the bathroom. He propped his hands on either side of her, where she stood with her back against the door, breathless and excited.

"I don't want this," she said unconvincingly.

"Yes, you do," he replied easily. "You think I am being unfaithful to the woman I intend to marry. It gives you a guilty conscience to consider allowing my embraces."

She didn't have to answer him. Her answer was plain on her face.

"As I thought," he said with a gentle smile. "You are so very young, *chérie,*" he added solemnly. He searched her eyes and then let his gaze drop to her parted mouth. "So young... so very, very young...."

The words went into her mouth as he brushed his lightly against it. She felt the warm hardness of his lips, the velvet tickle of the thick moustache. Then, slowly, his tongue probed her lips, parting them, darting past her teeth into the silky darkness of her mouth.

He felt her stiffen. He withdrew at once, and his mouth lightly brushed hers, teasing it back into submission. When she relaxed, he started again. She was totally innocent of such loveplay. He had to remember that, and be patient with her.

It was exciting to make love to such an obvious virgin. He smiled as he made her mouth lift to seek the deepening pressure of his. He felt her shy movements, the hesitant reach of her hands around him, against his silk shirt, warm through it as they sought contact with his shoulders. She came closer and he levered his body down into hers, using the door to hold her there while he maneuvered them into greater intimacy.

She wasn't protesting anymore. Her mouth opened to the darting sensual movements of his tongue. Her body submitted to the slow, blatant drag of his hips that let her feel the strength and power of his arousal. She tasted him, experienced him, as she'd never known another man. She gave him everything he asked for.

Even when she felt his long leg push between hers, when she felt him lowering against her even more, so that his hips were squarely over hers and they were as intimate as lovers except for the layers of fabric that separated them.

She made a husky, passionate little sound in his mouth, and shifted quickly to accommodate him. He pushed against her rhythmically, letting her feel how it would be.

It was almost too late to stop. He shuddered and she clung when he tried to draw away.

His lips moved against hers when he spoke. "For a thousand reasons, this cannot continue," he whispered unsteadily. "The pleasure is becoming too urgent, too sweet to deny. All I must do is loosen two fastenings, and you will know me completely, standing here against the door. Let me stop while I can. I am too aroused to give you tenderness. It will hurt."

She felt his mouth touching her face, gentling her, as he forcibly withdrew from temptation. He held her while he covered her eyelids with kisses to calm her.

She was shivering with reaction. But there was no shame in what she felt. Finally her eyes slid open and looked up into his, curious and shy and uncertain.

"You know very little of men, *n'est-ce pas?*" he asked huskily, searching her face with quick, sharp eyes. "Do you really think that I have experienced such violent, sweet desire with a host of other women? Do you think this is such a routine experience for me that I am completely unmoved by it when I release you?"

"I don't know," she said shakily.

"Brianna, once in a lifetime a man may experience something so earth-shattering and passionate, if he is fortunate," he explained slowly. "I have no wish whatsoever to turn our magic into a sordid tangle of arms and legs in a bed."

She flushed. "Oh."

"It is not sex. That is what you thought?"

"You seemed not to want to be close to me, after the night we spent together," she said demurely. "I thought you'd decided it was all a mistake and you only wanted to forget it."

"I went up in flames and all I thought about afterward was how quickly I could strip you and relieve the ache you leave me with," he whispered wickedly. "But afterward, it made me ashamed to want something so physical, when I knew how fragile and vulnerable you were in other ways."

"So you ignored me completely," she agreed.

"It was the only protection I could manage," he told her with a long-suffering look. "Now that Tad is here with us at night, and Lang has cameras in most of the rooms, it would be quite difficult to find enough privacy to satisfy ourselves."

"You did maneuver us into a bathroom," she stated.

"Where I came to my senses in time," he reminded her. "I care too much for you to use you, no matter how much you inflame me," he added. "I meant what I told you. A man must not allow himself to reach such a frenzy of desire when he pleasures a virgin." He traced her flaming cheeks. "He must become as the wind across the desert, slow and tender and caressing until she is prepared to receive him."

She felt hot all over as he spoke. Her eyes fell to his throat, where a pulse throbbed visibly.

"You still avoid my eyes. Why?"

"It embarrasses me, a little."

"When we have been naked together in bed?" he teased softly.

"We weren't lovers."

He drew her head to his chest and caressed her hair. "Oh, we will love," he whispered. "But not as conspirators hiding in corners."

"I don't understand."

"Did you think me such a rake, Brianna, that I could make love to you while I had a woman waiting at home, expecting to become my bride?"

She hadn't thought about that aspect of his behavior. She lifted her head and looked up into his eyes with quiet curiosity.

"Well, no," she confessed. "It did seem rather out of character. But Lang said—"

He put his lean forefinger over her mouth. "Yes. Lang said that I was impatient for this charade to be over because I wanted to marry. Indeed I do, with all possible haste, and there are more obstacles and difficulties than you can possibly imagine because of my choice of brides."

She scowled. Her finger idly traced a button on his white shirt. Under it, his heartbeat was quick and hard. He caught her hand and she held his eyes while she worked underneath it to unfasten two buttons, then three, then four. His lips parted as she reached inside the shirt and began to slowly caress the hair-roughened muscles of his chest.

"I love to touch you," she said unsteadily.

"Wait."

She lifted her eyes again. "Is it so uncomfortable for you?"

"Yes." He put her hand to one side, smiling ruefully. "I have no plans to marry a woman from my own country. Although it is of a certainty that the woman I marry must agree that the ceremony be performed there. I am a high public official. I cannot marry in this country in secret. Do you understand?"

"Yes. No. You said you were going to get married," she began.

"And I am. Oh, yes, I am," he whispered fervently and bent to kiss her hungrily.

"Then who...?"

"You, of course. Who else occupies my mind waking and sleeping...? Brianna, marry me!" he breathed into her mouth.

Chapter Nine

While Brianna tried to cope with what she thought she'd just heard, Ahmed made a much more thorough frontal assault on her soft mouth. She couldn't think at all. She answered his lips and her hands slid with waves of pleasure over his broad, hair-roughened chest, savoring the feel of his body under her sensitive fingers.

He groaned and lifted his head, stilling her exploring fingers. "You are killing me," he whispered.

"You asked me to marry you," she moaned, reaching up to try to capture his mouth again. "I'm saying yes...."

She kissed him. He half lifted her and deepened the kiss, making her knees go watery weak as the heat between them reached an explosive force.

"I feel I should tell you," a deep voice came from the wall beside them, "that we had to put microphones even in the rooms where we didn't put cameras."

Ahmed's head jerked up. His blazing eyes searched the

walls while fierce and probably obscene words rattled off his tongue like nails out of an air gun.

"I won't have our translator work on that." Lang chuckled. "Congratulations on your engagement. Now would you mind getting out of the bathroom and breaking this up? Some of us are turning to strong drink...."

Ahmed caught Brianna's hand and pulled her out the door into the hall. He was raging mad, and she had to muffle laughter at the expression on his face. She was glad her name wasn't Lang.

"He did warn us before we embarrassed ourselves," she reminded him.

He was breathing roughly and his cheekbones were ruddy with bad temper. His narrow dark eyes looked down into hers. He said something terse.

"Will you teach me Arabic when we're married?" she asked with a loving smile.

"Only when Lang is in another country," he promised, glaring at the walls.

"I heard that" came plainly from another part of the wall.

"Go away, Lang," Brianna said. "I'm trying to accept a proposal of marriage in here."

"Yes, ma'am," Lang said, and there was a clicking sound.

She looked back at Ahmed. "Are you sure?" she asked. "There will be so many problems. Americans aren't well liked in your country, are they?"

"My people will like you," he said with certainty.

"What if your king refuses you permission to marry me?" she asked worriedly. "He could, couldn't he?"

"He could make it difficult, if he wished," he replied dryly. "But I can assure you that he will not. He will find you ravishing."

She knew he was exaggerating, but the flattery made her feel warm inside. "I hope so." She touched the loose buttons on his shirt. "We'll have to live in Saudi Mahara, won't we?"

He nodded.

"All the time?"

"Most of it," he said. "I travel in the performance of my duties, but our capital city of Mozambara is my home. I hope that you will learn to love it as I do."

"What about Tad?" she asked suddenly.

"He will come with us, of course," he said, as if he wondered why she should even have asked such a silly question.

"It will mean uprooting him. And myself. We'll have to learn other customs, another language...."

"You brood about things which will fall naturally into place, *chérie,*" he said, "if you love me enough."

She stared into his black eyes with building hunger. He seemed to be waiting for something. Perhaps he was as uncertain as she was about the future. "I love you enough," she said huskily. "I love you more than my own life."

He drew her close and bent his dark head over hers, his arms bruising for a moment as he realized how much she belonged to him, and he to her. There had never been a time when he had considered the need to have someone of his own permanently to cherish. But he was growing older, and Mahara would need an heir.

"Do you like children, Brianna?"

"Oh, yes," she murmured happily.

He drew in a long breath. "There must be heirs. It is my duty to provide them."

"It used to be kings who had to do that," she said drowsily. "Now it's cabinet ministers, too. I won't mind at all. I love little babies."

He winced over her head. She didn't know his identity. He was tempted to tell her, but she might panic. It would be better to wait until he could settle the resistance there would surely be among his high officials and even among some American officials to this match. She would only worry and perhaps try to back out.

He drew away and looked at her rapt face. He smiled. "We will overcome the obstacles, together," he told her, reassuring himself in the process.

She pressed close and inhaled the faintly foreign scent of his cologne, secure with the heavy beat of his heart under her ear. "I'm twenty-two," she said absently.

"Yes, I know."

She lifted her head, curiously.

"Never mind how I know." He bent, smiling, to touch her mouth softly with his. "Go to bed. It is late."

"I'm tired. But I don't think I can sleep," she said.

"Lie down, at least," he said.

"Okay. But I'm undressing in the closet!" she told the walls.

There were good-natured long sighs among the men in the room next door.

Lang was repentant when he came to the apartment the next morning. Brianna had a tight hold on Ahmed's hand so that he couldn't do to Lang what his eyes threatened.

"Sorry about last night," Lang said. "Really, I am, but we thought it would be wise to warn you while there was still time. We can't afford to leave even one room unprotected."

"The sooner this is over, the better!" Ahmed said harshly.

"All of us feel the same way, believe it or not," Lang said, and Brianna noticed then how tired and drawn he looked. "We haven't slept."

"Don't you take turns?" she asked.

He shrugged. "It's still twelve-hour shifts. Manpower is scarce for constant surveillance. We're a government agency, you know. We have to beg for funding just like everybody else, and sometimes the politicians get it in for us."

"Ah, democracy at work," Ahmed taunted.

Lang glowered at him. "Well, at least if we don't do a good job, nobody herds us into the marketplace to be decapitated."

Ahmed was affronted. "I have not decapitated anyone for a decade. We are a progressive nation. We even have protest rallies, just like the West."

"I remember your last protest rally," Lang commented.

Ahmed shifted. "It was unavoidable. They stormed the gates of the palace."

"What are you two talking about?" Brianna asked.

"Your new home," Lang replied. He fixed Ahmed with a steady look. "When are you going to tell her?"

"When I have overcome the diplomatic obstacles," Ahmed said quietly. "And ascertained that she will not be assassinated along with me on the way back to Saudi Mahara."

"Good point." Lang stretched, big muscles bulging in his arms. "Well, I'm going out for a cup of coffee and then a quick nap."

"Are there any new developments?" Ahmed asked.

"Several. You'll have company inside as well as outside tonight," he commented. He stared at Brianna, who was looking uncomfortable. "You and Tad are pretty nervy people. Think you can survive a stakeout?"

"Sure," she said. "As long as I don't have to shoot anybody."

He smiled. "We'll do the shooting. But it won't come to that. I won't put any of you in danger."

"How about yourself?" she replied.

Lang shrugged. "I'm used to it. It's what I get paid for."

"Despite your eavesdropping propensities, I should hate to see you hurt," Ahmed added.

Lang grinned at them. "None of us likes taking chances. We're pretty sure they're going to make an attempt on you tonight. We'll be ready. With any luck at all, this will wrap it all up. If we're successful," he told Ahmed, "you could be on your way home by the end of the week."

Ahmed glanced at Brianna. "Yes," he said slowly. "So I could."

She didn't understand that look. It contained worry and apprehension, and she didn't think it was just because some enemy agents might make a grab for them.

The day passed slowly. Ahmed and Tad sat together in the living room, going over some new science magazines that Lang had provided, while Brianna reluctantly went to work. Her mind wasn't on her duties, though. It was on the danger they were all in, and especially on Ahmed's proposal of marriage. She wanted to marry him. She loved him. But until now she hadn't had to deal with the complications of marriage to a foreign national.

On her lunch hour, she went to the local public library and checked out every book she could find that dealt with Saudi Mahara. It was such a small nation that she had to choose general subjects to find out anything. Then she got a book on Arab customs and copied a magazine article on women's roles in the Middle East. This would give her some idea of the new life she was going to enjoy, she thought. It would be better for Ahmed if his new wife had foreknowledge of what would be expected of her. Not that she expected to wear a veil and walk three steps behind him, of course.

Ahmed and Tad were deep in a discussion of nuclear physics when she got home from work with her load of library books, and there were four government intelligence agents sticking out of her refrigerator.

She stopped dead at the sight of them.

Ahmed smiled complacently. "They have had nothing to eat since lunch yesterday," he explained.

"Oh, you poor guys!" Brianna exclaimed.

They turned and stared at her. One was holding a carton of yogurt. Another had a carton of milk. The other two were having a minor tug-of-war over a wrapped cheese slice. They all lifted their eyebrows hopefully.

"I'll cook you up a big pot of spaghetti and some garlic bread," she promised, dumping the books on the sofa and making a beeline into the kitchen.

"God bless you!" one of the bigger agents said fervently.

The others marched him out of the kitchen to let Brianna work. It was quick work, too. She had spaghetti down to a fine art. The sauce should have simmered for at least half an hour, she supposed, but those men would all pass out sooner than that. She handed them plates and forks and started dishing it up the minute she could combine the cooked pasta with the meat sauce. Ahmed and Tad managed to get a few bites, too, and while everyone was occupied, Brianna made a bread pudding for dessert. Even the crumbs were gone five minutes after it was taken out of the oven.

Lang arrived just in time for the dishwashing. He had a toothpick in his mouth, and the other agents all gave him accusing looks.

"What?" he challenged. "I had a fast-food hamburger. A little one, okay?"

They surrounded him. "We," the biggest one said, "had spaghetti and garlic bread, homemade and delicious," he added, addressing a beaming Brianna. "And for dessert she made us bread pudding."

"And you didn't save any for me?" Lang asked, horrified.

"You had a hamburger," the big agent reminded him with a grin.

"I'll never do it again," Lang promised. "Can't I have just a crumb of bread pudding? It's my favorite."

"Sorry. We ate it all," the big agent said. He didn't look sorry. He was smiling.

"Just wait until I have to write up this surveillance," Lang began.

"Oh, yeah?" one of the other agents said, with his hands in his pockets. "And what are you gonna say, huh?"

They all adopted the same pose. Lang sighed. "That you're a great bunch of guys to work with, and next time I'll bring four extra hamburgers back with me."

The big agent patted him on the back. "Good man," he said. "I'll recommend you for promotion when I get to be President."

"I wouldn't hold my breath if I were you," Lang advised. "You'd break the budget in a week, the way you eat."

"What did you find out?" another agent asked, and they were suddenly all government agents again, all business.

They went into a huddle. In a minute they began to disperse, setting up equipment and checking it.

Lang was very somber as he drew the three occupants of the apartment to one side. "We want you to act naturally. Do what you've been doing in the evenings since Tad came here. We've swept the place for bugs and cameras, and it's clean. Just try not to be surprised at anything that goes down, okay? One of us will be with you all the time."

It became real life then. Brianna had seen films of terrorists. They had automatic weapons and no compassion. They killed quickly, efficiently, and without mercy. She looked at Ahmed and Tad and realized that she could lose either or both of them in less than two seconds. Her face went white.

Ahmed pulled her close against his side. "This is no time to become fainthearted," he said quietly. "You must have the bearing and dignity of high office, even when under fire. It will be expected of you."

Because he was a high official of his country, she realized. She searched his dark eyes. "I'm not worried for myself, you know," she said gently.

"I realize that. Nor I, for myself."

She smiled at him. "I won't let you down."

He brought her palm to his mouth. "Cowardice is the last thing I would ever expect from you."

She beamed. "Same here."

"Could you stop exchanging praises and just go about your business?" Lang asked amusedly.

"Of course." Ahmed let go of her and went back to the science magazines he was looking over with Tad.

The boy was wearing a new pair of jeans and a white T-shirt. He looked healthier, but he was still pale and weak. Ahmed studied him, noticing that he was as game as Brianna.

"You make me proud that I shall become part of such a family as yours," he told Tad.

The boy smiled. "That goes double for me. Will we live in your country, then?" he asked, because he knew already that he wasn't going to be left behind when Bri married. They'd made a point of telling him so.

"Most certainly."

"I'd love to learn to ride a horse. They say there are no horses in the world like the Arabians."

"This is true," Ahmed agreed. "However, the horses I own are magnificent in their own right. They are bred in Austria, and I..."

The attack was so sudden that Brianna wondered for a space of seconds if she was asleep and having another nightmare. The front door burst in with explosive force and men in masks carrying automatic weapons were spraying everything in sight with bullets.

Ahmed pulled Tad to the floor in a spectacular tackle while Brianna dropped behind the counter as soon as she heard the explosion.

The exchange of weapon fire sounded more like firecrackers popping than like real guns. It was surreal. Brianna knew better than to dare lift her head. She curled up on the floor to make as small a target as possible and hoped that the government agents were accurate with those nasty-looking weapons she'd seen under their suit coats. She didn't dare think about Ahmed or Tad, or she'd go mad.

There was a cessation of noise. A clink of glass falling. There were quick, hard footsteps and then Ahmed and Tad were bending over her.

"Are you all right?" Ahmed asked quickly, rolling her over and gathering her up close. His eyes were wild, his face pale under its natural darkness.

"Yes. Are both of you?" she asked, her eyes going frantically from Tad to Ahmed.

"We're fine," Tad assured her, but he was pale and his voice was shaking. "Gosh, that was some... something, wasn't it?"

Brianna clung to Ahmed, shivering with aftershock. Those men had come to kill him. The bullets had been meant for him. She gasped.

"All clear," Lang said, repocketing his automatic under his jacket. He looked down at Brianna, his face still showing traces of ferocity from the ordeal. He glanced over his shoulder. "Don't let her get up yet," he told Ahmed.

"Haven't you caught them?" she asked fearfully.

"Oh, yes," Lang said, and there was something in his eyes that she didn't want to see. She looked quickly down again.

Ahmed cradled her in his arms and sat with his back against the cabinet. Tad started to peek around the corner but Ahmed jerked him back.

"No," he told the boy, and his face was unusually stern.

"Okay. I was just curious."

"Curiosity sometimes carries a high price," he was told. Ahmed looked down at Brianna's white face. "It is over," he told her softly. "All over. Lang told me earlier that he was in contact with my government. The perpetrators will be caught now. The coup attempt has failed."

"Your king will be relieved," Tad remarked. "Is he okay, do you think?"

"Oh, yes," Ahmed said absently, stroking Brianna's dark, damp hair back from her face. "The king has never been better, I am sure."

Later, when the devastation was cleared away and the enemy agents removed, Ahmed and Brianna and Tad were moved out of the wrecked apartment and into another.

Brianna had noticed stains on the carpet, but when she tried to ask about them, she was ignored.

"I'm not a baby, you know," she told Ahmed.

His smile was a little strained. "No. But I am older than you, and I have seen more. Believe me when I tell you that you need not know all of what has happened today. Trust me. Will you trust me, *chérie?*"

"Yes."

He brushed his mouth over her eyelids and left her with Tad while he moved out into the hall to talk to Lang.

"Well?" he asked the agent.

Lang was still high-strung from the experience. He leaned back against the wall, squeezing a hand exerciser to relax himself.

"I hate to be the one to tell you this," he told Ahmed. "But they've taken your sister into custody." He held up a hand when Ahmed tried to speak. "They haven't connected her to the takeover coup. They've only connected her husband. It was a preventive measure only. But you're going to have to go back with all haste and set things right. You knew that already."

"I knew. Brianna has not been told," he added. "She must not be. I need time to settle my affairs before I attempt to involve her in them. This, today, has been a salutary experience."

"It isn't the first time you've been shot at," Lang reminded him.

He nodded, looking darkly arrogant. "But it is the first time that she and Tad have," he replied. "For that alone, I have no regrets about the outcome."

Lang stared at the hand exerciser. "Assassination attempts are few and far between, you know. Your father had one. This is your second."

"This is connected to the same people, however," he said, "and they are now in custody. I must see what I can do for Yasmin. She would not try to kill me. I know this."

"Get a good lawyer," he was advised.

"I must," he said heavily. "Our court system is even harsher than yours, and we do not play dice with the death penalty. The ringleaders of this plot will be executed if they are convicted, and there will be no stays or appeals."

Lang whistled. "Harsh justice, indeed."

"The old ways are cruel," Ahmed agreed. "Brianna may not be able to accept marriage when she knows my true identity. It is regrettable that I could not tell her the truth from the beginning."

"That was our decision, not yours," Lang said.

He smiled ruefully. "Will it matter, in the end, who decided?" He moved away from the wall. "I will be ready to leave first thing in the morning." He paused, and turned back to face Lang. "Thank you for what you have done. And the others. Whatever they pay you, it is not enough for the risks you must take."

"We get paid enough," Lang mused. "The occasional pot of spaghetti and a bread pudding are icing on the cake."

"You are brave people," he said sincerely. "If your government ever fires you, you will always have a job in mine. I could use such a minister of justice."

"Ouch," Lang said, wincing. "A desk job, for a street man like me? Bite your tongue!"

"Commander-in-chief of the secret service, then." Ahmed chuckled.

"That's more like it, and thank you for the offer. One day I may need a job."

Ahmed leaned closer. "If you continue to put bugs in the bathrooms of unsuspecting people, I can almost guarantee it."

Lang chuckled. "I see your point."

Tad had trouble settling down for the night after all the excitement. He still didn't know what was going on, and he wouldn't rest until somebody gave him an explanation.

Ahmed took Brianna's hand in his while they sat on the sofa drinking coffee from the new pot Lang had scrounged for them. The apartment was furnished, but a coffeepot and coffee hadn't been part of the furnishings.

"Since you were forced to endure the unpleasantness with us," Ahmed told Tad, "it is proper that you know why. There was a coup attempt back home in my country."

"Not Mexico," Tad said with dry humor.

"Not Mexico," Ahmed agreed. "My home is in Saudi Mahara, a country in the Middle East. I have been in this country to represent my people in a contract for several jets from Ryker Air, the company for which your sister works."

"They needed a place to hide him until they could find the assassins who were trying to kill him," Brianna added, still a little shaky from the ordeal. "They thought that having him masquerade as a poor Mexican laborer, our cousin, was a good disguise, since everyone in the office knew that we hated each other. The last place any enemy agent would look for him would be in my apartment."

"You hated each other?" Tad asked, smiling. "Really?"

Ahmed looked at her with tenderness. "I was immediately attracted to her when she heaved a paperweight at my head. It was the first time in my life anyone had dared to attack my person."

"I find that hard to believe," Brianna murmured dryly. "You have a way of making people bristle, you know."

He smiled indulgently. "At times," he admitted. "But when I am at home, it is a crime to attack me."

"Your king must think very highly of you," Tad remarked.

Ahmed sighed. "At times he does. At others, he is rather disappointed in me, I fear." He looked at Brianna. "You have not changed your mind about marrying me?" he asked bluntly. "I saw the books that you brought home to study. There may be things in them that disturb you."

"They won't disturb me enough to take back my acceptance," she said firmly.

"You bet they won't," Tad affirmed, "because I want to learn to ride!"

She glanced at her brother, delighted to see the animation in his face. It made her feel wonderful to see him alert and alive and happy. It was like a miracle.

"Not just yet, however," Ahmed said somberly. "There is something I must tell both of you."

"Oh?" Brianna asked. "What?"

He studied their linked fingers. "I have to go home tomorrow. Alone."

Chapter Ten

There was a flattering look of misery from Brianna and Tad. It didn't really make Ahmed feel a lot better, however. He had no idea how Brianna would react when she knew what would really be expected of her. Marrying a foreign cabinet official might not be so difficult. But he was not that. His life was one of rigorous protocol and duty. Would she be content with such a rigid life? Would she be able to accept it for Tad?

He didn't want to think about it now. "It is only a temporary absence," he assured them. "There are some things I must deal with."

"They've caught the people involved in the assassination plot, haven't they?" Brianna asked perceptively.

He nodded. He stared at his hands. "One of them is my only sister."

She put her hand over his and moved closer to lean her head against his broad shoulder. "I'm sorry," she said sincerely.

"Me, too," Tad offered. "Gee, that would be tough. Why would she want to kill you?"

"I am not certain that she did," Ahmed confessed. "I think that it was her husband's idea and not her own. But I must find out."

"You didn't really answer me," Tad persisted, his blue eyes, so much like Brianna's, unblinking.

Ahmed's broad shoulders rose and fell. "The hunger for power creates madness at times."

"But you're a cabinet minister," Brianna began.

"I must make some telephone calls," he said abruptly, glancing at the clock on the wall. "You will excuse me?" he asked formally.

She let go of his hand reluctantly. He was keeping something from her. It disturbed her.

"Of course," she said automatically.

He smiled briefly and left them, going into the middle bedroom to make his calls. He closed the door firmly behind him.

"That isn't all," Tad said. "He's hiding something."

"Yes, I know." Brianna was worried. She didn't want it to show, but it did. "Oh, Tad, I hope this really is the end of the assassination attempts."

They had a quiet supper later that night, one that Lang and the guys provided—huge pizzas.

"This is our favorite food," Lang remarked, passing Brianna another slice. "We live on it when we're on stakeout. We know all the best places."

"You could have offered to bring us a pizza instead of a little hamburger yesterday," the big agent remarked to Lang.

Lang chuckled. "I fell asleep in the booth with half the hamburger in my hand," he confessed. "I guess I went without a nap too long."

"Poor guy," one of the other agents said. "You ought to get a decent job, you know."

"I tried, but only the CIA would hire me," Lang retorted.

Listening to their banter relaxed Brianna, but Ahmed was quiet and subdued. All of them, except Brianna, knew why he was upset. Even his standing would not save his sister's life if she was found guilty of treason. He hadn't told Brianna.

When the agents left, Tad went to bed, leaving Brianna and Ahmed discreetly alone.

But there was a new distance between them. He sat in the armchair across from her place on the sofa, looking terribly remote and sad. There was an aura about him that she remembered from their earliest acquaintance, when he and his entourage first arrived at Ryker Air. She'd thought then that he had a rather regal air, as if his position gave him great importance and he expected everyone to be aware of it.

"Are you sorry that you asked me to marry you?" she asked bluntly, her blue eyes worried.

His fingers idly caressed the soft fabric over the arms of the chair. "No. Of all my recent actions, that is the one which I regret the least. You delight me."

She smiled. "Will you have to be away long?"

He shrugged. "I do not know." He wouldn't meet her eyes. "The leaders of the coup have to be dealt with."

"Yes, of course, but why do you have to be there?" she asked, frowning. "Do the cabinet ministers act as judges in your country?"

He got up from the chair and paced restlessly. "You should study those books," he said, nodding toward them. "They will help you understand the way of my culture."

"I'll do that," she said. She smoothed her hands over her jeans-clad thighs. "It should be very exciting, living near the desert."

"It disturbs you, though," he said quietly, glancing at her. "It will mean many sacrifices. Perhaps you will not want to make them."

Her expression was unguarded, and looking at it made him feel wounded. He missed her already. He moved toward her and scooped her up against his chest, holding her cradled to him with his mouth hungry against her neck. "Do not look like that!" he whispered roughly. "I cannot bear to see you so! I am only thinking of your happiness!"

"Then stop trying to push me away," she whispered miserably. "You do it all the time lately."

"Not from choice," he said fervently. His mouth became sensuous as it moved up to her face. "I adore you. I desire you. You are my life...."

His mouth found hers and he kissed her very slowly, with a tenderness that was almost painfully sweet. Her hands traced his hard face, learning its lines, while she fed on the warm expertness of his mouth.

His hands went to her hips and lifted her gently into the changing contours of his body while he kissed her. She began to moan, moving closer of her own accord.

His fingers contracted, pulling, molding, and she shuddered.

He lifted his head. His eyes were glazed with desire, blackly glittering with longings that he could only just control.

"Would you, if I asked?" he whispered huskily.

"Yes," she said simply.

He stared at her swollen lips, her misty eyes. "I want nothing in the world more," he told her. "But I cannot risk the premature birth of our child. There must be no hint of scandal, no question of his legitimacy."

Her head was swimming, but the curious wording caught her attention. "You mean I mustn't get pregnant until we're married?"

He groaned. "That is exactly what I mean."

She cleared her throat. "Oh. I forgot. I mean, your country is much more rigid than ours about a woman's chastity, isn't it?"

"I fear so."

She moved away from him a little and managed a smile. "Okay."

He was trying to breathe normally, and failing miserably. He laughed despite his hunger for her. "Just like that? Okay?"

She colored. "I didn't mean it was easy."

"Nor is it for me," he confessed. "I want you very badly. But we will wait until the rings are in place and the vows spoken."

He bent and kissed her softly one last time. "Go to bed now. It has been a long and fraught day for all of us."

"Tomorrow will be worse," she said quietly. "You'll be gone."

"Not for long, I swear it!" he said huskily. "It will be the most terrible torment, to have to be parted from you even for a few days."

"How flattering," she said with a coy smile. "I'll plan a special evening for your return."

"Not too special, if you please," he returned. "We have our reputations to consider."

She reached up to his ear. "I'll have Lang come and bug the apartment." He made a threatening sound, and she burst out laughing, hugging him close. It was heaven, to be loved and in love. She hoped, she prayed, that it would last. If only there were not this feeling of foreboding.

Ahmed left the next morning, with his entourage surrounding him and Lang bringing up the rear. He and Brianna had said a quick and uncomplicated farewell before they left the apartment. He'd taken time to hug Tad, as well. But in his expensive suit, surrounded by his own people, he looked foreign and unfamiliar.

"He's elegant, isn't he?" Tad asked as they watched out the window. Ahmed climbed into a big white stretch limo with two of his henchmen, and Lang got into the front seat with the driver. They drew a lot of attention from people on the streets. It didn't matter now, the danger was over. Brianna hoped it was, at least. She was still worried about Ahmed going back to his own country safely.

"Yes, he's very elegant," she agreed.

"I think we're going to like living in Saudi Mahara," he said. "Is there anything in those books about it?"

She shook her head. "It's very small. They mention that it has a king, and they give some impossibly long Arabic name for the royal family, but little detailed information. It isn't what I expected," she added. "They're a pretty modern country, with industry and a structured society, and women are fairly liberated there. They're very European, in fact."

"All that oil money, I'll bet," Tad said. He sat down. He was weak, still, and tired easily. Brianna had telephoned his doctor the day before to make an appointment for today. The experience they'd been through had been upsetting, and Tad wasn't his old self yet.

"You have to see Dr. Brown at one," she reminded him.

"Do I have to?" he moaned.

"It's just a precaution. You aren't long out of the hospital. And yesterday was pretty shattering."

"Ahmed saved my life," Tad told her. "The bullets hit where I'd been sitting. Gosh, I hope nobody tries to do him in when we go to live with him."

"So do I, Tad," she said sincerely.

They kept his appointment with the doctor, who pronounced him well on the way to recovery.

Monday, Brianna went back to work, leaving Tad with an off-duty nurse—Ahmed's suggestion—and she spent her free time worrying about Ahmed. He'd telephoned twice over the weekend, but the conversation had been stilted and brief, and she felt inhibited trying to carry it on. He seemed to feel the same. His speech was more formal than she'd ever heard it.

The distance between them had grown so quickly, she thought. And Monday, he hadn't telephoned at all by the time Brianna had cooked supper and cleaned up the dishes.

Tad was skipping over channels looking for something to watch, while Brianna worked halfheartedly at crocheting a doily for the coffee table.

"Wow, look at this!" he exclaimed, pausing on one of the news channels.

Brianna looked up. There were uniformed men on horseback and some sort of procession in a Middle Eastern nation. At the center of the pomp and circumstance was a man in a military dress uniform with a blue sash of office across his chest, sitting on a throne while foreign dignitaries were presented to him.

"Why, that's Ahmed," Brianna exclaimed. "Turn it up!"

Tad did, very quickly.

"...looking very fit following an assassination attempt. His sister, the princess Yasmin, has been detained for questioning for some time. There is doubt that she was involved with the plot. Her husband's trial was brief and he was executed this morning. Questioned about the fate of the other conspirators, a spokesman for the royal house of Rashid said only that they were being dealt with."

The picture flashed off the screen. Royal house. Rashid. Ahmed, sitting on a throne.

Tad saw the expressions chase across Brianna's face. His own had gone pale.

"He's not a cabinet minister," Tad said slowly. "He's the king of Saudi Mahara."

Brianna's hands trembled and the crochet thread dropped in a tangle to the floor. *King.* He was the king. No wonder he'd been so well guarded. No wonder he expected people to jump when he asked for anything. *He was a king.*

"Do you think he really meant it, when he asked you to marry him?" Tad asked, putting her worst fear into words.

"How could he have?" she declared. "He's a king! He wouldn't ever be allowed to marry a woman from another country...!"

"The king of Jordan did."

"Many years ago—" she faltered "—and under much different circumstances. This...this changes everything!"

She got up and ran into her bedroom, closing the door. She collapsed onto the bed, tears running hot and copiously down her cheeks as she acknowledged the truth.

Ahmed had been amusing himself. There was no other excuse for it. She had been a diversion while he was forced into hiding to escape being assassinated.

The telephone rang when she was a little more composed. She went into the living room, shaking her head when Tad answered it. He got the message at once, punctuated as it was by her red-rimmed, swollen eyes.

"Yes, she's...she's fine, thanks. Yes, so am I." Tad sounded nervous. It must be Ahmed. There was a long pause. "Of course. I'll tell her. Sure. You, too." He put down the telephone.

"He said to tell you hello. He wanted to know how we were. That's about it." He grimaced. "Oh, sis, I'm sorry!"

She bit her lower lip, hoping that the pain would help stem the tears. "Me, too." She got control of herself again. "Is that all he said?"

"Yes. I don't think he knew we'd seen the broadcast. He didn't mention it."

"That was a BBC feed," she said. "He probably thought it was being shown in England instead of here, if he saw the cameras." She went to pour herself a cup of coffee. It was cold. She grimaced and put it in the microwave to heat up.

"He didn't tell us," he said.

"I know." She glanced at him. "Maybe he didn't know how," she added. "It must have been very hard for him, trying to live like a normal person when he was used to servants and luxury."

"I've never seen a king before," Tad said, trying to lessen the sad atmosphere. "It will be something to tell my friends when I start back to school, won't it?"

"Yes."

"You didn't take it seriously, did you?" he asked worriedly.

"Me?" She forced a laugh. "Don't be silly. I liked him a lot, but then, I didn't really want to have to live in some foreign country and learn another whole way of life, did you?"

"No." He shrugged. "Well, I would have liked the horses," he had to admit. "And Ahmed was a neat guy to have around. He liked talking to me about science. He knows a lot."

"He has degrees in chemistry and physics."

"Well, that explains it. I'd like to go to college one day," he said wistfully.

She heard the microwave buzz and went to take out her heated coffee. "You will," she promised. Her eyes swept over his pale face. "You're a walking miracle, did you know? I'm so glad that I still have you."

He looked embarrassed. "Yeah. Me, too." He searched her face warily. "You feeling better?"

She nodded. She sipped the hot coffee. "If Ahmed calls tomorrow, I, uh, I'd rather not talk to him. Okay?"

"Okay."

But he didn't call the next day, or even the next. Affairs of state, Brianna decided, must have claimed his full attention since his return. She tried not to listen to the news channels, but the temptation was too great. She suffered through political news and medical news and disasters just for an occasional glimpse of the king of Saudi Mahara. Once they showed him in his robes of state with a falcon on his arm. There was a very pretty young Arab woman in a designer suit with him. Brianna saw her take his arm, and she felt sick all over when the newscaster added that the woman was the widow of Ahmed's eldest brother, who had died many years ago in a yachting accident. Her name was Lillah, not Yasmin, so Brianna knew that it wasn't his sister. He was smiling at the woman, and she seemed very possessive of him. That was the last newscast she watched. She knew then that she was being an idiot. Ahmed had made it quite clear that he wanted nothing else to do with her. She might as well start living her life again.

The first step in that direction was to get her old apartment back. Now, with just herself and Tad to share it, there was no need for elaborate living quarters. Fortunately it still hadn't been rerented, and she was able to obtain it at the old rent.

Tad liked it better, mainly because there was a young man who lived on the same floor who became his shadow and idolized him—Nick, the boy whom Ahmed had befriended.

Brianna was still sad, but as the days passed, she began to enjoy life again, although not in the same way as before. She couldn't complain, she told herself. She'd had an adventure with a king, and she had her beloved young brother back. She really couldn't ask much more of life.

At work, she was promoted to assistant status and given a job working for one of the vice presidents. She'd hoped she might get to work with David Shannon, Meg Shannon Ryker's brother, who was a live wire and a delightful person. But instead, she was shifted to the office of the vice president of finance, Tarrant Blair, a rather crusty older man with a wife and four kids and a mind like a math calculator.

She didn't enjoy the job very much. Even less did she care for the way Mr. Blair treated her. He had no consideration for her time. He would think nothing of asking her to work overtime, despite the fact that he knew her young brother was home by himself, and when it wasn't really necessary. He had plenty of time to get his work done during the day, but he came in late quite frequently and spent an unbelievable amount of time on the telephone with his stockbroker.

"How are things going, Brianna?" Meg Ryker asked her one day when she'd stopped by the office to meet her husband Steve for lunch.

"Oh, fine, just fine," she lied. "I'm very happy about my raise in salary."

"How's Tad?"

"He's doing very well."

"I suppose the two of you are having a lot of fun catching up on the time you've missed together?"

Brianna grimaced. "We were. This new job requires so much overtime that I'm pretty well worn-out when I get home. It's challenging, though, and the extra money is wonderful." She smiled.

She didn't fool Meg, who continued to converse merrily until Steve showed up. Once she got her husband out of the building, she pulled him to one side.

"Why does Blair have to keep Brianna after work so much?" she asked bluntly. "Doesn't he understand that she's only just gotten her brother back from the dead, not to mention what she went through when Ahmed was being guarded so closely? And she still has not recovered from the aftermath of that situation," she added meaningfully.

He scowled. "Blair shouldn't require any overtime at all. He isn't the busiest man on staff."

"Couldn't you check?" Meg coaxed, tracing a button on his suit coat.

He smiled, bending to kiss her softly. "Yes," he said. "I can check."

She smiled back, her eyes adoring his face. "That's why I married you."

"Because I kiss so well," he agreed, bending again.

"Because you're so concerned for the welfare of your employees," she corrected, the words muffled against his mouth.

"Exactly." He forgot what they were talking about for the rest of the lunch hour.

But when he returned, he had a private conversation with Mr. Blair, one which he challenged the other man to repeat on pain of firing. After that, Mr. Blair no longer required Brianna to stay after work, and his telephone calls with his broker became a thing of the past.

Three weeks after Ahmed had left town, Brianna was almost her old self again. She'd put the whole situation behind her and was ready to face the future. There was a man in her department who seemed to like her. She wished that she could encourage him. But there was no sense of excitement in her chest when he looked at her. Wherever she looked, in fact, she seemed to see liquid black eyes looking back at her.

She felt particularly remorseful one Friday afternoon when she dragged herself into the apartment, looking as if she'd just lost her last friend.

"You're positively mournful," Tad muttered. "Honestly, sis, you just can't go on like this."

"I'm only tired, Tad," she said evasively. She smiled, moving into her bedroom to change into jeans and a loose, floppy, colored shirt. "How are the lessons going?'' she asked when she rejoined her blue-jeaned brother in the living room.

"My tutor says I'm bright and eager to learn," he said mischievously. "And that if I work very hard through the rest of the school year, and probably the summer," he added ruefully, "I'll be able to rejoin my age grade next fall. They've done lots of tests. He'd like you to give him a ring and go by and see him one afternoon at the board of education office." He pursed his lips. "He's thirty-eight, single and pretty passable to look at. I told him you were a ravishing model-type girl with no bad habits at all."

"Tad!"

"I didn't," he confessed, grinning at her. "But you might like him."

"It's early days yet," she said, averting her eyes. "What would you like for supper?"

"Macaroni and cheese," he said immediately. He followed her into the kitchen. "I'm sorry about how it worked out," he told her. "I know you're having a hard time getting over Ahmed."

She stiffened at just the mention of his name. "No, I'm not," she assured him. "I'm doing very well indeed since Mr. Blair suddenly decided to do his work instead of talking on the telephone all day."

"I noticed. It's nice to have you home. But..."

She turned and ruffled his dark hair. "I like having you at home. I'm perfectly happy and well adjusted. Now get out of here and let me work, okay?"

"Okay."

He went reluctantly back into the living room and started to turn up the television. But the buzzer rang and he went to answer it. Brianna knew that it was probably Nick. She was banging pots and pans and didn't hear

Tad's excited voice. She did hear the opening of the door a few minutes later.

"Is that Nick?" she called over her shoulder as she took a pan of rolls out of the oven and sat them on the stove, reaching to turn off the oven.

"No," a familiar deep voice replied quietly. "It is not."

Chapter Eleven

Brianna felt her heart race madly into her throat. She froze where she stood, afraid to believe what she heard. "Ahmed?" she whispered.

"Yes."

She turned, her big blue eyes wide and unbelieving. He looked drawn, as if the weeks had been a strain. There were three men with him, big, tough-looking Arabs who took up positions in the living room where Tad was staring at them in fascination. Ahmed was wearing an elegant three-piece navy pin-striped suit with a white silk shirt. He was impeccably groomed. But then, she remembered, he was a king.

"Hello," she said hesitantly, uncertain about how to address him. Did she call him "Your Majesty" or curtsy?

Her uncertainty showed plainly on her face, and he winced.

"I . . . would you like to sit down?" she asked. "In the living room . . . ?"

"Brianna," he groaned.

She moved back a step, struggling for composure. She plastered a smile on her face. "Tad and I saw you on the news," she stammered. "I'm glad they caught everyone. And your sister, I . . . They said that she wasn't involved. You must be very glad."

"Yes." His voice was suddenly dull, lackluster. "Very glad."

She glanced toward the living room. Tad was talking animatedly to one of Ahmed's men, who was smiling and answering him very pleasantly.

"Tad's doing fine," she remarked. "He's catching up quickly with his schoolwork."

"And you, Brianna?"

"Oh, I'm fine, too, as you see," she said. The smile was beginning to hurt her face. "Would you like coffee?"

"That would be nice."

"Your men . . . ?"

"They are content."

She fumbled down a cup with a crack in it and quickly replaced it, rummaging through the cabinet and her meager store of dishes to find something that would do for a king to drink out of.

He came up behind her, catching her cold hands in his. "Don't," he pleaded huskily. "For the love of God, don't treat me like some stranger!"

"But you are." Hot tears stung her eyes. She closed them, but it wouldn't stem the sudden flow. "You're a king . . . !"

He whirled her into his arms and bent, taking her mouth hungrily under his, oblivious to the shocked stares from the living room or Tad's voice intervening, diverting.

Tears drained down into her mouth and he tasted them. His lean hands came up to cup her face, to cherish it while he kissed away the tears and his tongue savored the sable softness of her thick eyelashes.

"So many tears," he whispered, his lips tender. "Salty and hot and sweet. They tell me, oh, so potently, that you love me, *chérie*."

She felt his mouth covering hers, and for a few seconds, she gave in to the hunger for him, the long ache of waiting. But she couldn't forget who and what he was. She drew demurely away from him and lowered her face.

He claimed her hand, holding it to his chest, where his heartbeat was strong and quick.

"They showed her on the television," she said quietly.

"Yasmin?"

She shook her head.

"Ah. Lillah."

She nodded.

He tilted her eyes up to his indulgent ones. "And you thought... Yes, I see what you thought, this sudden color tells me."

"She's very lovely."

"She is not you," he said simply. He touched her face as if he'd forgotten what she looked like, as if he was hungry to look at her. "I did not telephone you because it is too difficult to make conversation over the coldness of an ocean. I had to have you close to me, like this, so that I could see your eyes, feel your breath as you spoke to me."

"I thought that once you were back home again, all this might seem like a bad memory to you," she said.

"I have not slept," he said quietly. "I have worked for the release of my sister. There have been charges and countercharges, and many members of the military had to be dealt with to prevent there ever being a recurrence of this coup attempt. I have been busy, Brianna. But not so busy that I could ever forget the taste and touch of you in my arms.''

"That's nice.''

He tilted her chin up, searching her sad eyes. "You said that you loved me enough to risk marrying me. Do you still?''

She hesitated. "Ahmed, you're a king,'' she said. "I could...I could be your mistress,'' she whispered, lowering her shamed eyes. "I could be a part of your life that way, and you wouldn't be risking anything. There are so many people in your country who don't like Americans.''

"I do not have a mistress,'' he said gently. "I do not want one. I want you for my wife. I want you to bear the heirs to my name, my family, my kingdom.''

"They would be half-American,'' she pointed out, worriedly.

He smiled. "So they would. How politically expedient. Not to mention the benefit of having an American wife in the complicated thread of international affairs.'' He traced a line down her cheek. "I have made the necessary announcements, calmed fears, outtalked adversaries and placated doomsayers. All that I have accomplished since I left here. And I have arranged our wedding.'' He kissed her shocked mouth. "Even the vice president of your own country has promised to attend. So has Lang,'' he added dryly.

"It won't be just a small church wedding,'' she murmured fearfully, gnawing on her lower lip.

"Stop doing that,'' he coaxed, his thumb freeing the soft flesh. "You will make it sore and I cannot kiss you. No, it cannot be a small wedding. It will be a wedding of state. Televised around the world.'' He kissed her horrified eyes closed. "You will have a gown from Paris. I will have them send a couturiere to the palace to fit you."

"A couturiere," she echoed. "To the palace. The palace?"

He brushed his mouth tenderly over hers. "I am a king," he reminded her. "Most kings live in palaces, unless they are very poor kings. I am not. My country is rich. My people are cosmopolitan and our economy is excellent. We have only the occasional student protest. Once we had to deport some foreign students, but we later learned that they were deliberate troublemakers."

"I'm just ordinary," she protested.

He smiled. "So am I. Just ordinary."

"I'd be a queen," she said, just realizing it. Her eyes were like saucers. "Oh, dear."

"And Tad a prince," he reminded her. He glanced toward the living room. "Can you really not picture him in a crown?" he teased. "He would have the finest tutors in the world, and the best education we can afford for him. Oxford, if he likes."

She wondered if she was dreaming. Her eyes slid over his beloved face. So much misery, so many tears, and now here he was and he wanted her.

"There's, uh, there's just one thing," she said jerkily.

"Yes?" His smile was tender, indulgent.

She looked up. "Do you...can you...love me?"

The backs of his fingers drew slowly down her cheek to her mouth, under her chin, her throat. "These words should be spoken only in the privacy of a bedroom," he said solemnly. His dark eyes held hers. "Be patient. I have never said them."

Her lips parted, because what was in his eyes made her feel humble.

"Say that you will marry me," he coaxed. "Say the words."

"I . . . will marry you," she answered.

He smiled. He kissed her forehead with exquisite tenderness. "Now," he whispered, "it begins."

She had no idea what it would involve to marry a head of state. She and Tad were whisked away to Mozambara, the capital city of Saudi Mahara, like birds on the wind, leaving everything behind and all the details of closing up the apartment and shipping furniture to Ahmed's men.

Tad was given his own suite of rooms and a personal servant to look after him. He was dressed in the finest clothing, had access to the court physician if he so much as sniffled, and a tutor was immediately engaged for him. His head spun at the sudden luxury that surrounded him. His every whim was immediately satisfied.

That worried Brianna, who managed an audience with the king to complain about it. They were never alone now. They were constantly chaperoned and protocol was strict and unrelenting.

"He's going to be spoiled," she moaned when Ahmed dismissed her fears.

"He should be spoiled," he informed her with a smile. "He has had a savage time for a boy his age. Let him enjoy it while he can. And please stop worrying."

She glanced around the throne room. It always seemed to be full of advisers and visiting potentates and politicians. "Can't we even have dinner alone together?"

He pursed his lips and his eyes were sensuous as they searched hers. "Another week," he promised, "and we can be alone together all we like." His gaze dropped to her mouth and lingered there. "I dream of it every night, Brianna," he added breathlessly. "I dream of you."

"And I of you," she said huskily.

He drew in a long breath. "Could you leave now?" he asked pleasantly. "You are quite soon going to have a visible reaction on my composure."

She cleared her throat. "Sorry."

She turned and left, nodding politely to several curious men near the door who smiled at her.

The days were long. She was fitted for the wedding gown, which was so expensive with its imported lace and specially made fabric from Paris that she thought privately she could probably buy a yacht for less. It was a marriage of state, though, and this was necessary. Everyone said so. The queen Brianna must be properly dressed. Queen Brianna. She shook her head. That was going to take some time to get used to.

She spent some of her time with Tad, and the rest daydreaming about her forthcoming marriage in the lush garden with its fish pond and flowers. Just looking at Ahmed from a distance made her heart race. Soon, there would be the two of them together, with no prying eyes. She grew breathless at just the thought.

The great day finally arrived. She was dressed and a bouquet of orchids placed in her cold, trembling hands. Tad smiled at her reassuringly, as richly dressed as the handsome bridegroom waiting at the huge altar in the church.

There were newsmen and cameras everywhere. And the crowds were huge. The people of Saudi Mahara seemed not at all unhappy to welcome their new American queen. She hoped that their welcome was sincere, and not forced by the many armed guards who surrounded the area.

She kept her eyes on Ahmed as she entered the church. It was the longest walk of her entire life, and she was terrified. The terror grew as she began to recognize some of the people in the front pews, people she'd only ever seen on television newscasts. But she made it, her nerves in disarray but her head held high and her carriage perfect.

Ahmed's pride shone out of his black eyes as she joined him at the altar. He took her hand in his and they knelt before the high clergyman who was to perform the ceremony.

Later, she remembered very little except that the beauty of it made her cry. When they exchanged rings, and then were pronounced man and wife, she began to cry. Ahmed cupped her face in his hands and looked at her with an expression she knew that she would carry to her grave, held in her heart forever. He bent and kissed away every single tear, while their audience watched in rapt approval.

It was a fairy-tale wedding. Brianna entertained congratulations from visiting dignitaries until her hand hurt and her voice began to give way.

Ahmed stood at her side, tall and proud. The festivities went on long into the night and Brianna thought that she'd never been so tired. It disappointed her to feel herself wilting, because she'd lived for this night, for her wedding night, for so long.

When he led her to the royal suite, which they would share, she was almost in tears when he closed the door behind them.

"Ah, what is this?" he whispered, brushing away the tears as he smiled gently down at her.

"I'm so tired," she wailed, her eyes seeking his. "It's been such a long day, and I want to feel excited and strong and..."

He stopped the words with his lips. "You are telling me that you are too tired to make love," he whispered, "and I know this already. *Pauvre petite,* the demands of state are sometimes a great nuisance to bear. But this is only the beginning of our time together."

"But I want you," she whispered shyly. "And I've waited so long!"

"As I have waited." He kissed her eyes closed. "I shall undress you, and myself, and we shall lie naked in each other's arms all night long. Then in the morning, when you are rested, I shall make love to you as long as your body is capable of receiving mine."

She blossomed under his warm, tender mouth, allowing him to remove the exquisite dress and the even more exquisite silk and lace things under it. He lifted her in his arms, his dark eyes adoring her silky skin, and carried her to bed.

"Oh, how magnificent!" she exclaimed as he put her down on the canopied bed. It was gold and silver, with geometrical motifs that added to the allure. The curtains were black with silver and gold threads.

"The colors of office," he informed her, moving to the dresser to empty his pockets and unfasten his cuff links and tie clasp. He glanced toward her, noticing her nervous fingers reaching for the cover.

"No, Brianna," he said softly. "Let me enjoy you."

She blushed, but she subsided back onto the bed. After a minute, the shyness began to drain away and she found pleasure in the slow boldness of his gaze.

He divested himself of everything except his briefs. Then he turned, facing her, and let her watch him remove them. He was aroused, and her body shivered as she stared at him.

"A nuisance only," he said amusedly. "I require nothing of you tonight except for your closeness."

She could never remember being less tired in her life as desire suddenly overwhelmed her. She couldn't drag her eyes away from him and as he saw her expression, his chin lifted and his eyes narrowed.

He moved to the bed and balanced beside her with one knee. Her hand went to it involuntarily and shyly, hesitantly, traced up it. She paused, her eyes seeking his.

He nodded. She continued, her breath catching when she touched him.

He moved down beside her and his mouth eased over hers while he taught her hands to explore him gently, sensuously. The lights were all blazing, and if she'd ever thought of making love like this, she would have been horrified. But the sensuality of his hands and mouth, the lazy movements of his body, made her uninhibited and wanton.

By the time he shifted her onto her back and his body moved over her, she was mindless and totally receptive to anything he asked.

He kissed her while he made himself master of her body, feeling her shocked gasp as he began to take her. Her hands gripped his upper arms fearfully, her nails biting into him as the stinging pain briefly overcame her desire.

He lifted his head and his body stilled. "In the old days," he whispered to her, his voice a little unsteady in the heat of passion, "the old women would hang the bridal sheet out of the window the next morning to show the traces of virgin blood that clung to it. I am not supposed to know, nor are you, but they will take this one away and hide it tomorrow, so that for all our lives together they can prove that you had no lover before me, and that our children are legitimate."

She swallowed. "It hurt a little," she whispered tightly.

He smiled gently. "That is natural. But what I can give you now will make up for it. Shall I show you?" he whispered, bending.

She felt him move, shift, and his eyes held hers while he did it, until the right movement made her body jerk and her breath catch.

He whispered something in French, and his mouth began to cherish hers. She had nothing to compare the experience with, nothing to prepare her for the sudden fierce bite of passion into her body. She fought him because it frightened her more than the brief pain had. He laughed and lifted his head to watch her as he forced her body into an explosive culmination that arched her back and tore from her open mouth in a husky little scream. Only when he felt her begin to shiver in the aftermath did he allow himself the exquisite pleasure of joining her in that hot delight of ecstasy. It was, he thought as it racked him, almost too sweet to bear.

He felt as if he lost consciousness for a second or two. He became slowly aware of Brianna's whispery movement under the weight of his body. He lifted his head and looked into her wide, curious eyes.

He didn't speak. Neither did she. Her eyes went down to where his chest lay on her breasts and back up to his mouth and then his eyes with something like wonder. She took a soft breath and then moved her hips deliberately, so that she could experience again the pressure that it exerted in the secret places of her body. She flushed.

He touched her face, raising himself slightly on his elbows, and he moved his own hips, his knee nudging her legs farther apart. She gasped.

His hand slid down her thigh and curved around it. Holding her eyes, he shifted onto his side and gently brought her into the cradle of his hips so that they lay still joined together in intimacy. He smiled and pulled at her thigh, easing her into the rhythm. In this position, she was open to his eyes and he to hers. They looked at each other in wonder, and then their eyes locked and he caught his breath at the pleasure he saw in her face.

"Here," he whispered huskily. "Like this, my love."

He pulled her hips into his and pushed slowly until she accepted him completely. She blushed at the incredible intimacy of hanging there, between heaven and earth, while she seemed to see into his soul.

"Ahmed," she whispered, drowning in him. "Ahmed, I love you . . . so much!"

"And I you," he said unsteadily. "With all my heart."

He shivered, rolling slowly onto his back with her body still joined to his. His hands smoothed down her back, gently pulling. His body tautened under hers with each slow, delicate motion.

"Sit up and take me," he whispered.

"I don't think I can. . . ." she began nervously.

"You are my love. My life."

"And you are mine. But I . . . can't!" She hid her face against his chest, and he laughed with delight at her shyness. She was a rarity in his life. A woman with inhibitions.

"So shy," he whispered. "You delight me. Brianna, you . . . delight . . . me!"

As he spoke, his hands moved her hips, making her gasp, making her shiver with pleasure.

She felt his body pull and tauten. His jaw clenched and he arched in a sinuous movement that she found incredibly arousing. Her lips touched over his chest in shaky little kisses while his hands brought them both to the most incredibly tender climax of his life.

She bit him in her oblivious pleasure, and his short laugh was as much a groan of ecstasy as he gripped her bruisingly hard and held her to the rigid clench of his body.

She felt him relax suddenly with a rough shudder, and her cheek lay heavily against his damp chest. The hairs tickled her nose and she smiled wearily.

"Is it so good, always?" she whispered.

"I think, only when two people love," he whispered back. His hands made a warm, sensuous sweep of her back and he arched up to enjoy the silky feel of her against him. "*Dieu!* You exhaust me with exquisite pleasure and then, so suddenly, I want you all over again."

She smiled against his chest, lifting up so that she could look into his dark, possessive eyes. "We're married," she said with quiet wonder. "We can sleep together every night."

He smiled. "There will most likely be very little sleep obtained by either of us," he mused.

She traced the line of his jaw. "I like making love."

"I like it most of all with you," he said, sensing her quiet fears. "I never loved before. It is the most profound experience of my life to lie with you so intimately."

She relaxed. Her mouth brushed his and she lay against him, sated and weary. "Can we sleep like this?"

His arms enclosed her. "Just like this," he assured her. His own eyes closed in drowsy pleasure. And finally they slept.

Brianna found that there were difficulties despite her love for her husband, but none that she couldn't overcome with some patient tutoring and understanding. She got used to palace protocol and meeting visiting dignitaries' wives. She got used to the things that were expected of a queen, just as Tad rapidly adjusted to life at court. He grew and blossomed, and soon Brianna relaxed. He was going to be all right, just as Dr. Brown had predicted.

There was a grand ball a few months after their marriage. Brianna had a gown by Dior, reflecting the silver-and-gold-on-black motif of Ahmed's court. Her hair had grown long, and she had it pinned into an exquisite coiffure—one that, she knew from experience, would be quickly disposed with when she and Ahmed were alone. She wore diamonds and pearls, and the tiara of her rank, and she met with approving glances from even the most stern ministers of Ahmed's cabinet when she joined her guests.

She was dancing with her husband when she noticed an odd expression in his eyes. His hand on her waist was curiously exploring.

"What is it?" she asked softly.

He smiled quizzically. "Is there something which you wish to tell me?" he asked gently. "Something which you have perhaps thought to save until you visited our court physician?"

"Yasmin," she said, glowering toward a gleeful sister-in-law who was wearing a guilty but very happy expression.

"Do not blame her too much. She dreams of dynasties, even as I sometimes do." He pulled her closer, his eyes loving and warm. "Tell me."

"I'm not sure," she confessed. "I've been unwell at breakfast twice this week. And there were a few other things." She searched his eyes. "I didn't want to tell you just yet."

"Why?" he asked softly.

"I was afraid you might not want to make love to me anymore if we were sure," she said hesitantly, searching his dark eyes as her hand caressed his jacket. "I thought they might take me away from you...."

"Chérie!" He stopped dancing and bent to kiss her worried eyes shut. "They would have to kill me to separate us," he whispered fervently. "And as for the other...Brianna, I would want to make love to you if I were on my deathbed!"

Reassured, she smiled shyly. "Would you, really?"

"I find you a delightful pupil," he whispered. "Adventurous and mischievous and totally captivating."

"I love you!"

"I love you," he returned. His hand pressed slowly onto her flat belly and they stood staring at each other while around them, suddenly curious and then knowing eyes began to gleam with confirmed suspicions. Without saying a word, or making an announcement, everyone at court knew that Brianna carried the heir to the throne. And it was a credit to them, and protocol, that not one suspicion was voiced until the actual announcement was made some weeks later.

Brianna's little prince was born on a bright autumn day, and bells rang from the churches to signal the event. Ahmed stood beside her bed holding the crown prince Tarin in his arms, with a beaming Tad beside him. Brianna, tired but gloriously happy, looked up at the three most important people in her life with eyes that reflected her joy.

Sensing her appraisal, Ahmed turned his head and looked down at her. His eyes were full of wonder.

"He is perfect," he told her, while nurses fidgeted in the background and smiled at his expression.

"A king's ransom," she agreed, loving him with her whole heart.

"Ah, that is not quite so," he whispered, bending to lay the tiny child in her waiting arms. "For, while I love my son with a father's great pride, *you* are the real king's ransom, my darling," he whispered, and he smiled at her radiant expression as he bent to kiss her.

*   *   *   *   *

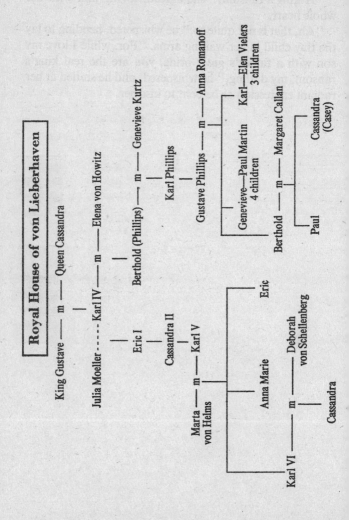

A PRINCE OF A GUY

Kathleen Korbel

Dedicated to
Lucia for letting me get away with it
and
Ronald Colman, who made me think
of it in the first place

One

Wouldn't it just figure? Stuck in a foreign country where they don't even speak English, and your car breaks down on the way up some ridiculously high mountain. And the next stop is at the top of that mountain. Casey readjusted the strap of her carryall and looked back to where she'd left the little bright red rental car to fend for itself on the negligible shoulder of a narrow, winding mountain road. Then she looked ahead to the tollgate just beyond her.

Moritania. The name of the tiny little country was ornately carved on the entryway. Two sleepy-looking guards manned the station, attired in rather antiquated-looking uniforms and plumed caps. Casey hadn't seen anything so quaint since the Vatican.

Approaching the guards, she turned again to her bag, intent on getting out her passport. She was talking long before she reached the men.

"I can't believe it," she said, riffling through the countless wads of currency and travel brochures that packed the oversized bag. "My first trip out of the States—out of New York, really—and my car breaks down in the middle of the Alps. I was coming up here to see the country—my family's supposed to be from here, ya know—but now I'm going to have to call a garage." Casey didn't notice that her audience was suspiciously quiet. "You do have garages here, don't you?" After seeing those outfits, she wouldn't have been too surprised if they'd said that there was no automation in Moritania at all.

She knew she'd stuck her passport in between her German phrase book and her traveler's checks. Where could it have gone? "Wait, my passport's around her someplace. It's a U.S. passport, and I really wanted to get a Moritanian stamp on it. For my mom. Just to prove the place exists. Who'd believe it?" Casey dug even deeper, the passport still eluding her. "I can't believe that I can't find it. I wonder if I left it at the hotel room with Sandra...."

Her voice trailed off as she finally got her head up to smile at the guards. All thoughts of her broken-down car and missing passport trailed away. The two guards weren't facing her. She wasn't even sure if they were listening. They were both bent at right angles, their eyes resolutely on the ground, their backs as stiff as wallboards.

Casey's eyes followed theirs. "Lose a contact?"

They didn't move. Quaint little country they had here. Maybe it was like Japan, she thought. They couldn't stand up until you bowed back.

She did. They didn't.

"Uh, excuse me?"

No reaction. Casey bent down until she was almost nose-to-nose with one of them. He still refused to face her. "Do you speak English?"

The man came up so fast that he almost collided with her. "But of course, my lady," he stammered, his eyes wide with apprehension. "It is the law." Then he went right back down.

Casey was flummoxed. Now, she realized that she hadn't traveled enough to become an expert on customs. Until she'd won the trip to Europe, she hadn't gone much farther than Brooklyn and midtown Manhattan. But for the life of her she couldn't figure out what this business was all about.

"Maybe I could just call the American consulate," she offered. "For my passport." Then she looked around. "Does a country this size have an American consulate? Does it have a pay phone where I can call the American consulate in the next country?"

"Please, my lady," the gentleman said, his eyes still on the ground. "Let me call."

Casey considered his position. "From there?"

"From the booth. I beg the privilege."

Still confused, she shrugged. It was getting hard not to giggle. "A country without much excitement, huh?"

Twenty minutes later, Casey occupied a chair in the little booth while the two guards scuttled around trying to find new and different ways to make her more comfortable. She assured them that there was only so much comfort one could find at a border crossing. All she succeeded in doing was making them more miserable. But when she asked whether the American consul was coming, or even a tow truck, all they did was exchange worried little glances.

"Soon now, my lady," the spokesman assured her. "He promised."

Casey shrugged again, thinking that she was doing a lot of that, and crossed her legs, resettling her wide denim skirt around her legs. Not exactly climbing clothes. But then, Julie Andrews had done the Alps in a habit.

"This is real *Sound of Music* country," she said, not really expecting an answer by now. "Of course, you guys were probably raised on Wagner and Romberg."

No answer.

"Romberg," she repeated, trying for some kind of reaction. "You know, *Student Prince*?"

"Cassandra, what on earth are you up to now?"

Casey lifted her head with a start at the sound of the new voice. Then her mouth dropped open. Now how had he snuck up on her?

The guards were back down again, and a new man stood in the doorway. Man? More like a miracle. He was breathtaking, the kind of man she was sure she'd never in her life run into on the streets of Brooklyn. Clad in a hunter's jacket of tweed and leather and a wool sweater over a snow-white shirt and navy blue tie, he looked more like an English lord gone to tour his estate.

Tall, maybe six feet, and slim. Athletic. Casey could imagine him on a polo pony or a yacht, the wind sweeping through his golden-brown hair. He had a face that would have made Cary Grant cry: long, with an aquiline nose, a strong chin and a well-bred brow. It was a cultured face with eyes the color of a summer sky.

A most practical child, Casey had never been able to figure how Cinderella could have been swept off her feet within the space of one dance. If this guy had been the one wearing the tights, it would have made perfect sense. She was in love before she even knew his name.

He turned briefly and dispatched the guards with a gentle word. The relief on their features was palpable as they straightened and departed.

"How did you do that?" Casey asked, getting to her feet. "No matter what I did they kept checking out their toes. It's kind of unnerving after awhile, ya know?"

Her guest considered her with frustration. "When are you going to stop? You're not going to make them better subjects by playing games with them. And you're certainly playing havoc with my schedule."

"Thanks for the interest," Casey said, smiling dryly. "What the hell are you talking about?"

"And where in heaven's name did you pick up that atrocious accent?"

Casey was bristling now. "From my mother. She has one just like it. Listen, my car broke down and I need a tow. And I forgot my passport back at the hotel. Otherwise I wouldn't have had you paged. Are you with the American embassy?"

He straightened a little, his head tilted at an angle of inspection. "Cassandra..."

"Nobody's called me Cassandra since the nuns... How did you know my name?" She shook her head, the confusion mounting. "Listen, I'll tell you what. If you're not with the embassy, just call me a tow or whatever. If this is an example of Moritanian hospitality, I don't think I want to visit after all. I'd have more fun in the Bronx on a Saturday night...."

Casey had more to say. Something about rudeness and insanity and lack of oxygen at high altitudes. She never quite got it out. As she was speaking, the gentleman's eyes widened with an incredulity that gave her pause. His lips opened in amazement, and he stepped up to her. When he laid a hand under her chin and lifted it, she fell mute.

His eyes caught hers and held them. His hand, graceful and strong, captured her with the gentlest touch. With just that contact, Casey found herself suffused with a sweet hesitation she'd never known. A languid heat, as if his eyes were stealing her strength. She looked up at him and forgot what she'd been about to say and why it had been important.

"Oh, my God," he breathed, the intensity of his gaze growing. His eyes swept her features, her attire, and then came back to rest on her face. "You're not like her at all, are you? Not at all."

Casey couldn't seem to drag her eyes away. "I... wouldn't know."

"Who are you?"

"Casey Phillips. Who are you?"

"Eric von Lieberhaven."

Their voices had grown soft somehow, intimate in the little room. It was Eric who broke the spell first, pulling his hand away as if he'd been scalded. Casey saw him rub it against his leg in what she was sure was an uncharacteristic gesture. She wasn't sure how she knew. She just did.

"But why did they call you?" she asked when he moved far enough away that she could breathe again. "You never told me. Do you work for the embassy?"

The smile he gave her was a bright one, rueful and wry. He had beautiful white teeth and a pattern of crow's-feet from the sun and wind that adorned his smiles with an endearing warmth. Casey smiled back without knowing why.

"No," he assured her. "I'm not with the embassy."

He did have an accent, but Casey wasn't sure what kind. Brooklyn had ruined her ear for distinctions, though she could instinctively mimic any accent if she wanted.

What she wanted, she realized, was to get to know Eric von whatever better. Fat chance, from the looks of him. He looked as if he'd been afforded more in life than a flat and a high school education.

Outside, the phone jangled, and one of the guards went to answer it.

"Your Highness?"

Eric turned to him.

Casey gaped. "Your what?"

"Yes, Franz?"

"It is the palace, Your Highness. They wish you to return immediately."

Eric nodded, Franz bowed and Casey continued to gape.

"Your *what*?" she repeated.

Eric smiled again. "A matter of formality."

Casey motioned to the guards. "The same kind of formality that has them inspecting their shoe tops, right? What kind of highness?"

He shrugged. "If you want the boring facts, I am Prince Eric Karl Phillip Marie von Lieberhaven."

She gestured to the surrounding mountains. "So you kind of own the place?"

His chuckle was easy and deep. She fell harder. "In a manner of speaking, I suppose. Although I do not stand to inherit the throne. I was a third child."

Casey scowled. "A prince is a prince. Which brings me to my first question. And my second and third. Why did they call you, and how did you know my name? And if they were bowing to you, why were they doing the same to me? Or is this just the most polite country in the world?"

She was rewarded with another chuckle. "Would you care to receive your answers on the way to the palace? I seem to have business to attend there, and I think you might like to come along. There are some people you might like to see."

She was gaping again. She'd never so much as been invited to a formal dinner, much less a palace in a European country, no matter that it was a country just about the size of Queens.

"Why?"

"Do you want your car back?"

"I don't have my passport with me."

His smile broadened. "One of the benefits of 'owning the place.' I can grant you immunity. I ask one favor, though. Don't say anything more to the guards for the moment."

Casey took a look down at the denim skirt and white cotton blouse that had been her traveling attire. Suddenly she would have preferred the habit. She looked as if she was headed to a roundup, especially with her sandy hair in its thick French braid. "Am I appropriate for a palace?" she asked. Then she laughed. "What am I talking about? I don't own *anything* that's appropriate for a palace. But then, I bet you don't have anything to wear to a Mets game, do you?"

His smile grew delighted as he took hold of her arm. "You look quite lovely."

Casey had to laugh. "Be careful," she warned as she followed him out the door. "You're fulfilling every one of my expectations."

Eric managed to pull a straight face for Franz and his associate. "Thank you for being so alert, Franz. You're a credit to the corps."

Franz was so pleased that his nose almost scraped his knees. Casey allowed the prince to help her into the

Bronco he was driving and resettled her skirt and carry-all.

"Is this what the well-bred prince is driving these days?" she asked. "I was expecting something a little flashier, maybe more along the lines of a Daimler."

He grinned and started the engine, turning the vehicle back through the gate. "I was out hunting. Daimlers just aren't built for the woods."

"So what does one call a man with four names and title?" Casey had the feeling she was babbling, but the situation had gotten beyond her when he'd unleashed those incredible eyes on her. She was strictly on overload now.

"Four names and three titles," he allowed. "Pick any one. I answer to just about anything. Where are you from, Casey? May I call you Casey?"

Casey caught him considering her again and decided that he could call her anything he wanted. "Casey's fine. I'm from Brooklyn, New York. Ever heard of it?"

"Of course. I traveled through it on the way to the airport a few years ago. Kennedy, I believe? I've never seen so many buildings."

She nodded. "That's Brooklyn."

"Have you been to Moritania before?"

She snorted derisively. "I haven't even been outside of the boroughs before. I won a trip to Europe at work and decided to stop by when I saw it on the map. The family story is that my great-great-grandfather came from Moritania. I couldn't believe it really existed."

Casey missed the quick look Eric shot her. "He did?"

She shrugged, looking out at the mountains in an attempt to get her pulse to slow down. He was too close to her, and his cologne was too enticing. She couldn't believe that she was reacting to him like nitro when it got too close to glycerine.

Practical, sensible Casey had always set her sights on the attainable goals. She'd made sure of it. She'd never once fallen head over heels for a suave, handsome prince from a foreign country. But oh, Lord, she had a feeling she was about to now. It just figured.

"That's what my grandfather said. They never talked about it much. They just kept saying that we're Americans now, we should concentrate on being good Americans. We have Romanov blood, too. Russian, Moritanian and Irish. Real Americans."

Eric nodded pensively. "It makes their decision to concentrate on the present an understandable one. The Romanovs certainly had nothing to look back for."

"The only thing I got from that association is a yearning for Fabergé eggs."

"Were you left any?"

She laughed. "All we got was the name. Somebody else got the money. I live in a flat with my mother and work as a secretary for an advertising firm. And I'm going to night school."

"College?"

"Three more years, then law school. I figure I'll be out of that sometime around menopause."

They were coming to the outskirts of a town, the quaint, square-gabled farmhouses giving way to more modern buildings. Casey could see a bit of glass and steel that was reminiscent of New York on a smaller scale. The streets wound in among the steep slopes of the mountains with the taller buildings crowding the base.

Casey still marveled at how houses clung to the sides of these mountains like limpets. There shouldn't have been any way people could have walked up those inclines, much less ride bikes or drive cars. But they did, herding their cattle and sheep and planting their gardens just shy of the tree line. People who had lived the same way for centuries and who had lived that way when her great-great-grandfather had been born here.

The thought gave her an unexpected thrill of belonging—of history past that of her family's time in America. After all, the farthest back she could claim there was the 1880s. Here she could claim back to Hannibal and beyond. These were the same people who had molded mores still practiced in her house. And the man sitting next to her was the heir of the men who had ruled when her family had lived here. Too bad she was too American to give that concept the respect she was sure her great-great-grandfather would have afforded it.

"If you'll pardon my saying so, Eric," she said, deliberately foregoing the title to see what he'd do, "you haven't answered my questions."

He didn't seem to notice her breach of conduct. His gaze firmly on the road ahead, he nodded, almost to himself. "I know. If you'll be patient, there's something I want to show you at the palace first."

Casey couldn't help but grin. "The floors, right? The penalty for being caught on foot without a passport in this country is a good wax and shine of the ballroom."

"You've read Cinderella once too often," he scoffed.

Not often enough, she said to herself. "Do you have little princes of your own?" Nothing like getting right to the point. As if it would make any difference. Grace Kelly she wasn't.

Eric laughed, that same soft rumble that had tickled her before. "None. My mother considers me the black sheep of the family. I've been so busy at the banks that I haven't had the time to settle down with a good wife."

"Hard to find that certain girl who can keep a home and grace state functions, huh?" She couldn't believe she was egging him on this way. But there was just something about her Brooklyn upbringing that made her go on the offensive when she felt intimidated. And how she felt intimidated! Her hands were sweating. The problem was that it wasn't his station in life that was doing it.

He laughed again, his eyes still on traffic. "Cheeky lot, you Americans."

"That's what kept getting us in trouble with the English."

She snuck a look over to feast on his smile. It just made her hands sweat more.

"Did your family talk much about Moritania?" he asked, swinging his gaze around just in time to catch her. Casey looked down abruptly, transferring her attention to the bag in her lap.

"Nope. Not a word. I thought it was a family joke until I saw the map. Which reminds me—" She made a sweeping gesture. "We've been by one town and two castles so far. We're running out of country. Just where is this palace of yours?"

His smile grew rakish. "Afraid I'm going to kidnap you?"

This time she faced him, her eyes giving no quarter. "Do princes still do that sort of thing here?"

For a moment Eric held her gaze, his own eyes suspiciously bright. Then he turned to the road again. "Not in the last hundred years or so. We just ply our women with wine and take them on the royal yacht."

Casey took a look around at the close-packed mountain peaks and laughed. "Yacht?"

"The French are nice enough to let us use the Mediterranean."

"Of course."

Just when she was sure they were heading into Italy, Casey noted that Eric was slowing for a side road. Not just a side road, one with another elaborate guard box. Obviously not the driveway to the local budget motel.

"The palace," he allowed, nodding and waving to the guard as the gentleman bowed in return. "It's actually the old hunting lodge, but we find it a lot more comfortable than the traditional castle that was built in the twelfth century. We let the tourists have that one."

They wound their way along a wide road that cut into a forest of the hugest, most stately trees Casey had ever seen. Every so often, for the next quarter of a mile, she could catch a glimpse of gables and old stone. But it wasn't until they made the final turn into the circular drive in front of the palace that she saw the whole building.

"Hunting lodge?" she asked, her eyes as wide as her mouth. "Who did you put up here, the Allied forces?"

The trees parted to reveal scrupulously maintained lawns that gently rose to the estate, a huge old building of high shingled roofs and old oak beams. Stone walls held a succession of tall, sparkling windows that reflected the lawns from the jumble of wings that made up the great building. It even had a turret or two.

The impression Casey got was of genteel age, of grace and loving care. The immense windows marched down each wall in lovely geometrics. The steps up from the driveway led to a great double door of heavy carved oak, crowned by a complicated crest carved in marble. Just the sight of it gave her the most intriguing feeling of belonging.

"It's not much," Eric said, grinning as he pulled the car to a stop before the great stairs, "but we call it home."

Casey couldn't help but shake her head with a rueful smile. "It's just a pity the conditions some people have to endure."

His laughter was delighted. "Shall we?"

When Eric helped her out of the car, Casey noticed a ring on his right hand, a heavy, ornate gold signet ring that had undoubtedly been passed from generation to generation. It made her envious. He had everything his heritage entitled him to. She had a couple of bitter old aunts and the memory of once having seen the woman who claimed she was Anastasia. Oh, well, not much she could do about it except enjoy every minute she spent under this exalted roof and then report back to Sandra when she resurrected the little red car.

Eric handed her up the steps before him as a silent groom appeared from somewhere and took the Bronco away. Casey half expected him to sweep the cobblestones behind them. When they reached the door, it magically opened, another liveried servant bowing and smiling as he passed them on.

"Rolph," Eric said, easing Casey along when she slowed, "is Her Majesty the queen available for visitors?"

"I shall check for you, Your Highness. Refreshments?"

He stole a look at Casey, who was rubbernecking the paintings on the walls with undisguised avarice. After a moment he nodded. "Yes, I believe they will be needed. In the Great Hall, if you please."

Rolph dispatched a discreetly questioning look, but bowed and moved away. Casey was still trying to take in the extent of the entryway.

Train stations were smaller. The walls extended up some thirty feet, decorated with what looked suspiciously like old masters and terminating in a high, vaulted ceiling that some brave painter had gotten his hands on. It was all light and froth, cherubs and swirling gold banners swimming around a vault of milky white. The floors were of pristinely kept white tile, and the effect was one of immense space, the inside of the building mirroring the image given by the outside. Quiet, understated grace and wealth. No need for ostentation here. It only made her want to see more.

"Like your decorator," she finally managed, casting a sidelong glance over to where Eric was enjoying her reaction.

"Moritania might not be big—" he bowed a little in acknowledgment "—but it is a country rife with good taste. I'd like to show you something, if you don't mind."

"The only thing you could show me to beat this would be the Sistine chapel."

Walking to the right side of the hall, Eric opened a great oak door. Casey walked past him into an even more impressive room. It was long, with six matched sets of crystal chandeliers and floor-to ceiling windows that reflected in the mirrors along the opposite wall.

"Been to Versailles, had they?" she breathed, coming to a stop.

Eric wouldn't let her. Instead, he took her by the elbow and gently propelled her down the parquet flooring. "I'm sure you don't know," he was saying, "but my brother just died recently...."

Casey immediately turned to him. "Oh, I'm sorry. I didn't."

He nodded with a sad little smile. "He was much older than I, and his heart was bad. The upshot of it is that next week his daughter, my niece, will become the new queen of Moritania. She is his only child, and his wife is also dead.''

Casey had no idea where the conversation was leading. He seemed so reluctant to tell her that she knew it was something important to him. She couldn't think of anything more to do but nod.

Then he stopped walking. Turning to her, he took hold of both of her arms, his eyes trying to communicate something of import. They had softened. Casey felt even more confused.

''What, Eric?''

''The portrait here at the end of the Great Hall has just gone up. It is a painting of the next queen of Moritania, Her Royal Highness the Crown Princess Cassandra.''

He turned her to face the painting. Casey's jaw dropped. Looking back at her from the canvas was a woman with delicate features, a gently molded face with deep, wide-set hazel eyes and a small, straight nose. A small mouth curved just at the ends as if she was amusing herself immensely with a private joke. Diamonds and rubies glittered in her mane of tawny hair, thick and styled sleekly away from tiny ears where teardrop earrings hung.

Casey turned to Eric and then back to the picture and then back to Eric again, unable to speak. Then she turned once again to the portrait and finally admitted what he'd been trying to prepare her for. She was staring at a portrait of herself.

''And here I thought losing the car was going to be the high point of my day.''

TWO

Behind Casey, Eric chuckled. "Pretty impressive, don't you think?"

Casey tilted her head to the side, trying her best to be objective. She'd never seen herself in satin and jewels before, and to be frank, it was an image she didn't mind. That stray Romanov blood peeking through, she guessed.

"She's prettier than I am," she finally ventured.

"Don't believe it," he told her. "She just has different priorities."

Casey had to grin, turning her head again. "And a great house."

She was about to ask about the rest of the puzzle when she was interrupted by an imperious voice coming from the doorway. It echoed through the room like the memory of an earlier century.

"My dear Cassandra, there you are. Aren't you quite ashamed of yourself for running off?"

Casey turned to see an elderly woman considering her with stern eyes. Elderly, maybe, but definitely unbowed. The woman before her stood ramrod-straight, as if refusing to allow herself to be overtaken by age. Her iron-gray hair was meticulously groomed, her designer suit impeccable and attractive. Casey had an image of the woman in high-necked satin and lace and a set of crown jewels and knew she was meeting somebody's queen.

Her Brooklyn upbringing and Irish blood responded.

"Mortified," she said, nodding easily. Maybe she'd have been more intimidated if the combination of her bloodlines hadn't destroyed her fear of titles. The Russians had them and couldn't use them, and the Irish had no use for them at all.

Eric stifled another grin as he stepped in, walking briskly over to his mother. With a sidelong glance, he begged Casey to follow. She did, her curiosity overwhelming even her rebellious nature.

"And well you should," the woman said, nodding back. "To take Eric away from his duties is—"

"A pleasure, Mother." He smiled, bending just a little to kiss her cheek. "I was merely murdering innocent birds with the bank's new board of directors."

She continued to glare, although her eyes softened suspiciously when they came into contact with her second son. Casey recognized the look. It had been the only way her own grandmother had been able to display affection. Harder to spot and more precious when given. Must have been part of that imperial training.

"This is not Cassandra, Mother," Eric continued, his hand on his mother's arm.

His mother's glare grew even more impatient. "Don't be impertinent, Eric. I, for one, am tired of your niece's little games."

"No more than I am," he assured her. "But this young lady is not she. Introduce yourself," he suggested, turning to Casey.

Casey stepped forward, knowing better than to hold out a hand. "My name's Casey Phillips, ma'am. I'm from Brooklyn, and my car broke down outside the border crossing. Eri—your son was kind enough to give me a lift to call for help."

Eric turned to Casey for the rest of the introduction. "Casey, may I present my mother, Her Royal Highness Marta, dowager queen of Moritania."

The queen squinted at her, then peered, her eyes like a wary hawk's. "Brooklyn," she snapped.

Casey nodded. "New York. America. I'm here on vacation. It's, um, a pleasure to meet you, ma'am."

For a long moment, nothing else was said. The three of them stood in a kind of tense tableau as Eric's mother studied Casey at her own leisure.

Behind them, another servant edged through the door. "Shall I serve here, Your Highness?" he asked diffidently.

The queen never turned, never took her eyes from Casey. "In the Rose Room, Gustave."

Gustave bowed and backed out.

"The eyes . . ." she finally said slowly. "They're quite different." She didn't say exactly how. "And Cassandra would never let herself be seen in such a getup."

Casey couldn't help a heartfelt scowl. So much for being invited for the weekend. The rest of her wardrobe wasn't a whole lot different.

Eric intervened. "Cassandra has a well-documented weakness for recognizable labels."

Hers was recognizable, Casey thought with a private grin. Everybody in *her* neighborhood knew who J. C. Penney was.

"You'll join us for some tea, young lady," the queen said. Not so much an invitation as an order, but the matter was moot for a queen. Who would ever think to turn her down? Just for a moment, Casey was tempted to decline, just to see what the old lady would do, but she was too curious to walk away right now. She wanted to learn about this mysterious twin of hers. And, she had to admit, she wanted to spend just a little more time studying the cool blue of Eric's eyes.

"Yes." She nodded. "Thank you."

Eric flashed her a smile of wry gratitude before ushering his mother out before him.

The Rose Room wasn't rose. It was more an eggshell white, with tapestries for decoration and a harp in the corner. Furniture somebody had actually sat on in the seventeenth century and hidden during revolutions and wars filled more parquet flooring, which was covered with a plush Oriental carpet in maroons and beiges.

The queen settled herself on a frail little love seat and motioned Casey to an adjoining wing chair. With the cosy marble fireplace next to them, it was quite an intimate little corner of a huge palace. Casey had the feeling that the queen had assembled it this way.

"Do you play the harp, ma'am?" Casey asked, watching as the servant assembled tea from a trolley behind the queen. Eric pulled up a satin-covered chair and sat alongside his mother.

"Heavens, no," the woman said. "My daughter did, though. Quite well."

Did. And there was a shadow in the stern blue eyes. Eric's family went young, it seemed.

"How did you come to visit Moritania?" she asked, accepting a cup and spoon from the servant.

Casey stole a look at Eric, but he was receiving his own cup. Royalty first, it seemed.

"Well, I won a trip to Europe and saw Moritania was near one of the areas where I was staying. I'd heard about the country from my grandfather as a child. He said that his grandfather came from here."

"Indeed. What was his name?"

Casey accepted her own cup and spooned in a healthy dollop of sugar. No artificial sweeteners around here. "Phillips."

The royal head came up a bit. "Phillips? That is not in the least Moritanian."

"I know. We figured he was renamed by one of the guys at Immigration who couldn't pronounce his real name. Happened all the time back then."

"He must have known the royal family," Eric said, smiling gently.

His mother dispatched another glare. "What trade did the gentleman practice in Moritania?"

Taking a careful sip from the fragile bone-china cup, Casey shrugged just as delicately. "I really don't know. We don't know much at all about him before he hit the shores."

The royal eyebrow arched. "Indeed. Do you know what trade he practiced once he did . . . hit the shores?"

Both Casey and Eric grinned at that. "Yes, ma'am. He was a gentleman's gentleman."

This time Eric's eyebrow lifted, his mouth struggling with an amused little grin. "It was probably his family's trade here, then. Which supports my supposition."

"Eric, really," the queen scolded him, her attention focused demurely on her tea.

It took Casey a couple of minutes to follow his line of reasoning. When she did, her head turned a little, wishing that from where she sat she could still see the portrait of the new queen of Moritania far down the palace hallway.

"You mean I have another royal line in me?" she demanded, not at all sure whether what she felt was pleasure or consternation.

"It's quite possible," Eric allowed. "It's not unheard-of for servant to have ended up founding a dynasty on the wrong side of the blanket."

She nodded pensively. "God knows half the American claim to royal heritage originated that way."

"Mine, too," he said, grinning with even more amusement. His mother was doing her best to ignore him.

Casey almost dropped her cup. "Excuse me?"

Eric laughed, and Casey felt it deep in her chest like a flutter. "My own great-grandfather was the illegitimate son of the king. We ended up with the throne when the old guy ran out of legitimate issue during a rather inconvenient war. My ancestor filled the gap so well that he was invited by the country to make it official."

Casey grinned, too, sharing not only the joke but the feeling of kinship with the handsome prince. "How intriguing. Must make for a great family crest."

She'd forgotten the queen. An outraged little cough brought her abruptly back.

Eric laughed again. "You can't intimidate this girl, Mother," he warned the old woman. "She's also a Romanov. And you know how those Russians are."

Casey wanted to tell them that it wasn't the Russian blood they should consider but the Irish, but she didn't get a chance. A new minion entered, wearing something akin to a morning coat, and bowed, waiting to be heard.

"Yes, Werner?" the queen asked without turning. He stood behind her, his anxious bureaucrat's eyes turned toward the prince instead. The man didn't seem comfortable meeting people's eyes. His own were poised somewhere about the third button on Eric's shirt.

"I beg your pardon, Your Highness." He spoke up in an appropriately hushed voice that made Casey think of funeral homes. "It is the princess. She is expected at the opening of the new children's hospital She is...um, late."

Casey could see the gentleman flinch, waiting for some kind of outburst. When it didn't come, his anxious stare turned toward her instead. She watched him with no more than curiosity as his eyes swept her attire and strayed close to her face. She had the most irrational desire to check her neck for dirt.

"She wasn't there?" Eric demanded, checking the slim gold watch on his wrist.

Werner allowed his gaze to swing to the prince before returning to Casey. "If you'll pardon my saying so, Your Highness..."

This time Eric comprehended the hesitation. "Oh, Werner, this is not the princess. This is Miss Casey Phillips from the United States. Quite a resemblance, don't you think?"

The gentleman's eyes grew very large as he gave a crisp bow, unwilling or unable by training to allow verbal surprise or doubt. "Quite, Your Highness. Welcome to Moritania, Miss Phillips."

He couldn't take his eyes off her. By now Casey was getting used to it. "My pleasure, Mr. Werner." Somehow, with the twang of Brooklyn in her speech, the stilted address sounded slightly ludicrous.

"And the princess..." Werner went on, once more turning to the prince for guidance.

"Should be soundly spanked," Eric answered absently, once again considering his watch. "When was she last seen?"

"Her maid helped her dress this morning, Your Highness. She then left the grounds in the Jaguar."

"That was five hours ago. What about her security?"

"Followed behind. They have not seen fit to report in."

Eric nodded briskly. "Get in touch with them. Have them dispatch the princess to the opening or present themselves up for dismissal."

"Eric . . ." the queen admonished quietly.

Eric acquiesced to his mother. "I know it's not their fault, Mother. But I, for one, am tired of baby-sitting the next queen of Moritania like a student on holiday."

Before leaving, Werner dispatched one more little nudge. "Also, Your Majesty has an appointment with the arts council."

The queen set her cup down with a brisk nod and got to her feet. "So I do, Werner." Turning, she took in Casey with a regal eye. "We hope you enjoy the rest of your visit to Moritania, Miss Phillips. Eric, please don't forget the benefit this evening."

Eric came to his feet, which brought Casey to hers. She figured if the prince got up it was a sure bet the commoner was supposed to, also.

"Of course, dear," he was saying. "Once we nab Cassandra, we won't let her out of our collective sights. Will we, Werner?"

Werner executed another of those bows. "No, Your Highness."

Werner made his exit only after the queen did. Which left the cosy little room to Casey and Eric. She didn't feel quite disposed to leave yet. Neither, it seemed, did Eric.

"More tea?" he asked with an intimate little smile playing across his lips.

"More information?" she countered with a matching grin.

"Our pleasure," he nodded, playing on the royal "we" his mother had invoked.

"Would it be an imposition to see a few more rooms?" she asked diffidently. "I mean, considering that my family line was evidently founded somewhere in one of them."

Eric laughed as he reached around and lifted the silver teapot to serve. "We'll bring our cups along. A frightful breach of protocol, but what can one expect from Americans, after all?"

"Just a bunch of cheeky colonials," Casey countered, accepting her cup from him. His hands were strong, their touch electric. She suddenly found herself staring down at them as if expecting them to give off sparks.

Eric, on the other hand, found his eyes on her face—on the softer lines of her eyes, the broader smile lines and more expressive mouth. If Cassandra had had the personality to craft that face, she could have been the most popular queen in Moritanian history, instead of merely its most notorious fashion plate. He ushered Casey out of the room, trying to figure out a way to see more of her before she had to go home.

Werner caught up with them in the game room. Game meaning dead animals rather than video. Casey wasn't terribly fond of all the beady stares and antlers that crowded the paneled walls. She'd seen *Bambi* one too many times to be comfortable with the deer, and preferred her bears stamping out forest fires. Eric traced the history of the room from the man who might well have been their common ancestor in the time of Louis XIV, his cultured tones invoking the privileged reminiscences of royalty.

"If it weren't for the present government," he was saying, "you could wander through the palace at St. Petersburg and tell the same kinds of stories."

Casey found herself shrugging, her attention more on his elegant features than the stories. "I'm afraid that once you've grown up without the exposure it's not the same. In my neighborhood, the kids would rather spend their time in a video arcade."

Eric turned, the afternoon light from the leaded windows soft on his face. "And you?"

Casey grinned. "I was video game champ for two months running."

"Video games," he mused, the look in his eyes too intense for the tenor of their talk. "I'll have to try them someday."

She felt the breath escape from her lungs. "Cheaper than stuffing bears."

For a second she saw the surprise in Eric's eyes. It still threw him off balance when someone spoke frankly to him. Then he dissolved into laughter. With an unconscious intimacy, he took hold of her arm and leaned over to drop a kiss on her forehead.

"I must stop in Brooklyn next time I fly into Kennedy Airport," he promised. "I've missed the most wonderful place in America."

Casey came to a shuddering halt at his touch, at the soft brush of his lips against her skin. It was as if she'd been without sustenance for a very long time and had just realized it. Damn, she thought with a growing sense of loss, why couldn't I pick a good boy from Brooklyn to succumb to? I've got to be an idiot and turn to water for a prince in a foreign country. Nothing like reaching for the attainable.

"Call me anytime," she heard herself saying. "The number's in the book." Then she smiled involuntarily, her wry wit saving her. "Under Displaced Royalty."

His eyes sparkled with delight. "With pleasure."

"Tell me something," she said a moment later, looking down the shadowy length of the great room. "Do you mind being third?" Neither seemed to notice that Eric had yet to recover his hand.

"Third?"

Casey nodded, her gaze straying to him, then away. "Do you mind not getting the throne? I know my nana said that her grandfather never quite got over it himself. He very much wanted to be Czar."

Taking a sip of his tea, Eric nodded thoughtfully. "Ah, yes. I can imagine. Actually, I'm quite content. Cassandra was born to nod and wave. I was born to banking, and that is where I am most needed. I don't begrudge her her notoriety in the least."

"Your Highness."

Eric turned, his hand still firmly on Casey's arm. Werner was back, looking more anxious than ever. He still couldn't seem to make eye contact.

"Yes, Werner?" Eric's tone wasn't quite as easygoing as before. Casey didn't realize that it had everything to do with her.

"Your Highness, I thought you would want to be apprised. When we tried to raise the security team, they failed to respond. Their auto has just been located west of Braz."

Eric stiffened, his grip on Casey tightening. "And the princess?"

Werner looked as if he wanted to dig a hole through the rug and hide. "Missing, Your Highness. A search is being mounted."

"You're sure it's not just another one of her . . . tests?"

"It is always possible." The little man looked positively sick. "But there was blood."

Casey heard a stifled groan. Eric began to slowly shake his head. "The economic conference begins tomorrow. The coronation is next week. My God."

"Yes, Your Highness."

Without hesitation, Eric snapped into action. "Not a word to the press. If the guard so much as sneezes at the wrong moment, heads will be on the block. I'll call the bank and tell them that I will be conducting business from the palace for the next few days to accommodate the ministers. Get hold of General Mueller. I wish to speak to him personally. Any unusual communications to the palace are to be funneled through me. Understood?"

Werner snapped off another bow. "Your Highness." Then he whirled around and left.

"Damn her!" Eric snarled, finally letting go. He began to pace, the filtered sunlight glinting in the rich depths of his hair as he passed the windows. Casey had the eerie feeling that the animals on the wall were watching him with patient eyes. We've seen it all before, they were saying.

"You have enough to do," she said hesitantly, hating the sound of her words. "I'll get on back to the hotel." It didn't occur to her yet that she still didn't have a car.

The sound of her voice brought Eric around. His eyes, those glacier-blue lights, fixed on her, studying her with an intensity that was disconcerting. They held her pinned to the spot and unable to think of anything redeeming to say.

"Would you mind waiting a bit?" he asked, his own voice colored by the thoughts whirling in his mind. The plans, the recriminations.

Casey shook her head, unsure and unsettled by the sharp consideration he leveled on her. "Of course not. If it's more convenient . . . I just thought that you'd want to see to the princess."

"I'd like to *thrash* the princess," he snapped hotly, then stopped, surprised that he'd voiced the reaction to an outsider. Only the royal family and loyal servants knew what trouble the Crown Princess Cassandra was. What surprised Eric more was that he felt comfortable elaborating. "If it weren't for Cassandra's insistence on playing little games with her country, this wouldn't have happened. She has the damndest idea that it's still the sixteenth century and she can act accordingly."

"You alluded to that before, I think," Casey said quietly. "When we first met. What does she do?"

He shrugged, pacing again. "She does a little disappearing act sometimes, dragging her security forces off on a merry chase to see if they can find her. Or she shows up unannounced to see if the citizens are following the latest law or whether they appreciate her station. She has most of the people of Braz terrorized."

"But is royalty really that much in control here?"

He nodded with rueful eyes. "Until she gets through with it, I'm sure. Moritania has always gotten along quite well with its royal family, and we with the country. With a place this size, if we didn't, we wouldn't have lasted a generation. She does have more control than most modern monarchs. Or she will next week when she's crowned." His eyes strayed toward the door through which Werner had disappeared, and his jaw tightened. "*If* she's crowned, that is."

"And if she's not?"

"The country is thrown into a fine mess of an economic crisis. The constitution demands that unless a new sovereign is crowned within twenty days of the death of the previous one, all legislation must be resubmitted for evaluation. Usually that gives us plenty of time. With the Sunday coronation, we had five days' leeway."

"It's so important?"

He stopped, leveling those eyes on her once more. "For a country that makes more money than Switzerland in banking, yes, I'd say it is. Our biggest selling point is stability. We haven't had a major disruption in government in nearly three hundred years."

Casey nodded, a bit numbly. "Yes," she agreed, wondering how she never knew that. "I guess it does."

He paced a few more times, then swung around on her, his eyes even brighter. "Would you mind coming along while I make some phone calls?"

"Sure. And if you need any help, let me know." She couldn't help but grin. "I'm the best secretary in midtown Manhattan."

Eric took her by the arm and turned her toward the door. "Casey, you may just have a deal, as you Americans say."

Casey watched in rapt silence as Eric conducted his business. Werner had already prepared what must have been the prince's study, a room of warm woods and hunter greens, for their arrival. Once there, Eric procured another pot of tea and some sandwiches and located the bank officers and the head of the Moritanian Guard.

The country didn't have an army per se. As in Switzerland, the entire male population was considered part of the reserve forces in the event of a war. The guard was simply the long arm of the law, as it were, protecting the palace and any foreign dignitaries working in Moritania and investigating the touchier problems that the police didn't quite know how to handle.

Casey heard Eric swear the general to secrecy in his search and then demand constant updates. She had the most intriguing feeling that she had tripped right into the plot of a thriller, except that everybody looked more exasperated than upset. She guessed that if it had been England the chances of a serious problem would have been a lot higher.

Then the bank business arrived, and Eric moved to that without hesitation, working the computer as a pianist would his keyboard. Casey was duly impressed. It seemed that very little could ruffle the man. He didn't so much as sweat as the reports came in from the field that the princess could not be found. Nor did he loosen his tie nor run his hands through his hair when the bank called to say that the representatives from the other countries were beginning to arrive for the conference and expected to see him that night at the benefit, an evening of opera and dinner at the royal opera house in Braz.

As the afternoon began to wear on, he did begin to pace, his long stride eating up yet another exquisite old Oriental rug and the hardwood floor beneath. Casey sat on the window seat edging the big bay window behind his desk and watched him, sipping quietly at her tea and wondering what she could do to help.

"The general is on line two, Your Highness," Werner announced.

"Will you complete the transaction with the bank for me, Werner?" Eric asked, going from computer to phone.

Werner, loaded down with other reports that were due for the courier, hesitated.

Casey sat down her cup and stood. "Go on, Werner," she said, smiling, "I'll do it."

He dispatched a look that she was sure wasn't in his guide to subordinates' manners, but when Eric waved him on, he went. Casey sat down at the desk and took a moment to study the figures scrawled on the pad by the screen. Eric turned to the phone, his fingers still pointing out different things to her as he greeted the general. She filled in the blanks with practiced fingers.

"Found?" Eric snapped, his attention suddenly on the phone conversation. "Where were they?"

Casey looked up, then went back to her work. Eric had forgotten her. Then she heard a sharp intake of breath and forgot the bank completely.

Eric stood alongside her, grasping the phone as if it were his last handhold on the Eiger, his eyes glittering. She could see the muscles jump along the line of his jaw as he received the news.

"Well," he finally answered. "It's her own damn fault. Of course, we must keep a tight rein on the information. Go right ahead with your investigation—" his eyes strayed to Casey, a new introspection in them "—I'll take care of the other. No matter what, no one else must know that this is what we are about, do you understand?"

He must have received the answer he'd anticipated, because he nodded rather sharply. "Keep me informed."

It was a moment after he hung up before Casey finally gathered the nerve to speak up. "I think all the numbers are in the right spaces, if you'd like to check. I can send it off then."

Eric's head snapped up. He stared at her as if surprised that she was still there.

"Is there anything else I can do?" she asked.

He smiled then, the light in his eyes brightening with a rueful wryness. "That isn't a question you should ask lightly just now."

"Oh?" She felt her heart thud oddly and then chastised herself for it. She was getting far too comfortable in this world of antiques and titles. It was high time to get back to her broken car and her off-the-rack clothes.

But Eric wasn't quite finished with her. Quickly scanning the screen, he punched the information on to the bank and drew her to her feet.

"I need a favor."

Then he led her back to the window seat and sat down beside her. "We have a problem," he began, his eyes still rueful. Casey couldn't believe that he still looked as if he'd just stepped from a fine restaurant. There had to have been more than his share of stress in that last call. She'd seen its impact. He could at least have had the decency to be rumpled by it.

She couldn't help but smile at him. "I also type and take shorthand. I do not get coffee, though."

His smile widened. Once again he had taken hold of her and didn't think to let go. She didn't think to tell him. He held her hand this time, and the warmth of his hand around hers was far too enticing.

"I'm afraid I had something a little more complicated than that in mind, Casey." He took a moment's glance at the mountains that climbed from beyond the window before returning to her. "How would you like to go to the opera?"

"The what?"

"The opera. Gounod's *Faust*. Then a formal dinner."

She shook her head. "Eric, I'm not exactly sure what you're driving at, but your mother pretty much said it all.

The getup I'm in is about as got-up as I get. I'm unfit for formal dinners *or* the opera. But thanks, anyway."

Idiot, she thought. You should have said, sure, I'll go. After all, look what Scarlett O'Hara did with just the drapes. Casey's rejection ate at her stomach like a knife.

Even so, Eric's smile refused to falter. "Let me complete my proposal first...."

She laughed with nervous energy. "Never say proposal to a girl from Brooklyn."

"Idea, then." He smiled. "Problem. I just finished speaking to the general, and the news was not all good. The security guards were found, unscathed except for nosebleeds. The princess was not."

Casey's smile froze. "What do they think?"

"No thinking necessary. They found a note. From a dissident group. The princess was kidnapped."

Casey couldn't help her own glance out to the majestic scenery, the closest she'd ever been to heaven. "You have dissidents here?" she demanded instinctively. It seemed so out of place.

Eric found himself smiling again. "My dear Casey, you can't organize a bridge club without dissidents, much less a country. These are a club of rather virulent socialists. They feel the monarchy must be banned."

"Socialists," she echoed rather stupidly.

He shrugged. "In a country with no unemployment, it is a bit difficult to comprehend. At any rate, they promise the princess will be safe if we free some of their friends in neighboring countries and proclaim to the world that a socialist government will be set up instead of Cassandra being crowned." His smile returned again. "Unfortunately, the way Cassandra has been behaving, I can hardly blame them."

"You don't seem terribly worried."

"Neither did the general. He knows these groups better than I, and he says that the princess is as good as rescued. The problem, of course, is that with the economic conference beginning tomorrow, we cannot allow word of this to leak out."

"Stability and all...." Casey nodded, getting her first glimmer of what Eric had in mind. Her eyes widened, her mouth dropped, and she took a look around the room.

"The opera?" she repeated slowly, her stomach and heart all of a sudden crowding her throat.

"If you wouldn't mind."

"But, Eric," she protested instinctively, "it couldn't possibly work. Listen to me. I sound like Rocky, not the future queen of Moritania. Me pose as Cassandra? Not even Hollywood would buy something that weird!"

"We'll say you lost your voice. You can nod and wave, can't you?"

She showed him.

He nodded briskly. "Excellent. We'll fit you in one of Cassandra's dresses, and I will escort you. No one will know."

Her eyes grew bigger. "You're nuts."

He shook his head without noticeable agitation. "Merely rather desperate."

"I don't know a salad fork from a tuning fork! What if I butter my bread in the soup bowl or fall asleep at the opera?"

"Cassandra has been known to do worse. All you have to do to create the correct impression is flirt shamelessly with everyone under the age of eighty."

Casey groaned. "I wouldn't know how to flirt if I saw a demonstration on videotape."

She didn't notice that his smile was a wry one. "I believe you greatly underestimate yourself." How could he begin to explain to her that her fresh exuberance was far more enticing than Cassandra's calculated cunning could ever be?

"Oh," he added, certain that he had a victory. "One more thing. You must act properly bored with Rudolph Van Dorn, Baron of Austerlitz."

Casey looked up, anticipating impending doom. "Who's he?"

Eric smiled. "Your fiancé."

She closed her eyes, capitulating. "Forget what I said. You're not the one who's nuts. I am." The breath she took to gather courage was a tremulous one. "I think I'm going to do it."

Three

"Do I like the opera?"

"You detest it."

"Thank God." Casey reached out hesitantly to pick a long white kid glove from the bureau where it was laid out for her. Holding it as if it was a dead mouse, she turned back to Eric. "I was afraid I was going to have to say something obscene like 'My dear, don't you just adore the mezzo?' I'd rather slit my throat."

Eric's smile was delighted. "After an evening of *Faust*, you may end up doing just that."

"How long do I have to get ready?"

He checked his watch again. "About two hours."

She nodded, her eyes back on the royal-blue satin gown that lay spread out before her. "It might take just about that long." Her bravado briefly giving out, she turned to him, the glove following like a ruffled wind sock. "Oh, Eric, I really don't think this is going to work. I'm going to fall off my heels or insult a world leader or something. Tell them that Cassandra is indisposed.''

With a hand on each arm, Eric faced down her rising panic with gentling eyes. ''You'll be marvelous. Just follow my lead and we won't have any problems at all. If you don't make an appearance tonight, there won't be any way to fight the kidnapper's propaganda when it hits the media. We have to try.''

''But I don't *look* like her!''

He reached up to brush an errant strand of hair from her forehead. ''You don't dress like her, that's all. And with Maria's help, no one will ever know the difference. Trust me, Cassandra. No one but us will know.''

She shook her head, her eyes wide. ''Both of us are nuts.''

''Possibly.'' He nodded, and Casey had the unsettling impression for a moment that he wasn't talking about their upcoming escapade. ''But it's the only idea I could come up with on short notice. Please don't back out on me now.''

She found herself ensnared within the clear assurance of his eyes. She'd never known anyone like him. He was so filled with purpose and confidence, so sure of them both that she felt helpless to do anything but be pulled along in his wake. Those eyes were sapping her panic again, soothing her and exciting her all at once.

''I wish I were back at the hotel,'' she whined with a heartfelt scowl, dropping the glove back in its place.

The next instant her head popped up and her mouth dropped. ''Oh, my God. The hotel. Eric, Sandra was expecting me to get back an hour ago. What am I going to do?''

This was obviously news he hadn't anticipated. ''Sandra who?''

"My friend. She and I have been traveling together. We were out late last night at a *hofbrauhaus* and she didn't want to see Moritania. She's waiting back at the hotel for me and the car so we can drive on to Switzerland tonight."

Eric let go of her for a moment, turning away to consider the new wrinkle in the plan. It didn't take him long. Before Casey could think up eight or nine arguments against not returning for Sandra, he turned back to her with a sly smile.

"Do you think she'd mind a short stay at the palace instead? I'm afraid she can't go along tonight, but Maria can see to her needs while we're out."

Casey almost laughed out loud. "Where's a phone? I'll call her."

Casey was sure that Sandra would still be expecting some kind of punch line when the chauffeured limousine came by to pick up her and the luggage, but at least it was all settled. She turned away from the short, rather disjointed phone conversation to continue transforming the ugly duckling into some semblance of a swan.

Eric presented a small, squat woman with rather heavy features and a sweet smile. "This is Maria. She is the Princess Cassandra's personal maid, and has been apprised of the situation. Outside of the military, no one but Maria, Werner and myself knows of your real identity. Of course, that's allowing for the fact that by morning every one of the servants will undoubtedly have figured it out. But they're unquestionably loyal. I hope this will be contained."

Casey wasn't sure Eric saw the brief scowl that crossed Maria's eyes. It seemed that princes didn't always appreciate their staff's loyalty as much as they thought.

"I'd put my life in Maria's hands before I'd put it in the general's," Casey said honestly, and was rewarded with the beginnings of a smile. "Now then, Your Highness," Casey said with an air of finality, "don't you have some dressing to do yourself?"

Eric smiled, a brief shadow over his eyes the only betrayal of his task ahead. Casey wanted very much to tell him it was going to be all right. She had a feeling that one didn't do that in front of the maid. Oh well, there was a lot to learn.

"Everything's going to be all right," she said anyway, as much for herself as for him.

His smile brightened as he bent to drop another kiss on her forehead, this one of gratitude. "You're right, of course. It's a brilliant plan. I only hope Cassandra behaves herself until we manage to get her free."

Maria's eyes rolled ever so slightly behind the prince's back, and Casey found herself stifling a giggle. "See you in an hour or so, Eric," she said, edging him out the door.

Then she turned back to the maid and a room that looked like one giant pink satin ruffle. Pink flowered wallpaper, pink canopied bed, pink ruffled tablecloths and dust ruffles on every stick of furniture in the room. It made Casey think of an exploded bottle of gooey pink stomach medicine.

"Your bath is drawn, Your Highness." Maria offered with a diffident bow. "Do you require assistance dressing?"

Casey gave her a wry smile. "Not since I've been three, thanks. Do you have to call me Your Highness?"

The little maid nodded. "Yes, ma'am. The prince insisted."

Casey nodded back, her eyes still wandering over the pink wasteland. Cassandra truly didn't have her tastes, and that was a fact. "Okay. Well, Maria, pull up a chair or something. I'm going to have to wash my hair before I do anything else. Half the topsoil of Austria is in it."

"Do you—?"

"No. I do that myself, too."

An hour later, Casey realized that what she couldn't do herself was manage to get her hair to look anything like Cassandra's. Along with all the pink was a gaggle of pictures of the princess, riding her horses, playing tennis, sailing the yacht, encrusted with family jewels at some soiree. In every one, her hair was sleek and leonine-looking. Not a stray hair to be found, even in the wind. Casey couldn't imagine how that could ever be done, if her hair was anything like Casey's.

For all the brushing, all the twisting and pinning and curling, her hair simply wouldn't behave. She stared briefly at the brush in her hand as if that were the traitor, and let out a healthy shriek of frustration, coming inches from hurling the thing at the mirror.

Maria saved mirror and brush.

"If you'll allow me, Your Highness. This is my responsibility always. It becomes easier to do if you put on the crown first."

Casey looked up. "The crown?" Her voice sounded very small.

"Yes, Your Highness. The dowager queen's tiara tonight, if I am correct. Diamonds and sapphires."

She was correct. By the time Sandra was ushered into the room thirty minutes later, Casey stood tall and regal in the blue satin gown, the tiara in place within the sleek chignon, the matching necklace and bracelet already donned. Casey didn't want to so much as move, sure that at least one clasp was faulty. She was just pulling up the white kid gloves when her friend arrived.

"Oh, I'm sorry. This must be—"

The tall brunette stopped in her tracks, looking from Casey to Maria and back before she could manage another word.

"Casey?"

Casey grinned brightly, turning so that the full satin skirt whispered around her. "None other. Like it?"

But Sandra hadn't taken it in. "Casey?"

"No," Casey said, scowling. "Catherine the Great. Sit down before you fall down, Sandy. Maria, this is my friend Sandra Vitale. Sandy, my new friend Maria."

Maria dropped a quick curtsy. "A pleasure, *fraülein*."

Sandy stared a little more. "Wanna tell me what's going on?"

"Did you like the ride?"

She nodded.

"If you liked the car," Casey said, grinning with an energy born of equal parts exhilaration and terror, "you'll love the prince."

As if called once again just by her words, Eric appeared in the doorway, attired in white tie and tails. Casey's knees almost gave out at the sight of him.

Sandra wheeled around just as he arrived, and her mouth dropped again. "Who are you?"

He smiled, and Sandra went dumb. "You must be Sandra. Welcome to Moritania. Has Casey explained the situation to you yet?"

Sandra couldn't even seem to draw breath.

"Don't mind her," Casey advised him. "She startles easily. Besides, I haven't had a chance to fill her in yet."

Eric nodded pleasantly. "Well, we only have about ten minutes before the car comes around. And you and I have much to discuss, Casey."

She nodded back, a sudden tightness in her chest. Eric looked as if he'd stepped out of the pages of a men's magazine. Casey had always liked formal wear on men. It added such an air of rakish elegance to them. But Eric, more elegant than anyone she'd ever seen, transcended the clothes. He moved gracefully in the sleekly cut clothes, filling them to breathtaking perfection. And she was going to be on his arm all night. Good thing she wasn't supposed to talk. She didn't think she was going to have the breath to anyway.

On his arm. Oh, Lord, she couldn't do this. She couldn't face those people and pretend she was somebody she wasn't....

Maria spoke up with the assurance of her position. "Excuse me, Your Highness. The princess has her earrings to put on yet."

"Earrings?" Casey asked, despairing at the thought that she had yet more precious stones to safeguard.

"Princess?" Sandra squeaked. Then she did sit down abruptly in one of the pink chairs.

Maria was going to assist Casey in their insertion when she stopped. "Which, er, site, Your Highness?"

Casey's fingers went to her ears and the three holes she and Sandy had made for various earrings. Maria cast a baleful look over at Eric.

"See if you can find a set that covers the extras," he suggested. "Any more quaint American tortures you've inflicted upon yourself, Cassandra?"

Casey grinned. "I bite my nails to the quick, but that's what the gloves are for."

"Well, make certain that you stay right with me the entire evening so that I can continue to prompt you. There are simply too many customs and protocols that you aren't acquainted with to brief you accordingly. I don't suppose you speak German?'' Her baleful look was answer enough. ''French? Italian?''

''Fettucine Alfredo?''

Eric nodded fatalistically. Sandra's head had turned back and forth so often she looked as if she was at Wimbledon. Casey presented her ears for Maria's ministrations, the new tenor of the conversation churning in her stomach. Dress-up time was over. It was on to the ball, and she didn't speak German or Italian. She didn't know which fork to eat with or when to applaud at an opera. Or if you did at all.

When all was finished, Casey presented herself for inspection. Eric stood before her, his face composed in a studious frown, searching, she supposed, for errors. The terror of anticipation grew.

She was wrong. Eric was struggling to cover his true reaction. Casey did, indeed, look enough like Cassandra to fool just about everyone. The face, the hair, the elegant clothes, all were perfect. But once again Eric was struck by the difference. Casey's hazel eyes shone like a child's with pleasure at her accomplishment. Her whole face radiated a warmth he'd never known from her namesake, a fresh, infectious vitality. Even the great size of Casey's eyes, reflecting her stark terror at the sudden undertaking, was beguiling.

He wasn't at all sure whether anyone else would notice. But he did. It made him realize that he wasn't sure if he really wanted to rescue the real Cassandra. If he did, this one would have to leave and he would be left with the cool isolation of his life.

Trapping Casey's eyes with the sweet sky of his, Eric approached her. He took her gloved hand in his own and bent over it, brushing his lips over her knuckles. Casey felt the whisper of his touch all the way to her satin-clad toes and knew that her eyes had involuntarily widened even more. She knew, too, that Eric couldn't help but see her helpless fascination when he straightened and sought her gaze once again.

"Her Highness is especially beautiful tonight," he said softly, his voice excluding the other people in the room.

Casey's eyes were radiant. "We thank the prince for his kind words," she answered, only a modicum of humor in her breathless voice.

"I know it sounds trite, Casey," he said, his eyes darkening with sincerity, "but you are doing my country a great service. We will never be able to thank you enough."

She managed a reply over the lump in her throat. "It's kind of my country, too, isn't it?"

"There is one thing," he said, the expression in his eyes playful, his hand still holding hers. "The Princess Cassandra has never been afraid of anything in her life."

Casey found herself offering a tremulous smile. He'd caught her wondering whether there was any way she could keep from walking out that door. "Just do me a favor and remind me of that when somebody wonders why I'm not paying attention when they address me in Italian. Or French."

Eric's eyes praised her as his words couldn't. "Think we'll carry it off, Maria?" he asked, his hand firmly around Casey's now.

Maria crossed herself. "God willing, Your Highness."

He smiled. "Indeed. Well, my dear, this is one show that cannot begin without us. Shall we?"

Casey slipped her hand into the crook of his arm and swung out the door before she had the chance to back out. "See you later, Sandy. Maria will take care of you till we get back."

When the rustle of Casey's dress receded down the long hall, Maria walked up to the girl who was still seated in stunned silence. Sandy looked up at her helplessly.

"You come with me," Maria told her. "We get some tea and talk about what goes on in this crazy palace, *ja*?"

With a very weak smile, Sandy got herself off her chair and followed out the door. *"Ja."*

The royal opera house was situated on one of those winding streets in Braz, a great mammoth creature of white marble that reminded Casey a little of Sacré Coeur in Montmartre. The inside seemed to have been decorated by the same muralist who had done the palace. Here, his art was wasted on ceilings so high that the cherubim couldn't be told from the seraphim. The grand stairway was crimson-carpeted, and the furniture in the lobby was French and frilly.

Casey had barely made it in the front door before she almost gave herself away. Her head went straight up in the classic tourist position, her eyes threatening to pop at the opulence she was to enjoy that evening due to the benevolence of the Moritanian people. Eric caught her just in time. With his hand to the small of her back, he gave her a little nudge in the kidneys.

"You've seen this before," he whispered in her ear as everyone in the room was bowing their hellos. "And you find it quite boring."

Casey smiled dryly, her hand to her throat in a gesture that she hoped would excuse the odd movement. "Of course I do."

Her eyes were on all the people caught in their deep obeisance as she and Eric passed. It made her want to giggle. As a rule, people didn't bow to secretaries in Manhattan, and the fact that it was happening here struck her as a bit ludicrous. So did the host of eyes that couldn't manage to look her in the face. She was sure it wasn't her décolletage, since she didn't have any. Must be the temporary title. If Eric's hand hadn't been so firmly in place to administer reminders, she would have been more tempted to tell these people that it was impolite not to look someone in the eye.

They reached their box without Casey tripping over the carpet, and stepped to their seats which had been crafted like small portable thrones. Casey quelled another urge to giggle. Eric kept her from sitting down until homage was paid by those already seated below and around them.

"Bow your head," he murmured, bowing his own with a smile as he gave a little wave.

Casey followed suit, feeling as if she was atop a float in the Rose Bowl parade. The audience straightened and waited. At another cue, Casey took her seat next to Eric.

"I'm beginning to feel like Jerry Mahoney," she complained under her breath.

Eric looked over. "Who?"

She grinned. "A ventriloquist's dummy. He made a lot of money, but he never had anything to say for himself."

If Queen Marta had not arrived just then, Eric would have burst out laughing. Everyone rose again in respect for the old woman, and the ritual was repeated.

Casey saw the queen peer questioningly at her, then at Eric. Obviously not much got past the old gal.

"Cassandra." She nodded, the arch of her eyebrow the only thing that gave away the fact that she knew exactly what was going on. "Nice to see you could join us."

Casey just nodded and smiled.

"Did Werner tell you that Cassandra has lost her voice, Mother?" Eric asked easily.

"He did."

Eric nodded. The queen nodded. Casey offered another pale little smile.

Only a few minutes later, the lights dimmed and the curtain went up. Eric surreptitiously slipped his hand in Casey's and gave it a squeeze of reassurance. Somehow, neither of them thought to let go during the first act of the opera.

Casey would have had enough fun just watching the audience, the building and the other royals during the opera. But she had to grudgingly admit that as the opera wore on, she became involved in that, too. She didn't know the language, couldn't understand a word that was sung, but there was something universal in the actions and the dilemmas that unfolded on the stage.

By the time the last strains of music echoed away into the vaulted ceiling, Casey found that the tight fear that had lived in her chest ever since Eric had first proposed this masquerade was beginning to ease a little. Her sense of well-being lasted only as long as it took to get to dinner.

They weren't just at the head of the table, they were seated on a dais so that every one of the hundred or so guests could see any mistake she made. Casey walked in alongside Eric, his hand once again firmly in the small of her back, the audience once again bowing, eyes downcast. There were Moritanians present, as well as the foreign bankers who were coming to the conference tomorrow. The wealthy and titled from neighboring countries and a few international celebrities were also in attendance. And all of them had come to see her.

"Your Highness." A bejeweled woman in her forties greeted her with a curtsy as they reached the dais. "I understand you've been a bit under the weather. I do hope you're feeling better."

Casey nodded and made a little rasping noise to go with her apologetic smile. A gloved hand went to her throat again. The woman responded with concerned eyes.

"I cannot begin to tell you how grateful we are that you attended the benefit," she gushed.

"It was a favorite cause of the late king," Eric put in, perfectly at ease. Casey wondered what would make that man sweat. She had the uncomfortable feeling that she was about to, herself. She wondered if she could escape to the solitude of the bathroom for a minute.

Then she wondered just where royalty went to the bathroom at these things. Did they use the public facilities, with a lady-in-waiting parked outside to make sure nobody viewed the royal bodily functions, or were you supposed to just wait until you got home? It certainly was a question she should have asked beforehand.

"Eric." She had enough forethought to make the word a low rasp.

He turned to her, somehow without excluding their hostess. She didn't quite know how to ask. Looking into the perfectly serene regard of those blue eyes, she lost her courage. With a wave of her hand, she changed her mind and let him return his attention to the woman.

That was when disaster loomed the second time. The hostess was reaching out to catch someone's attention in an attempt to make introductions to the prince and princess. When Casey caught sight of who it was, she almost passed out.

James McCormac. Star of screen, theater and Casey's bedroom walls all during her teen years. A ruggedly handsome man who had always had the knack of appealing to a woman's softer side, he had single-handedly carved out Casey's expectations of a man. The fact that she was going to meet him almost destroyed her.

Eric almost didn't catch her reaction in time.

"Her Royal Highness, Princess Cassandra," the woman was saying, her own eyes on the craggy features and gently silvering hair, "may I present James Mc-Cormac."

Casey's hand went out and her mouth opened. "Oh..."

Eric turned just in time, knocking into Casey with a force that took her breath away. The "O-o-o-o-h, my God, you're James McCormac!" about to come out died in a series of strangled little coughs. Eric succeeded in saving her from falling forward into the centerpiece as he covered the unfortunate lapse.

"Oh, Cassandra, excuse me," he purred. "Are you all right? You looked for a moment like you were choking."

Her answering glare was more than appropriately heartfelt.

"Jim," he said, smiling easily, turning back to the star. "Good to see you again."

Again. Not only was Casey expected to look reasonably intelligent in the presence of her childhood idol, she was supposed to have known him before. Marvelous.

"You're going to be sitting with us tonight?"

"That's what I understand, Your Highness. It will be my pleasure," McCormac said. Casey could hardly keep herself still at the resonant music of that familiar voice. When he turned to her with those incredible brown eyes, she wanted to run for the ladies' room. But she hadn't figured out just what she was supposed to do about that, had she?

"Your Highness." He bowed easily, his smile familiar and flattering. "It's a pleasure to see you again. You're looking more beautiful than ever."

She resorted once again to nodding and smiling. He didn't seem to mind.

"Oh, look, Cassandra," Eric said with some relish. "It's Rudolph. And I thought he wouldn't be able to make it tonight."

Casey turned to see a younger version of Herbert Hoover walk up, all spit, polish and starched collars. She wanted to laugh. Cassandra was going to marry this guy? He looked as if he was just about as much fun as a trip to the dentist.

Deciding that she was probably staying right in character, she walked over to James McCormac and slid her hand through his arm. Then, motioning to the table, she walked away with him.

"You probably ripped wings off insects when you were a kid, didn't you?"

Eric looked over to where Casey slumped in the seat next to him. They were riding through the winding roads back to the palace, the car as silent as the Alpine night.

"You did perfectly well tonight. Even Mother was impressed."

She snorted, sliding a finger up under her tiara to scratch at the pins holding it on. "Mother didn't have to walk into an ambush armed only with a tiara and a case of laryngitis."

Eric laughed, slipping an arm around her sagging shoulder. "Didn't you enjoy yourself? The opera was fairly good; the food certainly was. And, to be frank, the company was far superior to that at some of the benefit functions we must attend."

"James McCormac," she groaned, her eyes rolling heavenward. She'd done everything but drool down his shirtfront. It just wasn't fair. She'd dreamed about meeting him since the day she'd turned twelve, and Eric had stolen her moment of glory by not preparing her for it. It didn't matter at the moment that there wasn't any way he could have.

"You don't like James McCormac?" he asked.

She scowled again, her head back, her eyes on Eric. The shadows softened the contours of his face and all but hid his eyes. He still made her heart skip beats.

"Maybe you wouldn't find this in your frame of reference," she said, "but I've fantasized about James Mc-Cormac since I first went to the movies. He shows up tonight and I turn into mush."

Eric smiled down at her. "If you'd like, we'll invite him to the palace. He loves to use our stables when he's in the country. Cassandra has been known to ride with him."

Casey sat upright abruptly. "Are you crazy?"

"You keep asking me that."

"Cassandra is an exquisite rider, correct?"

He nodded, a smile playing at his lips.

"Well, pal, I can just about stay on. Brooklyn isn't exactly noted for its riding academies."

His smile grew. "You don't like to ride?"

"I've wanted a horse longer than I've wanted James McCormac."

Without their realizing it, they had pulled up to the front steps of the palace. Now the chauffeur bent to open the door for them.

"We'll finish the discussion inside," Eric said as he helped an exhausted Casey from the auto. The dress whispered against the cobblestones, and the faint lights caught in the jewels. Casey's throat gleamed a pearl white in the night air. It never occurred to her that she looked stunning. It occurred to Eric.

"Donna Reed," Eric said with a private little smile as he poured each of them a brandy a few minutes later.

Casey looked up from where she was trying to unwind her hair from the crown. It was getting too uncomfortable. "Pardon?"

He walked over and sat next to her on the soft leather couch. They had decided to sit in his study for a few minutes. "You said that you'd always dreamed of meeting James McCormac. I always dreamed of meeting Donna Reed." He handed her her glass and began to swirl the contents of his own, his eyes introspective. "I suppose as a boy I always wished she were my mother. She was always so..."

Casey waited for the rest, but after a moment Eric shook his head and took a drink.

"Loving," she finished for him.

He turned to her, surprised.

She smiled, wishing she could wipe the ghost of loneliness from his eyes with just a gentle hand. "My nana was raised in the imperial court. Your mother reminds me very much of her. A good mother, but one who doles out affection carefully. It must be difficult to understand as a child."

His voice, when he answered, was very quiet. "Were your parents the same?"

Casey shook her head. "No. My mother thinks that hugs should be world currency. And my father was famous for what we called attack kisses. He'd pick you up on the run, plant a kiss and be off."

"He is gone, too?"

She nodded, missing the big, gruff man. "About three years ago."

For a long moment, Casey considered the tawny liquid in her glass. Eric watched the shadows pass over her eyes and thought of the fresh air she'd swept into this stuffy place.

"Casey Phillips," he said softly, a hand beneath her chin. She lifted her face, her wide eyes mesmerizing in the half-light of the room, her lips soft. "Thank you for what you have given us. What you've given me. I'll never forget it."

Casey fought a surprising urge to cry. It was over, then. In the morning she'd give back the clothes, the bedroom and the laryngitis and go on to Switzerland to continue her trip. But she'd have to say goodbye to Eric. Suddenly the trip seemed empty.

"I won't, either, Eric. You've given me quite a day."

His eyes locked with hers, he offered a small, wry smile. "Even the kidney punch when you tried to shake McCormac's hand?"

She smiled back, her lips tremulous. "Even the goose-liver paté and caviar I had to choke down that I would have rather fertilized a garden with."

Without his realizing it, his face grew close to hers. She could feel his soft breath on her cheek. "I'm going to miss you, Casey. I wish you didn't have to go."

Casey found herself fighting the tears that welled in her eyes. "I do, too."

Once again, she was heard. As if it was preordained, both were startled to hear a knock on the door. Eric straightened to check his watch and shot Casey a puzzled look.

"Who could it be at this hour?"

She shrugged, hiding the tears with a nod toward the door. "One way to find out."

"Yes?" he called, setting his snifter down. Casey took the opportunity to drain hers, hoping it would ease the pain in her chest. It didn't.

Werner poked his head through the door. "I beg your pardon, Your Highness. We have some distressing news. The princess has been taken out of the country."

Eric came to his feet, his eyes on Casey. "That changes things, doesn't it?"

Werner's eyes followed. "I'm afraid it does, your Highness."

Casey found herself staring up at Eric with a mixture of dread and anticipation. They still needed her. She didn't have to leave yet, after all.

Four

Casey woke the next morning wondering where she was. It wasn't home, she thought, her eyes closed as she stretched beneath the deliciously warm linens. Not enough noise. At home there were sirens and traffic and airplanes on final approach. All she could hear here were...birds.

The trip. She was still in Europe. Was today Germany, Austria, Switzerland? After five countries in almost as many days, it was hard to keep track. She was covered in eiderdown, those lovely marshmallowlike comforters that enveloped a person more comfortably than a mother's hug.

Austria. They'd been in Austria. But weren't they supposed to head to Switzerland? She opened her eyes then and saw the pink. It was all she needed to remember.

She sat bolt upright to see that Maria had already been in. A set of clothes was laid out for her, including some beautiful peach silk underwear. Maria must have gone through the suitcase Sandy had brought last night and decided that absolutely nothing it contained was suitable. Casey felt uncomfortable at the idea of somebody else seeing her things. After all, not all of her underwear was in the condition that peach stuff was. And her favorite flannel nightgown had more than one worn spot. By now all the rest of the staff probably knew about it. Maybe even Eric.... She wondered whether Maria was supposed to report back to him.

Casey's thoughts wandered a bit as the notion conjured up pictures of Eric from the night before: circulating through the crowd in those impeccable clothes, protectively watching over Casey as they passed one crisis after another. Sharing his most private recollections with her in the still of the early-morning hours.

She had the unshakable feeling that this wasn't the kind of thing he did with just anyone. Why her, then? Was it because she reminded him so much of his niece? She wasn't so sure about that. He hadn't exactly professed an undying loyalty to the young princess.

Casey wanted to think it was because he was comfortable with her and valued her response. Did he start at her touch as much as she did at his? she wondered. Did he see her eyes as clearly as the sunlight when he thought about her?

Casey shook herself abruptly. This is not a Broadway musical, she admonished herself, throwing the covers aside. You don't get the prince in the third act simply because you're useful in the first. Grow up and get on with it.

She wondered where a person got fed around this place. Her stomach was telling her that it could use more than the goose-grown wallpaper paste she'd fed it the night before. Maybe Sandy would like to make a foray into the kitchen with her.

Casey swung out of the high old bed and padded across to the door. Sandy's room was across the hall. She'd been asleep when Casey'd finally gotten up to bed. Casey hoped she was ready to get up. She wasn't sure, since she didn't have a watch, but she thought it was still fairly early.

"Come in," Sandy answered to the quiet knock on the door. Casey walked in to find her friend dressed and sitting by the window.

Sandra looked up suspiciously. "Who won the '86 World Series?"

Casey snorted and closed the door. "Don't be silly. The Mets did. In the seventh game."

Sandy nodded. "Just wanted to make sure. Maria explained the whole situation to me last night, and I'm still confused."

Pulling up another chair next to Sandy, Casey sat down. "Think how I feel. I can't even wear my own clothes."

At this Sandy had to grin, gesturing toward the beautiful blue satin gown Casey wore. "Don't be ridiculous. With outfits like that, who'd want to wear their own clothes?"

Casey grinned back. "Did you get a load of that room I'm supposed to live in?"

"It *is* a little much."

Casey disagreed. "The *wallpaper* is a little much. The whole thing put together is a disaster. Where does she get her taste?"

Sandy's gaze strayed out the window. "She makes up for it in other areas, like her clothes. And her uncles."

Casey could hardly argue. "Yeah, he's real hard to look at, isn't he?" She didn't realize how suddenly wistful her voice sounded.

"I can tell you're having trouble with it. How was the party last night?"

"Come down to the kitchen with me and I'll tell you. I'll even tell you who I met."

Sandy turned to her again, cautious. "The kitchen? Are you supposed to go there?"

"I'm the Crown Princess Cassandra," Casey reminded her. "I can go anywhere I want."

Sandy nodded. "Good point. Let's go."

They'd gotten to the door when Casey thought to ask. "Do you have any idea where it is?"

Sandy grinned. "It's the one place in this maze I do know how to get to."

Casey did think to dress first, in a pair of gray wool slacks and a matching patterned sweater, but she didn't bother to do more than comb out her hair. She and Sandy sneaked down the back stairs, guided by the enticing smells of baking bread and the sounds of lively chatter.

When they appeared at the door, though, all noise ceased. The servants who worked in the great kitchen all came abruptly to attention and bowed, their eyes speculative enough that Casey had the feeling that they did, indeed, know by now that she was an imposter.

"You wish to inspect, Your Highness?" one senior-looking gentleman in white asked with hesitant deference. The rest of the staff looked as if they'd seen the ghost of Christmas past. It was obvious that the kitchens weren't a favorite haunt of the princess.

"No," Casey said, coming in. "I was starved and smelled the wonderful baking smells down here. I don't suppose you have any coffee and pastries or anything, do you?"

"But, Your Highness," the gentleman objected gently, his well-bred eyebrow arching with suppressed amusement at the broad accent. "It is only eight o'clock. You don't ever request your breakfast before ten. And you prefer it in your room."

"A change in habit can be good for the soul," she assured him blithely, feeling more at home here than among all the well-dressed people she'd mingled with the night before. "I won't tell anybody if you don't."

He bowed, still very unsure. "Very well, Your Highness."

Suddenly Casey started to sneeze. The staff looked as if they were about ready to drop to their knees to pray for her health. Holding up a hand, she tried to stop long enough to look around.

"Somebody's cleaning," she accused, sneezing again.

The culprit brought forth her bucket. "I was just going upstairs with my supplies, Your Highness. Is there a problem?"

Casey nodded, sniffling against the frustrating tickle in her nose. "Pine cleaner," she allowed. "I'm allergic to it. If you don't mind, don't clean my room with it for the next few days."

That seemed to appease everyone, and once the bucket of cleaner was gone, Casey's nose became reasonable enough that she was able to eat.

For the first few minutes, the staff was extremely uncomfortable having the two young women eating in their kitchens as they worked. It's probably like having someone you don't anticipate go through your underwear, Casey thought, taking a first bite from a cinnamon roll.

"Oh, my God," she breathed, her eyes lighting with the delicate taste. "Who made these?"

All activity stopped again. Casey looked up, motioning with the half-eaten roll. "Who made these?"

A great, broad woman stepped forward, her gray hair in a bun and her hands folded beneath her apron. Casey had a quick image of a nun on the playground at school. Except that this woman looked very nervous indeed.

"I baked them, Your Highness," she admitted in a soft voice, dropping a quick curtsy. "Is something wrong?"

"You bet there's something wrong." Casey grinned. "I'm going to end up gaining ten pounds by the end of breakfast, if I have my way. These are wonderful!"

The woman's face crumbled into a relieved little smile. She didn't seem terribly used to praise.

"I bet you make great blintzes," Casey went on, finishing off the cinnamon roll with dispatch and reaching for another. "My nana used to love blintzes."

"You would like me to make some?"

Casey's eyes rolled heavenward at the thought. "I haven't had good blintzes in ages. Do you make soda bread, too?"

The confused look on the woman's face was a giveaway.

"No, I guess not. That's Irish. I'll have to show you how. Great for breakfast, you know."

Within five minutes, Helga had the recipe for soda bread and Casey had finished off two more rolls. Sandy was still waiting to hear about the party.

"Your Highness, there you are."

Casey looked up to see Maria approaching in what for Maria was a dead run. The little woman scuttled past the rows of dangling copper pots and gleaming ovens to where Casey and Sandra sat.

"I was hungry—" Casey began.

Maria waved her explanations aside. "The prince is looking everywhere for you. There is a problem he needs to discuss with you immediately."

Casey looked around. "He couldn't come here for me himself?"

At this, Maria looked honestly perplexed. "A prince does not search through the servants' quarters, Your Highness."

"Oh," she answered with an arched eyebrow. "Excuse me. Can I at least finish my breakfast?"

"It is most urgent, ma'am."

With a resigned shrug, Casey got to her feet to follow. But as she passed the table where Helga pounded on bread dough, she leaned over.

"It's kind of, well, stuffy up there," she admitted under her breath to the surprise of the pastry chef. "Would you mind if I came back later for another roll or two?"

Helga didn't say a word. She merely patted the stool next to her station and smiled. Casey smiled back and followed Maria out.

Eric was once again pacing in his office when Casey and Sandra appeared. Casey noticed that he was in a navy pin-striped suit today, the banker off to business. Only this banker stopped her in her tracks. She wished he'd give her a minute to just feast on his eyes. They were so bright in the morning light. Crisp as autumn.

"Ever been to the kitchens?" she asked instead, the emotions he provoked scaring her. "Pretty nice down there."

He gave her a wry smile. "So that's where she found you. I was wondering."

"Did you think I'd sneak away in the night?"

"It's been known to happen."

"Not by me," she replied, grinning raffishly. "All that pink put me in a coma."

His answering smile was dampened. "Casey, there is a new problem."

"I did sleep well, thanks," she answered, wondering why she felt so compelled to antagonize him. He'd been nothing but kind to her. "And you?"

His eyes briefly touched hers, and she had the nagging feeling that there was something he wished he could say. But the moment passed, and his attention shifted.

"Fairly well. I was awakened this morning with the news that the dissidents have already made their statement that they have Cassandra."

Casey shrugged, seeing his strain now in a set of lines at the corners of his mouth, a tightening of his jaw. He had a habit of shoving his hands in his pockets as he walked. She wondered if it was to assume an air of indifference he didn't feel.

"You knew it was bound to happen," she offered more gently, wanting to reach out to him.

Eric nodded, his gaze returning to her. She felt that blue light like a shaft of sunlight on her face. "They produced pictures. Very convincing ones. And today is the first day of the economic conference."

It didn't take Casey long to follow his train of thought. "So what does a princess wear to the opening ceremonies of an economic conference?"

That brought him to a halt. "I'd wanted to have more time to brief you," he said. "To get you better acquainted with royal protocol before you had to interact on your own."

"On my own?" Casey's stomach dropped. "Aren't you going to be there?"

Eric shook his head. "Not like I was last night. I can't be by your side every minute this afternoon. And there is the press to contend with."

"Can I at least still have laryngitis?"

His smile was heartfelt. "The royal physician has been on the wire services already with the full story."

Casey nodded, trying to think fast. "Just how long do you think this whole thing is going to go on?"

Eric shrugged, coming up to her. "Not long, surely. The general assures me that it shouldn't be long before Cassandra's found. He, of course, cannot enlist aid from any outside sources, but he says that the kidnappers left a rather easy trail."

"Does this guy know what he's doing?" she asked.

"Under normal circumstances. My brother appointed him as a favor, but we've never had much quarrel."

"You've never had a princess kidnapped, either," she reminded him.

Eric didn't have much of an answer.

The opening left Casey even more drained than the benefit had. She felt like an understudy who had to fill a lead without benefit of rehearsal. Come to think of it, she didn't even know all the lines. At least her only job at the function was to nod and wave. She did do that well, facing the swarming press with the proper modicum of imperious disdain and greeting the gathered delegates with elaborate body language. But once she'd cut the proverbial ribbon, she sat back in silence to listen to what the princess was supposed to know about once she took power as the queen. The fact that she fell asleep during one of the long introductory speeches on interest rates and loans to third-world nations was excused by the fact that she was on medication for her indisposition. Finally, Eric collected her for the ride home.

"There's got to be a better way to make a living," she groaned as the chauffeur started the car.

Eric laughed. "You're a natural, you know?"

"No," she disagreed. "I'm a wreck. And Cassandra's shoes are too small."

He took hold of her hand with unconscious ease. "I don't know what I would have done without you, Casey."

She looked at him beneath the netting of the black-and-red hat she wore. "You would have dressed Maria up in black and a veil and said she was in mourning."

Eric smiled down at where Casey's head rested once more against the seat. Then, lifting her hand to his lips, he kissed it. "Anyone can impersonate a queen," he assured her, his eyes oddly intense in the shadows. "It takes a special woman to make a confirmed bachelor realize his loneliness."

For a very long time, Casey couldn't think of anything to say. She was trapped within the sudden exhilaration, the heart-pounding fear Eric's words had given her. She couldn't drag her eyes away, couldn't seem to smile or frown or speak. She was too afraid that he'd take back what he said and that she'd be left with half-realized longings.

"Eric," she finally managed, lifting her head and pulling her gaze from him, "do we have to go back right away?"

"What do you mean?"

She gave a little shrug, her heart still crowding her throat, eyes resolutely on the red linen of her suit. "The palace. Maybe you're used to it, but all those servants popping up when you don't expect them makes me a little claustrophobic."

Eric looked out at the late afternoon scenery, at the fiery sun crowding the mountaintops with fire, and smiled to himself. "Where would you rather go?"

"What about some cozy little coffeehouse?"

"Without advance notice?" He smiled ruefully. "Unthinkable. It would cause an unforgivable furor."

"I guess that means McDonald's is out of the question."

"No," he decided suddenly, reaching for the car phone. "I know just the spot."

They made one stop, where the chauffeur picked up a wicker basket from a corner store and townspeople watched respectfully from a distance, their smiles possessive and shy. Then the car turned onto a back road that wound its way into the countryside, neatly slipping in among the towering mountain peaks.

Casey slipped off her hat and held it in her hands, watching quietly as the farms and woodlands passed by them. Eric found no need to initiate conversation, and the silence deepened between them, a richly comfortable fabric that united them within the cocoon of the limousine.

Casey thought of passing time, of how by the same time next week she would be back at her desk at Wade, Simpson and Associates, the memories of these days solely hers. Due to the Russian and Irish blood in her she carried a fair dose of fatalism, and it manifested itself in her grieving for past beauty while still savoring it.

Time was fleeting, and her moment of beauty would be gone all too soon. Eric would return to his reality and she to hers, and they would never see fit to meet again. Unless, of course, Cassandra was kidnapped again. But Casey had the feeling that once Eric got his errant niece back he wasn't likely to let that happen again.

Eric thought of the delicious opportunities in chance. No more than three days ago he had been settled in a lifestyle designed from birth, orchestrated by only a limited amount of choice. As the second son, he was not born to rule. He had become the banker because banking was the military service of Moritania. It held the country's fortune and defended it against encroachment.

He had become an excellent banker because it was in his blood to lead. But he had remained a bachelor because, until he'd chanced upon the sandy-haired American with the free spirit, he had never met anyone he could say excited him. His circle of acquaintances was determined by bloodline and financial success, not necessarily personal dynamism. He'd never really had the opportunity to meet anyone who could manage to thumb her nose at everyone and everything as it was needed.

Casey was like a new light in his life, a means by which he could view his world from a different perspective. Hers were eyes unspoiled by advantage or prospective gain, and more and more he found himself wanting to share their view. He wanted to be able to continue basking in the freshness that had so long been missing from his world. A freshness that translated into a potent sensuality she didn't even realize she had.

The limo slowed a bit at another guarded gate and then swept on past, down a broad meadow that was lined with old oak trees. There were no farmhouses here. It was, however, well groomed, the broad lawns close-cropped and the trees trimmed as they swept toward the enclosing mountains.

"Is this where you were murdering helpless birds yesterday?" Casey asked, awed by the pastoral beauty around her.

Eric smiled over at her. "As a matter of fact, yes."

"And to think," she said with a little smile, "my relatives probably used to poach here."

The sound of his chuckle warmed her to a new smile. "If they were any kind of self-respecting Moritanians, they did," he assured her. "There's a spot a little farther on that's a favorite refuge of mine. We can enjoy our booty there."

Casey's idea of a refuge was a library room where everybody had to be quiet at once. Eric's was an immense expanse of garden, the product of centuries of development and care. Shrubbery bordered the area in precise geometrics, and a thousand well-mannered flowers spread a riot of color and scent over the center, right up to the exactly trimmed gravel walks and lily-laden ponds. From where they stepped from the car, Casey couldn't see the end of the gardens. They seemed to stretch on forever, a haven of solitude and birdsong where the world was kept at bay and reality in abeyance.

Unable to even wait for Eric, she wandered down the paths, drinking deeply of the mingled fragrances of roses and hollyhocks and dahlias—flowers she'd seen only in parks, in pictures in a book. She and her mother had grown some pretty scrawny chrysanthemums and tomatoes on the roof of their apartment building, all the while dreaming of lush gardens just like these. To have been dropped right in the center of all this, and not to have to share them with anyone else was as much of a dream as dressing up as a princess.

Casey didn't get any farther than the first arbor. Kicking off the black-and-red pumps that were beginning to cramp her feet, she sat herself down on the polished wooden bench beneath the clematis. The summer surrounded her and soothed her agitation.

"You found it." Eric smiled down at her.

Casey looked up with amazement in her eyes to see the deep gold of the late sun glint from his hair and warm the planes of his cheeks. He stood before her, basket in hand, looking like a schoolboy on a picnic.

"How did you manage to tap into my daydreams?" she demanded with delight. "This is the exact spot where I imagined I married James McCormac when I was twelve."

He laughed, the hearty music ringing out over the nodding flowers, and set the basket down. "This is the arbor I always escape to when the pressures get to me."

Taking a seat next to her, he spent a moment reacquainting himself with the place. Casey looked over to see the magic take hold in him and ease the lines around his mouth. His smile broadened dreamily as he surveyed what was his.

She didn't wait for him to come back from his reverie. Suddenly it seemed important that nothing interrupt his peace of mind. He had so little of it, she was sure. Even less with the kidnapping and the schooling of a barbarian in the ways of the royal family. Reaching into the basket, she drew out a bottle of chilled white wine and some cheese and set it between them. Then she reached in again for a couple of tins that completed the cache.

"Caviar?" she asked with a wrinkled nose. "I guess that's for you."

Eric looked over, the light in his eyes oddly intense for the peace he'd gained in the garden. "For you, actually," he said, a sly humor edging into his eyes. "You eat it every day."

Casey shook her head. "Not me, bucko. The only eggs I eat come from chickens, and I'm not overly fond of those. Ever since my first biology class in reproduction, I haven't been able to go near a fish egg. Not that I've ever had the opportunity until last night...."

He reached over to take the tin from her hand. "A class Cassandra should have attended, I suppose. She eats the damn things like jelly beans. Morning, noon and night. Beluga caviar, specially imported by one of our little gourmet shops just for her."

Casey held the offending food out to him like a dead mouse. "Then may she eat it in good health. I'm perfectly happy with the more mundane food groups."

With a corresponding smile, Eric made it a point to drop the tin back in the basket.

"How long of a break do we have?" Casey asked as Eric brought out the corkscrew—gold, she noted—and went after the wine.

"Break?" he countered with a sidelong look. "This isn't a break. I'm teaching you about protocol."

"I know all about protocol." She sneered, holding out the glasses for pouring. "You're the last one to show up, the first one to leave, and nothing gets done until everybody bows to you. Oh, yes, and you look down your nose like this—" she demonstrated with just a slight exaggeration "—at anyone asking a personal question."

Eric found himself laughing again. She was so right, and he'd never even thought about it before. The cork escaped with a definite popping sound, and he began to pour, his one hand around Casey's to hold the glass still.

"It's easy to see that there's imperial blood in you," he admitted, leaning closer than was necessary. Casey could feel his breath sweep her cheek. The warmth of his hand seemed to infuse her more thoroughly than the dying sun. "It's a good thing there isn't too much, though. You might begin taking yourself seriously like the rest of us."

Casey looked up at him in disbelief. "You don't really take all of it seriously, do you?" she asked.

Once again, when his eyes lifted to hers, she felt snared. Trapped in the reflection of the sunset in his eyes, eyes that were like pools of water on the edge of the sky. Her heart quickened and her chest tightened. The hand he held in his began to tremble without her even realizing it.

"Not so much since you've been here," he answered in a very soft voice. Once again they seemed to trap an electricity between them, and the air shimmered with anticipation. "Except for one thing."

She couldn't take her eyes away. Couldn't take her hand away, even though it was suddenly on fire like the rest of her. "What?"

The smile that edged into his eyes held surprise as much as pleasure. Eric set the bottle down and took the glass from Casey's numb fingers. Then, taking her face in his gentle hands, he bent to kiss her.

"I'm very serious," he finally said, lifting his head to consider her, "about you."

Five

Casey sat bolt upright, then fled the bench.

"Oh, no, you don't!" she objected with a voice that was just a bit too shrill. "No, you don't." She couldn't seem to stand still, striding over to the flowers and then back again, terror propelling her. Eric's kiss had set off the most delicious shower of sparks in her, chills that surprised her like a bright starburst against a night sky.

"No I don't what?" Eric asked with passive amusement.

She turned on him, leveling an accusing finger. "I've only known you a day. This kind of thing just doesn't happen in a day. I can't... You can't..." She turned away again, the promise in those laughing blue eyes steeling her outrage. What outrage, she demanded of herself? What she felt was stark fear of possibility. The too-good-to-be-true syndrome. Every nerve ending in her body was screaming at her to sit right back down on that bench. She wanted more.

Behind her, Eric didn't even stir. "In the last twenty-four hours," he said without agitation, "I've been more alive than I have in the last thirty-five years. What do *you* think I should do about it?"

She turned, her eyes wide, her breathing shallow. "I'm going home next week, Eric. Back to Brooklyn, remember? I'm the one who doesn't know what to call a duchess or what wine goes with chicken. I can't tell you who painted one of the pictures on your walls, or which king named your chairs. Hardly the person your mother the *queen* would choose to be seen consorting with her son. Besides, isn't somebody going to say something about a man having an affair with his niece?"

Eric's smile broadened. Casey's eyes widened in true outrage, this time at herself for voicing the thoughts that had been hovering just beyond consideration since she'd first set eyes on him.

"Oh, my God!" she wailed, setting off another march. "You've got me talking affairs now. Listen to me. Lord, my mother would slap me for even talking like that! Nobody in her family even mentions that word out loud."

"The Romanovs were always having affairs."

"Not in my house, they weren't!"

Eric finally got to his feet, the filled wineglass in hand, and approached her. Catching her in midflight by the wrist, he inexorably turned her to him. "Here," he offered, that wry humor still crinkling the corners of his eyes. "Have a sip of this. It might put things into better perspective."

"Better than what?" she demanded, even though she accepted the glass. Her eyes still challenging his, she took a sip and then another. The wine was smooth, refreshing and cool. Before she knew it, she'd finished the glass. Eric didn't say a word. He simply retrieved the bottle and the other glass and went about providing refills.

"How about a slice or two of cheese?"

Casey eyed him suspiciously. "Are you always this cool?"

His smile broadened over the rim of his glass. "Always. It's the mark of a good prince."

"I guess that's admirable," she admitted grudgingly. "Must not help your stress level much, though."

Eric laughed, drawing her back to the bench. "Stress is an American invention."

Casey suddenly found herself again seated next to Eric, his proximity doubling the wine-induced heat. She felt too much at ease with him, too seductively comfortable. Before she knew it, she was going to be expecting him to be there all the time.

"Oh, you're right," she scoffed. "Heads of small European countries have no stress. They say change of job is a big stress producer. I can't imagine what change of head of state produces."

He shrugged, slicing up the cheese. "Countries go on. Moritania certainly does." Then, turning, he held out a slice to Casey. "Fragonard."

Casey's head came up. "What?"

Eric's smile was intimate, gentle. "The man who painted most of the pictures in the front hallway. Fragonard. Somebody had a real weakness for him. And Queen Anne."

"She painted, too?"

He unceremoniously stuffed the wedge of cheese in her mouth. "No. She made furniture."

Casey found herself smiling now, too.

"Do you find me so disagreeable?" he asked, almost offhandedly.

Casey met his eyes without flinching this time. The truth was, finally, the truth. It was what could be done about it that was the problem. Taking the time to retrieve her cheese and take a delicate bite, she briefly studied the brickwork beneath her feet. "Just about as disagreeable as Cassandra finds caviar."

Pursing his lips with quiet satisfaction, Eric nodded, his eyes on his wineglass. He swirled it a little so that the wine rocked back and forth, distant sunlight sinking into the clear liquid and shimmering. Then he looked at Casey, and, in his eyes, she saw the fires that Eric seemed to always keep banked. They flared now, warm and sweet, a bottomless blue that held his secrets, contained his passions and remained very much his own. Casey knew without having to ask that this side of Eric was not one many people saw. She wondered, in fact, if any did.

"You've given me laughter, Casey," he said. "That's a precious gift. You keep surprising me. And I find when I lay in bed that I ache for the feel of you next to me."

"Eric, please don't...."

He held up a hand. "I want you to know that I've never said this to anyone before." A self-deprecating grin lit his features. "I don't make it a practice to lure susceptible young females to my bed." For a moment, his eyes drifted back to his glass. "To be perfectly honest, I had no idea I was going to tell you this. I didn't even have a clue I was going to kiss you."

When he turned his eyes back to her, Casey felt the sharp tug in her chest at the vulnerability there, the memories of loneliness and separation. Even though she was of the working class, in many ways Casey had it better than Eric.

As the moments passed, her resolve began to waver. The shadows had crept up to claim their corner of the garden, and the dusk breeze was growing chilly. Casey didn't feel the drop in temperature. She only felt the intensity of Eric's silence and her own inability to provide an answer.

Finally she sighed. "I'll tell you what. Could we maybe have this conversation again when Cassandra has her little fanny on that throne? Until then, I'm afraid that we could cause more problems than we'd solve by testing these, uh, waters." She faced Eric with silent entreaty and found that he understood.

"You have the control to be a princess," he admitted wryly. "Perhaps more control than I do. We'll work together."

Casey couldn't help a sharp little laugh. "That's what got us into trouble in the first place."

Even so, when they had gathered their things to leave, Eric stopped a moment and took Casey in his arms. She didn't stop him. The sure feel of his arms around her, the tensile strength of his long body against hers, stilled her. The searching heat of his lips compelled her. She brought her own hands up, holding him to her, and savored the delicious fire his kiss ignited in her.

A small breeze lifted Casey's hair. The evening birds were beginning to chatter in the trees, and somewhere Casey heard the bells on the grazing cattle. But when Eric finally pulled back, she saw and heard only him.

"We'd better get back," he said quietly, his finger straying over the outline of her lower lip, his eyes devouring hers in the dim light. "We have some time to do more instruction before the dinner tonight."

Consciously willing the fire to bank once again in her, Casey turned down the path with him to where they'd left the limo. They walked hand in hand, with Eric swinging the basket in time with their gait.

"Eric," Casey said a moment later.

"Mmmm."

"The limo's gone."

He nodded without noticeable agitation. "You didn't really expect him to have to wait for us, did you?"

She turned on him. "Well, if we have another appointment, how do you expect to get back to the palace in time?"

His grin was complacent and sly. "We walk. Don't you walk in America?"

"Only when the objective is in sight. You're less likely to get mugged."

"I don't think we have to worry about being mugged here," he assured her, turning into the lane where the late, lamented limo had sat. "Poached, perhaps. But not mugged."

"All right," she conceded. "I give up. Just how far away is the palace?"

Now he smiled, his even white teeth gleaming against his tanned skin. "You'll see."

She saw. They topped the rise to find that they were in the palace's backyard. Backyard being a relative term, of course. They still had a good quarter mile to walk, through a maze of hedges, fountains and reflecting pools and more flower beds, all illuminated with the most cunningly recessed lighting to make it look like a fairyland, mysterious and beautiful in the purpling dusk. The roses smelled stronger here, too. There must have been an immense garden nearby.

"Who does your yardwork?" Casey asked, coming to an amazed halt at the sight of the huge mansion rising from the far side of the terraces, patios and gardens. It was something out of a history book.

"A team of about thirty."

"Thirty." She turned on him with wry eyes. "My mother would die if she saw this."

"Maybe someday she can," he offered.

Casey shook her head. "She hasn't been out of Brooklyn her entire life. That's why Sandy came with me on the trip. I couldn't talk her into it. Besides, this is the last time for a while I'm going to be able to afford to do this."

She didn't notice the quick glance he dispatched as they walked on.

"Tonight is the dinner for the economic ministers," Eric said instead. "Pretty boring stuff."

"As boring as today?"

He laughed and squeezed her hand. "Hardly. Besides, if you nod off tonight, I'll be alongside to give you a nudge."

"I'm developing a bruise from the last nudge you gave me. Why don't you delegate somebody with less enthusiasm for the job?"

"Oh, I can't," he said. "That would absolutely shatter royal protocol."

"I'm absolutely shattering royal protocol by just being here," she reminded him. "Isn't there some kind of law about impersonating a princess?"

He chuckled. "It's been done all throughout history. Churchill even had it done during the war."

"And here Mark Twain thought he had an original idea. So why can't Werner do the nudging?"

"Because it is not allowed for anyone to touch a member of the royal family except under prescribed conditions."

She stopped, really amazed now. "Not touch them? For heaven's sake, why?"

With another wry smile, Eric shrugged. "Royalty is royalty because we're set apart. There are even rules about when we can be spoken to."

Now she had a disgusted scowl for him. "Like, 'Um, excuse me, Your Royal Highness, I beg the privilege to say Fire!'?"

His laughter was delighted. "Something like that."

"I was wondering why there was a circle of space around me. I just thought it was because of all the people Cassandra had put off."

They were walking again, their steps matching easily, the evening sky before them deepening to a peacock blue that cradled a lone star and a rising moon. Casey clutched at the moment with frantic yearning, wishing she could make it last forever. She had never known such peace, such exhilaration.

"It's a tradition that's centuries old," Eric explained. "From the time when rulers were omnipotent and often thought deified. They also had quite a few people to keep in place to protect their thrones. This was a way of keeping them at arm's length, I guess."

Hearing that hint of melancholy return to Eric's voice, Casey looked over. His eyes were on the great house where he was born and had lived his whole life.

"Not as much of a problem these days, I'd think," she observed.

"No," he answered quietly. "Not much. We don't even have much of the aristocracy left to entertain us. Just the customs."

"Do you have many friends?" she asked.

He nodded, surprised a little by the question. "A few. Back in England. I went to Eton for my schooling. And there are my teammates in polo and rugger."

She found herself squeezing his hand more tightly, offering her own friendship with the simple gesture. "That's not the way I'd run *my* country," she assured him with a definite nod of the head. "It's too isolated."

"After seeing New York," he retorted easily, "I'd have thought you'd like a little more isolation."

"Moderation in everything," she intoned piously.

With a chuckle, Eric slipped a companionable arm around her shoulder.

They had reached the first terrace before he spoke again. "How about a little accent coaching?"

Casey shot him a sharp look. "Why?" The tone of her voice was suspicious.

He shrugged with just a bit too much nonchalance. "You can't have laryngitis forever."

"I don't plan for my throat to clear up until I cross back over that border," she assured him.

"Just try it," he insisted. "For fun. 'The rain in Spain comes mainly on the plain.'"

She snorted, a bit unkindly. "Shouldn't I be learning how to say that in German?"

"Not necessary. One of Cassandra's pet projects is to see that English is Moritania's primary language. She'd already convinced her father to make it the new official language."

"How convenient. It wouldn't do any good, though. I'm sure Cassandra has definite speech patterns. I'd have to listen to those to even get an idea."

Her words were like a signal she didn't comprehend. Stopping in midstride, Eric grinned like a schoolboy and pulled her close for an enthusiastic hug.

"You're brilliant!" he announced with a delighted smile. "The tapes will be in your room within the hour."

"What tapes?" she demanded, feeling decidedly unsettled.

The tapes of any number of Cassandra's official functions, it turned out. On videocassette, on cassette tape, on compact disc. The woman had an obsession with her public image, and Casey, Sandra and Maria were forced to watch her repeatedly as they readied for the dinner.

"Haven't I seen this somewhere before?" Casey demanded as she scowled at the smiling, distant figure on the film.

"Yeah," Sandra agreed. "On Broadway. I think she played *Evita*. I'm surprised people have actually been fooled by you. You're not nearly enough of a witch."

Maria went on pressing and straightening without any change of expression.

"My dear people," Casey intoned, mimicking the accent and posturing for all she was worth. "It is our great pleasure to bestow on our uncle His Royal Highness Prince Eric the Order of Eternal Patience for putting up with our unspeakably juvenile behavior."

Sandra laughed. Maria almost choked.

"The chin a bit higher, Your Highness," she said with a carefully straight face. It was the merry sparkle in her eyes that gave her away.

Casey lifted her chin a little, looking far down her nose, much as she had for Eric. "Like this?"

Maria looked. "Like that, *ja*. Now you are like her. Was Your Highness an actress in this Brooklyn?"

This time Sandra almost choked. "No, Maria. She was just a troublemaker."

"I'm part Romanov," Casey said defensively. "Condescension is in my blood."

"You're not going to do something stupid, are you?" Sandy asked a moment later, after Maria had stepped out of the room.

Casey looked over from where she was still struggling with her dress. Maybe Cassandra was made for strapless. She most definitely was not.

"Something stupid like what?" she asked.

Sandy took a moment to answer. "This is all pretty heady stuff, pretending you're a princess. Nobody back on the block is going to believe it, that's for darn sure. And the prince is awfully handsome."

"Awfully," Casey agreed in a strangely subdued voice.

"And you have a knack for fantasy, you know?"

Casey's answering smile was a sad one. "Just because I was twenty-one before I finally admitted that James McCormac wouldn't marry me?"

Sandy's pale gray eyes were eloquent in their concern. "I just don't want you to be hurt. It doesn't take you long to fall."

Casey couldn't think of anything to do but study the way her hands rested in her lap. "You're right there," she said very quietly. "Took me all of one day this time."

She heard Sandy sigh. "I knew it. Casey, he's—"

Casey didn't even look up. "He kissed me today."

That stopped Sandy. "Please tell me you hated it. He has buckteeth and bad breath."

Casey just dispatched a dry scowl.

Sandy sighed again. "And?"

"I fall fast," Casey allowed. "But I've never thrown myself at somebody's feet." Then she had to grin. "With the possible exception of James McCormac, of course. I came real close last night."

"Casey," her friend pleaded, "be serious."

"What do you want me to do?" Casey demanded. "Walk away? Throw my drink in Eric's face when he tells me he cares for me?"

Sandy's eyes grew large. "He said that?"

Casey's eyes were on her hands again. Maria had applied fake nails, so that more and more of her was disappearing under Cassandra's facade. The whole situation was getting more and more alien, and it was becoming increasingly difficult to keep an even keel. "He said that he's been more alive since he's known me than in the last thirty-five years." Her voice dropped almost to a whisper. "And that he, uh, wanted me."

That brought Sandy to her feet. "Oh, my God...."

"Cool your jets," Casey retorted dryly. "Neither of us is going to do anything about it." She sighed with a shake of her head. "I can't even believe I'm talking like this. I feel like I'm becoming somebody else."

Sandy came over to her friend and crouched down beside where she sat, both of them in expensive silk gowns and coiffed hair that made them look as if they belonged here more than in their native streets in New York. When Sandy took hold of Casey's hand, Casey looked up at her, sudden tears glittering in her hazel eyes.

"Just be careful, honey," Sandy said. "You're the one who has to go home, not him."

And Casey nodded, the new pain exquisite in her chest. "I know," she said. "I know."

The soft rap on the door brought them both to their feet, Casey dabbing at her moist eyes with a tissue.

"Come in," she called.

The door opened to reveal Eric, in a dinner jacket this time. Cool, handsome, suave. Casey couldn't seem to speak for a minute.

He intuitively understood and entered, a bright smile of greeting on his face, his hands outstretched to the two women.

"Ladies," he said, "you look marvelous. It will be a pleasure to escort you this evening."

"You're just saying that because it's true." Sandy giggled, slipping a hand in the crook of his arm. Then, turning to Casey, she made a face. "Brooklyn was never like this."

"Well, you know what Dorothy said to Toto," Casey said, mimicking Sandy's move on Eric's other side. "We're not in Kansas anymore."

"Cassandra also never quotes movies," Eric warned her with a mischievous grin. "She finds them a waste of time."

"Does she read?"

He shrugged. "The odd cereal box, I'm sure."

Casey groaned. "Marvelous. That just about leaves the state of the hemline and horse etiquette."

"Do you know anything much about horses?" he asked, easing comfortably into his new role as Casey's straight man.

"Yeah." She smiled sweetly. "Where to sit."

He nodded placidly. "Should make for an evening of stimulating conversation."

"I'm still not recovered," she objected as they headed on down the great echoing hallway that bordered the royal apartments.

"Not according to Maria." He smiled slyly. "She said you sounded quite...inspired."

Casey smiled right back. "You try and get a peep out of me, and I swear I'll moon every one of the ministers at that dinner. And *that*," she assured him, "will make for a stimulating evening of conversation."

* * *

Eric watched Casey glide into the great banquet hall
and thought how she was beginning to grow into her assumed role. Heads turned as she passed, smiling and listening as if she were hanging on every word said to her,
and whispers followed her. He knew he should have
warned her to close off a little, slip a bit of ice into her
demeanor, but it was such a joy to watch what the monarchy could be like that he forestalled it.

"She is so lovely tonight, Your Highness," the Baroness von Richter confided as the two observed Casey
courting two of the more taciturn ministers on the other
side of the room.

Casey's eyes sparkled as she listened to the one gentleman describing his homeland. She urged him on with a
nod of the head, and a hand to the arm, and suddenly the
old man, who hadn't spoken more than a few words to
Eric in the ten years he'd known him, was opening up like
a schoolboy. Standing next to the plump baroness, Eric
found himself shaking his head with something akin to
wonder.

"It must be the drugs she's on, my dear Eleanor." He
smiled gently. "I've never known Cassandra to be so
generous."

The baroness allowed herself a small chuckle. "I would
never suggest that the princess should succumb to laryngitis more often...."

He smiled right back, embellishing the lie without effort. "Exactly."

It didn't really occur to Casey that she was having an
easier time of it tonight. She knew that the champagne she
drank before dinner had the most enticing fizzle to it, and
that when she caught sight of herself in the far mirrors she

couldn't quite believe that it was she in rose silk and diamonds.

And most of all she felt the unspoken support of Eric, no matter where he stood in the room. She knew that if she came within a foot of making an indiscretion, he would be at her side to bail her out. Whenever she turned to see where he was, his eyes were on her, that crystal blue compelling her as if there weren't another soul in the room.

"Your Highness." One of the strolling waiters approached bowing, his silver tray held rigidly in place. "Hors d'oeuvres."

"Oh..." she began to mouth, seeing the little piles of glistening black on each little cracker. The sight of it made her stomach turn. Then Eric caught her eye with a silent admonition. The charade could only be stretched so far, she thought.

She managed a sick little smile and reached for a cracker. Everyone around her immediately followed suit. Casey smiled again at them, trying to put off the inevitable as long as possible. She couldn't. They were waiting politely for her.

Closing her eyes, she popped it in and swallowed.

"My dear Princess." A voice spoke up at her elbow with all the upper-crust nasal condescension it could muster.

With a startled little gulp, Casey turned to answer. She found a small woman smiling, an hors d'oeuvre in hand, little color or intelligence in her eyes. She reminded Casey of that kind of pinched-nosed dog her mother said always bit.

Casey smiled, quelling a sudden stab of fear. Was she supposed to know this woman? Would she call up memories to share that Casey wouldn't recognize? Take a deep breath and nod, she told herself, just like all the other times, and hope that those vile little eggs stayed where they were.

She smiled with a bit more enthusiasm and nodded.

The woman hardly needed encouragement. "I must say that I cannot understand what your fascination is with the English language," she said. With a clipped and precise accent, she had all the hallmarks of a European native. Was she one of the aristocracy who survived into the modern era? Casey wondered.

Waving off her own remark with a gloved hand, the woman dove on. "Not precisely English anymore, anyway, is it? Of course, my Hans said that it was all because you were courting the Americans. I cannot ever imagine why. They're barbarians, hardly worth considering. Just because they have hamburgers and blue jeans, everyone thinks they are worth nothing short of devotion. It's an abomination, if you ask me, to usurp the majesty of German. Even the beauty of Italian for...for that..."

Casey forgot the caviar. All she could think of was how close she was to apoplexy. What a smarmy, self-righteous, condescending witch! There were so many things she wanted to tell her, so many threats and curses she'd like to hurl on her head for her archaic, self-serving attitude. A barbarian, was she?

But when she opened her mouth to offer a rebuttal, Casey saw the faces turned expectantly toward her. The waiter still hovered, certain she would want more caviar. Casey looked back at the smug and nasty little woman and tried again.

Nothing came. She choked, terrified of making a fool of herself in front of these people. What if they found out not only that she was not the princess but that she talked like the very people this woman was so spiteful toward? The fact that she was so terrified of someone this stupid only made her angrier.

"Of course," the woman went on, ignoring the definitely scarlet tint to Casey's cheeks, "I can understand that one must conduct world business, but really. I cannot think of any one custom, or person for that matter, that the U.S. has to offer that could possibly be . . . well, worthwhile. . . ."

"Cassandra, dear, I need to speak to you for a moment."

Feeling the gentle hand on her arm, Casey whipped around. She was sure Eric saw the wild rage in her eyes. He just smiled as if nothing had happened and turned to her assailant.

"If you'll excuse us, Countess."

The countess blushed, stammered and curtsied. Eric seemed to have a foolproof way of shutting up foolish old women.

"She's not worth it," he whispered under his breath as he led a scarlet Casey out to the renewed bows of their guests. "Just an old busybody."

Casey still couldn't manage a response, angrier at herself than at the busybody.

"Cassandra?" he asked solicitously as they neared the door. "Are you all right?"

She glared straight ahead, her color now closer to purple. They had almost made it to the door and safety.

"Say something."

Casey stopped just shy of the door, then turned to find Eric and the rest of the guests awaiting her answer. When she finally found her tongue, the results echoed from the rafters.

"Off with her head!"

Six

___

"How can you possibly be so in control?" Casey demanded of Eric.

"Years of study," he said, smiling gently.

The two of them walked the gardens at the back of the palace. It was late, the dinner having been over for a few hours, and Sandy was already in bed preparing for the hangover of the year.

"I almost decked that old lady," Casey admitted with a rueful shake of her head. "In fact, if she were here now, I'd probably still deck her."

"It wouldn't change her mind."

"It would support her claims." Casey lashed out at the soft night air, some of the anger still lingering. "Barbarians, indeed. Americans didn't invent the Inquisition or start World War II."

He couldn't help but grin. "But they did invent plastic lawn flamingos and Fred Flintstone."

"Bad taste doesn't make you a barbarian," she informed him archly. "If that were true, most of the European aristocracy would be guilty. I should have decked her."

"You should have done just what you did."

Casey had to grin. "What, a bad imitation of the Queen of Hearts? Is that what Cassandra would have done?"

"It's exactly what Cassandra would have done, and worse. You conducted yourself admirably tonight," he said, bringing her to a halt by one of the reflecting pools. Only the half-moon found its way into the water tonight. The unseen flowers permeated the soft night air with a thousand seductive fragrances.

The crown jewels still glittered at Casey's throat, and her hair was swept up in a soft mass off her neck. She looked the essence of sleek style. But her eyes, those deep pools that could entice a man to his death, still reflected the thrill and terror of what she'd just done more clearly than the water reflected the moon. It was that intensity, that clarity, that attracted Eric more than the classic beauty they'd transformed her into ever could.

He found his hands on her bare arms, his thumbs sliding up and down over the smooth skin.

"Tell me something," she said more quietly, her now-serious eyes looking into his.

His voice was barely more than a whisper. "Anything."

Casey found herself wanting to penetrate that cool demeanor, the tailored exterior of Eric von Lieberhaven that hid so well the person he didn't get to be. The little boy who'd longed for a normal mother, the man who had too few friends and too much responsibility. The prince who was fascinated by the freedom of a commoner.

"Don't you ever...oh, I don't know, let loose? Rip off that tie, slip on some old jeans and just raise a little hell?"

His answer was a bit wistful. "Oh, I think Cassandra raises enough hell for the both of us."

Casey couldn't help but scowl. "And what excuse did you use before she came along?"

He didn't seem to understand.

"For a younger son," she said softly, trying her best to make him understand, "you seem to have shouldered quite a load."

Eric smiled. His duties had been decided before he'd ever been born. "I have no choice. I have a responsibility to my country."

She nodded with an impatient little shrug. "And what about your responsibility to yourself?"

His gaze strayed back to the palace, that building that was so integral to the fabric of his existence. "I went to England to school. I got away for a while."

"What about now?" she asked. "What do you do now?"

"I play polo," he said. "And rugby."

"And have you ever done anything just for the hell of it?"

Again he didn't quite comprehend.

"Would you ever consider just telling off some old busybody just because it made you feel better?"

Eric didn't have to consider the question before shaking his head.

Casey sighed. "Do you even own a pair of jeans?"

"No."

She shook her head, frustrated that this man who gave so much could think so little of himself. Surely he should be able to inject a little spontaneity, to offset some of the crushing stress of his position. A bit of momentary madness.

The impulse was born even before Casey finished the thought. She could barely suppress the sudden smile. "You really should try it."

"Try what?"

Casey shrugged, easing a little closer to better her balance. Eric got the wrong idea and nestled against her, the fabric of his slacks whispering against the silk of her dress. She brought her hands up to his chest.

"Surprise," she said, with the innocent eyes of a siren. "You know, a little fun."

He bent his head a little lower; the soft timbre of his voice rippling along Casey's skin like a sultry breeze. "What kind of fun?"

Her smile blossomed, all mischief and glee.

"This," she said, and pushed.

Eric landed in the reflecting pool with a great splash and an outraged howl. Casey's laughter pealed out over the sleeping gardens.

"You little witch!" he yelled from his ungainly position, the water lapping against the sodden white linen of his once-pristine dinner jacket. His wet hair tumbled over his forehead. His pants were soaked and his shirt was plastered to his chest. The outrage on his face sent Casey into another paroxysm of laughter. Lights began to flick on at the other end of the garden.

"Why the hell did you do that?" he demanded, struggling valiantly against the laughter that was catching up with him.

"Just to see what you would look like," she admitted, still struggling for breath. Actually, he looked sexier than ever. The way that linen clung to his body showed her just how lean and athletic it was. Rugby must really make a man out of you. "It makes me nervous when somebody doesn't ever get mussed up."

"Is that so?" A smile now tugged at the corners of his mouth as he reached around to dig a sopping handkerchief from his pocket and mop his dripping face. "This was silk, you know."

"And you don't have another one to your name," she goaded.

Although Casey couldn't say how he managed it, Eric tucked the handkerchief away with a great deal of aplomb. "You could at least help me back up."

She held out a hand. She shouldn't have. Eric no sooner took hold of it than an identical smile appeared on his face, that of a pirate catching sight of a fat prize.

"Oh, Eric, no..." she began to protest. She never got the chance. Suddenly she was the one howling and Eric the one laughing. She landed right on top of him.

"You're right," he admitted after due consideration. "It is quite a sight." He reached up to brush the damp tangle of hair back from her forehead.

"This wasn't my dress," she protested instinctively, looking down at the damp mass of silk that did no more now than vividly outline her figure.

"And Cassandra doesn't have another," he said, grinning and wrapping his arms around her.

She laughed, rivulets of water sliding down her throat to mingle with the precious gems she'd borrowed. The evening breeze raised goose bumps in the wake of the water, and she nestled back against Eric's warmth.

"You get the hang of this stuff pretty quickly," she accused, still giggling.

He chuckled, too, not making any move to better his position. The two of them rested along the side of the pool, up to their waists in water.

"That's what I get for getting involved with a barbarian."

Casey let out another howl and turned in his arms, fully intent on giving him the due she'd been unable to give the old lady for the same kind of crack. Eric anticipated her.

Before she could retaliate, he pulled her to him. She gasped and struggled in vain to back off. It didn't do any good. With a deliberate smile, Eric brought her to him, his one hand cradling the back of her neck, the other firmly around her waist. His eyes open and laughing, he bent to kiss her, and she forgot about the cool breeze. He was igniting goose bumps all his own.

The soft command of his lips stole her resistance. The enticing rasp of his cheek against hers brought her hands up to circle his neck, and she ended up kissing him back. She heard his sharp intake of breath as she opened her lips to him. She felt his hand move from her waist, trailing the most delicious shivers with it. Her heart began to thunder in her ears, her breath stolen by the sweet play of his hands against her body. She could smell the heady tang of his cologne mingle with the flowers that surrounded them and taste the last of the brandy on his tongue.

Never in her life had Casey lost reason to the sensation of a man's touch. Never until tonight. When Eric's fingers reached for the soft swell of her breast, she could do no more than sigh, moving against him. His touch, so sure and sensitive, sparked lightning in its wake. Casey's hold on him tightened, her body aching to mold with his, to savor the textures, the strength, the hard angles of him. When Eric suddenly straightened, Casey was surprised by the sharp loss she felt.

She looked up at him, her lips still parted and swollen, her eyes wide and dark with his power over her. She was about to say something, but his eyes were suddenly past her.

Then she heard the discreet cough and considered diving underwater.

"We heard shouts," the voice behind her explained diffidently. "Is Your Highness all right?"

Eric never batted an eye. "Quite all right, thank you." He nodded evenly, never changing his hold on Casey or moving to get up. For her part, Casey couldn't manage any more than a stricken stare into Eric's soggy lapel, her back stiff with discomfort.

"Very well then, Your Highness," the voice said at descending levels. He must be bowing again. "If you won't be needing anything else."

A strangled little sound escaped Casey at that.

Eric smiled an easy dismissal beyond her shoulder. "I don't think so, Rolph. Good night."

"Good night, sir."

Silence returned at intervals.

"Is he gone?" Casey finally managed.

Eric grinned. "He's gone."

She dropped her head onto his chest and groaned. "I'm gonna die. The whole palace will know by morning."

"Probably within the hour," he allowed, still smiling with satisfaction.

That provoked another groan.

"I'm sure the servants have figured out that you're not my niece," he assured her, snuggling back into an intimate embrace, his head just over hers. "They won't mind our having an affair."

Casey's head came up, almost sending his teeth through his tongue. "Don't start that again," she warned.

"You started it," he retorted, his eyes all affronted innocence. Even so, his index finger sought out the puffy edges of her lips, which still betrayed his attention. "After all, you're the one who is responsible for the position in which I find myself. Not to mention the very enticing suggestion to enjoy a little fun."

His eyes returned to hers, soaking up the languid heat that still simmered there. Casey felt herself awash in that delicious blue, sinking without a trace within his charm.

"Well," she managed with a rather shaky voice, reaching up to pull his hand away, "you've had your moment."

Even soaked and dripping, Eric was able to retain his urbane air. He made waterlogged look like the upcoming fashion trend, and it was threatening Casey's breath again. Without blinking an eye, he turned the hand that had captured his and brought it up to his lips.

"But we might not find ourselves in such a conducive position again for so long," he murmured, his breath warming her palm and stirring the embers back to blazing life.

"Conducive to what?" she whispered, trying without much luck to keep an even keel.

He smiled and kissed her palm again. Casey couldn't feel the water anymore. Her body was alternately freezing and burning, the sharp yearning leaping like a brushfire in her. She felt herself lifting her lips to him again, letting them open to seek his warmth....

"Your Highness."

This time even Eric hadn't heard him. The two of them started like rabbits caught in a bright light.

"You do have some guts, Rolph," Casey rasped with a little shake of her head, still not able to face him.

"I truly beg your pardon, Your Highnesses. I was told it was vital I fetch you both."

"Thermonuclear war, I hope," she grated, her embarrassment complete.

Nothing fazed Rolph. "No, Your Highness. General Mueller. He awaits the prince in his office."

Eric's head came up at that. "The general?"

"Yes, Your Highness. He said it was important...." Or I wouldn't have bothered you, his pause said.

"All right, Rolph. Tell him we'll be there," Eric said, finally moving to get out of the pool. When he observed the condition the two of them were in, he amended his statement. "When we've had a chance to make ourselves presentable."

"Very well, Your Highness."

A good servant was a discreet servant, it seemed. By the time Casey made it up to the bedroom there was already a change of clothing set out for her and a bath drawn. She was relieved that Maria hadn't seen fit to stick around for the gory details. She was having trouble enough with them herself. Stripping off the ruined designer original, Casey found herself thinking about the man who was changing just down the hall from her.

It wasn't fair. It just wasn't fair. She was going to be twenty-five next July, and in all those years she had never found herself at a man's mercy. It had always been with a clear eye and a firm foothold in reality that Casey had viewed the men she'd dated. She had never found one to set off the proverbial fireworks or even to compel her so that she couldn't wait to be with him again. That had all come to a screeching halt the moment she'd laid eyes on Eric.

It wasn't enough that he was just about the most handsome man she'd ever laid eyes on. No one she'd ever gone to school or worked with could compare in any way. From the aquamarine of his eyes to the lean lines of his body, he was simply too good-looking to be true. If he'd lived in her neighborhood, the only way he'd still be single by the age of thirty-five would be if he were the parish priest. How the world's most eligible women had failed to net him by now mystified her.

But that had nothing on the fact that he seemed just as mystified with her. Her, Cassandra Marie Phillips, the daughter of a cabdriver and a grade school teacher. She, who'd dutifully ignored whatever lessons in gracious living her grandmother had tried so hard to instill on those painfully uncomfortable visits to the old woman's home. A man with more names than she had shoes was talking about having an affair with her.

Still shaking her head, Casey slid into the steaming water in the old claw-foot tub. It wasn't that she'd ever considered herself ugly. She figured she could stand up with the best of them in the neighborhood, especially if you went in for Tyrolean looks. She'd had dates to the prom and an offer to go steady while in high school.

But she wouldn't put herself up with any of the women she'd met at these dinners. They were world class, wearing their diamonds as if it was their right, easily conversing in any of four different languages about art and politics and the latest in society news. Casey could discuss Keith Hernandez's batting average and the cost of a snow cone on Coney Island. And she could only do that fluently in Brooklynese. She hated fish eggs and preferred the company of the staff to the guests. Eric had no business being attracted to her.

It did occur to her to wonder whether he might be putting on an act to better facilitate her cooperation. He did, after all, take his responsibility to his country very seriously. But that doubt didn't linger long, though whether from honesty or wishful thinking she didn't know. She simply couldn't accept the idea that a man with such sweet eyes could be so deceptive.

The next problem, of course, was what to do about his offer. Should she throw caution to the wind this one time and give in? The brief time she spent in his arms tonight promised a fulfillment she'd never dreamed of, never hoped for. She knew that she was finding life away from him less and less appealing. She knew that she celebrated his laughter and shared the pain that he allowed so fleetingly. And she knew that he made her feel more special than any of those jewel-encrusted women who could claim him by rights.

But, dear God, what would happen when she had to leave? Would it be easier to have committed herself to him during the time they had together—no more than a few days at best? Or would she survive more easily if she kept her distance, only suspecting what he could give her rather than being sure of it and missing it even while she held him in her arms.

Who was she to even consider it, anyway? An affair, even with a prince, was not something she took home to her mother. It would be something she would have to keep as her own for the rest of her life, unable to share it even with Sandy, because even Sandy wouldn't understand.

Casey opened her door to join Eric and the general without having come to any decision. As the time passed, the weight of it grew within her like a soreness that wouldn't go away.

She walked into the paneled office in tailored slacks and a silk blouse. She would have much preferred the denim jump suit she'd packed.

When Eric answered the knock on the door, he smiled at her appearance. She'd haphazardly pinned the curls back from her face, damp tendrils still clinging along her forehead and neck, and chosen to rest her feet from Cassandra's pointed pumps. The heather slacks and shimmering ivory-and-blue blouse that so flattered her lithe figure were complemented by bare feet.

"Come in, Casey," he said, guiding her in. "I was just speaking with the general. General—" he turned to the distinguished gentleman who was even now standing at Casey's approach "—Miss Phillips."

Instead of bowing like the servants or reaching for her hand like Eric, the general executed a swift click of the heels and a nod of the head. He was dramatically silver-haired and well tailored, a man carefully appropriate to his station.

"*Fraülein,*" he said in precise tones, "it is a pleasure to meet you. The prince was telling me what a service you have performed for our small country."

"No problem," she said, smiling a bit uncomfortably. "I always did like to play dress-up."

"The general was just telling me, Casey," Eric was saying as he moved back around to his desk, "that a new communiqué has been received from the kidnappers. Brandy?"

"Would Rolph have to come in to pour it?"

The general stared. Eric chuckled.

"I'll pour it if you'd like."

"Will I need it?"

He nodded. "Probably."

"Thank you, then. A brandy would be lovely." She sat down in one of the leather chairs without waiting for an invitation. The general sat more slowly in his, his still-raised eyebrows the only indication of his surprise at her appearance.

"They do keep odd hours," Casey said, restraining an urge to yawn, "don't they?"

"To keep us off balance," the general assured her.

She nodded as if she understood. "What do they want now?" she asked. "Safe passage to Disneyland?"

Once again it was the general who didn't seem to understand. Eric handed Casey her glass of brandy with a wide smile and perched on the corner of his desk.

"Actually, it's beginning to look better," he admitted. "They've retreated from their earlier demands."

Casey took a sip and thought that she really didn't like brandy, either. Too bad the prince didn't have beer in one of those little cut-glass decanters on his sideboard. "Why?" she asked.

Eric's smile grew sly as he took his own sip. "I have a feeling that Cassandra's making their life miserable. They've offered to let us have her back for a million Swiss francs—flat fee. No announcement, no coronation cancellation." His second sip was longer, and he came away with an even more delighted smile. "You know, I have a feeling that if we just left her there, by the end of the week they'd pay us to take her off their hands."

Casey scowled. "Don't get any ideas. I already owe her one dress."

"The general and I were just discussing that," Eric ventured, leveling those resistance-sapping eyes on her and setting down his glass.

"I don't think I want to hear this," Casey assured him, fighting a new urge to get up and run.

"The kidnappers are still eluding our grasp."

Casey turned to the general. "I thought this was going to be a piece of cake," she protested.

He frowned. "A piece of—"

Casey waved aside his confusion. "Easy," she clarified. "I thought this was going to be over before any of us knew it."

He studied his fingertips with regretful eyes. "I regret to say, *fraülein*, that the leadership of the group seems to have undergone a surprise change. We are dealing with someone we hadn't anticipated, and I fear he managed to move a step beyond our grasp."

Why did she feel as if the quicksand had just reached her hips? The more she helped, the more difficult the operation seemed to become and the more participation was required from her.

"Eric, I have to remind you..." She'd turned just in time to see him pull something out from a drawer. "What's that?"

"Try it on," he suggested, holding it out.

Casey shied away as if it was a snake. "No, thanks. I don't like the looks of that."

"It's only a crown."

She snorted. "That's what van Helsing told Dracula about the crucifix. Put it away."

The circlet of diamonds, sapphires and rubies glittered seductively in the soft light as Eric held it out to her. The symbol of everything her family had lost so many years ago, the wealth, the power of sovereignty. That last trace of royal blood, so long dormant in her veins, now called out to it, hypnotized by the lure.

"The coronation is Sunday," Eric was saying.

Casey deliberately shook her head. "I have to be back at work by Friday. Besides, Cassandra really would have my head if I stole her limelight on the biggest day of her career."

"What if we can't rescue her in time? Think of the turmoil."

Still she held fast. "No."

"Casey," Eric pleaded, "you don't understand. The entire economy is at stake. Taping rights have been sold to cable TV. The country will be out millions."

She shook her head, unable to work up the nerve to look at him. "I'll reimburse you. Small weekly amounts for the rest of my life."

The general added his weight. "It is only just in case, *fraülein*, so that the kidnappers cannot possibly have the upper hand."

Then Eric pulled the dirtiest trick he could. Pulling the crown away, he slipped it back into its case in the drawer, just as Casey had asked. A certain amount of light seemed to go out of the room. But then he turned his eyes back on her, and Casey forgot the glitter of those jewels. The jewels in his eyes were far more compelling.

"I can make arrangements with your company," he coaxed. "Stay, Casey. Just a little while."

"You'd go to pretty great lengths to protect your country," she answered. "Wouldn't you?" She couldn't help the note of hurt sarcasm that crept into her voice.

"Yes," he replied honestly. "I would. But I would never go as far as to hurt you."

For a moment it was as if the general wasn't even there. Casey and Eric faced each other, the intensity of their silent communication crackling between them like lightning. Any questions Casey had ever entertained regarding Eric's using her for his country's ends were laid to rest by the stark sincerity in his eyes. She knew that his plea was twofold. The sleight-of-hand idea at the coronation was real enough. But Eric wanted Casey to stay for him as much as for his country.

Emptying her glass with a suddenness that left her watery-eyed, Casey got to her feet.

"Why does it seem like I'm forever giving in to you?" she demanded.

"Because you know it's the right thing to do," the general ventured self-righteously.

"I wasn't talking about that," Casey advised him dryly. He had the good sense to remain quiet. "You might be able to deal with work," she said to Eric, "but you won't have a bit of luck with my mother. I'm going to have to take care of her."

Eric stood to join her. "I don't think you'll regret it."

The smile Casey gave Eric left him in no doubt as to her fears regarding that subject. "Oh, what the hell," she finally sighed, not caring that the general probably knew that she wasn't referring in the least to the charade he had asked her to play. "I might as well practice what I preach and do something just because I want to."

Taking hold of her arms, Eric smiled down at her, his eyes suffusing her with their warmth. "Then I know you won't regret it."

"Don't be so damn smug." She smiled back and left.

Seven

"Reports from the palace in Moritania today once again categorically deny as absurd the claims by the Moritanian Socialist Movement that they have the Crown Princess Cassandra held captive. A videotape of a woman claiming to be the princess has been received from the group at the same time the princess was participating in the state functions this week in coordination with the world finance conference being conducted in the small country."

Slumped in the leather chair in Eric's office, Casey punched the remote control, and the film of her nodding and shaking hands faded from the screen.

"Casey, it's getting out of hand," Sandy said diffidently from the chair next to her.

Casey shrugged. "I know. I should tell them all to take a hike, especially since Mr. Simpson refused to extend my vacation. I could be fired if I stay long enough to be crowned on Sunday. I guess princes don't carry the weight they used to."

"Come home with me tomorrow," Sandy prodded. "Let them play *Prince and the Pauper* with somebody else."

Without really answering, Casey got to her feet. "Let's go get something to eat."

The two of them had sneaked down to the office to watch the TV accounts of the situation while the rest of the palace readied for dinner. Two more days had passed in which Casey had spent the majority of her time at state functions playing charades and trying to ignore how much Cassandra's shoes hurt her feet. She'd called her mother and lied to her for almost the first time in her life, telling her that she'd lost her passport and wasn't sure they were going to let her get home the same time Sandy did, but not to worry. Her mother had worried, naturally. Sandy had rolled her eyes accusingly. All in all, it was making Casey pretty tired and crabby.

The longer she stayed, the more difficult it was becoming for her to go home at all. All she wanted to do was stay in this comfortable limbo where no decisions had to be made about her trip home, her relationship with Eric, her future. They played their games and conspired like children on a summer's evening, going out of their way to deny the transience of their time together.

"The bell will ring in a few minutes," Sandy finally said, not bothering to move. "You know, I really can't believe that somebody hasn't done more nosing around and figured out that you're fishy."

Now Casey was pacing. "An obedient people, I guess."

"No press is obedient," Sandy snorted.

"Well, maybe they're stupid!"

Sandy turned, her eyes a little wide. "Hey, don't take it out on me. I'm just the Greek chorus. Somebody's got to remind you where the reality line lies."

The turmoil bubbled up suddenly, surprising Casey as much as it did Sandy. Whipping around on her friend, she faced her with accusing eyes.

"I'm doing the guy a favor, okay?"

"You're playing make-believe."

"Of course I am!" she nearly shrieked. "He asked me to pose as his niece, so I'm posing as his niece until she's safely rescued."

Sandy got to her feet, just as upset. "I'm not talking about that, and you know it."

Standing her ground, Casey faced her, her eyes defiant. "Tell me what I'm supposed to do, Sandy."

Sandy never hesitated. "Leave. Get the hell out of this fairyland before it destroys you. You don't belong here, Casey. Pretending you do doesn't change it."

"I don't care if I belong here or not," Casey snorted with a wave of her hand.

Sandy's expression grew disbelieving. "You don't, huh? Then why are you practicing royal etiquette every day with Maria? Why did I almost hear you on your knees giving thanks this morning when they said they still couldn't find the princess? You don't want to go home." Pointing an accusing finger, Sandy made her final judgment. "I, for one, am glad I won't have to be here when it all ends." She didn't wait for an answer before stalking out of the room.

It was all Casey could do to remain in one spot. The fury of her anguish filled her with an unquenchable fire. In only a matter of days she had committed herself to something that she knew was a no-win situation. She knew Sandy was right. She could never stay here. She didn't belong in these echoing old halls. But she knew just as surely that, hour by hour, she was losing ground against the persuasion of Eric's gentle charms.

She should get out so fast that she'd leave the front door banging in her wake. But she couldn't watch Eric struggle day after day to maintain a country's precious equilibrium and desert him when she was his best chance of success. She suddenly couldn't bear to let him shoulder the burden alone, at least while she could legitimately be around to help. And, to be brutally honest, she couldn't bear to walk away from the life he'd stirred in her. It was impossible for her to go, but the longer she stayed, the worse she was making it on herself.

Furious tears welled in her eyes as the pain in her chest grew. Whirling around, she turned to the bookcases alongside Eric's desk. A vase. She picked it up, the need for a little destruction urgent. Hefting the large urn-shaped object, she went into a backswing, a sob escaping her.

"No!"

Startled, she turned, the vase still over her head. Eric stood in the doorway, a hand out to her.

"Not that one," he advised gently. "It's a Ming."

Walking over, he relieved her of it. Then he replaced it with a smaller, lighter vase of a darker green.

"Try this one. It's a lesser dynasty."

She should have given up the attempt. Somehow his words only made the frustration worse. With a little cry of rage, Casey hurled it against the far wall. It shattered with a dramatic explosion.

"Better?" he asked with a smile.

She made a furious swipe at the tears that had spilled onto her cheeks. "Who wants to live in a house where you can't even break anything, anyway?" she demanded crossly. "It's like living in a museum!"

Eric nodded. "Precisely."

"There you go again," she accused, the tears flowing faster. "I just busted your vase, pal. Can't you even get mad?"

He reached out to her. "You needed it. What's more, you deserved it. You've put up with an awful lot in the last few days, Casey. I'm awed that you've managed so beautifully this far." Tenderly he brushed away the tears. It only made matters worse. Casey ended up gulping and sobbing, trying to hold off the torrent his gentleness was unleashing.

"You really are amazing, you know," he murmured, easing her closer.

She would have none of it. "Knock it off!" she demanded, her control slipping farther with another major sob. "Just . . . knock it off. I don't want you thinking I'm wonderful."

"Why not?" he asked with a soft smile. "I do."

"Because . . . because it won't do any good. Sandy's right. I'm playing make-believe. I should get my fanny back to New York where I belong."

Without her knowing how, Casey found herself nestled against Eric's chest, his arms around her and his hand against her hair. She cried even harder.

"Don't even say that," he begged, his voice suddenly very quiet.

Casey lifted her head to see the pain in his eyes, the sudden tight set of his jaw. With a little hiccup, the tears just as suddenly died in her.

"Eric . . ."

He smiled then, his charming facade back in place. "Dinner's ready," he said with studied ease. "I came to get you."

She shook her head, the tears still glistening on her cheeks forgotten. She knew him better now, saw the tension he couldn't quite conceal. He was hurting, and it tore at her more sharply than her own pain.

"Wait a minute," she objected, snaring his eyes with her own. "You're not gonna tell me that you'll walk out of here and pretend everything's okay."

"It is," he argued carefully.

"It is not," she retorted just as carefully. "You're upset about something. And you can't tell me that it's going to all be okay if you just pretend you aren't and go out there and play the perfect prince."

The humor in his eyes was tempered by a wistfulness that brought loss to Casey's mind. "Ah." He nodded with another smile. "The famous American stress."

"Eric," she objected with a frustrated shake of the head, "get mad for a change. Throw something. Yell. It's not gonna hurt anything."

"That's Cassandra's forte, thank you."

"No," she disagreed. "She just takes advantage of the privilege. Did your brother ever scream?"

"Never."

"He might have ruled a little longer if he had."

She'd struck a nerve. She could see it in the darkening of the clear quiet of his blue eyes. There was a storm brewing in those calm waters.

"Yelling doesn't change anything. It doesn't get you what you want."

"What could you want?"

"I told you," he retorted, his hands tight on her arms. "You."

"I'm only staying this long because of you. You think I'd go through all this for Cassandra?"

"But you'll still go home."

"You're damn right I will."

Without either of them realizing it, their voices had begun to raise, their eyes sparking with confrontation.

"So you see? If I yelled at you or threw one of the vases, it wouldn't convince you to stay."

"Eric, how could I possibly stay?" she demanded. "Why should I forfeit my job just to drag out the inevitable?"

"Because I'm falling in love with you!"

The sudden silence was complete. Eric wasn't even sure he was breathing. How did she keep surprising him into admitting what he only suspected?

Once he'd said it, he knew it was true. He knew that he wanted this sprite to stay by him, to continue coloring his world with her brightness. But he knew just as well that this wasn't the time to tell her. She was having enough difficulty with the just task of subterfuge.

With an effort, he offered an easy smile. "Now you know why I don't think yelling is a good idea. One tends to say too much."

"You mean you didn't mean it?" she asked in a strangled voice.

He drew her closer. "I meant every word. But from the looks of you, I don't think you wanted to hear that right now."

Her answer was wry. "I guess the next time I goad you into letting off a little steam it'll have to be from a safe distance."

"What's a safe distance?" he asked.

"New York."

His thumb was brushing her cheek again, the movement bittersweet and intimate. Casey wanted nothing more than to close her eyes against it, to give in to the sweet weakness his touch wrought. For a very long mo-

ment the shadowy room remained silent, a silence that
weighed heavily between the two of them. The atmosphere of a gracious old home, of a class of people her
grandmother had known as a child. A class Casey had
never considered real as she'd grown up in her crowded
Brooklyn apartment.

She didn't belong here. But she was wanting more and
more to stay.

"I believe Mother is waiting for us to join her," Eric
finally said, his voice as intimate as his touch.

Casey lifted her eyes to his, basking in the mesmerizing
blue. "Well, I always said it doesn't pay to keep a dowager waiting."

With a soft chuckle, he bent to drop a kiss. "I'd advise
you to never put it quite that way to the queen."

They found the queen in the private dining quarters, a
room the size of only half a football field. The formal
dining room could have seated the United Nations without much crowding.

Tonight the intimate room with the twelve-foot leaded-
glass windows and the claw-footed sterling candelabra was
set for only six. Eric and Casey were the last to arrive.

Rudolph, the much-abused fiancé spoke up briskly
from where he stood next to the queen. "Cassandra, are
you quite all right? Your face is a bit puffy."

"Cold feet, my dear Rudolph," Casey shot back in an
arch tone of voice she'd copied directly from the tapes.
"Eric has been trying to remind me of my duty to my
country next week."

His eyebrows rose with surprise. "You don't want to be
crowned?"

"Don't be silly," she retorted, letting Eric lead her to
her place and give her over to Rudolph's rather diffident
care. "I didn't say anything about being crowned, did I?"

She had scored a point. Rudolph blushed, the queen frowned and Eric hid his smile behind the glass of wine he raised. Sandy, seated to his left, wouldn't be saying much for a while. To *her* right was the still-stunning Mr. Mc-Cormac. Casey looked over to greet him and felt her stomach give way. Damn Eric for throwing him into the pot tonight. Her first reaction was still to just sigh and stare, just as Sandy was doing.

"James, my dear," she said, smiling sweetly and leaning across to touch his hand. "It is so good to see you away from the press of a public function. How has your stay been?"

"Profitable, Your Highness," he admitted with a soft chuckle that made Sandy sigh. "There's something about touching base with one's money that stokes a person's feeling of security."

Casey batted her eyelashes, which sent Eric's eyes rolling. "Any service our humble country can be."

"Eric was saying that you hadn't had the chance to ride in quite a few days," he said as the servants began to circulate. James seemed to know just what to do with circulating servants. He moved around their serving with the grace of a ballet dancer. Casey just sat back, hoping for the best.

"A lot to do this week," she admitted. "I sometimes wish I'd decided to be crowned and married in the same dress. The fittings are absolutely draining me."

It was the eye signals from Eric that alerted her to the fact that one particular butler was standing behind her, awaiting her attention.

"Yes?" she snapped without turning. She wished she could remember the man's name.

"Your Highness, I must notify you that we have been unable to obtain your caviar for this evening."

Casey was a hairsbreadth away from giving herself away once and for all by throwing herself at the man's feet and thanking him with all her heart. Instead, she once again sought Eric's guidance. His brows gathered. She turned on the servant in a right snit.

"What do you mean?" she demanded, causing more than one flinch at the table. "There is always a supply kept ready."

The man bowed, and Casey saw the perspiration glistening on his forehead. It made her feel terrible. She didn't want to yell at this nice man. Maybe she could make it up to him when she came back out of the phone booth as Casey Phillips.

"It is my responsibility, Your Highness. I assumed that there was ample supply. When I found that not to be the case, I went to the shop where the palace obtains its supplies. The owner apologized, but he also has had an unexplained rush. He promises to have more in tomorrow."

Only Casey saw the abrupt stiffening of Eric's posture. It didn't dawn on her to wonder why. Later, she thought, and turned back to serve the little man's penance.

"Oh, very well. But if it isn't available at this table tomorrow night, you may serve your notice."

His latest bow was quick as he departed.

"You're becoming disconcertingly tolerant these days, Cassandra," Eric observed in a dry voice. "Could it be that the prospect of marriage agrees with you?"

Casey wondered what *intolerant* would have been like. "I'll whip him with rushes when the guests have left," she snapped just as dryly, and went back to her other guests.

* * *

"You do a most credible imitation of Bette Davis in *The Virgin Queen*, my dear," the queen stated dryly after the other guests had gone.

"Hardly the appropriate film if you're referring to Cassandra, Mother." Eric laughed from where he sat with his brandy.

She ignored the comment. "I must admit I considered Eric's scheme harebrained at first. It seems, however, to be serving for the moment. Have you heard from Mueller, Eric?"

Eric shook his head. "Not since about noon. They'd combed all of the known lairs for the MSM and come up dry."

The queen nodded with regal dignity. Casey, sitting off by the harp, couldn't help but wonder if this woman had ever let her dignity down and just played. Had she giggled like a schoolgirl when her young husband proposed, when he first kissed her? Or did she deign to be kissed? She'd grown up wondering the same about her grandmother. It had only been as the old woman had grown frail that she'd unlocked those memories that had reflected her human side.

"Very well," the queen said as she rose from her chair. Turning slightly so that she could take in Casey, seated very carefully in her antique chair, the china cup in her lap, the queen gave a quick nod of judgment. "When this is over, you must be our guest for a few days." An eyebrow arched. "The servants rather like you."

Before Casey could thank her, the queen swept out. Casey turned to Eric, the surprise still in her eyes. It was nothing compared to the surprise in his.

"Good God." He whistled, downing his brandy in a gulp. "She likes you."

Now Casey's eyebrow arched. "You make it sound like she shouldn't."

Standing, he poured another dose. "Not shouldn't. Doesn't. My mother isn't one to open up to people very quickly. One of the professional hazards of having power, I guess. She is very... careful. What you received was nothing short of the royal blessing."

"An offer of a visit?"

"Rest assured," he told her, "you're welcome here anytime. She might even take to inviting you to sip tea with her. And she hasn't made that offer to anyone since my Aunt Eleanor died."

Casey looked after the departed queen, then back to Eric with a little shrug. "Why me?"

He grinned. "She might just respect your gumption, my dear Casey. Not many people in this world are comfortable with her."

"Not many people in this world grew up with my grandmother," she retorted easily. "Now *there* was an old lady who could make you feel uncomfortable."

"Are you going riding with James tomorrow?"

"Are you kidding? And blow my cover?"

Eric laughed, taking a seat next to her. Slipping an arm around her shoulders, he prepared to get comfortable. It was not to be, however. A hesitant knock on the door brought his arm back around and him up off the couch.

"Come in."

It was all Casey could do to keep a straight face. She felt absurdly as she had the night her father had caught her necking on the couch with Mike Molloy after the junior dance.

Their guest was the butler who had put his head on the block at dinner that evening, the same one, she now realized, who'd first greeted her in the kitchens. A tall, distinguished-looking man, he carried himself like an army major. He entered and came to a stiff attention.

"You wished to see me, Your Highness."

Eric got to his feet. "Yes, Simmons, thank you. Sit down, if you'd like. I need to ask you a question."

"I'm sorry I yelled at you tonight," Casey apologized without thinking.

Simmons was coaxed into a surprised little smile. "You do have the knack, ma'am. We're all quite proud of you."

Casey didn't consider the various contradictions in his statement when she smiled back. "Thank you. Everybody's been really nice to me."

"And you they," he replied.

Eric finished pouring another dose of brandy and handed it over to the startled servant, an amused little smile playing around his eyes. "This will of course be held in strictest confidence, Simmons."

Simmons took a look at the liquor he held, took his seat and would have promised to have his tongue cut out.

"You spoke of the princess's supply of caviar tonight." Eric waited for a stunned little nod. "This is the first time to my knowledge that you've ever run out."

"Yes, sir," the man nodded emphatically. "I can't understand it myself. We had the full supply in. I checked it no more than three days ago. And suddenly tonight we show up missin' all of it. And the shop—you know the one—says they're out, too. Most unusual, sir."

Taking up his stride, Eric nodded to himself. "Most unusual. Who would have taken that caviar?"

"Oh, no one. No one really likes the stuff but Her Highness—" with a confused little frown, he turned to Casey "—Your Highness." Then he, too, drained his brandy.

"For just this evening, we might refer to the present Highness as Miss Phillips, Simmons."

"Yes, Your Highness."

"Who is allowed in the pantries?"

"The pantries, Your Highness? Why, any of us, you know. The cooks, meself, Rolph, when Her Highness wants a bit of a snack."

"Is there anyone you wouldn't trust implicitly?"

The words brought Simmons to his feet, the accusation sparking outrage. "Your Highness!"

Casey saw the set of Eric's shoulders ease a bit with the protest. She knew he was satisfied, but still wasn't at all sure what the whole inquisition was about.

"Thank you, Simmons," he said, stepping up to face the man, a supportive hand to his arm. "You've been a great help to me. I simply needed a little affirmation, and you provided it. Has anyone but the staff been near those pantries?"

Simmons took a moment to think that one over. "Well, sir, yes, now that you mention it. Werner's been nosing about a bit. Says he hasn't had time to get regular lunches and all, so he snitches a tin or two of something from the shelf."

"Werner." Eric's voice was almost hushed.

Simmons nodded uncertainly.

Eric nodded back, dismissing the man. "Thank you, Simmons. Good night."

Carefully setting his snifter down, Simmons bowed with a tentative smile. "Night, Your Highness—Your, er, Fräulein Phillips."

"Caviar?" Casey asked after the door had once again closed to leave the two of them to the cozy fire and each other.

Eric turned on her, the expression on his face a mixture of triumph and outrage. "Werner," he said, more to himself than to her. "It can't be."

"What can't be?"

He didn't return to the couch, so Casey got to her feet.

"The caviar," Eric prodded. "What do we know about it?"

Casey shrugged. "It's a source of protein, disgusting-looking and one of the few things I'm glad I can't afford."

"And who is addicted to it?"

At that Casey scowled, since she had been the hapless victim of that little passion. "You don't have to remind me. I've been the one taking her medicine while she's vacationing in the mountains."

Eric turned, his eyes bright with discovery. "And if Cassandra isn't eating it, and you certainly aren't—"

"Not unless somebody shoves it down my throat with a big stick."

"Then who is?"

She thought about it. It didn't add up. Simmons had already said that nobody else really liked the stuff. So it all pointed right back to Cassandra—who was missing.

"But how?" she asked.

Eric turned to the phone. "That's what I'm going to find out. I have a feeling that Cassandra is being supplied with her favorite junk food so that she remains manageable, and someone has to be able to get it for her."

"The shop was out, too," Casey remembered. "My God, Eric, you think somebody's been stealing it right from the kitchens to take to her?" Then it really dawned on her. "You think *Werner* has been stealing it?"

"We'll soon find out."

But they didn't. Eric called just about every official in the country, but he couldn't locate Werner. Off for the evening really meant off for the evening for that particular bureaucrat.

Next Eric tried General Mueller. After hearing the theory of the missing caviar, Mueller promised to look into it right away, since the update from his investigating teams hadn't yet produced anything promising.

Eric set the phone down to find Casey next to him, her expression as intense as his.

"What did he say?" she asked.

"He said, 'Good night, Your Highness. Sleep well.'"

Casey scowled. "In for a penny, in for a pound, my dear Eric," she said, mimicking his own speech. "How close am I to freedom?"

Now he was the one to scowl, stepping up to take her into his arms. "You're so anxious to regain it?" he asked gently.

Casey eased into his embrace without even thinking. Looking up at him, she saw the remembrance of their earlier conversations gleaming eerily in his eyes. Frustration, anticipation, a gentle reproach. He was so close to her, his scent filling her nostrils, his solid strength enveloping her. She felt whatever resistance she had left dissolving. All he had to do was hold her against him and she lost all interest in what happened to her namesake. All she could think of was what it would feel like to have this man make love to her. Slowly, gently, with a passion that only she could unleash, even as she had begun to unleash his emotions.

"Posing as your niece *is* a bit restraining," she admitted in a hushed little voice, her face lifting to his. "I can't even play footsies with you at dinner."

"What about now?" he asked, so close now that his breath stirred fire along her throat. She wanted his lips there, his hungry hands. Her body was beginning to thrum with wanting him. Her heart had begun to race.

"Now?" she echoed, letting her hands stray up his back, the expensive linen delicious against her fingers, as it kept her seeking hands from the steely strength of his back. "All I know now is that you'd better kiss me."

"I had?" he asked, and then dipped to brush her lips with his, the touch maddening. "Perhaps you're right."

His arms tightened. His eyes lit as he bent to recapture her lips. Casey closed her eyes, sighing against him. His lips tasted and taunted, and when he explored she opened to him, suddenly wondering why she hadn't liked brandy. It tasted so enticing on him.

He kissed her eyes, her cheek, her throat as she drew her head back, her hair tumbling over his hands at her back. Sparks flashed from his touch, skittering over her skin and sinking deep into her belly. She clutched at him as if afraid of falling, her fingers bunching into the fabric that covered his back.

"Eric, is this a good...idea?"

His hand strayed along her ribs, igniting chills across the silk-clad skin. She could hardly breathe for the freezing, burning fire he was unleashing in her. It frightened her, not only because she'd never known anything like it before but because she craved it so desperately. His fingers edged up toward her breast and she found herself wanting to urge him on.

"I think it's a wonderful idea," he whispered against her throat. "You can't imagine what it costs me to keep my hands off you."

"And here I thought those cold showers were a holdover from public school."

Eric nuzzled closer against the velvety skin at her throat, his tongue flickering against the soft crescent at its base. Casey gasped at the sudden lightning it unleashed, a liquid fire that swirled all the way to the edges of her fingers.

She never felt the buttons at her throat loosen. She just knew that for a moment his hand left her, and she felt it like the shock of loss. Eric's mouth was still against her skin, tracing tantalizing little kisses along the base of her ear. Casey felt the tight grip his other hand had on her waist, because without it she would have slowly sunk to her knees.

And then she felt his fingers skim her breast. Her breath caught. She arched against the agonizing thrill. He caught her nipple and teased it, his lips dropping to the ridge of her collarbone.

"Casey..." he groaned against her, crushing her to him, his patience lost. "I want you."

Casey recognized the power of his arousal against her and knew that her own sanity was vanishing as fast as his. With her last reserves of control, she took a deep breath. "Not here," she managed. "I'd never be able to sit down to tea with your mother again."

She surprised an abrupt laugh out of him. "Ever my practical Casey," he admonished breathlessly, his hold on her tightening.

"I want you, Casey," he repeated. "Now."

Casey felt herself nod, and couldn't believe it. Her lips were open, her eyes wide, her hair and dress disheveled. She felt as if she was sneaking around behind someone's back, but for the first time felt no shame. No guilt. She wanted Eric just as much as he wanted her, and she might never get another chance.

"Upstairs," she offered with a breathless little smile. "I have a bed that's wasted on just me."

With another kiss, he led her to the door. "Upstairs," he agreed.

No one else saw them walk arm in arm up the broad marbled stairs or down the long hall past the royal suites. Casey couldn't prevent the silly grin that kept plaguing the corners of her mouth as she thought about the man who walked next to her. Just the feel of his arm around her waist gave her a bright, giddy thrill, as if she was just soaring over the top in a Ferris wheel. She could see all the world, and it was spectacular.

They padded past the silent doors until they reached Casey's. Loosening his hold on her, Eric reached to open the door. The room beyond was dark, only a ghostly sky visible through the open curtains by the bed. Eric slid his hand along the wall for the light switch as Casey followed him through the door.

He never reached it.

Suddenly a shadow bolted up before them. Casey shrieked. Eric whipped around too late. The intruder's arm arced down, the blunt instrument in his hand connecting against the back of Eric's skull. With a groan, Eric slumped against the wall.

Casey turned toward the door. The intruder caught her by the arm and pulled her to him.

"Help!" she screamed, struggling to get free. "Eric, help!"

Eric didn't hear her.

Eight

The first sounds Eric could discern were the discordant sighs and grunts of struggle. It was dark. He couldn't remember much, just that he had landed in an ungainly heap on the floor where he lay wedged against a table.

The floor.

He remembered now. He'd meant to turn on the lights. He'd brought Casey up to her room....

Eric's eyes opened as the remaining memory returned—as did the pain, a tearing sensation at the back of his head as if someone with a pickax was at work. Over by the window he saw the shadows, two of them, tumbling around in silhouette against the gray sky, the sound of their breathing heavy and urgent.

"Casey," he groaned, trying to move in her direction. "God, Casey..."

He heard her muffled answering cry. Someone had a hand over her mouth and was trying to strong-arm her out the window. When she heard Eric she flailed out. Eric heard a resulting grunt of pain, then a surprised whimper from her as her attacker struck back.

Eric made it to his knees, then his feet. The room was spinning, the pain bringing on waves of nausea. One hand on the wall, he stumbled over to where Casey was kicking at her attacker.

Eric almost reached them when his hand made contact with a lamp. Without thinking, he flipped it on, then grabbed it.

Casey's attacker stopped. A heavy man, he wore a stocking mask and gloves. Eric didn't recognize him. But he saw that Casey was beginning to be worn down by the man's superior strength. She was going to be out that window in another minute.

"Let her go," he growled.

The intruder backed toward the window, Casey held firmly in front of him. Eric followed, trying to find an angle of attack. He could see the terror that welled up bright in Casey's eyes. It ignited a rare fury in him.

"Put her down or I'll kill you," he warned once again. The man laughed.

Casey took advantage of her captor's brief attention lapse. Relaxing against his hold, she threw him slightly off balance. When he moved to regain it, she shoved a hand straight up and struck his nose. He let out a howl, freeing one of Casey's hands. It was all Eric needed. Pivoting, he took a great cricket swing with the lamp and shattered it against the man's head.

It would have brought a lesser man down. It just stunned this one. Without letting go of Casey, he swung her at Eric, sending both of them tumbling against the wall. The man scuttled out the window.

Sandy got to the door in time to see Eric and Casey in a jumble on the bedroom floor.

"Really," she observed with an arch look, a hand on her hip. "Can't you two keep it a little more quiet? If the wind's with us, Switzerland probably heard your unbridled passion."

"Security," Eric gasped, trying once again to gain an upright position. "Let out the dogs."

For a moment, Sandy didn't answer. Then the truth sank in with a snap that brought her eyes wide open and a hand to her mouth.

"Oh, my God, Prince, you're bleeding!"

Tears still streaming down her face, Casey managed to get herself up in time to make the same discovery. Without any consideration for the room's real tenant, she whipped the linen tablecloth off the small nightstand and pressed it against Eric's head.

"Sandy, get help!" she snapped.

"Are you all right?" Eric asked, his back against the wall and his free arm around Casey. The other took over the job of holding the cloth. There was real fear in his eyes.

"I get sick at the sight of blood." She sniffed, trying to wipe her tears away. "Are you okay? You're a mess. You were great with that lamp." Another sob escaped her when she tried to grin. She was shaking. "Damn it, he hurt you."

"It could have been worse." Eric smiled, although he wasn't feeling appreciably better. The floor still tilted beneath him at regular intervals. At least he didn't have to move for a while. "You weren't bad yourself. Where did you learn that little move with your hand?"

Casey wiped away tears with the back of her hand. "From a marine D.I. I knew." When Eric's eyebrows raised, she defended herself. "Hey, pal, I live in New York. You learned how to ride horses, I learned how to ride subways. That was one of the lessons."

They held on to each other as they heard the burgeoning sounds of alarm gather in the great house. Suddenly Casey began to giggle.

"What's the matter?" Eric asked.

She motioned to the mess. "This isn't exactly what I had in mind when we came up here."

"I wonder if it was punishment for something."

Now Casey was laughing, the adrenaline still racing through her. "The nuns used to say that we'd get hit by lightning if we were ever caught messing around." She shook her head. "They never said anything about getting a blackjack to the back of the head."

They were so busy laughing that for a moment they didn't see the dowager queen standing in the doorway. When they did, it was to discover the real human fear she couldn't quite hide when she saw her only surviving son slouched in a pool of blood. For a painful moment, Casey was afraid the old woman was going to cry.

Not the dowager queen. "Rolph has called for Dr. Schmidt," she announced, only the quaver in her voice still giving her away. "I . . . presume the cut is superficial?"

Casey had the feeling that she simply couldn't bring herself to voice worse fears.

"I'm sure it is, Mother," Eric assured her in a rather washed-out voice. "It just feels like a bad hangover."

"You're ready to return to your room?"

"I think I'll just stay here for now, thanks."

She nodded, unable to leave yet unable to say more. For the first time, Casey felt sorry for her. There was a certain amount of loneliness in not being able to allow your feelings, especially for the person you loved most in the world. Watching this woman struggle with her control, Casey vowed that she would never raise her children that way. Rather than be an example, she was going to be an attack kisser.

"And you, Miss Phillips," the old woman finally said, turning to acknowledge Casey. "I hope you're quite all right."

"Thank you," Casey managed. "Eric saved me from being hauled out that window. That makes things pretty okay."

The sharp eyes sharpened. "Indeed."

"To think—" Casey scowled in Eric's direction "—I might have had to live on a diet of caviar and water. You saved my life, Eric."

Eric's reaction probably would have been a lot different had his mother not been there. As it was, he settled for a pained scowl. He thought the bleeding was slowing down somewhat. The dizziness was abating a little. It was time to reassert control. Releasing his hold on Casey, he slowly rose to his feet.

The queen's hand was out in protective warning before she could stop it. "Are you sure you—?"

Eric's eyes raised to those of his mother and softened. From where she sat, Casey saw a rare communication pass between them. The changing of the guard. For the first time in their relationship, the mother was not the one in control. She would never again hold the same authority.

"I'm not going to run after the gentleman, Mother." Eric smiled, easing himself down onto one of the ruffled pink love seats. "I'll just sit here until Dr. Schmidt shows up. The security people know where to find me."

His mother appeased, Eric turned to where Casey still huddled on the floor.

"Casey," he said gently, holding out a hand. "Come sit."

She gave him her hand, oblivious to the fact that it was still bloody. Now that all the excitement was over, she could feel the reaction set in. She had almost been kidnapped. Whoever had attacked her had certainly bounced her around enthusiastically enough. Everything was beginning to ache from her ribs to her shins. It would be nice, she thought, her eyes still on Eric's as if for the reassurance of that serene blue, when she could climb between the sheets and consign all that had happened to oblivion. It would be nicer if she could fall asleep in Eric's arms, but one look at the queen quelled that idea.

Casey's attempts to stand were a shambles. With Eric's hand for support, she tried to ease off the floor with half his grace. Instead, she ended up right back on her fanny, her knees as useful as antlers on a frog. She tried again, with much the same outcome. Her efforts only resulted in the reappearance of worry in Eric's eyes.

"I think I'm beginning to fall apart," Casey admitted in a very small voice.

He didn't bother to answer. He just stood up, his injury forgotten, and lifted her onto the seat next to him, holding her together with the force of his own control.

"I feel so stupid," she admitted, not noticing that the tears had returned. "You're the one bleeding."

Suddenly there was no one else in the world. "You're the one who was almost kidnapped," Eric said. "You have every right to feel a bit shaky."

"Shaky is one thing," she scowled. "Nonfunctioning is quite another."

He sat forward in his chair, an arm around her and both her hands in one of his. "I'm sorry, Casey. I would have never asked you to help if I'd known there would be any danger to you."

Casey snorted self-righteously. "There's more danger crossing the street in downtown Manhattan. I'll be fine. Although I've totaled another one of Cassandra's dresses." She exhibited the torn and stained teal-blue silk Eric's hands had so recently traveled over.

"I'll protect you from her," he said softly.

Casey felt so secure within his gaze, so safe and content. If only he didn't have to leave her side. She lifted her hand to the blood matted behind his ear. "Are you sure you're okay?" she asked, her eyes liquid with residual fear.

Before Eric could answer, Sandy reappeared, accompanied by the doctor, a short, florid man with half glasses he delighted in peering over. The queen had evidently decided that it would not be appropriate to be seen in her bathrobe, and was now missing from the assemblage.

Right on the tail of the doctor arrived the general, accompanied by his minions and brusque in his approach.

"Your Highness, the guards just notified me. Are you quite all right?"

Eric looked up from where the doctor was peering at his head. "I'll live, General. I don't suppose they caught the fellow."

The general's military posture showed definite signs of sagging. "I'm afraid not. I shall begin a thorough investigation in the morning concerning how he was able to get so close. I promise you, heads will roll."

Eric winced, whether at the doctor's ministrations or the general's choice of words, Casey wasn't sure. She took his hand without considering the company. He didn't seem to mind.

"He was right here in the bedroom?" Sandy was asking Casey in hushed tones, her eyes wide.

"How did the intruder manage to get into the grounds?" Eric was asking the general.

"The alarm system has been sabotaged," the general admitted. "It was just discovered."

"He had his hairy hands on my throat," Casey told Sandy.

"He wore gloves," Eric reminded her with a slight turn of the head.

"Poetic license," she allowed. "He did have a stocking mask. I don't have a feeling his looks would have improved appreciably without it, though."

Sandy grinned. "A real mouth-breather, huh?"

"It's amazing how thugs look the same the world over."

"A stocking mask?" the general asked.

"Support hose," Casey said, nodding. "His nose was within a millimeter of his left ear."

With a little clucking noise, the doctor finally straightened to deliver judgment. "Not a serious injury, Your Highness," he announced. "Although you will certainly feel some discomfort from it." Only Casey was in a position to see Eric's reaction to the obvious. "However, it will need to be sutured. I can do it right here if you'd like."

Eric cast a jaundiced eye around his niece's bedroom. "No offense, Cassandra—" he smiled dryly "—but I doubt sincerely whether this particular shade of pink is conducive to healing. I'll be more than happy to be treated in my own room."

Casey was glad. The only thing that made her sicker than the sight of blood was the sight of needles. The last thing they needed was for her to do a swan dive when the doctor treated Eric.

"You've already done quite a sufficient amount of damage to my room," she countered for the benefit of the doctor and a few guard officers who'd collected behind the general. "I'll never be able to get the disgusting stain off my wall."

"Don't try," he suggested. "Incorporate it into the decor."

"Would you like a sleeping draught?" the doctor asked, and Casey realized he was addressing her. She hadn't heard it put quite that way since her last gothic read. Didn't this country know about tranquilizers?

"No, thank you," she said, as evenly as possible. "A healthy dose of terror always puts me right to sleep."

Eric cast her a sidelong glance as he got to his feet. The doctor and general each took an arm to help him to his room. He shook both of them off.

"Perhaps your friend would stay with you for a while, Cassandra," he suggested, turning earnest eyes on her.

"I'll be fine," she assured him, her gaze not nearly as frigid as the tone of her voice. "As long as the general remembers to turn the alarm back on."

"I'll have a guard on the door," the gentleman assured her.

"Only if James McCormac volunteers," Casey retorted, and dismissed them all.

"So you've come to your senses and decided to come home with me tomorrow," Sandy said a little while later. "Right?"

Seated by the window, Casey gazed sightlessly out over the darkened expanse of back lawn and garden. The moon hadn't made it up yet, so the blackness was inky and unsettling.

"Right?" Sandy prodded from where she lounged on the pink bed.

"Wrong," Casey finally answered. "How could I leave when Eric's putting himself in danger?"

At that, Sandy sat bolt upright. "He's putting *you* in danger, you idiot. That guy didn't climb in here tonight to get decorating tips."

Casey waved her off, her own churning emotions distracting her. "I can't desert him."

"Casey," Sandy insisted, walking up to her. "We've gone way beyond blue eyes and great wardrobe here. You're starring in an Alfred Hitchcock movie, except that nobody's bothered to tell you how it's going to come out."

"As long as I get the handsome prince," Casey muttered half-heartedly.

"Casey..."

Casey turned on her friend, her patience disappearing. "Sandy, I already told you. I'm staying. I know it's a dumb thing to do, but I've done my share of dumb things before."

"Can't argue with you there."

"Then don't argue with me now. And don't run right over to my mother's when you get home and tell her what's going on. It's going to be hard enough to believe coming from me."

Sandy surrendered with a shrug. "You're the one paying for this shindig. I just wish I felt better about the whole thing."

Casey smiled as she got to her feet, weariness dragging at her. "I know. I'll try and be as logical as I can, Sandy. It's just that..."

"I know." Sandy smiled fatalistically. "I just wish I could stay and help."

"I'll be okay. I think I'd like to get some sleep now."

Sandy's silent reaction left Casey in no doubt as to her friend's opinion. But the goodbyes were given in hugs just the same. Then Casey was alone with memories of the kidnapping attempt and the unhappy realization that she'd caused Eric's injury.

After taking just enough time to soak out the first consequences of her struggle, Casey slipped out of the ruined garments and into one of Cassandra's less outrageous nightgowns. The sheets on the great mahogany bed were crisp and cool, and the eiderdown quilt as comforting as soft slippers on a cold night. Around her the palace sighed, its ancient walls whispering of the generations of emotion that had battered at it, the floors creaking beneath remembered weight. Casey lay in the luxurious bed and stared at another scrolled ceiling, unable for the first time in her life to get to sleep.

Soon the fear set in, the terror that hadn't had time to be fully realized while she'd battled her assailant and then struggled to maintain her composure before all those people. Her stomach churned and her chest grew hollow. Her hands began to shake until she clenched them in the soft quilt to keep them still. Her eyes stung with unshed tears.

Then the anger rose. Someone had actually tried to snatch her! Worse than that, he'd tried his best to make a soup bowl out of Eric's head. Lord, to remember her panic when she'd seen Eric go limp. When she'd called to him and he hadn't moved.

She'd really been afraid he was dead. The only reason she'd struggled so hard at first was to try to get to him. She hadn't really understood that the man was trying to take off with her. She just knew that Eric was hurt and some bozo in nylon and black leather was trying to keep her away from him.

And then they'd let him get away. Casey wanted to get her hands on that bastard. She wanted to pay him back for the blood she'd washed off her hands. And she wanted to pay the queen back because she'd let her relationship with her son wane to the point where she couldn't even hold him when he was hurt. She'd never even touched him.

Finally the frustration took over. Just what did she think she was doing here playing games with a country's future, doing Barbie Does Moritania while real hoodlums with real weapons were threatening its royalty? Was this the way it always was for Eric? Was he so calm because he was used to it? Maybe they got these kinds of threats all the time.

Well, she didn't. She was just a lousy secretary from Brooklyn with aspirations to someday graduate from law school and represent small claims if she was lucky. Nowhere in those dreams was there room for designer dresses and tiaras and customs about when you could be touched and talked to and people bowing and flinching at the sight of you for fear you'd do something to hurt them.

If she were going to be really honest about the whole thing, where did it say she had any right to somebody like Eric? She'd been telling herself that all along and hadn't believed it. She was born to marry a bus driver and have a few children to send off to school and ballet lessons. Her grandmother had been the last person she'd ever known who had even cared whether it was appropriate to wear white gloves or a hat to a function. Instead of attending high tea at the Savoy, Casey had grown up dining on hot dogs and soda at Shea Stadium.

But oh, Lord, how she wanted to have a chance. There had been such a life-giving incandescence in Eric's eyes tonight when he'd confessed that he wanted her. Such a heart-stopping hunger.

It didn't matter. She was going to be on that flight tomorrow with Sandy. She didn't belong here. Nobody really wanted her here. They hadn't even offered to clean up the mess once they'd escorted Eric off to be patched up. One little set-to and you really found out who mattered. She was going home where she meant something.

When Casey heard the door click open, she didn't move. She didn't have to. She knew just who it was, and her pragmatic resolutions flew right out the window. The hall light spilled over her, silhouetting her approaching guest. Then he closed the door, and the soft darkness enveloped them both once again.

When he reached the side of the bed, he stopped short. "I thought you'd be asleep."

Casey smiled ruefully. "I was just lying here thinking how I wasted a perfectly good vase earlier this evening. This is when I should be pitching things against the wall."

She sat up and scooted over, offering Eric a space to sit. He sat and leaned over to flip on the lone surviving table lamp. The pool of light surrounded them, glittering softly off the shards of glass clustered against the far wall as if they were paved gems.

Eric turned to take Casey's hands in his, his eyes tortured. "All you really all right?" he asked. "I wanted to be sure."

Casey sighed, furious that she couldn't better protect her determination from those sweet blue eyes. If only his forehead didn't crease just that way when he worried about her, or the crow's-feet appear when he smiled. If only he hadn't told her he was falling in love with her.

"It has been kind of an emotional day," she finally acknowledged, her gaze briefly straying to where her hands lay cradled within the warm strength of his.

"It has that." He nodded, and damned if those crow's-feet didn't show up. And that crease. Casey was losing ground fast.

"Maybe Sandy's right," Eric said quietly. "Maybe you should go home tomorrow with her."

Casey's eyes shot up. "How did you know about that?"

His smile widened. "There's not a whole lot that goes on around here that I don't know about."

Casey scowled. "Wonderful. I suppose you also know that she thinks I'm overdosing myself on make-believe."

"That's not why I think you should go. If anything happened to you, I don't know if I could survive it, Casey. I wanted to kill that man tonight."

"So did I," she admitted with a rueful grin. "Especially after he tried to dent your head." At the thought, she lifted tentative fingers to the area that had been hurt. His hair was freshly washed and combed, and there was no visible indication that the good doctor had been at him. "How is the royal concussion, by the way?"

He chuckled. Casey felt that sweet languor begin to steal through her limbs. "Probably just enough of a nuisance that I'll have to bring the royal aspirin to the functions tomorrow."

Casey's eyes sought his in outraged indignation. "Functions?" she demanded. "In my neighborhood, if you get a crack like that you spend the next day calling out for pizza and playing couch potato."

Eric's eyebrows lifted. "Possibly. But then, if Brooklyn had a finance minister he would not have the luxury to play any kind of potato. Especially if there were a big conference going on."

"Don't bet on it."

"I've put you through a lot," he admitted, his thumb drawing lazy patterns across her palm. "I just can't ask you to do any more."

Casey's eyes widened. Eric's were serious. He wanted her to go home. A great emptiness threatened to open within her. "You can't do that. Who's going to pretend they're Cassandra?"

He shook his head. "I'll worry about that."

"And if I say no?" She tried not to think about the fact that she had made the same decision no more than milliseconds before he'd walked into the room.

Still he wouldn't back down. "Then I'll deport you. You'll be on that flight tomorrow, Casey, so I know you're safe."

"And what about you?" she demanded, the tears threatening again. "How will I know *you're* safe?"

He kissed her hand with a gentle wistfulness that tore at her. "As soon as Cassandra is recovered, I'll be on a plane to Brooklyn to visit."

"And what about the meantime?" she asked. "Just how do you think you're going to manage without me?"

His smile was intimate. "I'll muddle through. It will give me something to occupy my time until I see you again."

Why was she so sure that if she left tomorrow she was never going to see him again? Was it just the fact that she could never envision Prince Eric Karl Phillip Marie von Lieberhaven walking into the drab little rooms on her street? Or was it the fact that when she left, all those ladies with their fine jewels and worldly demeanors would still be here to distract him?

Before she gave herself time to consider it, Casey turned her hand so that it could caress his face.

"How am I supposed to say goodbye to you tomorrow with all those people around?" she asked, her voice strained with the decision she'd just made.

Eric's expression softened, and he reached out to entwine her hair in his hand. "You could say goodbye tonight."

"Like we were going to do before?" she smiled. "Is your head up to it?"

His answering smile was so deliciously suggestive that it alone ignited the slow fire in Casey's belly. "My head doesn't have to be up to it," he assured her, his hand dipping around to trace the plunging neckline of Casey's ivory silk gown. "Especially if the rest of me is."

Casey rubbed her thumb over the rasp of his beard, thinking that this was the roughest she'd ever felt it. Thinking that she'd have to tell him that she liked it that way. And then praying she'd get another chance. If only the servants would understand and help her.

"In that case," she whispered, the beguiling smile on her lips drawing him closer, "let's part friends."

Nine

"**O**h, my God..."

Casey's fingers slowed at their task, the buttons of Eric's crisp linen shirt only half-undone. She had demanded the privilege, never having known the satisfaction of undressing a man. As Eric nibbled at the sweet flesh at her neck, she had managed to undo two or three of the tricky devils, made all the more difficult because the wildfire ignited by the touch of his lips set her hands to an unbearable trembling. His skin was so warm beneath his clothes, his muscles so tight and lean. And the golden hair that curled across his chest so delicious to the touch.

"What's the matter?" Eric mumbled against her neck, his words tickling.

Casey giggled, trying her best to draw in a stabilizing breath. He had pulled her down next to him on the bed, nestled atop those cloud-soft comforters, his hands at once taking command of her. She felt as if she was melting, her body reduced to a glowing, molten light stoked by the heat of his kiss and the hunger of his hands. She had never known her body could feel like that. Had never anticipated such agonizing delight at another's touch. Practical Casey Phillips was completely at Eric's mercy.

"You have a hairy chest," she managed with a smile, rubbing against him like a cat. Even through the silk of her gown, the feeling thrilled her breasts to a taut attention. She smiled and stretched again, surprised that she could elicit a moan from Eric by the action. "You never told me."

"You seem surprised," he murmured gruffly, his fingers twined in her hair, his lips teasing the base of her throat.

"I usually notice...that kind of thing sooner," she tried to explain. The buttons were all free, and she took to slipping his shirt off over his tight shoulders and hair-roughened arms. "But you never get casual enough that I can get a look at your chest."

Eric chuckled, deep in his throat where it vibrated against Casey. "Isn't this casual?"

She placed her hands flat against his belly, running up over the ridges of his ribs, the clean lines of his chest. He was so hard, so angular. The feel of him against her incited more fireworks—more of the molten fire that was turning her insides into water. "You have a beautiful chest," she murmured, dipping her mouth to it, tasting the throb of his heart. "You should show it off more."

Eric pulled her lips back to his, his eyes hot and possessive. "And you, my lovely Casey, have the most beautiful breasts—" he smiled, savoring the dark flavors of her as he discovered with his hand how her breasts anticipated him "—and the most lovely eyes, the most enticing mouth..." His fingers swept her nipples, dancing over the silk and lace and skin like the tongues of a spreading fire. His lips trailed after, along the edges of her gown, the moist tracks of his kisses sending her gasping.

Casey's head came back, her hands up to span the tight expanse of his back. Eric's head was just over her breast, the soft light glinting off his sleek brown hair, glowing off the tanned planes of his back. He bent to take a breast in his mouth, suckling against the slick silk. The hot possession of his mouth was agonizing. Sliding his other hand down along the contours of Casey's body, he explored her slightly concave belly, the ridge of her pelvis, the firm length of her thigh.

Casey was paralyzed. Nothing could have prepared her for the effects of his touch, nothing could have predicted this spiraling exhilaration. Eric brushed the filmy material away from her breast and just as easily slipped out of his remaining clothes. Casey watched with breathless wonder, intoxicated by the play of ivory light along his skin, desperate to know the hard, lean feel of him against her.

When he lay next to her, Casey felt him full and hard along her and her heart skidded. She held on to him, not even able to explore the delicious mysteries of his body as she wanted to. His mouth descended again and tore away her reason. All she could do was answer the urgent need Eric unleashed in her.

His hand moved up against her and her hips rose, pushing full against the flat of his hand. She ached for him, for the touch of him inside her to quell the fierce molten fire he had ignited. Her breathing was ragged against him, her heart racing. When Casey felt the gentle exploration of his fingers as they slipped beneath the tumbled skirt of her gown, she moaned, anticipating him, opening to him so that he could purge that agony.

"Oh, Casey," he gasped against her when his hand reached the dark recesses of her. "I've wanted you since the moment I saw you."

She could hardly draw breath to answer. His fingers plumbed her, dipping and stroking until she couldn't hold still against him. The agony was fierce, uncontrolled, a pain of yearning that only he could assuage. When he lifted his head to her, she managed a wild smile, her heart stolen by the tousled, unshaven face above her.

Casey didn't feel Eric ease up her gown. He bent to reclaim her mouth, and she became lost in the taste of him, the pressure of his hand against her leg. Wrapping her arms around him, she welcomed him to her.

The stab of pain didn't surprise her. It became lost within the explosion of sensation he ignited when he thrust into her. The firestorm broke over her, searing her, blinding her, bringing cries of release to her throat. Eric shielded them with his mouth, his own urgent groans mingling with hers. Casey felt her body begin to rock against him, arching against the fire that consumed it, molding with the overwhelming strength of Eric's. When he shuddered against her, his arms closing around her as if afraid to let her go, she held on to him. Felt him spill himself in her, knew the fulfillment of love.

Silence returned to the old room. Outside, the breeze rustled at the window and skittered through the trees. The floor of the room spoke again, and the walls answered. On the high mahogany bed, Casey and Eric lay intertwined, lost in the glow of contentment.

He lifted a hand to brush the hair away from her forehead. "You didn't tell me," he said with a little awe.

"What?" she asked with a smile. "That I was a virgin? Serves you right for not showing me your chest."

She surprised a smile from him. "Why?"

"Why didn't you show me your chest?" she countered, her own fingers splayed across his belly. "I don't know. Maybe you didn't trust me. Which was good judgment, actually. One look at it and I would have done this a lot sooner. Possibly right in the middle of that formal banquet the other night."

Eric scowled, running a finger down her nose. "You know what I mean."

Nestling a little closer, Casey sighed. "Did you ever hear about the little boy who didn't talk till he was three?"

"Pardon?"

"Not a peep, all that time. Then one day at breakfast he suddenly says, 'Mom, the toaster's on fire.' When she asked him later why he hadn't talked before then, he just shrugged and said, 'Because I didn't have anything worthwhile to say before now.'"

Eric chuckled, enfolding her in his arms. "You do have the most unique view of life, my lovely Casey."

"Just pragmatic." Casey smiled. She'd never really thought about her "state," as Sandy would have called it. It was just something that had never come up. She had always known in the back of her mind that there would be a time when this was right. Even two days ago she hadn't known that this would be it. Now, lying against the warm comfort of Eric's chest, she was glad she had waited.

"Pragmatic women don't push princes into lily ponds," he retorted. "Or let themselves be talked into parading themselves as a princess just to save the economy of a small country."

"They do if they were raised on the movies," she argued. "You've just been overdosed on duty all your life, my Prince. It tends to warp your sense of fun."

"Not totally," he said. "I know for a fact that what we just did was fun."

"A move in the right direction."

"It doesn't change what's going to happen tomorrow."

Casey nodded, hoping he didn't see the new light in her eyes. "I have no intentions of changing the plans."

Eric's hold tightened a little. "How would you feel about coming back when it's all over?"

"How would you explain me?" she asked, for she'd never had the nerve to ask before.

"As a long-lost cousin who just happened to show up."

"Right."

"I'm coming to get you, Casey," Eric warned, his hand absently stroking the satiny length of her hair where it tumbled over his chest. "I want you to know that."

Casey had to close her eyes against the hope that blossomed in her chest. The hope that he really would brave the streets of Brooklyn to find her. But in the last couple of hours she'd changed her mind about all that and decided not to give him the chance to back out, making the point moot anyway.

Eric didn't have a good morning. After slipping back into his own room just before dawn, he'd lain awake remembering the life-giving feeling of Casey in his arms, the worth of the gift she'd given him. Then he'd begun his day by issuing the orders that would send her away from him.

She didn't come down to breakfast. Eric sat alone at the great table, thinking how cold the room suddenly was, how bereft of the life her quick wit and irreverent manner brought. When Werner showed up for work, all Eric could think of was that Casey hadn't been able to believe he was guilty. She had given Eric the gift of seeing the people around him in a new light, and now he had to face them without it. The world he had inhabited because of station and duty suddenly seemed a less challenging one without Casey to share it.

"You've been seen in the pantry on more than one occasion," Eric said to Werner as the two of them sat in his study, the early-morning light honey-yellow on the warm wood. Eric kept waiting for Casey to walk into the room.

"Why, yes, Your Highness." Werner nodded, perplexed. "Is there some difficulty? I only thought that since the status of the palace is on alert, my services would be better utilized if I took less time for meals."

"Where were you last night, Werner?"

The older man frowned, leaning forward, his hands on his knees. "Have I done something to displease Your Highness?"

Eric eyed the pencil he was tapping against his desk. "We seem to be missing the stock of Beluga caviar that was kept for the princess. The local shop is also out. You have been seen at the pantry."

For a moment, Werner smiled. "Oh, sir, I can't tolerate the stuff. I've been eating the salmon, maybe some herring. Never the caviar."

"But the princess does eat the caviar, Werner. Caviar from that pantry."

The room fell silent. When Eric looked up, it was to see the hurt disbelief in his employee's eyes. Werner couldn't even seem to form the words to protest, so deep was the insult.

"I just had to ask, Werner," he said, feeling better. "Someone is getting that stuff to the princess, and right from under our noses."

Werner's astonishment could not have been manufactured. "A spy in the palace?"

"A kidnapper in the palace, I think. I'd like to quietly ask all the kitchen staff if they've seen anything unusual."

Now Werner could afford a weak smile. "Like my eating out of the pantry."

Eric allowed his own smile when he nodded. "If you would start now, I can help after the luncheon. I hate wasting time on that thing, but I'm afraid I have no choice. I have to make Cassandra's excuses."

Werner's eyebrows lifted again. "Miss Phillips won't be going with you?"

"She's not here, Werner. I sent her back home this morning."

"But she's down in the kitchens, Your Highness."

Eric's head came up, his eyes sharpening. "That's impossible. Her flight was scheduled to leave Zurich half an hour ago."

Werner shrugged. "I don't know, Your Highness. I just saw her on my way up here. She and Helga were concocting some kind of pastry."

Eric didn't say another word as he got to his feet and stalked out of the office.

It had been quite a while since he'd been down to the kitchens, since he'd snitched treats from the old cooks as a child. The room didn't seem quite so cavernous as it had when he'd been young. The walls still gleamed their immaculate white, and the flagstone floor shone spotlessly.

Activity in the great room stopped when Eric walked through the door. He didn't even see the ten or so people bow. Nor did he see the grins of anticipation on every one of their faces.

"Just what do you think you're doing?" he demanded, coming to an abrupt halt by a gleaming steel countertop.

Her nose smudged with flour, Casey looked up at him without noticeable discomfort. "Showing Helga how to make soda bread," she smiled, giving her dough another sound thump. Standing alongside, Helga didn't look quite so unconcerned. She dipped a quick curtsy, then kept her eyes firmly on Casey's work. "At least I think I am," Casey scolded. "I'm doing this all by memory."

"I told you to go home today," Eric persisted, his eyes as stormy as the North Sea.

Casey raised innocent eyes. "Now how can I do that?" she asked. "I have a luncheon to attend with the conference delegates and a cocktail reception this evening. And we still haven't found my caviar yet. Werner didn't take it, did he?"

Eric's breath escaped in a frustrated sigh. "Casey..."

Assuming an elaborate pose, arms akimbo, Casey mimicked his tone of voice. "Eric..."

"You can't stay. You could be in danger."

"You could be in danger, too," she countered. "I don't see you on the next flight from Zurich."

"You could lose your job."

She flashed a challenging grin. "You could lose your policies."

Eric turned on all the servants, his brows knit. "I suppose you all helped her."

Another round of bows and curtsies. "Yes, Your Highness."

"Fine," he snapped. "You can keep her in line. I give up."

"Excuse me, Your Highness," Maria spoke up from the door. "The seamstress is here for the fitting on your dress."

"And you," Eric said accusingly, whipping around. "I expected more sense from you, Maria."

"Yes, Your Highness."

"Don't go blaming Maria," Casey objected. "I strong-armed her."

Maria's placid expression belied the statement, but there was nothing to be done about it. Eric turned on Casey again.

"I could have you arrested, you know."

"Arrest your own niece?" she asked, eyes wide. "What for?"

"If you please, Your Highness," Maria said diffidently. "The fitting is important. We only have so much time."

"Casey," Eric tried one last time in a reasonable tone, "there really isn't any reason for you to stay."

"Yes, there is," she argued with an infuriating smile. "I decided that I can help you step off that throne a little more often. See how the real world lives. Who knows? Maybe it'll make you a better prince."

"I'm a finance minister," he shot back. "I know perfectly well how the real world lives. I control the economy of this country."

"Big deal," she retorted. "Have you ever tried to get a bus transfer in Manhattan? Find your luggage at La-Guardia? You have a hundred people to take care of you. You can't get a good taste of reality living like that. You can't even have any fun. It is my duty to change all that, Your Highness. I even found you a pair of jeans to wear." With a powdery hand, she pulled her long apron aside to exhibit a well-worn pair of denims and a cotton blouse from her wardrobe. "Just like mine."

"We'll talk about it later," Eric snapped, knowing perfectly well that he'd let her stay. "Now, go with Maria. You only have three days to get your dress fitted."

"Four," Casey automatically countered. "The coronation's Sunday."

He allowed a sly smile. "But the wedding is Saturday."

Casey's face fell. "What?"

"Your wedding to Rudolph. By law, you have to be married to rule. The wedding's Saturday and the coronation's Sunday."

She gaped. "You didn't tell me."

"Still want to stay?"

For a long moment Casey stared at him, then around at the staff, who had carefully gone back to their tasks. Finally she faced Eric again. "Do you promise you won't keep from rescuing Cassandra in time just to get even with me?"

It was rather disconcerting to see her sly smile mirrored on his face in answer.

The luncheon was held in the formal dining room, patrolled by Simmons and his cadre of servants and organized by Werner's accomplished hand. By the time Casey showed up to fulfill her duties, the guests were already seated and chattering among themselves. When she entered, they all stood and paid obeisance.

"Nice to see you all," she said, privately amused at the arched eyebrows. She'd refused Maria's help today, and satisfied herself with a simple French braid for her hair, and an unornamented Adolfo suit of raw emerald silk and matching pumps.

"A hat," Maria had very nearly wailed, the suggested implement in her fluttering hands. "The princess would never attend a luncheon without a hat and her gloves."

"Well, it's about time she did," Casey informed her, and headed for the door.

Eric appeared now to guide her in to eat, his own expression a study in bemused control

"Asserting your independence?" he asked under his breath.

"You're lucky I got the whole-wheat flour out of my hair," she smiled sweetly.

He got back at her by seating her directly across from the little woman from the other night. An ambassador's wife, it turned out, Countess Brader was not one to let a few days interrupt a train of thought. As Eric settled himself in next to Casey, the woman plopped down on her chair, returned to her half-finished roll and waved it in the general direction of Casey.

"Did you think about what I said the other evening, Your Highness?" she asked. "I was sure that once you did you would come to the only logical conclusion concerning the abysmal surrender to the crass Americans this country has arranged."

Bracing herself against a surge of irrational fury at this pompous, bigoted woman, Casey smiled with glacial control. Alongside her, Eric turned a warning eye on her.

"Indeed I have, Countess Brader," she announced, and quite a few heads turned. Most of the people here had been at the banquet. "I can well understand the pain you feel about having to converse in such a dismal language. Unfortunately it is the law, passed by my dear late father, so I am not at liberty to alter his intents. At least until I am on the throne. Therefore, since I do not wish to cause you any discomfort, nor do I wish to dishonor the memory of my father, I have come to a decision."

The woman's eyes brightened with cautious triumph. Casey smiled back.

"You do not have to speak in English. As a matter of fact, you do not have to speak at all."

The woman's face crumpled. "But, Your Highness—"

Casey raised a hand, seemingly oblivious to the delighted grins of the rest of her guests. "No, Countess Brader, it would not be fair to you. From this moment, I think it would be better if you never speak in my presence. That would suffice to satisfy both our problems, I think."

As Casey turned to begin her salad, she had to admit that she had gotten quite a kick out of the power she had just wielded. She'd never had the wherewithal to make a person she didn't like shut up, and to see that woman red-faced and silent was enough to make up for all the discomfort of charading as Cassandra these last few days.

She didn't think she'd done a bad job of carrying it off, either. Turning to take a sidelong glance at Eric, she found her hopes confirmed. His eyes were dutifully on his meal, but it was all he could do to keep a straight face. Others on down the table were having less luck. Casey could hear amazed chuckles ripple through the room, then the buzz of surprised conversation. Within moments the atmosphere of the room was just as it should have been for a state luncheon. At least the kind of state luncheon Casey would want to attend.

Eric spent at least the first fifteen minutes of his meal trying to maintain his composure. All he could think about was how glad he was that Casey had outwitted him and stayed off that flight. He wouldn't have wanted to miss this scene for all the world. Until now, no one in either Countess Brader's country or his, including her precise, pleasant little husband, had been able to put a curb on her sharp tongue. To see that woman reduced to frustrated silence was a satisfaction that he would enjoy for years to come.

And to think that the secretary from Brooklyn had been the one to finally discover the diplomatic words to shut her up. He couldn't believe it. The girl was brilliant. She was outrageous. And, he realized anew as he stole a look over at her in her sleekly simple attire, she was more beautiful than Cassandra could ever hope to be.

"Nobody looks you in the face," she complained later as they walked back down the long halls from the reception area.

Startled from his own reverie, Eric looked over at her. "What?"

"The diplomats," Casey elaborated with a frustrated little sigh. "They haven't once gotten their eyes higher than the level of my collarbone. Doesn't that drive you nuts?"

His hands in his pockets as he walked, Eric gave a little shrug. "I never really thought about it. It's the way they are."

"But if they won't look you in the eye, how do you know whether they're lying to you?"

He chuckled. "My dear Casey, in government you simply assume that *everyone* is lying to you and go from there."

Casey shot him an outraged look. "That's silly. You should make a law or something to change that."

"Don't forget," he advised, "you're dealing from centuries of tradition. At one time your head couldn't even be level with mine."

"Yeah, I know," she nodded offhandedly. "I saw *The King and I*."

Eric smiled, hooking his arm around hers as they strolled the long corridors of the first floor. The hallway was wide, the floor a checkerboard tile. Alcoves were

spaced along the walls with old Greek and Roman statu-
ary, anonymous torsos that had long since lost limbs and
faces to the ravages of time. It had been a place he'd enjoyed in his childhood, conjuring ghosts of dead centuries and popping out from shadows to scare the servants.

"Have you ever thought of getting used to the customs
instead of just arguing about them?" he asked with a
mischievous smile.

"Not when they don't make sense." Casey shook her
head. "Can't touch a princess, for heaven's sake. That's
one of the most archaic things I've ever heard of."

"Could you get used to them for me?"

That stopped her, the echo of her clicking footsteps
dying along the corridor. "That's like my asking if you'd
mind having the neighborhood over when you show up
for dinner at my house. That's the custom there, you
know. Especially if a native daughter makes it to twenty-
five without prospect of marriage."

Eric laughed. "I'd be delighted to meet the neighborhood. What would I wear?"

Casey smiled back. "It's a dead cinch that you wouldn't
get a block in black tie and tails."

"Then I'll wear some jeans," he said. "Just for you.
Will you allow people to wait on you—just for me?"

"I am," she argued.

"Now—" he nodded "—because it fits your role. What
about later when we're married and you have to keep
house and grace those social functions?"

Casey had been all set to turn on down the hallway for
the Rose Room, where the dowager queen awaited them.
Eric's words first stopped her, then swung her on her
heels.

"Did I ever tell you that this was my playground when
I was a child?" he asked offhandedly, looking around

with fond eyes. "I didn't have the luxury of a neighborhood park I could attend or a mother who had the time
for me. So I played in among the statues. They became my
friends." He paused a moment as the ghosts returned,
both happy and sad. "I'm glad I won't have the pressure
of ruling. My children will be able to lead a more normal
life."

Casey finally found most of her voice. "I thought you
weren't getting married."

"No." He shook his head. "I said that until now I
hadn't had the time to get married. I guess what I should
have said was that I hadn't found the woman I wanted to
marry."

When he turned his gaze on her, Casey felt the impact
of his decision. His eyes were bright, alive, almost merry.
His whole being radiated anticipation. He really meant
what he'd said.

Trying to remember how to breathe and stand up at the
same time, Casey said the only thing that came to a mind
unable to come to grips with his words. "Eric, I think
your plane just overshot the runway."

Ten

Eric laughed, taking Casey into his arms. "It never fails to amaze me how you cut to the quick of an issue."

Casey was glad he was holding on to her. She had serious doubts about whether she could stand. His smile, even more than his surprise words, had robbed her of any strength. As for her brain, it had gone straight into meltdown. She couldn't pull a lucid thought from anywhere to dispute or agree with anything Eric said. Except one.

"You're nuts!"

"I believe we established that a long time ago." He smiled, his delight in her growing. "This time I think my insanity could save me."

"But Eric," she protested instinctively, "I have no business being married to a prince!"

"Why, just because you have more sense and style than half the people who were in that room today?"

"When somebody asked me how I thought Schmidt did in Germany, I told them I didn't know they played baseball in Germany!"

"A technicality."

"I told the Minister of the Exchequer how nice I thought it was that England provided clergy for old grocery clerks!"

"He thought you were cute."

"Oh. Is that what 'I beg your pardon' means?"

"Do you love me?"

That stopped her cold. Casey looked up into those azure eyes and knew she was lost. All she could think of was how Eric's arms felt more like home than anything in her life ever had. How he had supported and goaded and cherished her until she almost felt as if she belonged here.

Long ago, when she was a daydreaming teenager, she had anticipated what it would feel like to love a man. She hadn't had any idea what that really meant. A heady anguish was building in her chest, the pain of hope, of possibility. Eric had just threatened to make dreams come true she'd never even known she'd had.

"Do you love me?" he asked again, his voice just as gentle.

"Love?" She tried to bluff. "That's not love. I always blush and stammer like a high school sophomore when a handsome man with a continental accent touches me. Or it could be all the pink in that room. I wake up and think I'm in a Barbara Cartland novel. And the outfits—you can't count out the outfits. Dinner jackets were invented to drive women into frenzies. You can't count on anything I do when I'm in the same room as a dinner jacket—"

"Casey..."

"Yes." She finally wound down with a stunned little shake of her head. "I love you. I have from the first moment I laid eyes on you."

"Then what is the problem?"

"Eric," she objected, finally finding the hurdles, "if I weren't playing the role of your eminent niece, I couldn't even touch you. I couldn't talk to you without being asked. Doesn't that say something about how appropriate our marriage would be?"

Just saying that word ignited a new ache in Casey's chest. She pulled away, walking over to one of the statues. It was an armor-clad torso, its navel just level with her eyes, the long years having smoothed the marble into a mere suggestion of anatomy. Casey saw it and thought of the tight power of Eric's sleek muscles, the delicious taste of his skin. She flushed and turned away again.

"I don't mind," he said from behind her. "Why should you?"

"Marriage," she moaned, closing her eyes. "Boy, you do move at a brisk pace, don't you? Just the other day we were talking affairs. And if you'll remember correctly, I was having trouble with *that*."

"You weren't having any trouble last night." He smiled with just a touch of roguish charm. His troubles earned him a scowl. "I've been alone for thirty-five years, Casey. I realized it when I met you. I don't see any reason to wait anymore when I know I love you."

"But you're a prince!" she retorted, turning toward him. The fact that they'd known each other such a short time no longer seemed relevant.

"And if your ancestor had been handy when the crown prince disappeared back in 1870, you might have been in line for the throne instead of Cassandra. You have as much right to be here as I do. Probably more." He grinned rakishly. "You have at least one *legitimate* royal line in you."

Casey couldn't quite bring herself to look at him. "You really didn't have a playground to go to?"

Eric smiled, pulling her to him. "I really didn't. I had the stables, of course, and the nursery. But I never had a set of swings."

"My kids are going to have swings," she said. "Every kid deserves the chance to get stitches by the time he's four."

"I agree." Eric nodded, easing her closer to him. "And a pony."

"And a baseball team to belong to."

"We'll start a league."

"What about piano lessons?"

"We have several. Mozart played on one of them, come to think of it."

"I can't marry you."

"Why not? We agree on how to raise children."

"What about your mother?" she asked, closing her eyes against his chest. She felt so content in his arms. "What would she say?"

"She has no say in how we raise our children."

"Eric..."

"Besides, she loves the piano."

"But would she like Brooklyn accents in the ballroom and baseball on the TV?"

"Why don't we go find out?" Eric challenged, holding her back to get a good look at her. Casey's eyes were wide, glittering with the maelstrom of emotions he'd unleashed. He brushed a thumb across the soft edges of her lips, remembering their taste with new yearning. He wasn't about to give her the chance to back out.

"I know just what she'll say," Casey argued with a futile shake of her head. "She'll look way down at me and say, 'In-deed.' Just as if I'd told her there was a mouse in the throne room."

Eric found himself laughing. Casey had once again painted a scathingly accurate picture. It was just what his mother would do. But he wasn't in the least worried, he had the feeling that Casey was more than a match for his mother.

"Come on," he coaxed, slipping an arm through hers and guiding her down a side hall. "We'll go by way of the nursery."

"Your other favorite spot as a kid."

He grinned. "Kind of a foregone conclusion, wouldn't you say? I really wish our children could enjoy it like I did. Of course, we'll move elsewhere."

"Children." She sighed with another shake of the head. Repetition of pertinent words sometimes helped clear an overloaded brain. It wasn't doing much for her this time.

The hallway they took ended in a short flight of stairs and then another hallway. Just as airy, this one was decorated with paintings. Portraits, the subjects decked out in a progressive series of costumes from the time when men had first charted the oceans. Casey scanned the paintings in passing, wondering if these were family or friends or maybe enemies hung in a back hall to remind the ruling government what they were on alert against. Maybe some of them had been related somehow. Noting the patch of powdered wig on one rather dandified gentleman, Casey almost hoped not. He would be kind of hard to explain back on the block.

Suddenly she stopped. "What is this, the Corridor of the Butlers? What's his picture doing up there?"

Eric came to a halt beside her, his eyes following hers. "Whose picture?"

"My great-great-grandfather."

Eric's eyes were still on the stiff features of the young man, the large dark eyes and the bristling blond mustache, the formal morning suit and the pearl stickpin in the cravat. Eric's eyes slowly swept around to her.

"Who's your great-great-grandfather?"

Casey pointed toward the eyes that watched timelessly over her head. "Him. I have an old picture of him from New York. That's him, even down to that funny scar on his face."

"The Heidelberg scar."

She turned then, to see Eric stunned for a second time. His eyes were also on the portrait, but they weren't examining. They were introspective, calculating.

"What's the Heidelberg scar?" she asked.

"From dueling," he allowed, still not facing her. "It was quite popular. Are you sure this is your great-great-grandfather?" he demanded. "What was his name?"

"Mmm, let's see," she mused, counting back generations on her fingers. "He would have been . . ."

"Berthold," Eric said for her.

Casey turned, surprised. "Yeah. How did you know?"

"Berthold Phillips," he said, his eyes widening as much in humor as surprise. Casey saw a true delight take hold in him.

Casey scowled at him. "How did you know? You sure as heck couldn't pull that one out of the air."

"I didn't have to." He grinned excitedly. He'd just dropped a kiss on her forehead when he suddenly backed away, his hands up in the air, his lips curling with wry delight. "Oh, excuse me, Your Highness. I exceeded my privilege in touching you without your permission."

"Eric, knock it off." Casey scowled. "What are you talking about? How did you know his name?"

"Casey," he said, grinning broadly, "the gentleman in this picture was the Crown Prince Berthold *Phillip* Karl Eric von Lieberhaven, the rightful heir to the Moritanian throne. He disappeared in the year 1870, and my ancestor took over."

Full realization took her a moment. "You mean *I'm—*?"

"The legitimate heir to the throne. You are a crown princess, my lovely secretary."

"In-deed," the queen said when they told her sometime later. Neither Casey nor Eric could face each other for fear they'd laugh.

"And what was your great-great-grandmother's name?" the old woman asked, her eyebrows still raised in stiff disbelief.

"Oh, gosh." Casey sighed, thinking back. Names weren't a long suit in the Phillips family. "Kurtz? Is that the one? I remember hearing that her first name was Genevieve."

Mother and son exchanged enlightened looks.

"So that's where he went." Eric grinned. "After all these years, we finally know." Turning back to Casey, he continued. "Berthold disappeared during a border dispute between Moritania and Austria. There was a faction within the aristocracy that sided with Austria. The Kurtzes were such a family."

"So old Berthold ran off with one of the bad guys?"

Eric shrugged. "It would seem so. The marriage was probably forbidden by his family and hers, and they ran off rather than give in."

Casey couldn't manage much more than a raised eyebrow. "Indeed." She turned to Eric as if the queen weren't seated just across from her. "Does this mean we really don't have to ask your mother..."

Eric's laughter echoed around the small room. "It means we probably have to get permission from *your* mother in order to get married."

To her credit, the queen picked up on that right away. "Eric," she snapped, her eyes swiveling frostily to Casey. "Explain yourself."

"Quite simple, Mother." He grinned, enjoying himself much more than Casey was. "I plan to set all your longstanding fears about my bachelorhood to rest. Casey and I are going to be married."

Casey and the queen objected in unison, Casey because Eric was making rash assumptions and the queen because he was making those assumptions about Casey. The queen won out.

"But she's—"

"The rightful heir to our throne, dear." He smiled. "If she pressed it, she might be able to dump the whole lot of us right out in the snow."

"Be serious," Casey objected. "That couldn't happen. Could it?"

Eric shook his head. "Not really. But I can't wait to threaten Cassandra with it. She'll go mad. Speaking of which, I have to make a few calls on that very sore subject. Would you ladies excuse me?"

Dropping a kiss on Casey's forehead, he strolled on out of the room, oblivious to her rather desperate eyes. The door closed, and the room fell into silence. Gathering her courage, Casey turned to the queen. The diamond-hard gaze that met her was enough to make her flinch.

"You may pour tea," the old woman announced, her posture, if possible, even more regal. She wasn't going to let a little change of plans throw her off. After all, in her mind it wasn't *her* family that was illegitimate. "We shall discuss this rather startling news."

"Startling's a good word," Casey nodded halfheartedly as she got to her feet. She missed the glint of calculating worry in the queen's eyes.

Almost two hours later, Casey found Eric back in his study.

"You left me alone in the lion's den," she accused, plopping down into one of the leather armchairs and kicking her shoes off.

"And I wager you did beautifully," he said, smiling.

"Well, she didn't bite me. Then again, she didn't offer to come to Brooklyn to meet my mother, either." Rubbing at a set of sore feet, Casey tilted her head to the side. "Actually, it isn't that important. Seems to me we're getting way ahead of ourselves here."

Eric's head was still bent over some paperwork he was doing. "Ahead of ourselves?"

"Yes. As in 'the bride-to-be hasn't said yes yet.'"

He looked up then to see the sly mischief in her eyes. "She will," he assured her with a maddeningly complacent smile, and returned to his work.

She matched his complacency. "What's it worth to you?"

"Me?" he countered easily. "Nothing. You? Now that's a different story."

"Why?"

Eric didn't say anything. He just held up a suspiciously familiar-looking passport.

"That's kidnapping!"

He snatched the little book away just in time. "That's such an ugly word. We in government prefer... protective custody."

Casey's eyes narrowed. "And what are you protecting me from?"

"Your own misconceptions. I was wrong to want to send you away. You belong here with me, and I'm afraid I'll just have to keep a watchful eye on you until you realize that."

Casey was going to protest, possibly even go after the passport again, when his next words brought her up short.

"Well, actually Werner will for the next day or two."

Casey straightened. "Werner? Why?"

Eric smiled, and Casey found herself caught in the throes of an overriding desire to throw him on the carpet and reexplore that hair on his chest.

"After the reception tonight, I'm going to be... out of touch for the next day or so."

Something clicked when he said that. Something Casey didn't like. Eric was looking suspiciously pleased with himself, and the last thing he'd said he was going to do was check up on Cassandra.

"Explain 'out of touch,'" she suggested carefully.

"I'm taking your suggestion to get to know how people live a little better," he announced. "I'm going out into the real world."

That was when Casey realized something else. Eric was dressed all wrong. He didn't have his suit on, nor his tie. He didn't even have on one of those hand-tailored linen shirts she'd grown so fond of. He was clad in a dark gray Aran-knit sweater. Casey's eyes narrowed even more. Her heart rate also took a quantum leap. How could anyone possibly look so good?

"See?" he said, pushing his chair out. "I even found those jeans you got for me."

Find them he did indeed. At any other time or place Casey would have been mortified to find herself staring in such a southerly direction at a man as he got to his feet. It wasn't, after all, very polite. But she truly couldn't help herself. Eric, who had virtually redefined elegance for her, should not have looked quite so nice in casual clothes. After all, he had been born and bred to fine tailoring and expensive materials.

Not true. The jeans hugged his lean frame as if they had been painted on, outlining any number of powerful muscle groups with breathtaking effect. Combined with the sweater, the outfit made him look twice as handsome, twice as sexy. Casey found herself shaking her head, her palms already slick.

"What's wrong?" he asked. "Don't I look right?"

She couldn't help a rueful laugh. "It's not fair."

"What isn't?"

Her grin broadened. "Give me an hour or so and I'll show you."

Eric's answering smile was broad. "So you think I'll blend right in."

"Nope."

"But you said..."

"I said you looked great. And I meant every word. The problem is you still don't look like anything but a prince."

Moving around to her, he slid his arms around her waist. "And you, of course, have a suggestion."

Casey did her best to ignore the rising temperature in the room. Eric's denim-clad thighs were insinuating themselves against her silk-clad ones, and it was the most interesting sensation. Tantalizing...

"Where are you going?" she asked abruptly, trying to ignore the tongues of flame snaking their way up her thighs.

Eric's smile was enigmatic and enticing. "Out."

She would have no part of it. "Out where?"

"I'm not about to tell you. You'll just try and tag along."

She tried to make her shrug nonchalant. "Walk out like that and you'll be spotted in a flash."

Eric was doing his best to keep his mind on the subject. He'd made a mistake when he'd taken hold of her. His body couldn't care less for Cassandra's problems and the duties of the country when it got this close to Casey. It simply wanted to satisfy that age-old need that kept men and women having the next generation of men and women.

The whisper of Casey's silk-clad legs against his was setting off warning bells, the soft fragrance of her hair filling his nostrils and driving all logical thought before it. He wanted to bury his face in its honey-hued depths, exploring the dark treasures of her delectable body with his hands. The fierce ache for her flared hard in him, almost taking his breath. For the first time in his life he very nearly shut the door on his obligations and spent his day exploring the delights of afternoon lovemaking on an Oriental carpet.

"Eric?"

"What?"

Casey smiled, sure of her power over him, an instinct that needed no practice to surface. It didn't hurt that the evidence of his arousal was so obvious, either.

She rubbed against him just a little. "You were going to tell me where you were going."

Just in time, Eric reeled his senses back into the safety zone. "No, I wasn't," he disagreed with a grin, dropping a kiss on her very pliable lips. "Witch."

Casey's voice remained soft. "Does this have anything to do with Cassandra?"

"It has to do with us."

Her eyebrow lifted. "I think I'm going to enjoy this."

The corners of his lips curled. "The sooner Cassandra's back on the throne, the sooner we can uncover your existence and arrange a proper wedding."

"I still haven't said yes."

His next kiss was not as fleeting. "You will."

"I'll say yes faster if you tell me what's going on."

"You don't give up easily, do you?" Eric had to smile at the determined look on her face. It would probably be easier in the long run to let her know now. "Simple. I got in touch with the shop owner, who said that the same man comes in for the caviar each day. He gets there right about five. I'm just going to see where he goes."

"Why can't somebody else do it?"

At that, Eric's face shadowed over a little. "Let's just say I have some questions that I need answered for myself. Don't worry. When I find out what I need to know, I'll call in for help."

A strange chill chased down Casey's spine. "How could General Mueller agree to such a thing?"

Eric's smile didn't quite touch his eyes. "Princes outrank generals."

She didn't feel any better. There was a whole lot of something Eric wasn't telling her, and she had the feeling that it would put him in danger.

"How about if I come along?"

"No. I'll be back in time for dinner."

She scowled. "That doesn't mean anything. They hold dinner for you. We could still be sitting there at four tomorrow...."

"Casey. I'll be fine. Let me have my moment of excitement."

She deliberately eased back into his embrace. "I thought I was your moment of excitement."

Eric would have none of it. "Go on and get dressed for the reception. I'll escort you before I go."

She made a face. "'And the condemned man ate a hearty meal.'"

For the first time since she'd been playing this little game of Cinderella goes to Moritania, Casey snapped at Maria. Then she snapped at Werner and Simmons. It had all begun with her decision to stay. Somehow, just that action had changed her participation in the game from a passive to an active role. If they wanted her around, they were at least going to have to let her have her two cents' worth.

She turned a bit surly when Eric insisted on playing detective without her right after asking her to marry him. Casey still hadn't figured out just how she was going to break the news of the wedding to her mother, and now he was putting the whole thing in jeopardy.

The worst part was the effect his proposal had had on her emotional stability. From the moment she had realized he was serious, an explosion had ripped through her. A tremor that could surely have been felt on the Richter scale. Within the period of—what, days?—she had progressed from lusting from afar to yearning from close up to the frustration of futile hope to the shock of certainty. She had, quite literally, fallen in love at first sight, and amazingly, unbelievably, so had he.

It wasn't supposed to happen this way. That only happened in fairy tales and movies. Her mother had known her father for five years before she'd "known," as she put it. How could Casey know in a week? How could Eric? But, inexplicably, she did.

And how had she managed to outsmart reality by meeting and falling in love with Eric in the first place? It couldn't be real. It just couldn't. And yet every time she looked at him, she fell even harder. Every time he reached out to touch her as if to make sure she really existed, she felt his power over her grow. She melted before the intensity of his eyes and ached for the touch of his skin. No matter if he'd been a cabdriver who'd picked her up on the way to the airport, she would have loved this handsome, vital man.

But, and this was the final twist that fueled even more emotional quakes, he was a prince. The kind who lived in a palace and played polo just for fun. The unreality of it only fueled even more Casey's unconscious decision to make her own place in the palace while she had the chance.

So when Maria had come to inform her that it was unseemly for her to sit sipping coffee with the cooks while dressed for a formal occasion, Casey had informed her that since she was willing to show up on time for the functions they needed her to attend, the least they could do was to let her pass her time her way in the meantime. Especially since it wasn't bothering anybody to begin with.

Then Werner and Simmons approached to apologize for a few glitches in the proceedings, and she had told them both to chill out a little.

"What are they going to do if the flowers don't get here for their reception, overthrow the throne?" she demanded. Swinging on her heel, Casey shook her head in exasperation. "Everybody takes things to damn seriously around here."

"Certainly not you," Eric said, smiling tolerantly as he approached.

Casey turned to see him in yet another three-piece suit, this one gray with a scarlet silk tie. All of her irritations fled as if just the sight of him were soothing water where one bathed one's fevered brow. Eric did have the knack for settling her feet a little more surely back on earth and putting her priorities back in order. After all, what could be a problem if she could be with him?

"How long are you going to stay?" she asked, her voice unaccountably husky. Casey was thinking suggestive thoughts again, which inevitably led to the devious ones. He did look so delectable in gray.

"Just an hour or so. That's all that's expected of us."

She nodded and took his arm, and he turned with her into the main ballroom.

The doors slid open to the glittering assembly of the rich and famous, all suspended in the mirrors along the walls. The chandeliers sparkled and the late sunlight slanted in, gilding the room. The chatter echoed down the marbled floors and back again from the great portrait that hung at the far end of the hall. When the doors opened, everyone stopped.

Casey ran a nervous hand down the side of her mauve sheath dress, thinking how if Eric had his way she was going to have to get used to this. Then she decided that Eric couldn't possibly be serious after all. He couldn't really mean that she could fit in here.

They were announced, and Eric let go of her arm. The crowd turned to her and bowed, only the sporadic tinkling of ice against glass betraying the fact that they'd already started the party.

Casey scowled. "Eric, this is ridiculous," she said under her breath.

He turned without speaking.

"I'm getting real tired of this bowing garbage," she elaborated. "I've seen more bald spots than a toupee salesman!"

His abrupt chuckle brought some heads up. Casey's next announcement brought up the rest, most with startled expressions on their faces.

"Oh, for heaven's sakes, let's dispense with this," she announced, trying to catch the attention of even one pair of eyes. "I'm not going to banish anybody just because they didn't bow. It's a waste of time."

"But Your Highness..." one voice said automatically.

"Look me in the eye when you speak to me," she snapped. "Nobody looks me in the eye. How can I possibly know what you're thinking?"

Their first reaction was to bow acceptance. Half the room hesitated halfway down and straightened with some embarrassment.

"Thank you." Casey nodded briskly. "This is the way I'll conduct business from now on. It'll keep me from getting a swollen head."

Before she moved into the room, Casey turned on a very amused Eric. "Let Cassandra straighten out *that* when she gets home," she said, grinning wickedly.

Eric was still chuckling over Casey's actions two hours later as he finished dressing for his little journey. Lord, wasn't she just what this place needed? She was right. Cassandra would have a seizure when she got back and no one thought to bow when she stalked past. He couldn't wait to see it.

First, though, he had to get her back. He knew Casey was right. He shouldn't be playing amateur spy, but until some things were settled he saw no other way. Once he discovered where they were keeping Cassandra, he could gracefully back away and let someone else handle it, just as he'd planned to do all along. Then he'd come back and thoroughly ravish the young lady he'd just asked to marry him.

He was just buckling his belt when he heard the knock on his door. His attention still on the task, he walked over and opened the door. Casey never gave him the chance to protest.

"This is just what I expected from your room." She smiled brightly as she kissed him with determination on her way past. "All dark wood and teal blues. Very masculine. Very sexy."

"You're supposed to be at the reception," he accused, one look at her denim-clad figure enough to stir objection. "And just where do you think you're going?"

"With you," she replied, stuffing the cap she'd borrowed from Simmons, and was saving for the end of negotiations, into her back pocket. "You need an operative familiar in street work."

"I need to put a guard on you," he retorted. "You can't come."

"You can't go like that," Casey assured him with a practiced eye. Walking up to him, she unbuttoned the two top buttons of the cotton shirt he'd opted for, arranging the edges just so that the hair that curled at the base of his neck was visible. "*Very* sexy," she said. Then she mussed the shirt a little to negate the meticulous care the servants took of his clothes.

Eric couldn't help reaching out to gather her into his arms. "You think that will make the difference?" he asked skeptically, his mind more on the deliciously soft feel of her against him.

"No. But this will." And then reaching up with her hand, Casey proceeded to completely rumple his hair. It looked so good that she found herself wrapping her arms around his neck.

Eric's eyes immediately yielded, a languid heat rising from their depths. He pulled her closer and dipped down to claim her lips, thinking how honey-sweet they were. How eagerly she responded to him, opening her lips to him and curling her fingers in the hair at the base of his neck.

Eric groaned, the need flaring sharp and insistent. Casey's breasts pressed full and were against his chest, the nipples taut. He could feel the sudden staccato of her heart against him, counterpoint to his own. His hand strayed to it, his fingers cupping the swell of her breast and searching upward to claim the button-hard pleasure of her nipple. Stretching, she eased herself more fully into his grasp. The passion he had controlled for so long in deference to his position threatened to overwhelm him with just the satiny feel of Casey's hair against his fingers, the soft mewling sounds he tore from her throat, the bold evidence of her arousal in his grasp.

Just as he was about to lose all control and lift her onto the heavy canopied bed, Eric pulled away, his breathing still ragged.

"No." He shook his head at the desire in her eyes. "I have to go."

Casey's expression crumbled, her eyes still filled with the fierce desire Eric had unleashed in her. He held his hand against her breast as if unable to pull completely away from her. She felt the tingling contact of him spread throughout her and knew she didn't want him to leave.

"I've never said this before," she managed, her voice husky, "but if you go now, just know that I fully intend to encourage you to finish this later. I ... think I'm addicted to you."

Eric's smile was intimate and soft, his eyes intense. "I'll hold you to that, my lovely Casey. And then I'll have the time to make love to you thoroughly and tenderly, just as you deserve. We'll make it a joint addiction." His smile grew slightly rakish. "Now what is that in your pocket?"

Chuckling at Eric's deliberate choice of words, Casey reached for the cap and set it square on his head. It brought the picture to an attractive completion. With the cap on, he looked more like a tourist than a prince of anything.

Stepping back, she considered her handiwork. "Sunglasses and a camera would help. Do you have cash?"

Eric pulled out his money clip with a grin.

"Where's your wallet?"

He shook his head. "I usually don't carry one."

"Are you kidding? Where do you carry your credit ... ?" Reason kicked in. "Never mind. I don't suppose you need identification, either, do you?"

His smile said it all.

"Maybe I wouldn't mind living with you so much after all. When do we leave?"

"I leave now. Alone. I'm not a total idiot, Casey. Believe it or not, when I fulfilled military training, I took a bit of espionage."

"You still haven't ever grocery-shopped for yourself. Besides, if you leave me here, I'll just continue to embroil myself in one scandal after another until you return." Casey's eyes grew lazy. "You might not even have a throne to come back to after I get finished with it."

Eric stared at her, thinking how beguiling she looked with her beribboned, full-flowing hair and how infuriating her determination was. "You would, wouldn't you?"

It was Casey's turn to smile.

"Maybe I *am* crazy." He sighed in resignation, taking her by the hand and pulling her to him. "Because I think I am going to do it."

Eleven

"I didn't know you wore glasses."

"Only when it suits me." Casey pushed the offending lenses up on her nose and took another look up and down the street. She and Eric were seated at a sidewalk café just next door to the gourmet shop that sold Cassandra's caviar. After convincing the shop owner to point out the caviar buyer for them, they had taken seats beneath the colorful umbrellas to observe. Their conventional tourist attire and Casey's exaggerated Brooklyn accent made them all but invisible to the average Moritanian eye.

"I still can't believe no one recognizes us," Eric offered as he took a drink of his beer.

"People see what they expect," Casey told him. "We're the last thing they'd look for in a sovereign. Take pictures everywhere we go, and remember to let me do the talking. Another preconceived notion about tourists."

Eric grinned and raised the camera to snap a shot of her biting into a pastry. "Only if you'll promise to stay out of the way when we finally get where we're going. That's my area of expertise."

Casey nodded, pushing the wide-brimmed straw hat back a bit on her forehead. With her hair knotted up under the hat, it was virtually impossible to see the telltale locks, and her face looked noticeably different with the owlish glasses she wore for distances.

"So," she said after letting the delectable chocolate-and-sugar confection dissolve to her satisfaction. "What do you think of your country from the other side?"

Eric flashed a smug smile. "Pretty well-run place, if you ask me."

Casey giggled. "The romantic out-of-the-way spot for the tourist who wants something different from his vacation."

"Or the investor who wants something different for his money."

Eric's eye strayed to a long-legged Slavic beauty who strolled by with a matching set of Afghans on leash. The street was lively with foot traffic, and the specialty shops were decorated in traditional Bavarian motifs, painted gingerbread and leaded windows. A white-gloved officer stood on a box at the intersection directing traffic—and watching the blonde with the dogs—and a flower vendor paced the corner behind his bright wagon. Overhead, great puffy clouds skirted the mountaintops and chased lengthening shadows along the narrow streets. If they hadn't been here to follow a possible kidnapper, it might have been an idyllic afternoon for two lovers to spend in the small Alpine community. Soon the cowbells would begin to clatter as the herds moved to their food, and the citizens emptied the streets for their homes.

"He's here."

Casey's head snapped around. "I thought you were watching the blonde over there."

A fleeting grin touched Eric's lips, his eyes resolutely on the wide window of the gourmet shop. "A good sovereign is an observant one. Let's go."

Casey's eyes followed around to get a quick impression of a slightly scruffy young man in fatigue jacket and jeans. Nothing, really, to set him apart from any of the other wandering youth in Europe.

"Eric, wait," she warned as he got to his feet, intent on the young man who was just nodding thanks over his package.

Eric turned to her. "C'mon, Casey. We don't want to lose him."

"We also don't want to draw attention to ourselves," she retorted quietly. "Which we will do if we don't pay."

Eric had the grace to offer a rueful smile. But when he pulled a ten-pound note out to drop on the table, Casey shook her head.

"This country should be bankrupt," she groused, exchanging the ten for a one and standing up after him.

That was when she bowed to Eric's area of expertise. She was going to walk right after the young man. Eric held her back until their prey had rounded the corner.

"Give him a little room to move," he suggested. "He won't be so suspicious."

"Hey, yeah." She nodded enthusiastically. "That's the way they always do it on TV."

Taking her by the arm, Eric turned down Wilhelminstrasse and around to the little side street, Kirkenstrasse, where the cathedral sat. The crowds thinned out a little bit here, since there weren't as many shops or businesses and no services were scheduled. It was more of a residential

street, with old gabled homes sharing space with more
modern apartment buildings. At the center of the block,
St. Cyril's jutted in soaring gray stone. Just like anywhere else in the ancient cities of Europe, the modern auto
accommodated itself to streets laid for horses by parking
halfway up on the sidewalks. A walk along the street was
a bit claustrophobic.

Casey immediately spotted the young man half a block
up as he walked resolutely along past the old Gothic
church. He held the bag to him as if protecting treasure,
his attention alternately on his way and the street around
him. He was obviously anticipating unwanted company
along his trek.

"I wonder where he's going," Casey mused.

"Nothing down this way but..." Eric's voice trailed off
a moment, his own eyes scanning briefly around as if to
reacquaint himself with his capital. "Of course."

When he wasn't forthcoming with an explanation,
Casey nudged him. "Of course what?"

"The train station. It's another block down."

Casey nodded, a strange exhilaration blooming in her
chest. The anticipation of the hunt, the thrill of adventure. For a midlevel secretary from New York, she had
had more than her share of adventure for a lifetime, yet
here she was on another escapade that made her feel like
a movie heroine. First she wondered just when she was
going to wake up. Then she had what she considered to be
the good grace to wonder whether having a good time at
Cassandra's expense was quite proper.

"Casey."

Casey turned to see that Eric's attention was still resolutely on their target. "Yes?"

His eyes never shifted. "I'm having a hell of a good
time."

"Chasing a kidnapper?"

"We're going to have to do this again sometime."

She couldn't help but giggle. "I'm not sure Cassandra will be so anxious to cooperate just so we can play cops and robbers."

"Not just that," Eric retorted with a quick shake of his head. "This is probably the first time I've been out without the entourage. Even in school I had servants and attendants and spies to let my family know whether I was behaving myself. This is . . . well, liberating."

Casey grinned as his eyes strayed briefly to her. "It is, isn't it? If we could only throw in a passionate interlude on a white rug in front of a fireplace where Rolph can't find us, it would be damn near perfect."

"Don't even suggest it," he begged, his eyes alight. "I might be sorely tempted to let this guy go."

The train station had been built with the kind of ostentation that made one think of Roman temples. This was a temple to transportation, with crowds gathering at regular intervals to worship progress, and trains clattering and wheezing like great behemoths captured to entertain the populace.

Casey and Eric followed their young gentleman straight through the great vaulted lobby and out the back door to the platform. The young man was heading for the waiting train.

"He bought his ticket ahead of time," Casey marveled. "Good planning."

Letting a respectable number of people come between them, Eric and Casey followed the young man onto the train just as the conductor pulled in the steps. The cars were about half-full with tourists and commuters. The young man took his seat at the very back of the car so that he could keep an eye on everyone else. Taking hold of

Casey's hand, Eric walked blithely past and sat in a seat farther up.

Settling into a window seat, Casey turned to him. "So how do we keep an eye on him?"

"He can't go far," Eric retorted easily. "At least until the train stops." The station was already sliding slowly past the window as they picked up speed. "Do you have a compact?"

"A what?"

He motioned with his fingers. "Powder. Makeup."

Casey scowled. "I'm not Doris Day, Eric. The first time I wore powder in ten years was when Maria made me. Why?"

He scowled right back. "The mirror."

Reaching into her purse, she couldn't help a wicked grin. "And if I hadn't come along, how were you going to keep an eye on him? Or do *you* have a compact?"

Eric didn't dignify that with an answer. His eyebrows did raise a bit when Casey handed him a small mirror in a plastic case.

"I do brush my hair on occasion," she retorted before he could get a word out.

"Then do it when we pull into the next town."

"*Guten Tag*, your tickets please."

Both Eric and Casey turned to the congenial voice at their elbows.

"Tickets," Casey breathed in surprise.

Eric turned to her, then back to the conductor. "What?"

"We forgot."

"You don't have a ticket?" the gentleman asked. Gray-haired and short, like the classic image of a brewmaster with a ruddy nose and sparkling little eyes, the man didn't seem terribly upset.

Eric leaned close to Casey. "What do we do now?" he asked quietly, his gaze slipping out the window to where the narrow valley was speeding past in a pleasant blur.

Casey motioned to the old man. "Buy them."

That seemed interesting news to Eric. "We can do that?"

Casey's eyes rolled. "Oh, for heaven's sake. Excuse him," she said to the conductor. "He's been in the monastery a little too long."

"For what stop?" the little man asked, bringing out his ticket book.

"For what stop?" Eric echoed.

Casey couldn't come up with any ideas. "It's *your* country."

"Not anymore." Eric smiled at her. "We've just crossed into Switzerland. Moritania has a special provision that allows free travel between the two countries."

"What stop, *Bitte*?" the conductor prodded patiently.

"Lucerne," Eric replied. "I've always wanted to see it."

"Lucerne," the little man repeated, nodding.

"I don't want to go there." Casey whined in her best Brooklynese. "We've been going to all the cities you want to go to, Howard. I want to go someplace different. Conductor, is there anyplace that's on the way that's not so big?"

"Oh, *ja*. There is a festival in Holman this week, and quite a few lovely *hofbrauhausen* in Thusis or Haustock. Almost any town along the way is lovely."

Casey made the pretense of thinking. "We-e-e-ll. Maybe we can go to those on our way back to Italy. What I'd really like to find is a plastic cuckoo clock with a silhouette of Elvis on it. Don't they make clocks somewhere in Switzerland?"

The poor little man didn't know quite what to think. Eric didn't give him the chance. "Lucerne will be fine, thank you. How much?"

The little man returned hesitantly to his book. "For the two of you, eighty-four francs."

Eric looked up from his money. "That much?" he retorted sincerely. "Why, that's outrageous."

Casey just rolled her eyes and kept silent.

A moment later, Eric cast a jaundiced eye in her direction. "Howard?"

She graced him with her best hundred-watt smile. "Do you like it?"

He smiled right back. "I love it. Mildred."

The scenery they passed was, as promised, lovely. Breathtaking. The tracks followed a river through the valley, the water glinting sharp cobalt and magenta with the setting sun. The mountains thrust up beyond, sudden and majestic, their crowns still mantled in the pale blue of late snow. The farms they passed were neat and tidy, the fields carefully tended and the animals robust. A perfect pastoral scene. Casey found it difficult to believe that such prosperous, ongoing rural life could exist in such peaceful fashion in the same small country with great cities like Zurich and Geneva.

Alongside her, Eric's attention was alternately on the man who sat six rows behind them and Casey's profile as she looked out the window. The longer he knew her, the more Eric wondered how he could have so completely mistaken her for Cassandra that first afternoon. She was as different from Cassandra as a brightly feathered bird from a cat. Casey was all light and laughter and common sense, scattering her offhand compassion before her like a rainbow from a prism. The sun had been caught in her, and it shimmered from the depths of those soft hazel eyes.

And standing within their gaze he suddenly felt like a man freed after years in his own prison.

For the first time he knew that his secrets would be safe with someone. That his insecurities would be attended and his accomplishments celebrated in such a way that their intangible worth would be greater than any riches he had ever known. True, he still had to convince her to say yes, but as he sat alongside her, away from the fishbowl of the palace, he couldn't believe that she would ever say no. He loved her far too much to consider a life without her.

When Eric took hold of her hand, Casey turned bright eyes on him. He knew she was enjoying herself as much as he. Now all he had to do was convince her that she could enjoy herself as much as his princess.

The train passed through three towns before their quarry made his move to get off. Eric spotted it as they were pulling into Holman, the little village all decked out for its summer wine festival.

"This is the spot," he muttered, his eye on the scrap of glass in Casey's hand.

She turned surprised eyes on him. "How do you know? We haven't stopped."

"He's getting nervous. Picking the bag up and putting it down. He hasn't done that before. And this is the first time he's been interested in what's outside."

"What do we do?" Casey asked, trying to decipher the same signals Eric seemed to see.

"We get off first. Doesn't that look like an interesting little town?"

"Oh, Howard," she immediately whined, picking up the cue. "Look at all the people. I don't want to go all the way to Lucerne tonight. I'll bet we could stay here. Let's go to their fair. Maybe they have the clocks here."

"Mildred . . ."

"Well, I'm getting off. If you don't want to, fine."

Pulling her purse over her shoulder, Casey stood just as the train came to a shuddering stop. Grumbling about women and whims and trying to find available rooms on the spur of the moment, Eric clambered to his feet and followed her down the aisle. Sure enough, their friend followed right behind.

Tucked alongside a narrow lake in the high Alps, Holman was alive with celebration. Even as the sun set and the sky lost its crisp edge, crowds of people wandered streets lit up by Japanese lanterns and decorated with fresh flowers and bunting. The buildings were all immaculately whitewashed, every window boasting a flower box overflowing with geraniums. The untidy swell of voices spilled from open beer halls, where the revelers were already sampling local fare and music. Stepping onto the platform, Eric and Casey were greeted by a young woman in Tyrolean attire who handed out flowers and smiles. The picture was enchanting.

Casey wished she could stay here and show Eric what life was like in the real world. But, as they stood basking in the young woman's smile, their quarry was heading down the main street. They had no choice but to follow. Eric took hold of Casey's hand and began to weave his way through the crowd.

They would have been successful if it hadn't been for the ebullient partyer who wanted to share his bonhomie. Just as the suspect was turning down one of the streets halfway up a winding hill, a man stepped from one of the open doors that spilled music and took Eric by the hand, then by the shoulder. Casey couldn't understand his German, but she did understand the universal body language. Here was a man who felt happy with the world and wanted to know that everybody else was. He offered some of his beer, then some companionship inside the noble establishment and then, when Eric struggled to get away, a rebuke for wasting such a wonderful festival.

By the time they broke free, their prey was gone. Hurrying up to the cross street, they turned, only to find an even denser crowd. Eric strained to see something familiar. He dragged Casey on through the crowd, then up and around several side streets. He even asked some of the partyers if they'd seen the young man. They struck out at every turn.

"What do we do now?" Casey asked, their failure gnawing at her. They'd been so close.

Eric took one more look around to see that nothing had changed. His shoulders slumped and he shrugged. "Try again tomorrow, I guess. He has to go back."

"Maybe we can get a microtransmitter or something," Casey offered.

Eric grimaced. "That only happens in movies, Casey. We have to rely on footwork."

"But what do we do tonight?" she asked.

"Get back on that train."

She shook her head. "Not tonight, we don't. There isn't another train going our way until morning. I heard the conductor tell one of the passengers."

Eric made another sweep. "Then I guess we stay here."

It turned out that their friend the happy partyer was the one who guided them to lodgings for the night. After exhausting all his luck at finding a place to stay on his own, Eric had opted to rest at a little *hofbrauhaus*. Their friend had chosen the same one to move on to.

Apologizing for their earlier rudeness, Eric and Casey found themselves sitting with him and sharing a drink. And that was when he gave them the good news. It just so happened that his cousin Gerta had lost a customer that very evening in the finest of the rooms she kept over the restaurant. If they'd like, he'd introduce them as his very dear friends—after they'd all had a drink together, that is.

Four drinks later, Eric and Casey finally climbed the steps to a cottage on the slope above a little restaurant. Of typical chalet construction, the cottage had a balcony that overlooked the celebration and the lake below, and two complete little apartments for guests. Frau Voelker showed them into the one with the fireplace.

Casey stepped over the threshold and came to an abrupt halt. "Oh, my."

Eric stopped next to her. "A rug."

"A *white* rug." She nodded with the beginnings of a smile. "Right in front of the fireplace."

"I suppose we'll just have to settle for this place."

She nodded again, chills of anticipation already racing through her. "I suppose."

After Eric paid Frau Voelker in cash, the little woman didn't mind in the least bringing the magnum of champagne he requested up from the restaurant. She didn't even mind adding a few hors d'oeuvres. The festival was a good time to sample the local food, she reminded the couple gently. Eric assured her that they would. Later. She smiled and backed out the door.

The apartment consisted of one small sitting area and a bedroom, both filled with heavy old furniture. The walls were whitewashed and the fireplace was stone. Casey immediately fell in love with it.

"Well," she mused, looking around, "it's not the palace...."

Eric slipped his arms around her waist and pulled her against him. "We also don't have to worry about Werner interrupting us, or Rolph, or another intruder...."

"Enough said," she murmured, rubbing her cheek against the crisp cotton of his shirt. "Just what did you have in mind for that champagne?"

Eric flipped her hat off and sailed it across to a chair. "It's to be sacrificed," he said wickedly.

Casey looked up at him, her heart already beginning its erratic acceleration. "Sacrificed."

He nodded very slowly, his hot blue eyes boring into her with relentless intensity. "I plan to offer it up in the hopes that I can talk you into marrying me."

"Planning on getting me drunk?"

His attitude was all innocence. "Never. It is merely a—"

"Bribe."

"Refreshment. Our negotiations could, well, become...heated."

As Eric spoke, he reached up to unpin her hair, pulling it down to cascade over his hands. He ran his fingers through its satiny lengths, igniting fresh shivers along Casey's spine. She couldn't seem to breathe correctly, and her heart was pounding.

"And what about poor Cassandra while we're... arguing?" she asked, her eyes ensnared within the sorcery of his.

Eric smiled, and the message of his smile shot through her like hot, living fire. "She has caviar. We have more important things to discuss."

His hands had strayed from her hair, making slow sweeps along the curve of her spine and the gentle swell of her hips. Where his hands traveled, her skin sang, the music seeping into her very core until she felt her entire body thrumming with the special song of his touch.

It was as if her body was a stranger to her, it responded with such frightening intensity to Eric. Casey had never felt that white-hot explosion from just the dance of fingertips against her throat, never known the sudden keen lightning in her belly that flickered throughout her limbs with only his glance. When Eric bent to take her lips, she went liquid and rigid at once, burning to hurry his touch, terrified of the pleasures he was unleashing. She had always been terrified of what she couldn't control, and there was no controlling the firestorm this man was unleashing in her.

"How 'bout that champagne?" she stammered, straightening abruptly.

Eric let his hands rest at the small of her back where the skin was so soft and intimate beneath the material of her blouse, where nerve endings sent rippling messages down Casey's legs. She tried to pull from his grasp and couldn't. Her legs had lost the will to leave.

Eric's smile contained his full power. "I thought I'd like to see you in the firelight first."

Casey started. His words had sent the lightning through her again.

"Casey." His voice was soft. "Look at me."

She had no choice.

"What are you afraid of?"

Trembling before the onslaught to her senses, she was afraid she was going to cry. "I . . . I don't know. It's just so much. . . . It scares me to feel this good."

His smile turned to a low chuckle, brimming with comprehension. Casey could feel his need for her, the steely strength of him alongside her. But his hands were patient, his temper gentle.

Instead of answering right away, Eric gathered her to him once more and recaptured her mouth. His lips were so sweet, like the water from a spring. His beard chafed her cheek with delicious effect. Casey could taste the smoky flavor of alcohol and smell the tang of his after-shave. He eased her lips open to fully explore the dark pleasures of her mouth, and she sank into his embrace.

Just the communion of his mouth, the hungry plundering of his tongue, sapped Casey's resistance. Her blood rang in her ears and her knees trembled with the effort to stay upright. The winds took the fire in her and spread it.

"I need you, Casey," he whispered into her ear, his tongue flickering against the soft shell and igniting shudders of pleasure. "I've never needed anyone like this before. Tell me you're not afraid of me."

Casey's hands clutched at the steely contours of his back. Her chest heaved with the exertion of control, the panic that couldn't be told quite so easily from exhilaration anymore. She squeezed her eyes shut against the spell of his, but she could feel that piercing blue right through to her core.

"No, Eric," she managed, her face against his chest where she could feel his heart and the strength of him around her. "I'm afraid of me. I've never let myself go like this before... before you, anyway."

"Doesn't that tell you something?"

"Yeah. It tells me that you cast spells. I'm not normal around you."

Gently Eric lifted her face to him, and she saw the full scope of her power over him. "Maybe you're just beginning to realize what normal is. I love you. Tell me you love me."

Casey couldn't manage it. His words compelled tears, tears that lodged in her throat and stung her eyes. She clung even tighter to him.

Eric wouldn't be dissuaded. He returned to claim her mouth, exploring it with a thoroughness that left Casey moaning against him. Then he let his lips trail to her throat, his touch unleashing showers of sparks that settled in her breasts and brought her nipples to attention.

"Tell me you love me," he repeated.

"I love you...." She couldn't think past the heat of his touch, the intimate play of his hand along her back. Then his lips discovered the soft hollow of her throat and his hand roved upward toward her breasts.

"Tell me you'll marry me."

"Eric..."

His fingers rasped against her blouse, teasing her breasts with fleeting contact. His fingers circled her nipple and then swept outward again. Again she moaned. Eric's tongue was drawing designs of fire at the base of her throat, and Casey's head was thrown back to better receive it.

"You'll marry me."

"All right! All right, I'll marry you.... Oh, that feels so wonderful."

"You won't be afraid?"

She brought her own hand around to seek out the hair that curled at the base of his throat. When she found it, she let her fingers luxuriate in it, thinking that she had never known how delicious the texture could feel. How enticing. Casey wanted to stretch against it like a cat.

"Terrified," she finally admitted with a hesitant little smile. "But I don't think I care. I want you, too."

Taking her face in his hands, Eric brought her hesitations to an end. "Well, my beautiful Casey," he murmured, "you have me."

Easing Casey back onto the soft white rug, Eric settled himself over her. The wait was difficult for him, but he knew that this time was for Casey. This time he wanted her to understand what he wanted to be able to give her, what lovemaking would be between them. When he undressed her, he did it slowly, his eyes devouring the soft, sleek lines of her body as he uncovered it layer by layer, as his fingers sought to come closer to the core that fueled the hot light in her half-open eyes.

She was softened with her arousal, her lips puffy with his attentions, her breasts straining against the lacy bra that contained them.

Eric ran his hand up the firm lines of her calves, her thighs, only her panties keeping him from that mysterious silken flower that beckoned. He swept trembling fingers along her hips, her belly, the line of her ribs, aching to taste the muskiness of her as he excited her. She reached up to unbutton his shirt, but he restrained her. That would come later. Later when he'd thoroughly maddened her and he saw that entreaty for release in her eyes.

Casey writhed before his touch. Eric pinned her beneath his weight, his mouth commanding hers, his tongue tasting her lips, her throat, sketching shivers along her shoulders and down her collarbone. His hands finally savoring her breasts, he rubbed the tender nipples with thumb and forefinger until lightning leaped to her toes.

The fire spread; the tremors began to build. Casey arched against Eric's touch, only to find that his mouth had replaced his hand, his tongue and teeth drawing out new moans as they teased and tasted and tempted her breast through the filmy material. She ached to feel him bare against her, to feel his passion-heated skin alongside her, to touch him. To open to him and ride the crest together with him. The fire crackled in the fireplace and seared her with his touch.

When Eric slid his hand in past the material at her hips, Casey writhed against him, desperate for his fingers against that sweet, hot ache he'd ignited. So warm against her, they dipped into her, fled, then dipped in again. She was whimpering now, desperate, her hands clutching at him. She swept his hips, his legs, the straining power of him where it met her thigh. Her eyes open and barely seeing, she rushed to free him of his clothes.

His hands never seemed to leave her, but suddenly he rested above her, naked, his lean body golden in the firelight. Casey let her hands discover the hard muscles, the whorls of golden hair on his chest that tapered toward his flat belly. She devoured his body with her hands, much as he had hers with his eyes, taking it to her as if she might never have the chance to have it again. The sight of his arousal awed her. The smile in his eyes captured her.

Casey felt his hand on her thigh, an invitation and a command, and she opened to him, letting him ease the panties free and away. Then the bra, so that her breasts were free for him. He tasted her skin, then, the soft mound of her belly as it curved toward her navel. He reclaimed her breasts with his tongue and let his fingers dance against the satin petals he sought to enter. Casey eased tentative fingers to bring him to her and he groaned, a sound that maddened her even more.

She couldn't bear the agony any longer. Her body was now screaming for release. She had to have him in her, feel him drive into her and fill her with himself.

"Eric, please..." She strained against him, rocking against the exquisite pain of his touch. "Take me. Please take me."

And then his hand was gone, his mouth, which had so sweetly tormented her. She looked up and found that he would return to her, easing over her, his eyes trapping her with their incandescence. She opened her lips and her thighs to welcome him, and he entered her.

This time there was no pain. But the hot fullness of him in her sent her into shudders. A rhythm took over she didn't understand. She rocked against him, her breasts crushed against his chest, her mouth ravaged by his, her entire body quaking with the climax that swept nearer.

Eric sheltered Casey's cries and offered her his harsh groans, his hands tight against her buttocks, driving her closer against him, driving him deeper inside her. Casey's head went back; her fingers dug into Eric's back. Convulsions of fire racked her body, torrents of shattered light and heat, as the world whirled away into a liquid center where she and Eric embraced. Then he shuddered against her and called her name, and she collapsed within his hold, where a floating euphoria filled her like late-afternoon light in summer.

Twelve

"And to think," Eric mused, running a finger along the edge of Casey's breast, "I didn't even have to resort to the champagne."

"Don't make rash assumptions," she warned from where her head rested in the hollow of his shoulder. The fire still crackled, and the white rug cushioned them with its thick, delicious warmth. Outside their window the moon was just topping the mountains across the lake, the sky that sheltered it a deep indigo. Casey couldn't remember ever having been so content.

"Resort to champagne for what?" she asked a moment later, lifting her head. A shower of honey-colored hair cascaded over Eric's chest.

"For getting an answer to my proposal," he said with smug satisfaction, his finger straying to outline Casey's softly pouting lower lip.

She frowned a moment, trying to remember what she'd said in the previous few minutes. She hadn't exactly had all her senses in working order. Most had been on Receive instead of Send.

But send she had. It came back to her in a rush. Not only her promise, but his method of extraction.

"Coercion," she protested with laughing eyes. "No judge in the world would honor a promise made under duress."

"Duress?" His eyebrows lifted. "Are you telling me you were tortured?"

"Tormented is a closer word. I never stood a chance, Your Honor. The plaintiff used underhanded and foolproof methods of extracting the promise."

"And just what were those?" he goaded with a smug grin.

Casey looked up as if in thought. "Well . . . severe and prolonged kissing . . . expertly applied embraces . . ."

"Are you telling me you won't marry me?"

"Are you telling me I don't get any champagne?"

"You can have some if you'll marry me."

"Then it *is* a bribe!"

"A reward," Eric retorted.

Casey grimaced. "All right."

He grimaced right back. "All right what?"

"All right, I accept your lame argument *and* your proposal."

Eric laughed, pulling her tightly against him in a hug that was almost fierce. "That has to be the most unique acceptance I've ever had."

Casey looked up slyly. "You've had others?"

He deposited a kiss on her upturned nose. "None I've enjoyed half so much. Now after we decide when we'll have the wedding, I say we should go down and get something to eat."

"Champagne first," she retorted.

Eric scowled at her. "You'd almost think you liked the stuff."

"I never had the chance to find out until a couple days ago. No wonder jockeys drink it for breakfast."

His eyebrows rose again. "How do you know that?"

"Books," she said. "The one really democratic place in New York is the library. Anybody with a library card can get in and get all the knowledge they want."

"And you wasted yours on jockeys."

They were both grinning, enjoying their moment of freedom. It seemed the first time their conversation wasn't governed by what Cassandra did or where she was.

"And Irish and Russian history. Want to know about what Cromwell did to Ireland?"

"I know, thank you. Interesting combination of interests."

Casey shrugged, her breasts brushing against his chest. "I'm weak on geography—which you know—and social graces. And I wouldn't know a Picasso from a pizza. But I can quote the opening line from just about everything Dickens and Breslin have ever written." She considered him with calculating eyes. "You know, you really don't know that much about me."

He brought his hand up to stroke the soft skin of her cheek. "I know that you speak your mind, that you aren't afraid of anything and that I love you."

"But for all you know I could paint myself blue and worship trees. All I've done since I've been here is play Cassandra."

Cupping her chin with a gentle squeeze, Eric eased both of them to a sitting position. "In that case, I can't think of a better way to use up champagne."

And they did just that. Drinking the first half over questions of Casey's life story and preferences in pastimes—baseball and swimming coming quickly to mind, and horseback riding still a strong dream—they sat side by side on the rug, voices and companionship quiet and completely comfortable. The second half was saved until after dinner was obtained down the slope in town.

It was there that Eric really opened up. It might have been the champagne, or the fact that he was just another anonymous reveler in the happy crowd, but by the time the two of them climbed back up to their chalet he'd made seven or eight friends, joined in any number of community sing-alongs and come away with someone's Tyrolean hat. When Casey saw the sparkling life in his eyes, she knew he had never been so totally free.

As she'd watched him lose an arm-wrestling contest with a farmer, she'd promised herself that if she really married him, she'd see he got out for these little weekends regularly.

"But my home is in Brooklyn," she said quietly some time later. They sat on an old cushioned couch on the balcony, the champagne propped in a bucket at their feet. Eric still wore the hat, now at a rather acute angle so that the little feather at its crown was close to his ear.

Steeped in the champagne, the beer from the festival and the gemütlichkeit of the day, he looked drowsily over at her. "Would it be so bad to live in Moritania?" he asked.

Casey shook her head, her eyes suspiciously misty. "I don't know," she admitted. "I haven't had the chance to miss the old block yet—my friends, my family."

"You have a lot of cousins?"

She nodded. "Oh, yeah. Tons. And they all come over for Christmas and St. Patrick's Day. We all grew up within a few blocks of each other."

"Then we'll invite them to the wedding."

She turned to him. "Eric..."

He made his decision with a definite shake of his head. "If they are important to you, they will come. Your cousins, your friends, Sandy, your mother..." He nestled closer to her, slipping an arm around her shoulders and resting his head against hers. "I want our wedding to be the happiest day of your life."

Casey didn't even notice the tears that started to trickle. "I don't know, Eric. I just don't know."

He faced her, his eyes far more sober than they should have been. "Do you love me?" he asked very quietly, his own avowal there in the depths of his eyes, lighter than a morning sky.

Casey didn't flinch. The soft mountain breeze tickled her hair and carried the sound of distant music and the cowbells that were so much a part of the mountains. She'd come to love those sounds, so tranquil and pristine, so much a part of Eric. Somewhere in town a church clock chimed eleven, its notes rolling gently out over the water. It surprised her to realize that she didn't even miss the cacophony of traffic anymore. She wondered whether walking through downtown Manhattan would ever be the same.

"Yes," she whispered. "I love you. I love you enough to give up Brooklyn without a second thought. But my mother's there, too, Eric. And she's alone."

"Then she'll come stay with us."

"You don't know if you'd like her."

Eric's eyebrows went up. "The woman who thinks hugs should be world currency? How could I not like her? Casey, there is nothing I wouldn't do for you."

Her voice grew very small. "You really mean that?"

When Eric smiled, the entire worth of what Casey had given him reflected in his eyes, she knew his answer without words. "I can't wait to meet your cousins," he said simply. "Or your mother."

She felt the tears then, hot and sweet as they coursed down her cheeks. She felt Eric's arm tighten around her. Their lips met. Soft, probing, intense. He eased her mouth open and plundered the honeyed depths with his tongue. Casey never felt her empty champagne glass slide from lifeless fingers, but did recognize the sharp shaft of light that ignited in her belly as Eric's other hand reached for it.

She braced herself against him, her hands flat against his chest where she could feel the suggestion of curling hair beneath his shirt. Her fingers immediately went to work on the buttons, and this time he let her. Casey ached for him, for the remembered lightning of his touch, the soft seduction of her name on his lips. She wanted desperately to feel that cherished union with him, to hear his hoarse cry and feel him shudder against her as he gave himself completely to her in a way no other man had. And then she wanted to fall asleep within his embrace and watch him wake next to her in the morning. You don't miss what you've never had, they said. Suddenly she missed it fiercely and knew that Eric was the only man who could provide it.

When Eric lifted Casey from the couch, he carried her in to the antique bed to lay her amid the soft embrace of goose down. And then he returned to claim her.

It amazed Casey that Eric could be again so different in his lovemaking. Tonight there was a kind of desperation to his touch, an urgency to his kisses, as if he had to make up for lost time or protect them from an uncertain future. He slipped her clothes off quickly and let his follow close behind. When he had her beneath him, he let his hands and mouth prowl over her as if to memorize every hollow and curve. His hands cherished her, stirring her skin to a fresh molten glow and feeding the fierce ache in her belly. He bent to taste her breasts, one after the other, nipping at the tender skin, suckling and caressing until the nipples rose taut for him. He let his hand foray down past the downy triangle at her thighs to once again inflame her to begging.

Casey's body thrilled with the mounting shudders, the breathless, bright incandescence Eric's hands provoked. Her own hands roamed as hungrily, tracing muscle and sinew as a sculptor would his own perfect creation, her fingers curling in the hair on his chest and sweeping across his flat, hard belly. She tested the turgid length of him, his brutal groans at her touch making her bolder. She teased and tormented him much as he did her, learning just what would drive him mad and what would bring him to her. Finally Eric shifted on top of her, and Casey looked up to see the blue of his eyes. She took the privilege of guiding him home.

His mouth claimed hers. He wrapped her within steely arms, entered her with the pent-up longing of a man who had waited his whole life for the one woman he would claim as his own. Casey gasped at the intensity of his entry, at the fierce, primal rhythm he set, crushing her to him and capturing her moans with his fevered mouth. She wrapped around him, his fever infecting her, his drive compelling her until she rocked with him, faster, faster, her fingers clutching helplessly until the nails left scratches, until her moans became gasps and her gasps cries, her eyes open to Eric's and her body brilliant with his fire.

Slowly the night returned, and Casey could hear the cowbells on the wind and a few boats out on the lake. The world outside was peaceful, sheltered in starlight and bathed by the moon. And inside, cradled within the comfort of Eric's love, Casey slowly fell asleep.

She woke the next morning before the sun. Curled in the protection of Eric's embrace, she watched the day slowly take hold and thought how very much she had grown to love the mountains. They began the day in shadow, indigo like the distant night and stark against the brightening sky. But as the sun rose behind them, their shape and hue began to change. The snow was eared soft, muted robin's egg that edged the peaks in severe slashes. Then the mountains themselves, blue, then gray, then green, the high crags a nutmeg brown. The lake mirrored the sky, wisps of coral skimming the azure surface, soft morning mist rolling off it and obscuring the edges.

The town woke slowly, first the roosters, then the cows, strolling out from their barns to the tune of their bells, and then the people. Casey thought that she had never been so content to hear so little. Not one plane, not one ambulance keening off to disaster. Not a single screaming neighbor or blaring television. Of all the things she would miss, she realized those wouldn't be on the list.

She didn't realize Eric was awake until he reached up to stroke a hand through the tumbled mass of her hair.

"Quite a nice day outside," she ventured softly.

"Then it will be the day we call your mother and invite her to the wedding," he decided.

The hesitation returned with his words. The feeling that no matter what she wanted there was no way this all could come true. "What if she won't come to live with us?" she asked, her hands up to the solidity of his arms as if steeping herself in his strength. "She hasn't even left Brooklyn her whole life. Her family's there."

"She will," he assured her with a kiss to the top of her head. "We'll convince her. Right after we figure out what to do with Cassandra."

"Oh." Casey grinned mischievously. "Her."

"I imagine Sandy's told her by now."

"Cassandra?"

"Your mother."

"Then we should get our buns in gear and get her back."

"Your mother?"

Casey giggled. "Cassandra. Don't you have cousins?"

Eric didn't seem to have any trouble following her train of thought as his fingers roamed along Casey's bare arm. "Distant ones," he admitted. "The von Lieberhavens weren't great propagators."

"Should have had a little Hapsburg blood in you. They propagated half of Europe."

"We do."

"Oh. What about your sister? The one who played the harp?"

"Anna Marie," he said, his voice suddenly wistful. "She was like a second mother to me. Never married. She died when I was ten—a plane crash. It nearly did me in." His words were a lot more matter-of-fact than his voice. The woman who had inspired such regret in the dowager queen's eyes must have been a special person. Eric still missed her.

"You're an only child?" he asked.

"I didn't say that." Casey's voice suddenly sounded defensive.

Eric's hand stopped moving. "You're not?"

Casey kept her eyes on the mountains. Solid, unchanging, dependable, unlike some people.

"I have an older brother. Paul."

"You sound angry."

She sighed, snuggling more deeply into Eric's arms. "Confused, I guess. Hurt. He, uh, left home quite a few years ago, and we haven't heard much from him since."

"He ever say why?"

"Why he left, or why he hasn't bothered to find out his father died?" Casey pursed her lips for a moment, angry that she'd let her voice rise. "He never said," she admitted. "When he left he just told me he had to do it and that I'd be all right."

"I'm sorry, Casey."

Lifting her face to his, she smiled. "Well, at least if I live in Moritania I won't have to worry about his dropping in unexpectedly. He always thought the country was a joke, too."

Eric rewarded her with his first kiss of the day.

The first train to Moritania was at eight-thirty. After making certain they purchased their tickets, Eric and Casey wandered off. Hand in hand, they strolled the winding little streets, sometimes stopping at shop windows, or pausing to greet someone they'd met the night before. Casey couldn't remember how, but quite a few people had found out that she and Eric were engaged and had ended up being invited to the wedding. She couldn't wait until they got their invitations.

Frau Voelker insisted on serving them breakfast since it came with the price of the room, so they dined on hard rolls and cold cuts, the Germanic version of the continental breakfast. To be perfectly truthful, Casey had gotten to the point where she looked forward to the fare each morning. It went well with the strong coffee and tea that were so popular in Europe. After serving them in the timbered-and-plastered room that Casey was sure dated back to the Hundred Years' War, Frau Voelker extracted her own invitation to the wedding.

"This is going to be one of the most novel royal weddings of the decade," Casey confided to Eric with a grin as they finally left, fortified with the Frau's blessings and hearty handshakes.

"It's *our* wedding," Eric returned with a mischievous grin. "Why shouldn't we be allowed to invite whomever we wish?"

"What's your mother going to say?"

He rolled his eyes. "Don't worry. Since you don't speak German, you'll never know. It's the only language she uses to curse."

The day was another sparkler, the sun climbing fast over the mountain peaks to burn off the mist and a fresh breeze swirling along the brightly decorated streets. A few shop owners were already out sweeping their stoops, waving a greeting as prospective customers passed. Tourists strolled along aimlessly, and out on the lake a flock of birds lifted into the sun.

Eric took Casey's hand as they walked toward the train station, each of them eking out their last moments alone. It seemed as if the world was conspiring to make these last peaceful moments bittersweet in their beauty. In this tiny Alpine town, for at least these few hours, they were no more than a young couple in love. They had no tradition to uphold, no honor to consider, no title to think of. It made Casey just a little more frightened of what Eric was asking her accept for him.

"The post office," he said suddenly. "I have to call the palace and let them know our schedule."

"Don't let them suggest sending a car," she advised.

"Don't worry." He gave her a quick kiss. "I won't. I'm not telling them where I am, just that I'm on my way back."

Casey elected to stay outside, preferring the view there to the precise paneled cubicles inside. Leaning back against the whitewashed wall, she let her gaze wander aimlessly. She saw the meat shop where the butcher spread wood shavings on the floor, the flower shop with its riot of color and scent, the town square with its expertly manicured garden. All around her she heard German and English, Italian and French, Japanese, Arabic, Swedish. It was a delicious symphony of sound, a delicious bouquet of aromas on the mountain breezes.

Suddenly she froze. Jeans and a fatigue jacket. No, it couldn't be. He was walking right toward her, right into the post office where Eric was making his call to the palace. Casey's heart started thumping and her hands dampened. It was definitely the man they'd tailed the night before. And here he was walking right at them.

Looking around wildly, Casey tried desperately to think of something brilliant. Should she hide? Should she brave it out and stand her ground, pretending she'd never seen him before? She took a quick look into the dim interior of the post office to see Eric at one of the phones, his back to her. At least he was keeping his voice down. If their friend wandered too close, he wouldn't find out too much.

When she turned back to the street, he was almost on top of her. Keep calm, Casey, she told herself. Take slow breaths and look right through him like you don't know him.

He was walking right into the post office!

Summoning all her courage, she took a slow breath and nodded an impersonal greeting as he passed. He nodded back, his features pleasant and noncommittal. Then he walked in the door. It was all Casey could do to keep from following him. She wanted to throw something at Eric to get his attention, but his back remained resolutely to her.

The young man walked up to the window and greeted the teller like a friend. The teller smiled and handed over a batch of envelopes. Replies from other kidnapping attempts, Casey thought blackly. How could he seem like such a nice guy? He had a crown princess stashed someplace. Throwing a familiar wave and farewell over his shoulder, he headed out of the building.

Casey barely let him get by before she whipped into the office.

"That young man," she said to the official, "I think I know him. Does he live around here?"

The man shrugged easily. "For the summer, you know. I think he's been up in the old Gasthaus Reifsteck on the Lake Road."

She nodded. "Has he?" Then she turned to watch his progress through the window. "I could swear I know him. Do you know his name?"

"Of course. Hans Gerdman. I believe he's Dutch."

"Thank you." Casey smiled brightly at the tall, very bureaucratic-looking man with uniform buttons that had been polished to a blinding gleam. "I'll have to look him up while he's here. I think we went to school together."

The man smiled a vague response and returned to his work. Casey turned to Eric. "Get off the phone," she muttered, an eye to the official.

Eric looked at her, still speaking to someone on the other end about quotas and deadlines.

"He was just here," she insisted, making motions toward the desk and then out the window. "The—" her voice lowered dramatically "—kidnapper."

Eric's eyes widened. The young Herr Gerdman could be seen chatting with the florist across the street. Without so much as an "Excuse me," Eric hung up the phone and followed Casey toward the door.

"He's living up at the old Gasthaus Reifsteck on the Lake Road," she said quietly. "Now all we have to find out is where that is."

Eric turned amazed eyes on her. "How did you find that out?" he asked.

Casey couldn't help but grin. "Another lesson from TV."

The young Herr Gerdman didn't seem to be in any kind of hurry. Picking up a handful of flowers, he wandered a few stores down and haggled with the baker over some fresh-baked pastries.

"Stoking up for his next encounter with Cassandra, no doubt," Eric said dryly. "Well, let's go out ourselves and do some quiet questioning. We might just make it back to the Gasthaus before our friend there."

The Gasthaus, they discovered, was in the process of renovation. A group of very nice men had spent the summer working on it, supervised by a quite proper gentleman who spoke very practically about his investment and his relationships with the town nearby. Set on a bluff above the lake, it was an old lodge built in the 1400s and since then in service as any number of restaurants and hostels. The town was glad to see an energetic group of people working on it. The quickest way to get to it was via the footpath at the edge of town. The scenic route, of course, was along the lake.

Eric and Casey chose the lake. It was a cinch Herr Gerdman didn't consider scenery a high priority, so there would be less of a chance of them meeting unexpectedly. Setting off at a brisk pace, they walked along hand in hand. No one paid the slightest bit of attention.

"All I want to do is assure myself that Cassandra is indeed in the Gasthaus," Eric said as they topped the first rise, where the lake spread out in a long finger beyond them, the sun glistening off its waters.

"And if she is?"

"We come back and call for help."

Casey nodded, as satisfied as she could be.

"You will not get involved," he warned. "I plan to set you in a safe place while I search the area. Is that understood?"

She turned anxious eyes on him. "But I can help...."

"No." He came to an abrupt halt, pulling her to a stop alongside him. "I let you come along this far because you insisted that you could help with the everyday world."

"I have, haven't I?"

"Yes. You have. But I will not expose you to any more danger than I can. I would have left you back in town if I'd thought you wouldn't hotfoot it right down that footpath to meet me."

Casey had to allow a sheepish grin. "You *do* know me pretty well, don't you?"

With a flash of affectionate frustration in his eyes, Eric delivered a quick kiss. "Yes," he said. "I do. So I want you to promise me that you'll stay where I put you until I come back to get you. No matter what."

"What if—?"

"Promise!"

Casey pouted, a real four-star lip-curler with an added bonus of downcast eyes. "All right. I promise. But don't fool around and take too long. I have a much-too-vivid imagination."

"I won't." Eric knew he was taking a chance by trusting her, but he couldn't think of another way to appease her and still keep her from getting too involved.

Fifteen minutes later, they turned to see the Gasthaus Reifsteck tucked back in the trees to their right. An uninspiring structure, it was a basic block with open timbers and plaster, the windows now boarded up. Behind the main building, just as at Frau Voelker's, a few lesser buildings spread out up the hill to accommodate guests. There were stacks of lumber and equipment scattered over the area, making it look as if it would be a beehive of activity on a working day. This didn't seem to be one of them.

"There are people living in the guest houses," Eric said quietly, pointing out open windows and intact power lines. "I wonder if anybody's in the restaurant proper."

"Only one way to find out."

Eric took Casey by the hand and led her across to the front door of the main building. They had just reached it then they heard someone approaching. Eric yanked on the door. It came open easily and the two of them slipped inside.

The restaurant was empty, old and half-renovated. Tarps lay everywhere, and plaster dust coated every exposed inch. Most of the walls and parts of the floor were finished. The two fireplaces appeared to be in the process of a major cleaning. Casey could imagine the enormity of the job. You could pack a lot of soot up those babies in five hundred years.

Their footsteps echoed hollowly across the floor. No one appeared to challenge them. Casey felt some of the tension ease out of her chest. She started breathing again.

"Well, looks like nobody's home," she whispered. "Can we go now?"

She'd no more than said it then they heard a grating sound along the outside front wall. Eric wasted no time. Pulling Casey into the kitchen, he found a pantry and threw open the door.

Somebody was using it as a cleaning closet, hiding brooms and mops and cleaners. Eric shoved Casey right in.

"Stay here," he ordered. "If anyone comes along, make a noise like a broom."

She didn't even get a chance to throw him a scowl before he closed the door. All right, she thought disparagingly. Here I am in a broom closet. What do I do now? Casey felt absurdly like a clandestine lover trying to hide from the wife. She prayed she wouldn't be found. Not so much because of the danger—she refused to consider that—but because of the embarrassment. How do you explain standing all alone in the broom closet in a closed restaurant?

Casey had only been in there a few seconds when she first smelled it. Pine. Somebody had left a big bottle of pine cleaner in there. She stood very still, her hands stuffed in her jean pockets, and wondered how long it was going to be before her body ran amok.

The restaurant's front door opened. Casey froze, the pine already tickling at her nose. She wrinkled it up in defense, but that didn't help. Somebody was coming, and she was in desperate danger of sneezing.

She heard approaching footsteps, heavy, precise, measured. No panic, so they hadn't found Eric yet. She wondered where he was. She wondered why she'd insisted on coming along. Then the floor creaked out in the kitchen and she lost interest in everything but holding her breath.

That pine cleaner. She had to do something, push it out of the way, bury it under something, dilute it in water. If she didn't she'd give herself away.

The footsteps grew nearer. The burning grew along her nasal passages. Casey's entire face wrinkled involuntarily. She opened her mouth to cushion the blow.

And then, just as her visitor drew abreast of her very door, her body betrayed her. Casey let out the sneeze of the century.

Immediately the door flew open. Light flooded in, silhouetting a tall, ramrod-straight figure. Delicately rubbing at her still-burning nose, Casey managed a sheepish smile.

"You know, you Swiss really know how to organize a broom closet," she bluffed heartily, stepping right out and trying to get past her visitor.

"But I'm not Swiss," the man said, and Casey turned toward him, recognizing his voice, sparking unhappy recognition.

There before her, one hand on the open door, his other on her arm, stood General Mueller. He had a smile on his face that told Casey he had visions of dollar signs dancing in his head.

"Uh-oh," she moaned, "is Eric going to be mad at me now."

Thirteen

Eric had never meant to get this involved, but it had been so easy. Coming out of the restaurant, he'd spotted a thin, blond young man heading toward the nearest building, possibly a sentry inspecting the grounds. Eric followed discreetly until the young man entered the building to join another person for what looked like an ongoing card game. They never noticed as Eric skirted around to complete his reconnaissance.

The other chalet was in use but presently empty, the phone working. After calling the palace for a little backup, Eric returned and took care of the two guards, a simple matter of making a little noise and greeting the responding man with a gun to the back. He'd carried the small automatic without Casey's knowledge and without intending to use it, but it turned out to come in handy in a situation like this.

It also fortunately turned out that these particular band members weren't the stuff of action-adventure films. When the one saw his partner with his hands up, his hands did a matching salute, his playing cards fluttering forgotten to the floor. There hadn't even been any guns in the room.

From that point it had been quite easy to find out that Cassandra was closeted in a third-floor bedroom in the restaurant proper, guarded by a third man. Hans, it seemed, hadn't made it back yet.

After getting the rest of his answers, Eric tied the guards securely, stuffed them in the cellar and prepared to return to the restaurant. He'd send Casey to meet the guard team when it reached town and guide them back. Then he'd position himself to make sure nobody entered or left the restaurant that held Cassandra until help arrived to free her. After that, he'd deal with General Mueller.

Just as Eric had come to suspect, the general was behind the whole plot. The general had contacted the MSM with the idea for the kidnapping and had helped them set it in motion, claiming to adhere to their principles. Eric had an idea that it had a lot more to do with the million-franc ransom. The general might be wily and crooked, but there was one thing Eric would swear to in court. Politically, the general placed himself just a bit to the right of Genghis Khan, and that end of the spectrum had little room for socialists.

While keeping an eye on the upstairs window, Eric crept across the yard and up the back steps to the kitchen. He couldn't wait to get his hands on Mueller. And not so much for endangering Cassandra. Knowing her, he felt sorrier for the cardplayers, who had undoubtedly had to put up with her tantrums. He was furious because he had trusted the general only to be made a fool of. If he hadn't had that itch to call the gourmet shop and double-check on the caviar, he never would have discovered that the general hadn't questioned the shop owner at all, much less followed up on the tip any other way. Eric might have trusted the general enough to have paid out the million in ransom.

Eric cracked the back door and peered through. No one was inside. No sounds, no movement. There were plenty of footprints on that dusty floor, but nobody to immediately claim them. He slipped inside and headed carefully over to the broom closet.

"Casey..."

No answer. Eric opened the door, expecting to have to fight off a barrage of her questions. The mop was crammed to the side of the closet, and the pail was up-ended. But Casey was gone.

He'd told her to stay where she was. What the hell had she disappeared for? She'd better not have tried to follow him. There was still Hans and that third man to account for.

Preparing to slip the gun back beneath his sweater, Eric suddenly stopped. His head turned as a frisson of fear slithered down his neck. What if she hadn't disappeared on her own? What if that third man had somehow found her? What Eric had seen so far didn't exactly add up to a top-notch terrorist operation, but all the same she could be in danger. He let the door swing silently shut behind him.

Looking quickly around, Eric tried to decide what to do, his heart suddenly in his throat. He couldn't wait for the team to get there from the palace. It could be an hour or more. He had to find Casey, and find her now.

Eric crept through the room, looking for a possible hint as to where Casey was and whether she'd gone voluntarily. The footprints were no help. There were too many of them, accumulated over too long a period of time, to follow one set. He decided to check the two sets of stairs that led up from either end of the front room.

The sound of footsteps brought him to a halt. Crouching low along the wall, he raised the gun. There was somebody coming downstairs. Eric prepared to greet him.

Then he saw who it was.

The general came into view, slowly taking each step as if trying very hard to maintain a difficult balance. Eric immediately saw why. He had Casey.

Mueller carried her in his arms, a gun in one hand pointed so that it could kill her. Casey's hair swung limply alongside him as he negotiated the steps, her neck arched over his arm, her face pasty-white and slack. She was unconscious. Eric came to a shuddering halt, his heart dying in him.

"What have you done!"

"Ah." The general smiled in genuine delight. "You're here. I wondered."

Only that gun, pointed right at Casey's face, kept Eric from going for Mueller's throat. If the General had done anything to hurt her, Eric would kill him.

"Don't be a fool, General." His eyes struggled to stay away from the pale face in the man's arms. "The team is on its way. You can't have the ransom. You know that now."

"I know no such thing," he said agreeably, coming to a stop at the last step.

"If you hurt her..."

"Prince Eric," the general said indignantly, "I am an officer and a gentleman. I do not *injure* innocent ladies. I do pacify them, however. It makes then so much more agreeable, don't you know."

"Bring them both down now, and it will go easier on you."

He shook his head. "I don't think so. But I will make a deal with you. I will give you one and keep the other."

"But there's no way out." His expression carefully nonchalant, Eric was feverishly trying to think of some way to neutralize that gun. After that, he could maybe get past the general to get both Casey and Cassandra. An impossible task, with Casey unconscious and Cassandra in who knew what condition? But he had to do something.

"If you would be so kind as to drop the gun, I won't be forced to do something...disagreeable," the general threatened in an absurdly congenial voice. "After all, I'm in a most unpleasant position. It makes me seriously consider acts I would otherwise have no part in."

It was the cold amusement in Mueller's eyes more than the words he used to threaten Eric that convinced him to drop the gun. The general had no qualms about doing what he had to to save himself.

"Now you may let me by," he continued with a grateful smile, "so I can conclude the hasty negotiations you and the young lady have precipitated."

"Know this," Eric snarled. "If you harm her, I'll come for you."

"The queen mother was right, then. You are quite besotted with the girl."

"You heard me."

There was a scuffing sound out back, and the general's eyes momentarily strayed to it. It seemed to be a signal, for at the sound of it a great smile of triumph bloomed on the general's features.

"In that case," he said happily, "here. I give you a gift."

Before Eric could move, the general pushed Casey directly at him. Eric leaped forward to try to catch her. The general had outsmarted him, though. Eric was able to get his arms under Casey, but the momentum was too great, and they ended up sprawled on the floor. With a great laugh, the general scooped up Eric's gun and scooted right past.

"The other one is now worth two million. And I know you'll pay it."

Eric pulled the limp body into his arms, desperate to find a pulse. His fingers went to Casey's throat, when his eyes widened. Suddenly he was unceremoniously dumping the still form on the floor.

"Mueller!" he howled, coming to his feet. "I'll get you!"

One hole. There had been one hole in the earlobe. The general had kept Eric's attention with Cassandra while his cohort had somehow gotten Casey out of the house. Suddenly she was the hostage, and Eric was truly frightened. Frightened and enraged.

The general might correctly assume that Eric wouldn't think twice about paying an exorbitant amount to ensure Casey's safety, but he didn't realize that Eric's feelings for her transcended state and family honor and responsibilities. Eric would gladly kill Mueller with his bare hands.

His only thoughts now on rescuing Casey, Eric turned to search out some kind of weapon, leaving Cassandra in an ungainly heap on the dusty floor. Absurdly enough, the only thing he discovered was a set of fencing foils over one of the fireplaces. Marvelous. The best he could hope for was for the general to run quickly out of bullets and for none of them to end up anywhere in him. Eric pulled one foil down and headed for the door. It was better than nothing.

The general hadn't taken the time to free his two men from the chalet. He and one other man were hustling Casey back down toward the Lake Road, possibly to where they had a car waiting. She was gagged and her hands were tied behind her, the partially buttoned raincoat Mueller had supplied flapping around her like a sail in an uncertain wind. Without a thought for his own safety, Eric ran after them.

"I'll shoot!" the general shouted.

"Go right ahead!" Eric shouted back, gaining ground.

Her eyes like saucers at Eric's wild taunt, Casey managed an outraged shriek behind her gag. Her arms were pretty well tied up, but she did land a couple of good barefoot kicks at her captor's knees.

The man who pushed her was none other than the mouth-breather she'd gotten so acquainted with at the palace a few nights before. Even without the stocking mask, she'd recognized him right away.

"Well, hi there," she'd said brightly when the general had pushed her into the room. "Nice to see you again."

He'd liked her witty repartee so much he'd stuffed a gag in her mouth. Then the general had told her to take her clothes off. It hadn't, in truth, been the high point of her day. Casey had seen Cassandra asleep in the bed across the room and had wondered if that was how dying people felt, looking on at themselves as they drifted away. She'd even pulled the gag out and objected, but Bubba—she'd decided to dub him—had taken care of that with dispatch.

"Either you take your clothes off," the general had said without much agitation, "or he will."

Casey had gone right for her buttons.

So here she was stumbling along in her bra and panties and somebody's raincoat, wondering whether it would be worth it to sell the story for a miniseries and then realizing that she'd been right the first time. Not even Hollywood would buy this one.

Another shot echoed behind her, and she whipped around, throwing Bubba off balance. Eric bobbed and weaved, the sun glinting off the long sword he carried.

Casey's heart sank lower. Swords were impressive. She'd seen Douglas Fairbanks trim all of a castle's candles without putting out a single flame. But in any book in the world, a gun still beat a sword. She was terrified that she was going to see Eric stumble to his knees, a crimson blossom appearing on his shirtfront. Bubba grabbed her by the arm and she landed another kick.

The general hadn't picked Bubba for his patience. Letting out what Casey was sure was a curse, he flipped her over his back and headed off again. She took up kicking at his chest, her hands helpless behind her. The general got off another shot over his shoulder before following. Ducking behind a tree, Eric could be seen edging closer.

Eric gained ground as the one man labored to stay up under Casey's struggling weight. The general fired two more shots just as they turned onto a path a few hundred feet shy of the road and headed away from town. Eric ducked successfully both times, weaving in and out of trees to keep the general's target at a minimum.

He wasn't quite sure what he was going to do if he got close enough. The general seemed to have an unlimited supply of bullets. But Eric had the overwhelming feeling that if he didn't free Casey right now, he wouldn't be able to again. It was a lot more difficult to work up the courage to kill a crown princess than it was a secretary.

Eric saw the car as he rounded a corner, parked a ways up the path and facing the road. Mueller would have reached it by now if Casey hadn't managed to plant both knees in her captor's solar plexus and get him to drop her.

Casey was fighting tooth and nail now, knowing somehow that once she got to that car it would be all over. Eric still stalked them. She could see him through the trees, approaching relentlessly even as the general continued to fire shots. Would Mueller really try to kill him, she wondered, or just injure him to make a point? Somehow the latter thought didn't make her feel any better. An injured Eric, here away from the town, could die before help got to him. And she'd be the cause of it. The fire that lit in her chest propelled her limbs faster against the implacable Bubba.

The general had had just about enough of it. Turning briefly to her, he threatened, "Either stop or I'll hurt you, young lady. I have plenty of ammunition for the both of you."

Only the gag prevented Casey from telling him just what she thought. She even tried to land a kick in his direction, but Bubba wrapped a steely arm around her struggling frame and dragged her toward the car.

Turning back to Eric, Mueller fired off another shot. Eric dived for cover, not even feeling the sudden sting on his shoulder for the pounding his body took trying to go to ground. Why didn't somebody hear the shots and call the authorities? Scooting across from tree to tree, he advanced as the general struggled with his companion to get Casey into the car.

A vehicle rumbled along the road below them, and Eric heard her get the breath to let out a muffled scream. The general hit her for it. That was all Eric needed. Discovering a log just in front of him, he opted for it over the sword. Hefting it before him, he made the final run for that car.

The general turned and aimed. Eric heard the report and felt a thud in the wood he held. He ran faster. The general fired. Nothing happened. It was like an old movie. The general looked at the gun as if it had betrayed him and considered throwing it at Eric. The other man was still struggling with Casey's flailing arms and legs in the back of the car.

Smiling, Eric stopped. The wood was heavy in his hand, a satisfying feeling of justice. The general stared at him and then the gun as if in a daze.

"Why don't we be civilized about this?" Eric offered one last time before the impulse to crush the general's head overtook him.

Mueller suddenly smiled back. "Absolutely not."

He raised the gun again. Eric shrugged, and began to swing with the wood. The general pulled the trigger. The log connected with the gun just as it went off.

Bubba stopped just long enough to see which man yelled behind him and why. Casey needed just that long to kick him hard where it counted. Screaming in agony, he hit the ground and stayed there. He deserved every groan. But the silence beyond that car terrified her, and she had to discover its outcome.

Her heart thundering in her ears and her breath coming in ragged gasps, Casey made herself peek out over the window. Then she screamed.

She did have the courtesy to step over the writhing man before she launched herself into Eric's arms. The general lay dazed at his feet. He'd landed there after he'd made the enraged rush at Eric's throat, only to be met with a well-swung log to the side of the head. Eric opened his arms to Casey, gathering her trembling body to him as if afraid that she weren't really there.

"Are you all right?" he asked, his voice rough-edged and hesitant. He should never have let her talk him into taking her along. He'd almost lost her. "Did he hurt you?"

It wasn't until he held her back to see the disdainful look in her eyes that he remembered that she was gagged. He immediately beamed.

"You know, it does occur to me that I might prefer you this way. At least I won't get any back talk from you."

The threat in Casey's eyes grew dramatically direr the longer Eric chuckled at her. He paused only long enough to pick up the guns so that he didn't have to worry about trouble from that quarter, before reaching around to pull down the gag and remove the wad of cloth from her mouth.

Casey immediately took to spitting. "I think they used Bubba's old socks. Blah!"

"Bubba?"

She grinned up at him. "Our late-night visitor over there. Since he didn't have the manners to introduce himself, I made up a name for him. Untie me, Eric. You're bleeding."

Eric looked down in surprise to see that she was right. There was a ragged hole in his sleeve just below his shoulder, and a lengthening scarlet stain on his shirt. He supposed he was going to feel it soon. He didn't now. All he felt now was relief.

"I'll make a deal with you," he said easily. Both of them ignored Mueller's groan. Eric pointed the gun in the appropriate direction, his eyes still on Casey. "I'll only untie you if you promise, once and for all, to marry me."

"You're doing it again!" she protested.

Dropping a kiss on her very tight lips, he smiled agreeably. "I know. It seems the only time I can get you to make sense is when I have the . . . advantage."

Casey struggled to keep that scowl on her face. Eric deserved a resounding no for his smug attitude. But she couldn't refuse him. Relief and giddy joy bubbled through her like that champagne she'd gotten to like. She hadn't made any sense around him so far. Why should she change now?

"Oh, all right," she snapped, turning to let him at her hands. "I'll marry you." Bending down, she nudged the still-dizzy general at her feet. "Did you hear that, General? He's going to want a witness."

The general groaned.

"He heard it," she said over her shoulder. "Now let me loose."

"Just a minute," Eric said, his hand to her neck. "I'd better check."

Casey shot him a look that somehow bordered on the lethal and the delirious all at once. "Check what?"

Eric fingered the soft little lobe of her ear. "He fooled me once already, and I certainly wouldn't want to let Cassandra out of such a manageable condition. I wouldn't want to marry her, either."

"Neither would I."

He bent for a closer examination that somehow entailed the flicking of his tongue against her skin. Casey almost ended up on the ground next to the general. "Hmmm," he murmured. "Three holes. Who won the 1986 World Series?"

She allowed a certain amount of exasperation. "The Mets. If you don't let me loose right now, I'm going to make sure you bleed to death."

Eric not only let her loose, he whirled her around for a resounding I'm-glad-you're-safe kiss that left her dazed.

"Yes." Eric nodded, his eyes happy and bright. "You're all right. You scared me for a while there. I was afraid he wasn't going to be as nice to you as he was to Cassandra.''

"He made me take my clothes off!" Casey retorted indignantly, a self-righteous eye on the general's still form on the ground.

"To give him time to get you away. He dressed Cassandra up in them."

"What a ridiculous idea." Then a grin teased the corner of her mouth. "Speaking of which, what happened to the sword? I thought this was going to be a real swashbuckler."

Eric nodded sagely. "A good prince is also a flexible prince. Besides," he added, easing her more tightly into his grasp, "I couldn't see myself eulogized as the prince who lost a duel between a foil and a .38."

"The last of the great romantics."

The sunlight sent feathered shafts through the trees, gilding Casey's hair and warming Eric's face. The day was really going to be a beautiful one, full and sweet, just like the life that now stretched ahead of them.

Eric stood with Casey in his arms, wondering how he was going to keep the general and his crew peaceable until the team arrived, when he heard the crashing through the trees. Letting go of Casey, he turned to see Hans come to a sudden stop, the deer in sight of the hunter. Without more than a second's hesitation, the young man whirled around and was gone. Casey moved in his direction.

"Forget it," Eric suggested. "Let's just get home."

"What if he goes back for Cassandra?"

"Then he's either a lot dumber or braver than I think."

"Speaking of which," she said, "where is Cassandra?"

* * *

"You certainly took your sweet time looking for me!" Seated regally in the back seat of the limo as it sped across the countryside, Cassandra once again checked her appearance in Casey's hand mirror. "And then to leave me just lying there in all that...dust while you went gallivanting off after...her!" The sidelong glance she shot at Casey said it all.

Casey looked over at the woman opposite her and then at Eric. "Yeah, Eric. We're going to get along just great."

Cassandra didn't deign to notice the comment.

"Be careful, Cassandra dear," Eric said, "or we'll give you right back."

"Don't be absurd, Eric. I am the crown princess."

"And Casey's been impersonating you for a week without anyone being the wiser."

This time she did cast an eye on Casey, albeit a jaundiced one. Lifting the royal chin with icy disdain, Cassandra returned to the mirror. "Hard to believe."

"I agree," Casey said evenly. "I'm much thinner."

They pulled through the sleepy streets of Braz to scattered waves and smiles, and proceeded to the palace. Casey looked forward to seeing the lovely old forest again, and the gardens and, surprisingly enough, the queen. Today, she knew, she would finally break the news to her own mother. The sun was settling onto the tops of the western Alps, shedding a liquid golden light over the valley and gilding the palace windows. Eric had his arm around her, and they were coming home.

Eric spoke up as they came to a stop at the front door. "Cassandra, I think you'll find that there have been some changes since you've left."

"Changes?" she challenged. "Dear Eric, what could change here? An invasion by Austria, a foreclosure of the banks? Nuclear confrontation?"

Cassandra waited until the chauffeur opened the door before stepping out. Behind her, not only Eric and Casey but the chauffeur smiled.

"Worse," Eric assured her. But his niece didn't hear.

A moment later, the assembled staff greeted their crown princess without so much as a nod of the head, and she began to shriek.

"I hope the staff doesn't mind the fireworks," Casey apologized with a barely suppressed smile as she and Eric stepped into the foyer.

"Certainly not, Prin—Fraülein Phillips," Rolph said from behind her. "It does the young princess good to be unsettled once in a while. Welcome back, Your Highness."

"Rolph," Eric said with a smile, "I assume everything has been going well since we've been gone."

"Yes, Your Highness. Her Majesty the queen would like to see you—and Fraülein Phillips—in the Rose Room. And then the kitchen staff is expecting Fraülein Phillips in the kitchen to taste-test their attempts at making soda bread."

Casey reached a hand out to the very proper little man's arm. "Thank you, Rolph. I'll be there."

Eric took her hand and led her into the Rose Room, where the queen sat alone by the fireplace. The old woman didn't acknowledge their presence until they were seated a moment.

"Cassandra is safe?" she asked without preamble.

"You mean you didn't hear her?" Eric asked incredulously.

"It was a foolish risk you took, Eric," she snapped. For a second her eyes strayed to the patched arm he held gingerly by his side. Then she returned her attention to the fireplace. "General Mueller has been dealt with, I assume?"

"He has. And now, if you don't mind, Mother, I think I'd like to shower and change. There is still a government to run."

Her hand came up even as he moved to get to his feet. Eric eased himself down again. "Another matter. We must talk, I think, about the marriage."

"What marriage, Mother?" Eric asked. "Cassandra's? Mine?"

"Do you really think the country would be served by your flaunting a twin to the queen so soon after this incident? Do you think Cassandra would tolerate it? Surely it would be better if no one knew Miss Phillips existed."

Casey, for one, couldn't think of anything intelligent to say. Eric maintained his princely control.

"What are you driving at, Mother?"

She turned to him, her eyes the eyes of a queen who must make a difficult decision. "We do not have the luxury of some countries to have comic-strip princesses and tabloid royalty. Our country depends on the stability envisioned in our government by very conservative business leaders. If they thought we were susceptible to blackmail, we would lose their trust and their business. If the people of this country thought we would deceive them we, the royal house, would lose their good will. And we would have at best a puppet royalty."

"I assume there's a good reason for bringing this up now," he said with tight control.

"To be frank," the queen admitted, "I am . . . fond of Fraülein Phillips. I did not wish to cause her pain. But I hoped that the two of you were merely caught in an emotional thrall of the moment, and that once Cassandra was back you would realize how impossible it is for you to continue your relationship. I have gone to the lengths of consulting Frau Phillips concerning my decision, and she agrees with me. Neither of us advise this marriage."

It was Casey who stood first. "You talked to my mother?"

"It was only in your interests, child. I have a car and a plane standing by to take you safely home as soon as you are packed."

Casey turned to Eric, her eyes filled with pain where they had been so bright only moments before. "But we haven't even told her."

"I want you to consider this, Eric," the queen said. "You have more than yourself to think about. You have a country."

Standing to face his mother, Eric smiled icily. "I *have* been thinking of my country, Mother, my entire life. It's about time I think of myself for once."

"But as queen, Cassandra surely won't allow it. Think of the damage to her."

He shook his head. "I don't really care. If Cassandra thinks she can run this country without me as her finance minister, that's fine. I'm going to marry Casey, and that's final. I don't care if it means I have to renounce my title and move to Brooklyn with her." His voice softening, he turned to smile encouragement into Casey's stricken eyes. "Maybe I could learn to play Space Invaders."

"Oh, Eric . . ." Casey protested.

He silenced her by taking her hand.

"Surely you can't dismiss the situation so blithely," his mother objected, her own eyes now uncertain. "Why would you even consider making such a rash sacrifice?"

When he smiled then, it was at Casey. "Just because I want to." Eric turned to level an uncompromising gaze on his mother and all she represented. "It's your decision. I'll stay long enough for Cassandra to be installed, but if my wife isn't welcome in my family, then neither am I."

Fourteen

Eric had been right when he'd said that Moritania was rife with good taste. Cassandra's wedding was the proof. Filling the cathedral with bright and beautiful guests, the event galvanized the little country into a day of widespread celebration. Garlands of fresh flowers decorated the buildings, and the citizens dressed in the bright hand-sewn finery of traditional costumes. Flags and bunting flew, banners hung from the gray stone of the cathedral walls, and every policeman and guard member had been shined and pressed to a razor-sharp finish.

Braz was alive with color and music and life. Even though Cassandra was not a favorite in the royal family, even though no one really anticipated her becoming the queen, it was still a chance to reaffirm the ancient traditions that helped bind the small country together. The royal family belonged to each and every citizen of Moritania, and they were pleased to show them off. Even the camera crews from the cable company had been situated so that they didn't mar the scene.

At precisely noon, the procession started out from the palace. The Moritanian Guards led on horseback, then the palace guards on foot and the intricately designed carriages that carried the royal family.

Eric sat alongside his mother, resplendent in the full uniform of the guard. As the prince, he was the traditional head of the unit and entitled to its benefits. He sat regally straight in the pristine white uniform with its polished brass buttons and high-crowned cap. A saber lay at his side, and his feet were shod in glossy black boots. More than one female citizen could be seen blowing kisses at the handsome prince. His mother, alongside, was attired in traditional queen's garb—a matronly blue dress and an awful-looking feathery hat. Casey figured it must be some kind of tradition of its own.

After the last of the procession wound its way into town, the chauffeur helped Casey and James McCormac into the back of the limo. Eric had asked James to escort a now-silent Casey so that she could at least enjoy the festivities before she left. From the expression beneath her wide-brimmed hat, Casey wasn't at all looking forward to it. Even the addition of James, now even more attentive than when he'd thought she was Cassandra, couldn't lift her spirits. Casey had the depressing feeling that once Cassandra was queen, she had every intention of dropping the last sandbags into Casey's hot-air balloon.

There was a crowd all along the route, and by the time they reached the narrow Kirkenstrasse there was no way to get through. The people packed the available space along the street and down the two blocks to the station in the hope of hearing the ceremony through the loudspeakers outside the church.

Quite a few tourists swelled the crowd, good for the economy of the little country. Casey only knew that the cheering rose precipitously when Eric stepped from his carriage, flowers arcing through the air toward him from his adoring subjects and tourists alike. After that, Cassandra's reception was something of an anticlimax.

Cassandra noticed it, too. Stepping from her carriage with the help of her uncle, the princess stopped to bathe in her people's adoration, only to realize that it wasn't quite as forthcoming as it had been a moment earlier. Breathtakingly beautiful in a satin-and-beadwork gown and a tulle veil, she seemed distracted and nervous, something Casey had noticed the last few days. The staff had noticed it, too, speculating on its causes over the coffee they shared with Casey. Even James had commented on it, noting that Cassandra's usually perfect porcelain complexion seemed a bit wan, her bare shoulders sagging above the expanse of the exquisitely designed gown.

"Maybe she finally realized just what she's in for," James said, smiling wryly as he guided Casey along to a side door in an attempt to miss the cameras.

"Being queen?" Casey asked, her hand held firmly in the crook of James's arm. She should have been swooning by now. He was in a morning suit and top hat, his famed brown eyes sparkling and seductive. And his attention was all on her. Why couldn't he have managed to do all this before Eric dropped into her life?

With a flash of white teeth, James motioned to the front of the church, where Rudolph, Baron of Austerlitz, waited. "Being married."

He almost succeeded in getting Casey to giggle as the two slipped into a side pew about halfway back. Casey could see heads of state from where she sat, royalty, jet-set luminaries and what she assumed were the wealthy and notable of European society. Her marriage to Eric would have been different, she thought with a rueful little smile beneath her concealing veil. They were going to invite whomever they wanted.

High above them, the organ swelled to a thunderous crescendo that echoed through the soaring church, and heads turned to see Cassandra standing at the back. Candlelight flickered, rich ornaments glittered in the yellow light streaming in from the huge rose window behind the altar. The scene was magical. Casey should have been properly awed, as she'd been the first time she'd attended one of these functions. Instead, she watched Eric walk sedately up the aisle alongside his niece and thought that her heart would break at the sight of him.

Casey turned away, her eyes on the ice-blue kid gloves in her lap, which matched her tailored dress, a soft geometric print in blues and greens and ivories that fell from padded shoulders and skimmed her figure with delicate attention. The sleeves were long and fitted, the matching hat a delicious shade of blue-green that matched the ocean on a sunny day.

Casey would never have the chance to wear something this fine again. She would never be invited to functions like this or be treated with quite the same deference by the people who ran the world. But she didn't care. The Russians and the Irish were right. It all ended. Even while you were enjoying it, savoring it, it was coming to a close.

"What the—"

Casey's head came up at James's bitten words. He pointed over toward the center aisle. Confused, she followed to find that everyone's attention was ahead of her. A hush had fallen on the crowd.

Just shy of the steps to the altar, Eric stood with his head bent toward Cassandra's. She was at a dead stop, her head shaking, making some kind of point. From the angle of her face, Casey could see that she was watching the less-than-impressive Rudolph.

The organist faltered, then picked up the melody again with a bit less enthusiasm. The bishops and priests who crowded the altar waited with frowns on their studious faces. The audience began to shift in their seats. Rudolph waited at rigid attention.

Suddenly Cassandra pulled herself free of Eric's hold. "No!" she shrieked, loud enough for the cable viewers to hear. "I won't do it! He's a worm!"

Casey's eyes rolled. Beside her, James did his best to maintain his composure. Up on the center aisle, Eric was doing his best to talk some sense into his niece.

"That girl does know how to throw a tantrum," Casey admitted under her breath.

James heard and chuckled. Outside, the crowd had grown very quiet. Casey looked up to the balcony to which the commentator had been relegated. He was hot at his microphone, his avid commentary probably more appropriate for a title bout than a wedding. Maybe if Casey waved now, her mother would see her.

"Oh, the hell with the crown!"

Casey's head came back up with a snap. You could have heard a pin drop as Cassandra's peevish words echoed throughout the cathedral. One of the priests had taken to mopping his brow.

Without warning, Cassandra turned on the audience and flipped her veil back. To everyone's surprise, the famously composed face was tear-stained.

"The crown isn't worth it!" she shouted to everyone. "Free yourselves of it! I am! I'm renouncing this sham of a marriage and that anachronistic title of queen to become Mrs. Hans Gerdman! People of Moritania, unite behind me!''

Before Eric could catch her, she fled down the aisle. Actually, Casey wasn't sure Eric wanted to try. The look on his face left her in no doubt as to his opinion of Cassandra's latest little act.

"Hans?'' she squeaked in delighted surprise, a hand to her mouth.

"Who's that?'' James demanded in her ear.

"One of the dissidents who kidnapped her,'' she giggled, thinking of the thin, earnest young man who had spent so much time at the florist's. She hoped Cassandra could find him again. The way he'd been running when he'd gotten away made Casey suspect that he wasn't about to stop until he reached the Mediterranean.

"Well, leave it to Cassandra to throw out the baby with the bathwater.'' James grinned, easing back in his pew to enjoy the proceedings.

Up at the side of the altar, Rudolph had gone white. He was looking around as if planning the least public means of escape. The archbishop looked as if he was going to faint. The commentator up in the shadows almost fell off the balcony in his excitement as his cameraman swiveled frantically in Cassandra's wake. As usual, it was left to Eric to rescue the situation.

Without noticeable agitation, he stepped up to the altar and turned to face the audience. "Excuse me,'' he said. "It seems we have an abdication on our hands.''

Casey saw the sharp expression on his mother's face and knew that she was outraged. Roll with it, honey, Casey thought with a grim smile. He's probably the only person who can save your royal position right now.

"I do apologize for Cassandra's timing,'' Eric went on with a smile to the audience, carefully checking out the church. "She's had a rough week of it, though. I asked her to consider putting her decision off, but she refused—in her inimitable style."

A rumble of laughter could be heard from outdoors.

"So," he continued, looking for a moment at the plumed hat he held in his hands. "We seem to have a country without a monarch. I'm afraid that just leaves me."

When Eric looked up, Casey felt James move beside her. She turned a bit to see his hand lift just enough for Eric to see. Her heart leaped. What were those two up to?

"Stop that," she hissed, batting at his arm.

James smiled. His task had been accomplished. A great grin broke out over Eric's face as he stepped down off the altar and approached. Casey's eyes went very wide. So did the queen's. The commentator was speechless.

"I hope you as our guests at this most auspicious occasion won't mind," Eric was saying as he walked, "but I have to consult with my subjects on a matter of some import. I'll be right back."

He walked right up to the end of Casey's pew and held out his hand. A thousand pairs of eyes turned to her. She blushed scarlet beneath the veil, frozen to the spot.

"Casey?" he asked, smiling with those beguiling eyes.

"Go on." James nudged from behind her.

Before she knew it, she was on her feet walking toward Eric, and a fresh buzz of excitement broke over the audience. She had no idea where Rudolph had gone, but the bishops were toughing the whole thing out.

The crowd that met them was jubilant. They knew better than anyone what Cassandra's abdication would mean. The minute the door opened, pandemonium reigned. Flowers filled the air and adults held their children up to see. Some were clapping, stamping their approval. Some were singing and crying. Eric silenced them all with a raised hand.

"As I'm sure you've all figured by now," he began, "if Cassandra refuses to rule, it's up to me. I have always been willing to serve my country any way I can."

A fresh wave of cheering attested to that.

"But now," he continued, "I must ask for something in return. I must ask for your understanding in a matter that has been transpiring for the last week." With one last, lingering look at Casey, he turned back to them and went on. "You see, I'm afraid that the reports of Cassandra's kidnapping were absolutely true. She had been held all week, only having been freed yesterday. As you may also know, she has been seen repeatedly at functions in Moritania. I'm afraid that we, your government, sought desperate means to preserve the stability of the country, and had to do it behind your backs. I ask your forgiveness. I would also like to introduce you to the young woman here, a distant relative of the family, who flew in to help us in our hours of need."

He never gave Casey the chance to object before whipping off her hat. Beneath, her hair was swept up and she had pearls at her ears. The crowd gasped at the resemblance. Casey stood rigidly still beside Eric, torn between the desire to run and the desire to collapse into a little pile right there on the stone steps.

"Now, certain advisers claim that revealing Fraülein Phillips's identity would be deleterious to the benefit of the country. Under normal circumstances, I would agree. But you see, I have decided that unless she can be my queen I cannot rule. I ask your permission."

The man was pure magic. He barely got the words out before the crowd went wild again, now showering Casey with the flowers and the well-wishing. There was very little question about their feelings concerning her, especially since she'd come in contact with quite a few of them the week before.

"Now just a minute," Casey objected to Eric.

"You promised," he said, eyebrow raised.

"I didn't know you were going to be a king."

He shrugged. "The vagaries of power. Take it or leave it."

"What about the wedding we'd planned? My mother and Sandy?"

Eric held up his hand again and received the crowd's attention. "One thing. My lovely fiancée wants to wait for our wedding so that her family and friends may attend. Can we put this marriage off a bit?"

They cheered.

"What about my career?" she asked then.

His hand went up.

"College," he said. "She demands that she be allowed to finish college and practice law."

"Before the wedding?" somebody asked.

He turned to her with inquiring eyes.

"No." She smiled sheepishly, then turned to the crowd and repeated herself. "No. After."

That was fine with them.

Eric laughed. "Fine, then, if it's all right with you, how about a coronation instead today?"

"Coronation?" Casey demanded. "How can you be crowned without being married? I thought it was the law."

It was his turn for a sheepish grin. "Only for women," he admitted.

Casey bestowed her best scowl on him. "Now I *know* I'm going to finish college. You guys have quite a few laws around here that could use a little updating."

Her audience approved. Eric approved even more heartily. Turning her into his arms, he bestowed the first official, public royal kiss, which had not only Casey but every other woman in sight weak-kneed.

The crowd went wild.

Early the next morning, before anyone else was up, Eric and Casey went out riding. He presented her with a roan mare with a very solid disposition to carry her, and Casey fell in love a second time. The two of them cantered over the grounds back to the manicured lawns beyond the gardens. As the sun appeared to first burn off the dew, they settled on a blanket under a vast oak tree and considered their future.

"Your mother wasn't far from a stroke yesterday," Casey grinned from where she lay nestled in Eric's arms watching the brightening sky.

"She'll grumble about it for at least a week," he said, his hand already fingering her hair. "Then she'll go along, just as always. Especially when she realizes that the country will survive."

"There's no chance Cassandra will change her mind and dethrone you?"

"Why?" He grinned. "Looking forward to wearing that crown at all those state functions?"

Casey grinned back a bit dryly. "I'm already measuring her old room for a couple of Space Invaders machines. Beats all those pink ruffles."

"Cassandra is long gone," Eric assured her. "And quite impotent to change things once the entire staff lined up to witness her statement of abdication. Werner admits to having signed twice."

Casey chuckled. The picture was an amusing one.

"She's gone. Off to live on love," he assured her. "And the fifty thousand pounds she took from the office safe."

"Love comes expensive these days," Casey admitted. "Good thing I have simple tastes."

"Hot dogs instead of caviar."

"Beer instead of cognac."

"I can't wait for our first barbecue."

She giggled, her fingers seeking out the delicious expanse of hair that curled through his open shirt. "I can't wait for the wedding."

"When does your mother get here?"

"Friday. She refuses to make any decisions about moving. Says maybe *I'm* going to be a queen, but that doesn't mean *she* wants to live like one."

"All in good time," Eric murmured soothingly, feathering kisses across her cheek. "All in good time. After all, look how far we've come in a few days."

"Yes." Casey sighed, Eric's touch suddenly stirring the embers that glowed in her belly. "Just last week I was a frog." Her legs were shot with sudden fire, her arms reaching for him. "Now I'm going to marry one."

Eric chuckled. His finger trailed along her throat to the open neck of her blouse. "I'm the king now, remember. I can have you beheaded."

Casey stretched against the sweet lightning of his touch. "I thought you were going to ply me with wine and take me on the royal yacht."

Eric's mouth followed the trail, eliciting surprised little gasps. "That's only for mistresses," he said, his tongue descending the valley between her breasts as he mastered her buttons.

With a wicked grin, Casey twisted her fingers in his hair and gave a yank. "What about queens?" she asked with deliberate sweetness when he yelped.

"They get this."

His mouth descended to her breast, hot against the cotton and succulent against her flesh. Casey gasped, arching, the fire crowning without warning, liquefying her with impatient desire. She scrabbled at his back with her hands, dipping to slip them in beneath his shirt, pulling at it to free his chest to her. He leaned against her, his own impatient fire burning the length of her thigh.

Eric dipped a hand to her jeans, sneaking in flat against her belly and tempting the curve of her thigh. Casey moaned, the sun bright in her eyes, Eric's body hot against her hands.

"Eric . . . won't somebody . . . find us . . ."

He lifted his head long enough to answer. "Just poachers. Everybody else knows exactly where we are and why."

"Wonderful . . ."

It was, though. She didn't care who knew. Her body had already sought its new rhythm, arching against the torment of Eric's touch, seeking the feel of him with hungry hands. Casey ran hands along his thighs, the tight square of his buttocks, so firm and tempting, then up the sleek expanse of his back. She buried her mouth into the delicious texture of his chest and let the rasp of it against her tongue and lips inflame her even more.

She felt his hands at her hips, sliding her jeans down. His fingers galvanized her. She lifted to him, aching to feel his hard, strong hands against the soft, sensitive skin there. Impatient to lie naked and vulnerable before his sight.

It was the light of his eyes that praised her the most, their smoky arousal prowling her skin like the touch of a hot wind. Every time he aroused her, Casey wondered how such a flame could be quenched. And yet it was, again and again, and she found herself aching just to awaken the fire again, each time better, each time special for the loving passion in Eric's eyes; in the steely length of him within her.

Her skin was moist with his kisses, her legs trembling for the control, for the fever that raged in her. He bent to take her mouth, mingling sighs and savoring taste and texture. His body was hard against hers, his hair-roughened chest agonizing the tender nipples that strained against him, his thigh chafing hers. His fingers danced in a maddened flight against the hot, slick center of her until she cried out in agony. Casey's body quivered with the impending cataclysm. Her eyes opened to Eric and the sun. Her heart, long lost to him, swelled to bursting for happiness.

"Ah, my fair king," she gasped with a smile, her hands tangled in his soft golden-brown hair, "I am yours. I only ask the chance to try and provide a worthy heir."

For just a moment, Eric's eyes went wide. "You're..."

"I said try. Again and again ... and again ..."

Her hand blindly seeking, Casey found Eric rigid and waiting, and taunted him even more. He gasped at her bold touch and returned the favor. Easing his hand down her thigh, he invited her submission. But again it was Casey who took the initiative. Rolling a surprised Eric on his back, she eased herself on top of him. Then, her eyes wide and tempting, she began to rock. Eric groaned. He brought his own hands up, to her breasts, to the hair that shimmered in the sunlight like rare gold, to the soft, milky skin of her shoulders.

"Witch," he groaned again, the light of laughter in his eyes. "You're a witch. You've cast a spell on me."

"Damn right," she moaned, the hard power of him inside her filling her with light, with unspeakable agony and joy. "And I'm not going to let you go again, either."

They reached the peak together, their names intermingled on the soft summer wind, their arms tight around each other as the light broke over them in shimmering waves like the summer sun.

At the edge of the clearing, a doe appeared and stopped. Paused in that breathless moment before flight, she considered the intertwined couple across the lawn with wide, curious eyes. And then she bounded away, startled by the renewed whispering.

"So I guess I'll have to be queen," Casey said softly, her hand once again stroking Eric's silky hair.

"Do you mind so much?" he asked.

Casey was surprised to see that he was serious. She kissed him, once again nestled within his embrace, the sun warming her skin and the breeze cooling her heated body. Beyond them, the Alps rose in majestic silence and the sky arced into infinity. The calm in the air was palpable.

"No," she said, smiling. "In fact, I'd almost venture to say..."

"Say what?"

"Oh, you know, that we'll..."

His brows knit. "We'll what?"

"C'mon," Casey scoffed with a mischievous smile. "Don't you read fairy tales? What's the last line of everything from Cinderella to Snow White?"

Eric's eyes sparkled with mischief. "The end?"

She scowled. "And then Casey Phillips married her Prince Charming—"

"*King* Charming, if you don't mind."

"...and they lived..."

"In Moritania and Palm Springs."

"Eric!"

He mimicked her pose. "Casey!"

"You're not very romantic."

"I'm lying naked in an open field with you in the middle of the day when I'm supposed to be at the bank," he objected. "What would you call that?"

"Wanton."

Reaching over, he drew a lazy finger along her breast, raising a new crop of goose bumps. "I've always been a man of action," he explained, dipping to taste her swollen lips. "Not words."

She giggled, bringing her hand up to his cheek. "Can you interpret it for me then?"

An hour later, as Casey once again lay nestled in Eric's arms, she decided that she liked the way Eric ended a fairy tale a lot more than the way the Brothers Grimm did. After all, this Prince Charming did a lot more than dance. Now, if she could only teach him about baseball...

* * * * *

A Note from Marion Smith Collins

Dear Reader,

The idea for *Every Night at Eight* actually began with my
first book for Silhouette. *Another Chance* was set in Rome,
and I was fortunate to travel there for my research. On the
way back to the United States, I decided to stop for a few
days in Monaco. I admired Grace Kelly as an actress and
when she became Grace, Princess of Monaco, I devoured
the pictures and stories of her wedding, a live fairy tale in a
fairy-tale setting. Could anything be more romantic?

The principality, though small—only 570 acres—has been
ruled for many years by the Grimaldi family. A tiny country
with densely packed villas climbing steep mountains from
the rock-hewn shores of the Mediterranean Sea, Monaco
and Monte Carlo are exquisite. The gardens are lined with
paths, neatly mowed and lush. Flowers in every color bloom
profusely; rich bougainvillea drips from balconies in every
shade from pink to dark vermilion. And all this in January!

When I asked, the weather pattern was explained to me as a
visualized ski jump. The chill of winter in central and
northern Europe blows down the mountainsides and takes
flight over the coastline, missing the small country perched
on the shores below. The palace itself was regal, evoking
lovely daydreams.

I stored the memories, the brochures and the books, knowing
that one day I would use the images—fictionalized, of
course—in a book. But it had to be just the right story.

My only marriage-of-convenience theme had been
the first fiction I wrote, a Harlequin Romance novel,
The Beachcomber. I won't tell you how long ago that was!
But eventually the favorite theme for so many romances and
the beautiful setting seemed destined to come together as
Every Night at Eight. I hope you find it as romantic as I did.

Happy Reading!

Marion Smith Collins

EVERY NIGHT AT EIGHT

Marion Smith Collins

To Tara Hughes Gavin.

Chapter One

Nicholas Saber looked out the cabin window. The definition of the runway was blurred not only by the aircraft's speed but also by a heavy rain. The nose of the sleek private jet lifted and Nicholas felt the aerodynamic pressure push him gently against the back of his seat. Suddenly, as though plucked by a celestial string, the plane climbed quickly into the air, past the clouds, into the blue afternoon sky above Boston's Logan Airport and leveled off.

Saber unfastened his seat belt and rose to his feet. He stretched his long arms over his head. His fingers brushed the ceiling. He had changed from comfortable traveling clothes, in which he had crossed the Atlantic, to a dark suit, white shirt and tie. The journey was almost over. This was the last leg, this comparatively short hop from Boston to Washington, D.C.

"I'll be damned grateful to get out of this airplane," he

said to his companions, a man and woman who were the only other passengers.

A white-jacketed steward appeared at the curtain that divided the cabin from a forward compartment. "Would you like hors d'oeuvres or drinks, sir?" he asked.

Saber indicated his guests. "Bree? Ryan? What will you have?"

"I'd love some coffee, thanks," Bree O'Hara answered. Lovely, dark-haired Bree wore a simple silk dress in bright crimson, her best color.

"I might like—" began her husband, Ryan.

"Black coffee," Bree finished for him. "Watching our weight, remember?" She smiled sweetly at her husband's frowning face.

Ryan O'Hara was the police commissioner for the city of Boston. When Saber had first met the couple nearly two years ago, Ryan had just been appointed to the position and was responsible for security during Saber's visit to the United States in his official capacity as Karastonia's foreign minister. They had remained good friends.

The police commissioner had been determined to continue active participation. But he'd since learned the bane of administrators everywhere—all paperwork and no action. Blend that with marriage—a contented, happy marriage, as he'd told Nicholas—and fatherhood, and before he knew it Ryan had gained fifteen pounds.

Saber watched them carefully, a small cynical smile on his lips. When love was involved, marriage became a crapshoot, a roll of the dice. But his friends seemed to be making it work. Maybe they were the exception that proves the rule.

True to Saber's expectation, Ryan couldn't maintain a grumbling facade under the force of that sweet smile. "Damn desk job," he growled good-naturedly.

Nicholas laughed. He'd already heard this complaint. "Coffee for all of us," he told the steward.

The steward returned with a tray and set it down on the table between the seats. When they'd been served, the man disappeared again into the forward compartment.

"Now, Saber, do you want to tell us what this is all about?" asked Bree. "Not that we aren't delighted to spend a weekend in such distinguished company—"

Saber snorted. "Bree, you of all people?" Then he smiled. In the presence of his friends he was beginning to relax.

Bree kept a straight face. "I was referring to your position as distinguished Godfather to one April Nichole O'Hara. Is there something else you do?" she asked with mock innocence.

Saber laughed. "That's right. Put me in my place," he quipped. But, as usual, any mention of the adorable six-month-old tyrant who ruled the O'Hara roost provoked a reflective, melancholy feeling within him. "I'm getting married," he announced without further preamble.

"Who is she? Do we know her?" Bree and Ryan both spoke at once. They had visited Karastonia on several occasions, including Saber's inauguration as the first elected president of the country, and had met a number of people, so Bree's question came as no surprise. She was clearly delighted at the idea. "Was she at the inauguration?"

"No, she was unable to be there," said Saber brusquely, remembering the inauguration festivities with a feeling akin to aversion. In fact, during that hectic week he had begun to formulate the plan to remarry. He'd had it brought home to him just how much he needed a hostess, a companion, a wife, at his side.

The king of Karastonia, who had no direct heir, had decided two years ago to set aside the monarchy in favor of democracy. Foreign Minister Saber was the king's cousin and could conceivably have made a case for ascension but he had absolutely no ambition in that direction.

Besides, he agreed wholeheartedly with the king, who felt the time had come to join the worldwide march toward government by the people. He had not agreed with the king, however, that all the plans could be implemented and elections held within one year. But as long as his cousin ruled, he was bound to obey.

It had been a heady and exhausting experience, playing midwife at the birth of a brand-new democracy. And it had not been an easy delivery. Though most of the dissident voices were now grumbling their acceptance, there were still people who thought Karastonia should continue under the centuries-old monarchy.

When the elections were held—at the end of the prescribed year—the majority of his countrymen felt that Saber was the logical choice for president. Admittedly, he had the experience, the dedication and the love for his country. But now, after one year in office, he was beginning to wonder about his endurance.

He was tired. And he was lonely. And so he would take a wife. "You probably don't know her, but you'll meet her this weekend. She's from Virginia," he answered Bree's first question at last.

"She's an American?" asked Ryan, his brows lifting in surprise.

"Her mother is. She has dual citizenship. She's the daughter of our hosts this weekend. Her name is Selena Mastron."

Selena Cybele Victoria Mastron's image rose in his mind as smoothly and as effortlessly as his breath filled his lungs. She was pretty enough, though not a beauty as he remembered her. But she had other, more valuable qualities. Statuesque, dignified, she was extraordinarily intelligent, had natural poise and warmth, a sense of humor and—he added to himself with a slight quirk of his mouth—a good body. Her smoky gray eyes held a hint of sensuality without being unseemingly seductive.

Selena's calm, perceptive intelligence and traditionalism were contributions from her father, retired Karastonian ambassador to the United States. Her grace, as well as her freewheeling independence—the only characteristic that gave him pause—were inherited from her American mother, a former prima ballerina.

Saber had considered long and carefully before coming to the conclusion that Selena would be a perfect wife for him despite her occasional tendency to be a bit too forthright and outspoken. The job he needed her to fill required her cosmopolitan attitude, her dignity, her enterprise, her vitality.

And, at thirty-four, she was mature enough not to expect a vow of eternal love—which was the one thing he couldn't offer.

He described her to his friends, then he went on to explain, "Her father is Karastonian but she was born here and grew up here." He hesitated. "There's one small obstacle," he added soberly. "Selena doesn't know that her father and I have arranged this marriage."

His words were greeted by a long silence. He noted that Bree set her cup down with great care; Ryan's jaw had gone slack.

"An arranged marriage?" murmured Bree, disconcerted. "I didn't know that sort of thing still went on."

She cleared her throat and gave a little laugh. "She sounds extremely... appealing but, Saber, you may be in for trouble."

He smiled at their uneasy exchange of glances. "That's why I especially wanted you two to fly down to Virginia with me for the weekend. I know that American women are different, and I want your advice as to the best way to handle it."

Selena pulled into the four-car garage between her mother's Lincoln and her father's Range Rover. The other vehicle was a sporty runabout model. Her car looked like a poor relation in comparison. *Poor old Pinto,* she thought to herself, as she switched off the engine. As long as a vehicle worked properly and got her where she wanted to go with a minimum of fuss, she didn't particularly care what kind it was.

She sighed, got out of the car and stepped from the building into the last rays of fading sunlight. She shivered; though spring had officially arrived three weeks ago and new blooms seemed to pop out daily, a slight chill remained in the air. She took her small suitcase out of the back.

The sight of her family home, as always, warmed and soothed her. She smiled. Located in suburban Virginia outside Washington, D.C., the two-story manor-style house was an island of peace and quiet set amid rolling lawns and shaped boxwood, formal gardens and bridle paths. The pebbled walkway crunched under her sneaker-clad feet as she headed toward the house; she inhaled the fresh, sweet scent of the early jasmine vine that shaded the trellis near the side door.

Spring break. To her students it meant a trip to the beach; to Selena it meant going home. She could look forward to being pampered for a few days. She smiled, too, at the memory of her adolescent resentment and rebellion toward the attention and coddling she received as an only child.

But no more. She wouldn't resent the coddling this week. This week she was going to revel in it. Her steps quickened in anticipation.

Thank heavens the long, tedious interval of professional pressure at the college where she taught was over. No more interviews, conferences, discussions, no more scrutiny of her private life to judge whether she was worthy, in the eyes of the college administration, of tenure. All the questions had been asked; all the testimony given. Now she simply had to await the verdict.

There was competition, of course, and she would have to live with the uncertainty for a few more hours. A friend of hers, Van Styles, was also under consideration. She liked Van; at one time she'd thought he might have become more than merely a friend. But she had been with the college nearly two years longer, and, to be honest, she was a better teacher. That was one of the reasons the relationship hadn't worked out.

The decision of tenure was taken very seriously indeed by the committee that recommended candidates to the board of governors of the college. After tenure was offered and accepted, the board expected the tenuree to remain with the school until he or she died or retired, whichever came first. The committee weeded out the persons who might not be fully appreciative of that singular honor, and once they made their recommendation, the matter was as good as settled. The committee, however, had been unable to arrive at a decision.

This morning she'd been informed of yet another delay. This latest holdup didn't bode well for her cause, she knew, and she was angry over it. But she managed to control her impatience.

The side door leading to her mother's morning room was locked. Odd. Selena rattled the knob, shrugged and headed around to the front entrance.

Though the members of the committee hadn't come right out and admitted so, this latest delay in the promotion process was prompted by the fact that she was an unmarried woman. The subject of her marital status had first arisen earlier this week. The men wanted guarantees that she was not planning marriage. The question was such a surprise, that she'd hesitated.

They had not been pleased at her hesitation. Their prissy little comments about things like biological clocks and maternal instincts had been almost comical. She'd recovered quickly, reassuring them that she had no plans at present for marriage or a family.

But the damage had been done. She could tell by their frowns and thin-lipped silence. She'd had to remind them, subtly, of course, that such questions on their part were illegal as hell.

She climbed the shallow steps, crossed the broad veranda and tried the front door. It was locked, too. Perplexed, she pushed the bell, and pushed it again.

The man who opened the door was an unsmiling stranger in a three-piece suit. His demeanor and his thorough scrutiny screamed security.

Selena was not unfamiliar with the type. "Ah-h-h, hello," she said, more puzzled than alarmed. Having grown up in a home where a person of any nationality was apt to turn up at any time, entourage in tow, she wasn't particularly surprised.

"You're Ms. Mastron?" demanded the man sharply.

No accent. That was interesting. His dour face was inscrutable. He was not extremely tall but his broad shoulders almost filled the doorway. He examined her very carefully, as though she were a specimen with which he was unfamiliar. That could very well be. She wasn't exactly dressed for visitors. Her faded blue denim slacks were casual and worn enough to be comfortable, and her blue shirt was rumpled. The pretty pink sweater vest, knitted by her mother, was the only decent-looking item of clothing she wore.

By the time he had concluded his appraisal of her, she had the feeling of having been dissected, examined and laid out to dry. "Dr. Mastron, actually," she said, wondering if she had proclaimed her title in an effort to establish some degree of credibility with this person. If so, it hadn't worked.

"Won't you come in?" he said woodenly.

Before she could recover from the amazement of being politely invited into her parents' house by a total stranger, and a mean-looking one at that, her mother emerged from the drawing room.

"Darling, I thought I heard the bell. I'm so glad you're here."

"Mother, is anything wrong?"

Selena was enclosed in a warm, fragrant hug. "Nothing, dear," said Jayne Mastron, a hint of laughter in her eyes as she drew back and looked at her daughter. She frowned, but it wasn't because of the clothes. Jayne was accustomed to her daughter's traveling wardrobe. "You look tired."

Before she could assure her mother that she was indeed very tired, Jayne took her under her arm and waved her free hand toward the stranger.

"And this is Mr. Smith."

Sure he is, thought Selena. And I'm Minnie Mouse. She nodded her acknowledgment of the introduction. "Mr. Smith."

"Saber is going to visit us over the weekend," Jayne went on to explain. "He should be arriving within the hour."

Selena did not like the little skip of anticipation that her heart delivered at the news of Nicholas Saber's imminent arrival. She reminded herself that she'd recovered from her adolescent fascination with the handsome widower long, long ago.

Nicholas Saber was the president of Karastonia, the tiny, beautiful country on the Aegean Sea that was her father's homeland. She looked around to discover that Mr. Smith—she'd been correct about his security status— had melted away.

With a philosophical shrug Selena laid aside her expectations for a relaxing holiday. She certainly wouldn't be pampered, not with Saber around. She wouldn't be able to throw on another old pair of jeans and ride wild over the countryside whenever she felt like it. She wouldn't be able to pour out her frustrations over her job to her mother—who would understand—and her father who wouldn't understand, but who would comfort her, anyway.

On the other hand, things seemed to...happen... whenever Saber appeared. He had a knack for bringing excitement in the room with him, as though he donned it with his clothing. And wherever he went, whether he sought the attention or not, he became the focal point of any gathering.

"Saber's friends from Boston, the O'Haras, are coming, as well. Do you remember us mentioning that we met them at the inauguration?"

She caught her breath. "Yes," she said softly. But the name O'Hara brought forth an uglier, more vivid memory. "Isn't he the police commissioner who helped save Saber's life when he was in Boston several years ago?"

Jayne chuckled but her eyes were serious as she laid her hand on her daughter's chilled cheek. "To hear Ryan tell it, Saber didn't need his help." She glanced at her watch. "You have plenty of time to change later, Selena. Leave your bag, and come into your father's study for a few minutes. We have a fire in there. I hope it's the last one of the season."

Selena dropped her bag at the foot of the stairs and followed her mother down the hall. "Where is Daddy?"

"He's—"

"Right here, my darling," said a voice from behind them.

Selena turned to be immediately warmed by her father's smile. He'd just come in from outside and his hair was windblown. She noted that he was moving stiffly as though he'd pulled a muscle. He'd probably been riding his rascally old stallion, Black Snow.

"Hi, Daddy." Again she was enveloped in a hug, this one secure and enthusiastic and smelling of rich pipe tobacco. She hugged him back, her enthusiasm equal to his; she adored him.

But when she drew away to look more closely at his face she noticed a pale cast to his skin that hadn't been there the last time she was home. She was probably imagining things. She schooled her features into familiarity and affection. "How are you?"

"I'm fine," he said heartily—too heartily.

Turnus Mastron was not quite as tall as his wife or daughter but he managed to take both of them under his arms and together they entered the room where a fire blazed merrily on the hearth. "Your mother told you that Nicholas is coming for the weekend?" There was a hint of pride in his voice. His close friendship with the charismatic leader was a point of pride to him.

Selena tried to reclaim some of her earlier animation as she held out her hands toward the fireplace. "Yes, she did. I am properly impressed, I assure you. Is this an official visit?"

"Not this weekend, no. He will spend the better part of next week in Washington attending to state affairs but he has some personal business to attend to first," he answered with a satisfied expression.

Jayne shot her husband a speaking look.

"A vacation weekend," he amended, trying to disguise the pleasure in his accomplishment. He went to a serving cart that held the makings for drinks and began to prepare a Scotch for himself and two small, stemmed glasses of dry sherry for Selena and her mother.

Selena had intercepted the look that passed between her parents but she chose to ignore it. Most likely there was some minor crisis that Saber wanted her father to advise him on and her mother was cautioning discretion. Though Turnus had retired as Karastonia's ambassador to the United States, he was often called upon for consultation. Her mother said it kept him young.

She turned her back to the fire, took the glass her father offered and sipped tentatively. The liqueur was really too heavy for her taste but her father thought all women should drink sherry and all men, Scotch. She'd long ago given up arguing with him.

"Well, Selena, are you going to keep us in suspense?" asked Jayne, leaning forward from her seat on the sofa. "Did you get your promotion?"

Selena sighed and set her glass aside as she joined her mother on the sofa. "I still don't know. Now the committee says they'll announce their decision this week."

"But that's what they said last week," protested Jayne.

Selena nodded. "And the week before that. They've raised a new question now," she said, unable to keep the irony from her voice. "I'm afraid the old maids are worried that I might be hit by the nesting urge."

"The old maids?" said Turnus, clearly puzzled. "I thought the committee was made up of men."

Her father had lived in this country for thirty-five years and he rarely had trouble with idioms, but Selena smiled and explained, "They *are* men, Daddy, but they are old maids in any case. To translate—they're wondering if I will want to marry and have a family." She shrugged. "I tried to tell them that the thought never entered my mind, but they don't want to hand out tenure to a woman, anyway. And to convey the honor and have her resign in favor of a husband and a baby would be a disaster."

"I can understand that," said Turnus thoughtfully.

"Daddy." She shook her head in resigned amusement and looked at her mother, who seemed to be choking on something. "I don't know how you put up with him," she added, laughing. "I suppose I'd better change my clothes before the distinguished guests descend upon us." She rose and crossed to her father's side and kissed him on the cheek. "You old chauvinist," she said fondly.

It was an accusation that had been made many times in this house when she was young, she recalled as she climbed the stairs to her room. But the amusement had long since replaced her adolescent rancor. She still had trouble comprehending her mother's acceptance of the old-world, male domination that seemed inbred in Turnus.

But Selena had her own life now; her father's chauvinistic standards didn't affect her any longer, thank goodness.

* * *

The dining room had grown relatively quiet as the people around the polished mahogany table addressed their food. The civilized clink of silverware on china, and the soft muffled footsteps of the butler as he served, removed, and kept the wineglasses filled, were the dominant sounds. The occasional murmur was almost a surprise accent to the hushed atmosphere.

Something was up, thought Selena, as she chewed thoughtfully. Her gaze traveled from one of her dinner companions to the next; she seemed to be the only one who wasn't knowledgeable. From the moment they'd gathered together, she'd sensed a watchfulness, a cautious expectation emanating from the other five. The aura of expectation was so strong that it sang in the air and seemed to envelop the whole house.

She would have been worried about a world crisis of some kind, if the others weren't all so—so—*jolly* was the only word she could come up with to describe their behavior, but it wasn't really a good description.

Even her father seemed in excellent spirits, and she was convinced now that he was not feeling well. Over a succulent bite of quail, smothered Southern-style, her eyes met those of Bree O'Hara. She smiled with her eyes.

The smile was returned, but the pretty brunette was as edgy as everyone else and—Selena didn't like this observation—she thought she saw sympathy in Bree's eyes.

Ryan interjected with a remark about the food and the visual contact was broken before she could really judge it. She set aside the disquietude prompted by that look, deciding she must have misread it.

She had avoided looking at Saber, seated to her left. But he'd had no such reservation. In fact his eyes had widened in surprise when he'd greeted her. Now she felt his gaze resting often on her profile.

She was dramatically aware of him. Warmth seemed to emanate from his large frame, his deep voice sent shivers through her, and the fresh, clean smell of his distinctive after-shave drifted toward her. She began to wish she had worn something more conservative than the rose silk that left her shoulders bare.

She hadn't seen him in over a year but he was as handsome as she'd remembered. No, he was more so. Maturity enhanced his looks as well as his self-confidence. Though the silver strands in his hair were more numerous now than the last time she'd seen him, the gray was insignificant in his thick hair. He was still physically powerful, as well. Strength radiated from him. And his dark eyes still held a hint of sensuality and, surprisingly, laughter, even beneath the burden of arduous responsibility that was reflected there.

On her right, at the head of the table sat her father, another disturbance. He had barely touched his dinner. She was beginning to worry seriously about his health.

"Selena?" Her mother's voice interrupted her thoughts.

Selena resented the rush of color that stained her cheeks. "I'm sorry, Mother. Please forgive me for being such an automaton tonight," she added to the others around the table.

Bree came to her rescue. "I understand you are waiting for news of a promotion?"

Now, how in the world had Bree O'Hara known that? "Yes. The dean of the history department retired unexpectedly last year, leaving some gaps in the faculty. I'm hoping for tenure." She couldn't explain further without going into all her frustrations, and such complaints were hardly acceptable for dinner-table conversation. She waved her hand dismissively. "The politics of academia are sometimes hard to explain."

"As are politics in general," inserted Saber smoothly. He went on to tell an amusing anecdote about a French representative to the United Nations, known to be a rather snobbish gourmet, being stranded in a small southern town in the United States and being forced to breakfast in a café called Mom's. Saber swore that the man was now trying to corner the export market on grits.

The others laughed and Selena sent him a grateful glance.

"Would you like something else, Nicholas? More wine?" asked Jayne when they'd finished with dessert.

"No, thank you, Jayne," Saber answered, distracted once more by a movement from Selena next to him. He'd noticed the fatigue that touched her lovely face—that face that had been such a shock to him—and wondered what had caused it. He hoped to hell she wasn't troubled over a love affair. That could complicate things. He was unaware of the frown that chased across his brow.

"Then, shall we have our coffee in the living room?" Jayne rose.

Saber got to his feet and held the chair for Selena. She threw a polite, if absent, smile of thanks over her shoulder and preceded him out of the room. Just before they reached the door to the living room he stopped her with a touch at her elbow. "I need to talk to you alone for a few minutes." He leaned forward and spoke in a low voice so the others wouldn't overhear. He realized suddenly that his lips were only inches from her bare shoulder. The skin there was unblemished, as smooth as creamy satin. He straightened abruptly to meet her blank expression.

"Now?" she asked as she turned. She had spoken too sharply, drawing the stares of the others.

He frowned and ignored the sudden silence and varying looks from the other four people. Turnus's smile was confident; Jayne's was anxious; Bree and Ryan still wore traces of the initially stunned, then dubious, expressions with which they had greeted his announcement on the plane this afternoon.

He'd dismissed the warnings of his friends that convincing Selena to marry him would be a difficult task. Not that he'd ever really believed it would be easy, but he knew his own powers of persuasion and he was confident that Selena would agree to be his wife. He regretted the need for haste but the obvious fact that she was disturbed about her job might be a plus. "If this is a convenient time for you," he said formally.

Selena's tired look turned into one of concern as she saw him frown and she realized that she had become the

focus of attention. ''Well, no. I mean I don't mind.
Would you like to talk in Father's study?''

Saber nodded. Aware of the sudden uneasiness that
chased across her features, he gave her a reassuring smile.
''Thank you.'' He glanced at Jayne. ''Will you excuse
us?''

''Certainly,'' she answered quickly. ''Shall I have coffee sent to you?''

Saber hesitated. ''No, we'll join you shortly.''

Jayne nodded and led the others into the living room
while Saber followed Selena down the hall and into the
study.

Chapter Two

As he entered the study behind Selena, Saber's mind registered several things, the first of which was her unforeseen and unexpected sensual appeal. He'd always known she was attractive but this beautiful, sexy woman was not the one he'd remembered when he'd made his plans.

Her hair, thick and lustrous, was pulled into a severe chignon. He wondered what it would look like spilling down her back. She moved gracefully, the rose silk of her dress made a rustling sound against her legs and her perfume was heady. She gave him a dubious glance.

With the door closed, the room became intimate and cozy. He paused, relished the silence, the peace, the opportunity for a moment of gentle distraction in the world of hard government business. The draperies had been drawn. The darkness in the room was broken only by a hooded desk lamp and the soft glow of firelight.

"Would you like a brandy?" she asked, moving to a sideboard.

"If you'll join me."

She smiled. "You looked very serious back there. Am I going to need it?"

"Possibly."

He should have thought before he answered. With the word, her hand, holding the decanter, halted in midair. She secured the bottom with her other hand, and he could see that both hands were shaking. "I've had the impression all evening that something was simmering just under the surface of the dinner conversation. Please tell me, is there something wrong with my father?" she asked. Her voice had dropped to a frightened plea.

"No, of course not, Selena. I give you my word."

Silently he admonished Turnus. He hadn't missed the former ambassador's anxious mood during dinner. He wasn't sure what had caused the show of nerves that was so unlike Turnus. Mentally he shrugged—only child leaving home, he supposed.

But Selena had noted it, as well, and thought her father was ailing. He took a step toward her, then halted. He felt uncertain as to how to proceed. Such feelings were alien to him.

He opened the button of his dinner jacket and thrust one hand into the pocket of his trousers. "What I have to say is personal. It is a subject to be discussed between you and me."

Her alarm turned to puzzlement. "You and me?"

Nicholas nodded to the sideboard. "Pour the brandy and let's sit down."

If thirty years ago, Turnus had taken his family back to Karastonia to live, he thought irritably, this would have been so much easier. Everything could have been arranged with a minimum of commotion.

The Karastonian practice of arranging marriages was not carried out with barbaric inflexibility, but it was common. Traditional. No Karastonian father would ever force his daughter—or son—into a distasteful alliance. But an advantageous marriage was something that the parents were responsible for providing for their children, just like food and clothing, shelter and an education. The children grew up expecting it.

And the system worked extremely well. The divorce rate in his country was one of the lowest among the Western nations.

But here in the United States he was faced with a drastically different situation. He was confronting an independent Yankee who just happened to have Karastonian blood in her veins. Instead of the calm, logical conversation he'd anticipated, instead of the cool, reasoned arguments with which he'd hoped to present his plan, he'd managed to alarm her.

Sounds registered in the silence, which only moments ago had seemed so peaceful. The light clink of the decanter against the glass, muffled footsteps on thick carpet, and quickly she was standing in front of him, holding out a heavily cut balloon glass.

Saber's hands were large and well kept, Selena noticed. And warm, she added to herself, as his fingers brushed hers. "My father doesn't really approve of women drinking anything but sherry," she said, indicative of absolutely nothing. As she released the glass she was distracted for a moment by the clean scent of his after-shave. He'd managed to defuse her worry with his quick denial and now she tried to relax, but, under the best of circumstances, relaxation wasn't easily accomplished around this man.

She settled into one of a comfortable pair of red leather chairs that flanked the fireplace. He took the other. The fire popped, the leather creaked. She was grateful that his features were in shadow. But she was also surprised to note that she didn't need to see him to be affected by his nearness.

Saber was as sexy as he'd ever been. What was his age now? Forty-two or three? Somewhere around there. She remembered his being slightly less than ten years older than her. No matter. At eighty, Nicholas Saber would be sexy.

She wondered what he wanted to discuss with her that couldn't be discussed in front of the others. But she folded her hands in her lap and waited patiently. If Saber was like the other men she'd known from her father's homeland, he'd tell her in his own time; pressing him wouldn't do a bit of good.

Nicholas took a breath. Good Lord, he'd faced diplomatic antagonists, business competitors and political rivals with a lot more assurance than he felt right now. What could she do? Say no? Then he'd just have to begin looking for someone else. No big deal, as the Americans said.

"Selena, have you ever considered marriage?" he asked, partly to break the ice, partly to give himself an additional minute to read her reaction.

His words were greeted with a soft, husky chuckle. "That's one way to open a conversation." She shook her head in amusement.

He felt his features ease into a smile.

"My father says you are a master at the unexpected diplomatic ambush, but I am neither a diplomat, nor am

I a distracted prey. I have no idea what you're leading up to. Why don't you just come out with it?''

Saber deliberately set aside his glass and slouched in his chair, crossing his feet at the ankles and linking his fingers over his stomach. The position brought his face out of the shadows and allowed her a view of his expression. ''I am here to ask you to become my wife.''

That part had been Bree's idea. Ask, don't tell.

She laughed.

He liked her laugh, he decided. He found the sound to be like a soothing, satisfying melody.

Saber frowned again, realizing that he was noticing too much. He remained silent.

''You're not serious,'' she said, amused.

''I assure you, I am very serious.''

She was still more amused than concerned. ''But why would you ask such a thing? You don't love me.''

His expression grew hard. ''Of course not. Love doesn't enter into this at all. That should be clarified from the first.''

The lovely smile faded from her face to be replaced with a perplexed frown. ''You'll have to excuse my being so dense. I don't quite understand, I'm afraid.''

She was stepping carefully, he noticed. He almost laughed—she clearly didn't want to offend him. There was plenty of her father's talent for diplomacy in her, after all. ''I also find myself somewhat at a loss.'' Hoping to get this over with as quickly as possible, he gave her what he hoped was a reassuring look. ''You know, Selena, this is the first time I've ever proposed.''

''But you've been married,'' she protested, her confusion mounting. Suddenly her brow cleared. And her eyes narrowed suspiciously. ''Oh. That was an arranged marriage, wasn't it?''

Dangerous ground, thought Saber. Bree had also cautioned that, above all, he should *never* let Selena know that he had arranged the marriage with her father. "Most American women would be deeply offended by that sort of arrangement," Bree had said. She had then added, "You have to give her a very good reason to give up what sounds like a promising career."

"Yes, my first marriage was arranged," he said calmly. "We were both very young," he added, hoping the excuse would defuse the situation, so he could go on and give her his 'very good reason.'

She straightened in her chair. "Did my father know about this?" she demanded.

"I discussed the offer with both of your parents, yes," he answered carefully.

"Did you also know that my father once tried to arrange a marriage for me?" she demanded, those smoky gray eyes flashing.

Her anger, swift and unanticipated, seemed to have come from nowhere. Damn it, Turnus should have warned him. No wonder he'd been nervous at dinner. Saber maintained an even tone. "No, I didn't know that. Clearly you didn't appreciate his efforts."

She shot him another glare. "Of course I didn't appreciate his efforts. It is an outdated and rather insulting custom." Then she shrugged and struggled to control her annoyance. "Well, no matter. I appreciate your offer of marriage, but the answer is no."

"Is there someone else?" He spoke quickly, irritated by her instant refusal.

"No," she answered, just as quickly. "I simply don't wish to be married." She sat forward as though she were going to leave.

He'd expected her reaction. "I hope you'll hear me out," he said smoothly. "At least, give me a chance to explain my position to you. You know, Selena, that this suggestion didn't simply come out of nowhere."

She watched him warily but didn't object further. Instead she eased back in the chair and waited.

He picked up his glass again and absently swirled the amber liquid around, watching the motion. "I knew when I stood for election that the office of president would be demanding, especially since we were still feeling our way along in regard to many issues."

He sipped from his glass. "Over a year has now passed since the election. We'll soon celebrate the first anniversary of our democracy."

He hoped that he wasn't revealing too much of his weariness, but he sighed, aware that he had to be honest about his reasons if he were to have a chance of winning her acceptance. "In reality, the office of president is even more arduous than I had anticipated," he admitted wryly. "I find that I genuinely need a woman at my side. A woman like you. And not only for companionship. I need the guidance of someone with your experience. Though the birth of democracy has brought about many positive changes, it has also been a strenuous transition." During the pause that followed his words, he rose to return his glass to the bar. The brandy was potent and he was tired enough to appreciate its relaxing benefits, but he needed his wits about him. "It's been particularly difficult for the women."

Selena had her mouth open to reiterate the fact that she had no intention of accepting Saber's proposal, but at his last statement, she hesitated. "The women?"

He shrugged and returned to the chair facing her. "Men seem to take naturally to freedom. Women don't," he said carelessly.

She stared at him, unable to find words to express her wonder at this whole conversation, particularly his last, negligently offensive, comment. She shook her head helplessly.

He took the gesture for another negative and went on, "I hope you won't refuse without considering the good you could do. The women of our country—and especially the young girls, the women of tomorrow—need a strong intelligent role model." He leaned forward in his chair and rested his forearms on his knees; his urgency communicated itself to her in his posture and in the steady way his eyes met hers. "And I want—need—a wife to share my life." He paused, one corner of his mouth turning up in what might have been a small smile of regret.

Selena remembered his wife, Lisha, so beautiful, dying so young. The gossip had been that Nicholas Saber was devastated. From her own observation, she didn't doubt it for a second. That must be the reason for his statement about love not entering into this. He would never love anyone the way he had loved Lisha.

Then she had another thought. What would the people of his country—she couldn't think of it as her own, even though legally it was—think when he married again?

"So this would not be...what did they call it in Victorian times? A marriage in name only?"

"God, no! That would be a very uncomfortable situation."

Despite herself she was both flattered and stirred by his prompt denial.

"I hope you don't imagine that you have to be in love with someone to feel desire and physical enjoyment," he went on. "Love is a dangerous emotion."

She wasn't sure how to answer. Her blood warmed quickly under the deep tone of his voice and the intensity of his gaze as he let his eyes roam over her.

"I won't hurry you into bed." He exhaled heavily and sat back again. Once more the shadows claimed his face. "You must understand, Selena. I haven't lived the life of a monk and I don't intend to start now. But, if you marry me, I give you my word that I'll be faithful."

Selena sighed, linked her fingers and leaned forward, unconsciously mirroring his former posture. "Saber, I am not unaware of the honor you do me, and yours is an appealing offer." Without thinking she had slipped into the more formal cadence of continental English. "But I must answer with a definite and final no. I have a life, a career, family, here in the United States. I have no wish to leave." She spread her hands in a gesture of finality. "I'm sorry."

His eyes were black as sin, she thought, fascinated by the glare of displeasure she saw in the dark, brooding gaze. This man didn't like to lose. And then, as quickly as the expression had appeared, it vanished, making her wonder if she'd imagined it.

"I understand," he said noncommittally. Then he stood up, a signal that the conversation was over. "I suppose we should join the others."

Clearly he felt no real regret. Selena was surprised at the sting of disappointment she felt at that. "Please make my excuses to the others. I am really tired and I think I'd like to go to bed now."

"Certainly." He crossed to the door and held it open for her. "Good night, Selena."

"Good night, Saber." She paused, thinking that she might add something. But what could she say? Finally, she shook her head and left him.

* * *

Saber's brain was still functioning in another time zone. He knew he would be unable to sleep, so when he reached his room he didn't undress.

He had brought plenty of work with him but, after a few minutes, he realized that his papers weren't going to hold his attention. He thought about reading, but nothing on the shelves appealed to him. He flipped on the television, and flipped it off again. Restlessly he wandered the large bedroom.

The house was too damned quiet. From a chair, he picked up his discarded jacket and tie and stood for a moment looking down at them. Then he dropped them again.

He'd been rather surprised at his let-down feeling and had fought to keep it from showing as he'd made Selena's excuses and carried on a conversation with the others over coffee.

Thank God none of them had dared to question him concerning the results of his interview with Selena. Considering the mood he was in, he would probably have bitten off a head or two.

Odd. He hadn't realized that her refusal would affect him in that way—in *any* way. Maybe because he hadn't expected her to refuse. Damn it, he needed her. *Karastonia* needed her, he amended.

He paced for a moment, trying to come up with an alternative. Thoughtfully, he searched his mental list of acquaintances for another woman who could fulfill all his criteria. He couldn't come up with a single one who was as appropriate as Selena.

What had happened to his celebrated powers of persuasion? he asked himself. Where were the smooth words when he needed them? Where were the diplomatic finesse, the savvy, the skill, the subtlety?

He rolled back his sleeves another notch and marched determinedly to the bookshelf. To hell with it, he thought as he pulled down a book and let it fall open in his broad hand. He'd find someone else.

He paused, book forgotten in his hand, and stared into the middle distance.

There was no avoiding it. Selena Mastron had seemed tailor-made for the role of Mrs. Nicholas Saber.

The household was quiet. Selena had heard the footsteps in the broad hallway, the soft good-nights and the closing doors, only because she was listening for them. She was wide-awake, unsettled by Saber's astonishing proposal. Unsettled, as well, by her own response to the idea. True, she had no interest in marriage, but if she did have, Nicholas Saber would certainly be a leading candidate for a husband.

She thought about the beautiful country that held a number of members of her family as well as half her allegiance. The women she had known from there were bright, cosmopolitan. Saber must be exaggerating the problem. And yet, if there was a problem, she was flattered that he thought she could be part of the solution. As a matter of fact, the more she thought about it, the more flattered she was by the whole proposal. *Nicholas Saber*...

When the telephone rang at midnight, she had almost forgotten she was expecting a call. She snatched up the extension on the table beside her bed, hoping the sound hadn't awakened anyone else.

The conversation lasted no more than a minute, then she hung up.

Had the telephone rung more than one time, Saber would have answered the extension in his room. He was accustomed to being awakened at all hours, but he wondered who in this house was expecting a call so late.

As a rule, midnight phone calls signaled an emergency. *Or they were from a lover.*

Bree certainly didn't have one of those. He doubted that Jayne had ever had an unfaithful thought in her life. Which left Selena. Had she lied to him about being involved with another man? Was she even now whispering soft words of passion into the telephone?

Or was there something amiss in the household? He went to his door and listened.

Selena grumbled under her breath as she leaned into the refrigerator. Surely there was some strawberry jam; her mother *knew* she loved strawberry jam. There had always been a standing order for the stuff.

She reached to the very back, knocking over a jar of mayonnaise in the process, and brought out the only squat jar she could find. Raspberry. Well, that would have to do.

When she turned, she almost dropped the jar. Saber stood in the doorway, still dressed in his tux pants and white shirt. "Saber! You scared me."

"I'm sorry." He eyed the jar she held. "I heard the telephone."

Selena gave a fleeting thought to her own attire and then dismissed it. She'd pulled on her jeans with the faded Redskins shirt she slept in. Not glamorous but certainly modest enough. "I'm sorry it woke you. The call was for me."

He seemed to stiffen. "I was awake. A problem?" he asked casually.

She went to the drawer that held the silverware and took out a spoon. "No." She set the jar down hard and screwed off the top. Then she hooked a stool over with her bare toe and plunked herself down, anger in every aspect of her movements. "Well, yes. A co-worker called."

Van Styles had tried, but hadn't succeeded, to keep the triumph out of his voice. "I didn't get my promotion," she stated curtly.

"Ah, Selena, I'm sorry," he said. He sat on the stool across from her and folded his arms on the counter. "Your mother told me how much you had been counting on it. Aren't you going to put that on anything?" He nodded toward the spoonful of jam she was raising to her lips.

She tasted the sweet fruity mixture before she answered. Not bad. "No, I like it straight. Though I prefer strawberry. Would you like—?" She indicated the jar.

He smiled, but shuddered inwardly at the thought. "No, thank you."

They sat that way for a minute, neither of them speaking. Saber's mind was turning over the news about her job. Could he use it to his advantage? He lifted his head and what he saw sent all self-concern out of his thoughts. A couple of glistening tears hovered at the corner of her eyes.

She looked over and caught him watching her. She lifted her chin and blinked furiously to stem the tears. But the action merely served to dislodge them. They tumbled down her cheeks. "I'm sorry," she whispered, swiping at the wetness with her fingertips. "I half expected this after my last interview with the board of regents. I shouldn't let it upset me."

And that was his undoing. She looked so vulnerable. It was the first time he'd ever seen her look that way. The legs of his stool scraped the floor noisily. He circled the table and pulled her gently to her feet. "Ah, Selena, it's not worth your tears."

She felt dainty in his arms and smelled of wildflowers. Her hair was silky against his face. He held her for a long time. She was no longer crying, but she seemed to respond to his support. He ran his hand down her back to her waist and back up again.

She lifted her face and Saber couldn't resist. Without thinking, he covered her sweet naked lips with his. The kiss was brief, light. When he lifted his head to look down at her, he saw that her eyes were slightly burnished to a dark pewter color. The reaction warmed him clear through and gave him hope. She hadn't exactly returned the kiss, but she hadn't protested, either. And the kiss had affected her; he could tell by her eyes.

Selena drew out of Saber's arms, holding his gaze and searching for something to say. She appreciated his tenderness and comfort, accepted the support of his strong arms willingly, without hesitation. She couldn't deny that, but now there was this moment of stinging awareness between them as a result of the kiss. She couldn't let him think that one kiss would change things.

Before she could speak, the refrigerator kicked on, startling them both. He looked around for the source of the disturbance. Their gazes met again, clashed with a note of self-consciousness, parted.

"Do the people at the school really appreciate your talents, Selena?"

It was such an odd question that Selena laughed, a bit shakily, but she laughed, nonetheless. "Obviously not." The moment of awareness had passed, she thought with some relief as he moved back around the counter to his stool and she resumed her place across from him. It was a great deal more comfortable that way, she told herself as she plucked a tissue from a box on the counter and blew her nose.

"Then let me urge you to reconsider my proposal." He held up his hand when she would have spoken. "You don't have to answer me now, but I would ask that you think about it. I promise that if you can bring yourself to accept, you will be appreciated not only by me, but also by the people of Karastonia."

She looked at him, the automatic protest dying on her lips, and she thought about what he'd said. She hadn't really given him a fair hearing, she decided. Dangerous as it was to listen to this charismatic man, she was interested and concerned.

"Tell me more about the problems the women are facing, Saber." Surprisingly she slipped easily into the Karastonian language with its rounded vowels and softly rolled consonants.

He, too, switched languages. "This may take a while."

"And I'm sure you're tired from your long trip. I should have thought of that."

He smiled, activating the deep, sexy slash in his cheek. "I'm still on Karastonian time and that makes it early afternoon. Are you sleepy?"

That smile of his was intensely potent; she must never—ever—let herself forget the overpowering infatuation she used to have for him. Because no matter how potent, that smile was also rare—most of the time he wore a look of grim determination. "No."

Facing her across the counter he began to talk. "From the moment he began to plan toward the change in government, my cousin knew he didn't want to bring along the baggage of the past. We wanted women fully involved in the governing of the country. The vote, once it was given, would be given to everyone over the age of twenty. It was never our intention to exclude women. We encouraged registration, but it wasn't until the first elections that we discovered that most of the people who had registered were men. And that won't work in a democracy. We need to produce an informed female electorate, as well. I feel the best way is by example. As my wife, you would be a highly visible woman and good symbol of what we wish to accomplish. You have the experience of having lived in a democracy all your life. You are a teacher. And from what I hear, a good one, despite the opinion of your board."

"I might consider taking a teaching job there," she said tentatively.

He shook his head firmly. "You can teach if you like. In fact, I would encourage you to do so. But you wouldn't be as effective as a role model. If we were married, you would be much more visible, much more influential." He reached across the counter and took her hands. His own were warm and slightly rough. "I know your inclination is to refuse again. I'm not asking for an answer immediately but I'm urging you to think seriously about marrying me. The proposal may have sounded impulsive but, I assure you, it isn't. I've thought this through very carefully. I'm offering you another kind of opportunity, Selena." He released her and folded his arms on the counter. He fixed her with his sin-dark gaze. When he spoke again he was serious and sincere. "You can make an important and significant difference in our country. If I didn't believe that, I wouldn't say it.''

''Why me?'' Her voice was not as strong as she would have liked it to be.

''You're the perfect choice. You're Karastonian.''

''I'm American, too.''

''You have dual citizenship,'' he said.

''But *marriage,* Saber?'' Selena took another spoonful of jam and switched back to English. ''We're not talking about going out for a casual date.''

Saber dropped his chin, closing his lips as though to hide a smile. She glared at him and cleaned the jam off the spoon. It tasted sweet in her mouth. Almost sickeningly so. When he raised his gaze again, she saw no sign of amusement.

''I realize that you and I are not very well acquainted. We would maintain separate quarters for a while, to allow ourselves time to get to know each other. I won't rush you into a physical relationship before you're ready. You are a lovely woman, Selena, and I'm very attracted to you but I realize that you can't possibly feel the same way.''

Oh, no? came the unbidden thought. I've been half in love with you since I was twelve. Her mind reeled with reminiscences—the memory of herself as a daydreaming, besotted girl; the newspaper pictures she'd collected of the charismatic foreign minister, the dry-throated responses when they'd happened to meet—and the possibilities he was laying before her now. But a schoolgirl crush was one thing; marriage was another.

She realized suddenly that this was the explanation for the sympathetic look in Bree O'Hara's eyes. Not to mention the worry in her mother's, and the satisfaction in her father's. She wasn't sure she liked that. She replaced the top on the jar of jam. "Your Excellency..." The title had slipped out.

For the first time since he'd arrived, he laughed. The sound was rich and very masculine. Ribbons of awareness wove heat around her spine. She wondered if he realized how lusty his laugh was.

"Forget the titles, Selena. We did away with those along with the monarchy. You called me Saber before. Or—my given name is Nicholas. Will you reconsider?" he added mildly.

She was disgusted with herself; she had known that his title was obsolete. Still she didn't know what she wanted to call him. She took refuge in propriety. "Very well. I would have to have some time, however, to think it over."

"Of course." He hesitated, then went on. "If you decide to marry me, I will also make it financially worth your while." That had been Ryan's idea.

Unaccustomed to feeling as ambiguous as she had felt for the past thirty minutes or so, she was grateful for the excuse to be annoyed. "I'll give you one piece of advice for free, Saber," she said, reverting automatically to Karastonian again. She rose, keeping her expression noncommittal. "Of all the ludicrous statements I've heard during this long, long night, an offer of money is the most offensive so far. I've told you I will think about it. Now, if you'll excuse me, I'm going to my room."

Back in her bed, she closed her eyes, only to see his face swim before her. She couldn't help considering the intimate aspects of marriage to Saber. His strong mouth— how would those lips feel against hers in a really serious kiss? He would give her time, of that she had no doubt.

And neither did she doubt that a physical relationship with him would be satisfying. She couldn't accept. Of course, she couldn't.

What a shame.

Chapter Three

After a sleepless night, Selena arose before six, pulled on an old bathing suit and beach robe, picked up a towel and made her way through the silent house.

The brass handle under her hand was cold as she let herself out through the French doors of her father's study; the early-morning air hit her bare skin with a chilly, but not unpleasant, bite. Though the darkness was already ebbing in the east, a few of the brightest stars still winked in the western sky.

The pool would be heated, though; even this early in the season her mother swam every day. She paused at the edge of the patio, then sprinted the last twenty yards, shedding her robe as she reached the edge of the coping, and jumped in, feet first.

She came up laughing. Lord, it was colder than she'd expected. She struck out toward the far end of the pool with a vigorous stroke.

She had done as Saber had asked; she had considered carefully—all night long. But, no matter what, she couldn't see herself as his wife. This morning she would have to tell him so. Maybe.

But first she would swim laps, a lot of laps. Perhaps the cold shock of the water temperature would jump start her brain and wash away this absurd and uncharacteristic indecision. Maybe the exercise would clear out the tension which seemed to have been building within her all night. And maybe she would find a calm and firm reason to convince herself, so there would be no mistaking her determination.

Nicholas watched Selena from his bedroom window. Her body, even in the old tank suit, was superb. He mused once more about how different she was from what he'd expected.

He had returned to his room last night, confident that, although he'd made a blunder at the end, he'd reasserted his diplomatic finesse somewhat. He'd been clumsy in his first attempt after dinner—perhaps too sure of himself. When she'd turned him down flat, it had surprised him, not pleasantly. At the same time, he'd accepted that he needed to reevaluate his efforts. He'd done much better with the second opportunity.

The atmosphere in the kitchen had been more informal, and informality always helped. Every good diplomat knew that more was accomplished on the cocktail circuit than around the meeting table. The call from her school, which had left her depressed and vulnerable, hadn't hurt his case, either.

Yet, he had a premonition that in the full light of morning, Selena would again refuse, this time unequivocally.

Damn. If there weren't so many restrictions on his time he could have eased her into this idea of marriage. Last night she was tired and worried, not at all in the mood for a proposal like his. He should have known she'd turn him down flat the first time. Talking her into putting off her decision, into thinking about it for a while, hadn't been easy.

And then he'd ruined it all by his offer of money—though he still wasn't sure why.

What else could he do to convince her?

Unbidden, his subconscious suddenly suggested a fairly intriguing idea. He considered for a minute, then dismissed it. While it might appeal to her, it would be offensive to him. But the idea kept pushing at his mind, demanding to be given consideration.

It might work. At least it would give him the time he needed. And it would give her the out she needed to save her pride, autonomy, whatever it was that made American women so damned independent. He chided himself for the adjective. Her independence, "damned" or not, was just what he and his country needed at this time.

Five minutes later, Nicholas strolled to the edge of the pool and watched as Selena swam toward the far end, turned with one smooth movement, disappearing beneath the water for a moment. When she surfaced again, she resumed her long even strokes, her arms pale and smooth in the early-morning light.

Selena had seen him immediately. It was a tribute to her experience that she hadn't suddenly floundered in the water. She maintained the smooth, demanding rhythm of her strokes, but her senses were tumbling out of control.

She'd never seen Saber in jeans before. In fact, she'd never seen him in anything except a business suit or formal attire. Even last night in the kitchen without his jacket he'd still maintained his air of formality.

She had always considered him a remarkably handsome man. Dressed casually, he was devastating. He stood, legs planted apart, hands tucked into the back pockets of the jeans, watching her. In the dress shirt, the same one from last night, now badly wrinkled, his shoulders appeared twice as broad, his forearms twice as muscular.

She finished the lap in the shallow end of the pool and when her feet touched the bottom she stood slowly, keeping her back to him. She climbed the steps and, moving nonchalantly, reached down to scoop up her robe and towel. Robe belted, towel wrapped around her wet hair, she felt ready to confront him.

They stood, facing each other across the water, for a long minute. The surface, disturbed by her activity, calmed, settled into its natural drift.

"Would you like to swim?" she asked finally breaking the silence. "I'm sure there's a suit in the cabana."

"No, thank you. I came out to apologize."

She shrugged. "Apology accepted."

"I'd also like to talk to you."

Blunt to the end, thought Selena. Well, she could be just as blunt. "We've already talked, Nicholas. I thought you wanted me to think this over."

"One or two things have occurred to me. They would be advantages, I believe, from your point of view. Things that might—" He stopped, oddly at a loss.

"Sweeten the pot?" she said evenly.

He hesitated over the idiom but it only took a second for him to grasp her meaning. His lips thinned in annoyance. "I didn't mean to insult you when I offered to pay you a salary. As my wife, you will be performing many services for the country. Why shouldn't you be compensated?''

"Good God, Saber." She spun away, heading for the house but her course intersected his and his legs were longer. He caught her arm as she tried to pass.

"What is the matter with you, Selena? I'm only offering—''

"To *pay* me. Like—like a woman off the street." She tried to free her arm.

"No! You can't think that! You would be paid for your educational expertise, for your service to the women of our country, not for sharing my bed. Selena, you can't have thought—'' At that he grabbed her other arm and brought her to within inches of his body.

She caught her breath. His gaze dropped to her mouth. Time seemed to hang suspended between them. He was warm, his body radiating heat. She suddenly felt an urge to warm herself in his arms, to seek comfort there as she had done last night. She couldn't control the shiver that went through her, and he noticed.

"You must be cold." He dropped his hands and his voice was heavy. "Let's finish this discussion inside over a cup of coffee."

She led the way to the back door and kept right on through to the hall. "I'm going to get dressed." She had made it to the second step leading upstairs, when she realized he was following her. She stopped. "I won't keep you waiting long, I promise."

But he wouldn't wait. "Selena, what I wanted to say was this." He raked his fingers through his hair in a gesture of frustration. "I've been trying to look at this from your point of view. And I don't want to force you into a situation where you will feel caged or imprisoned. So I've come up with another idea. We can put a time limit on this arrangement. If, after a certain period—say, a year—you don't feel that our marriage has a chance, I will arrange for you to divorce me."

Selena looked at him for a minute, wondering what it had cost him to make such an offer. She had an idea that it was a lot. At last, she nodded silently and turned away. As she headed up the stairs she felt his gaze on her back. She had the strangest feeling that—no matter how this situation was resolved—something, tentatively and potentially precious, had been lost forever.

By the time she returned to the dining room her father had made an appearance. She poured coffee for herself and joined the two men at the breakfast table.

Turnus was unusually reserved and Selena soon realized that Saber had made her father aware of what had passed between them. She should be annoyed but for some reason she was not. He'd discussed his proposal with her parents. She supposed that the parents should also be apprised of the consequences of said proposal.

With her father's next statement, however, she realized how wrong she was. Clearly Saber hadn't told the whole story. "We are all to attend a dinner at the Karastonian Embassy this evening." He laughed under his breath. "Nicholas attracts the media like honey attracts flies, and there is bound to be speculation. With your mother and I along, it would give the press a chance to get used to seeing you without questioning your presence."

"That is, of course, if you will agree to let me escort you." Saber's words drew Selena's attention and she met his even gaze. He was giving her an opportunity to say no.

Turnus seemed to be under the impression that this was a done deal but Saber knew better, thought Selena sourly. She opened her mouth to contradict her father's assumption, but Saber spoke instead. "It isn't necessary for Selena to go unless she wishes."

Go with him to an official function? That made things seem awfully definite. "I'd love to go," she said perversely. Then she wondered why.

Saber didn't hesitate. "Fine. We'll leave at seven."

Bree and Ryan joined them then and there was no chance for more conversation.

Selena was late. She had tried on and discarded several dresses before she finally decided on a blue-gray chiffon which was an old favorite of hers. She kept most of her formal things here. Aside from the occasional command performance at the home of the college president, most of her socializing at school was casual. With its classic cut and simplicity, the blue dress gave her self-confidence to meet whatever lay in store for her tonight.

She had arranged her hair in a looser chignon than she usually wore and pulled several strands free to brush her neck. Now she clasped a small but glittering blue butterfly in the arrangement.

She examined the effect, turning her head from side to side. This was ridiculous. Trying to make herself look like a romantic heroine for a man who had to have half a screw loose. Butterflies, for heaven's sake. At thirty-four she was much too old to wear butterflies in her hair. She pulled the pins from her hair and reached for her hairbrush. She was going to make them all late. What a way to start— She broke off the thought. To start what?

Nothing, she told herself. This wasn't the start of anything.

When Selena descended the staircase five minutes later, Saber caught his breath. Her glorious hair, dark as midnight, was caught up away from her face on one side by a

tiny sparkling butterfly no larger than his thumb. The rest
of her hair spilled down her back in loose, easy curls. His
fingers literally itched to touch the silky mass. She was
wearing a smoky blue, soft, floaty gown that drifted
around her legs when she moved. The effect was arrest-
ing. He wished he *could* find something to criticize.

From the moment this morning when she'd left him
standing at the foot of this same staircase, he'd looked for
a limitation, a shortcoming in this woman. Because, as
he'd gazed down into her face, framed by the damp towel,
without a smidgen of make-up, he had suddenly and inexplicably grown warm and aroused. He'd quickly tried
to distract himself, explaining the idea he'd come up with
to put a time limit on their arrangement. As she'd climbed
the stairs, though, he'd had the feeling that he had somehow made another serious mistake.

Not offering the time limit, but in the selection, itself.
Selena created too many extraordinary emotions within
him.

Too late; he'd already asked. But, he was beginning to
suspect, this woman could have an effect on him emo-
tionally and that was the last thing he wanted. He had
stood there like a slab of wood, watching her climb the
stairs in her bare feet and he had wondered if it wouldn't
be better if she turned him down. Now, as he watched her
descend that same staircase, looking so very different, he
was almost sure of it.

The rest of the party was frozen into silence by her appearance. For some reason the fact annoyed him even
further.

"I hope I haven't made us late," she said when she
reached the bottom of the stairs.

She didn't rush with her apology, he noticed, wryly. She knew she was late but like all the beautiful women he'd known, she expected to be forgiven.

"Not at all," he said smoothly. "The car is waiting. Shall we go?"

The reporters had gathered outside the gate to the Karastonian Embassy. How in the world they found out he was here was always a mystery to him. As the car turned in, he could hear the shouted questions. Cameras were thrust against the window of the limo, their flashes momentarily blinding those inside. But the driver and the guards assigned to the gates knew their jobs and soon the car drew up to the chancellery entrance. The ambassador was waiting at the foot of the steps. He was alone.

Nicholas bit off a frustrated curse. This was what he was battling. Damn it, he'd sent a prescript to all the embassies. He hadn't worded it too strongly, of course, but had merely made a suggestion that the women should begin to take their places beside their husbands, greeting the guests of the country.

The world was so complicated these days. The women of Karastonia had to step forward and take their places beside the men if there was to be any hope for the democratic government to succeed. He knew they were capable of doing anything they wanted to do. He also knew that their fathers, brothers, husbands, needed to encourage them. That was another problem.

He deliberately paused after he emerged from the car to assist Selena. With a hand at her elbow, he shortened his steps to keep her even with him.

Selena could see the surprise on the face of her host. She knew exactly what Saber was doing; she was half-

Karastonian, after all. She had observed the traditions and customs of the country firsthand.

"I hope your wife is not ill," said Saber when they reached the ambassador. His voice could have frozen hot fudge.

"No, sir. I mean—" The man fumbled for a minute more. Then he turned and motioned toward the door. His wife, a rather plain woman who knew her place—was standing submissively in the background. At her husband's gesture she hesitated for a second, then came forward. "We're honored to welcome you, Mr. President."

Saber charmed them both, presenting Selena as though she were the honored guest here tonight. She wasn't particularly enamored of being the subject of his object lesson, but she smiled to herself, understanding what the demonstration was meant to convey and applauding his sincere intent.

She had been unnerved by the reporters at the gates, had seen the muscle in Saber's jaw jump once in reaction to the clamor. For the first time the magnitude of his responsibility dawned on her. He was determined to wrest a democracy from the remnants of a monarchy, to turn a patriarchal society into a strong, modern nation, ready to take its place among the other democracies of the world. His was a formidable task.

She had a chance to study him briefly as the introductions were performed. If anyone could do it, she decided, he could. And then all chance for speculation was lost as they entered the building. The party was a large one. She realized immediately that the reporters at the gate were the foot soldiers. The big guns were here inside. Among the approximately one hundred and fifty guests, she counted one anchor, two newspaper correspondents, including one whose regular beat was the State Department, a well-known producer-star of a weekly television interview program, and the president of a network.

Saber accepted two glasses of champagne from the waiter, handed one to Selena and waded into the melee, keeping her by his side. He milled about. He spoke to people as though he had all the time in the world. He knew everyone here, called most by their first names, asked about everyone in their families, down to—it seemed to Selena—a mother's aunt's uncle's first cousin, twice removed. "How do you do it? I've forgotten most of the names already," she murmured once in an aside.

He grinned, a most un-Saberlike expression. "Practice, practice, practice. Isn't that how it goes?" The grin faded and he added, "I'm a politician, after all."

She was surprised by his teasing. In the car it had been obvious that something had happened to annoy him and it appeared to have something to do with her. The tension had been so thick it could be cut with a knife. At first she'd thought he was irritated because she had been slow in getting downstairs, but she knew she hadn't been more than a minute or two behind her mother and father.

"You seem to have learned your trade well."

He shrugged. "I've known most of these people for many years."

She also knew a few people here, leftovers from the days when her father had been the ambassador. As the bids for Saber's attention increased, she realized that her presence was slowing him down. When she saw the U.S. Secretary of Commerce edging purposefully toward them, she touched his sleeve. "You don't have to baby-sit me, Saber. I'll be all right on my own."

He looked around dubiously, then nodded. "This trade agreement I'm here to discuss with your Department of Commerce is important, and there are some people I should speak with. But don't go far away,'' he said, his gaze intensifying as he looked down at her. For a mere fleeting instant they looked into each other's eyes and the time seemed to stretch as the room receded from around them.

At last Selena interrupted the spell. "I won't," she said, wondering about the breathlessness in her voice.

Not more than a moment had passed, surely, when she felt, rather than saw, the curious members of the press begin to move in on her. Nothing overt—they were here as guests and behaved properly. But they were, after all, journalists. The network anchor reached her first.

The questions were polite but probing and finally the producer-star of the weekly television news program came right out and asked what they had all wanted to ask. "Are you and Saber an item?"

"I don't know what you mean," she answered calmly. She wasn't about to make this easy for the man.

"Saber has quite a reputation. He's dated a number of American women. I just wondered if you were his latest." The man's expression was almost sneering.

"Saber and his friends are spending the weekend at my parents' home in Virginia," she answered with dignity. "We are all his guests. As are you, I believe."

Mercifully, dinner was announced. She looked around to see Saber making his way through the crowd toward her.

"That reporter's tie must be too tight—it seems to have cut off the flow of blood to his brain," said Bree's voice from behind her.

Selena laughed.

"What's funny?" asked Ryan.

Saber reached her side. He lifted a brow and looked from Bree to Selena.

Bree linked her arms with her husband's. "You don't have to worry about this one, Saber. She can handle herself."

Selena wondered how long Bree had been standing behind her while she talked to the journalists.

As the evening progressed, Saber realized that he was again searching for a flaw in Selena. He chastised himself for the effort. There was much to be admired in this woman. She handled the curious and the speculative with equal aplomb.

He, on the other hand, needed to get his temper under control. As if he didn't have enough on his mind, the trade agreement he had come here to sign was in jeopardy. There had been pressure on the United States, from a country much more powerful than Karastonia, not to sign the treaty as it was written.

His country desperately needed this agreement. When he'd inquired, the U.S. Secretary of Commerce had reassured him about the president's commitment to sign, but he wasn't encouraged. He knew the havoc politics could play.

After dinner they were first entertained by a classical violinist. Selena listened to the brilliant performance with only half her attention. The other half was focused on Saber. She had watched his expression grow more serious with each passing hour until lines of strain were deeply etched around his eyes and mouth.

He'd disappeared twice during the entertainment for brief intervals—one time with the ambassador, another time with a group of people that included her father and the Secretary of Commerce.

Both times, when he'd returned, Saber's visage had been a bit blacker. Whether from aggravation or apprehension, she couldn't tell, but clearly something was wrong. She felt a swell of compassion for him and sympathy for his position. He couldn't even enjoy an evening out without being badgered by his responsibilities.

At last, a pianist concluded the final performance to enthusiastic applause. Saber slipped back into place beside her just before the lights came up. She turned to him with a smile as she clapped her hands.

There was no logical explanation for what happened next. As the illumination grew gradually brighter, he looked down at her, a perfunctory smile on his lips. And suddenly, to her astonishment, as though the mere sight of her was somehow comforting, the lines in his face eased, his troubled expression relaxed, his dark eyes, which had been clouded with worry, miraculously cleared. The token smile became a grin of genuine pleasure.

"Was he good?" he whispered.

"*She* was terrific," she answered, and almost laughed aloud as Saber did a comical double take.

Then he gave her a rueful smile. "Sorry. That was unforgivable. Thank you for saving me embarrassment."

She felt warmed to her toes by the change. For the first time she began to reflect on the possibility that she could help, that her solace and support might be of value to this man. It was a startling thought.

He carried heavy burdens. Did she imagine she could do anything to ease them? Did she want to? It gave her a lot to think about.

The moment was interrupted by the Karastonian national anthem and they all rose to honor the flag. They said their goodbyes and the limousine was brought around.

"I shall await your convenience tomorrow, Mr. President," said the ambassador.

Saber was standing beside the open door of the car. The rest to them were inside but Selena could hear him plainly.

"I'll be here early tomorrow morning. Move the first meeting up from Monday to tomorrow night. If that is possible."

"I am sure I can arrange it."

Saber nodded and shook the man's hand. He climbed in beside her and the limousine started down the curved driveway.

Jayne and Bree were discussing the evening. Turnus and Ryan were arguing good-naturedly about the merits of living in Boston versus Washington.

"I didn't realize that you would be leaving so soon," said Selena softly. Her words, under the conversation of the other four, were inaudible except to his ears. It seemed she wouldn't have as much time as she thought to mull over the events of the evening.

"I had planned to stay until Monday morning but we have discovered an unexpected obstacle to the trade agreement I was to sign. It will take some effort to straighten out the difficulties."

"I understand. I'd like to talk to you before you leave."

Saber looked sharply at her. He was struck by the quickening of his pulse, but he could read nothing from her expression. "Shall we have a brandy when we get back to your parents' house?"

"That would be fine," she answered.

Selena linked her fingers in her lap and waited for Saber to pour the brandy. There was no fire tonight and the room seemed chilly.

Then he was standing before her, his hand extended with the balloon glass in it. "Thank you."

Saber looked down at her face. She was outwardly composed but, he noticed, she turned the glass in her hands not even aware that she was doing it. He waited.

She sipped from the glass and set it aside. "Saber," she said, hesitating. She had to crane her neck to look up at him. "Please, sit down."

A faint smile played around his lips as he took the chair across from her. She looked like she was waiting for the hangman.

She took a long breath. "Well, Saber, with certain conditions, I am prepared to accept your proposal."

A light flared briefly in his eyes. He sat back in the chair and folded his arms across his broad chest. "You seem nervous."

"Well, what do you expect? Of course I'm nervous. And not completely convinced that I'm doing the right thing."

Saber hid a smile. He'd not seen her nervous before. "What are the conditions?" he asked, intrigued.

"Well, I couldn't leave until after school is out for the summer."

He nodded thoughtfully and continued to struggle to keep the smile off his face. He'd never heard her preface a sentence with "well" and now he'd heard three. Obviously indicative of a certain state of mind. When they were married it would be a useful fact to know. "When is that?"

"The third of June." She watched him warily.

"And did you feel that I would object? Selena, I am not unreasonable." He leaned forward and took the glass from her. Then he gripped her hands between his. His voice lowered as he tried to convey his satisfaction. "You won't regret your decision, Selena. I'd like to take you home with me when I leave on Wednesday, but I understand that you have a commitment to your position at the school," he said gently.

She seemed to draw some comfort from his attitude. "Saber, I would also hope—and I want us to promise—that we be honest with each other. You said that if I wasn't happy, I could..." She paused.

"You could divorce me," he finished for her. "And I meant that, Selena. You will always be free to leave and I will make it as easy as possible for you."

She squeezed his hands. "And I want you to have that freedom, as well, Saber. If you aren't happy with our bargain, I want you to tell me. I couldn't stand it if we weren't honest with each other. You may find someone someday that you may be able to love. Please promise to tell me, Saber."

His features hardened again at the mention of the word. "Very well. If you need me to say it, I will. I promise to be honest with you, Selena."

She inhaled and smiled. "Thank you. And I accept your proposal."

A corner of his mouth turned up. "Thank you, Selena."

The bargain was sealed, not with a kiss, but with a handshake.

Chapter Four

The head of the history department, Dr. Wrens, summoned Selena to his office for the second time in a week. As she waited in the anteroom, she was well aware of the looks she was getting from her colleagues as they passed through the office on their way to classes, to their homes, to conferences. She was getting looks from everybody these days—the students, the janitor, the man who filled the soft-drink machine. Ever since her picture had appeared in *USA Today*—one of those taken through the window of the limousine—she seemed to be fair game for whispered speculation and long assessing stares, even from her friends. So far, she'd managed to escape the cover pictures of the tabloids, but that would probably be next.

Sometimes, despite her determined demeanor, she wanted to shriek. Was she becoming paranoid? No, actually she was simply mad as hell.

She maintained her expression of calm and congeniality when the secretary called her name. "Dr. Mastron, Dr. Wrens is ready for you."

She smiled. "Thank you."

As she passed the young woman's desk, she caught the wink, the grin, the crossed fingers.

Somehow she kept herself from doing or saying anything rash. Earlier in the week when she'd been called in to this same office, she'd had to endure the girl's gushing congratulations on her engagement, the knowing and rather surprisingly cunning look, the outlandish but probing questions that stopped short of asking how her fiancé was in bed. But not very far short.

She continued to be shocked at the almost-indecent curiosity that surrounded the life of Nicholas Saber.

Her father seemed to want to reassure her, calling every night to explain that this kind of thing didn't go on in Karastonia. Clearly, Turnus was afraid that his daughter, a mercurial mixture of two divergent cultures, would lose patience and call the whole thing off.

In reality, the tempest served to strengthen her determination. If she decided to call off this marriage, it wouldn't be over something as trivial as overly enthusiastic journalists.

"Have a seat, Dr. Mastron," said Dr. Wrens as Selena entered the room.

His head was bent over some papers. He didn't bother to look up or to rise. She sat across the desk and pondered his shiny bald spot. At last he raised his head and pinned her with his bright blue eyes. "What are we going to do about this situation, Dr. Mastron?"

"I don't know, sir," answered Selena honestly.

"The distinguished gentlemen of the press are causing some rather complicated problems for the school."

And for me, thought Selena, thinking of the gamut she had to run to get inside her home in the evenings, of the telephone that rang constantly.

And the mail was voluminous. Some of the letters were official and congratulatory but many more were from acquaintances, even strangers, asking for money or intervention.

But the man across the desk seemed to have no perception of the problems she might face. He certainly gave no sign of sympathy or understanding. "The distinguished gentlewomen are causing their share of problems, as well," she observed mildly.

The look he gave her was puzzled and she had to bite her lip to keep from laughing out loud. Even now, he didn't get the point.

"Since we have your resignation in hand, the dean has suggested that I get in touch with Daniel Summers, to see if he can finish out this term for you.

Selena became very still. Here it was, then. She had handed in her resignation, effective the end of this term, but they wanted her out immediately. Dr. Daniel Summers had retired from teaching. He lived in a nearby community, however, and he had filled in when flu had devastated the college faculty this past fall.

Selena had thought she was reconciled to her decision but the idea of severing all contact with this place suddenly made her feel very sad and melancholy. She had many good friends here; she'd enjoyed her work. It was difficult to remember the frustrations or the irritations at a time like this. And the thought of leaving it behind forever made her very sad.

The long-distance telephone connection was so clear that Saber might have been in the next room. Still, he didn't seem to understand. He had been silent since she'd told him seconds ago that she had been asked to leave the campus because of the commotion engendered by the announcement of their engagement. "Did you hear me, Saber? I've been fired, axed, dismissed."

He chuckled. He actually chuckled!

If he *had* been in the next room she would have choked him. Was he really so unfeeling? What had she gotten herself into? "Saber," she said quietly. "I am not in the best of moods and I find nothing in the least amusing about this situation."

"I was laughing at my own blunder, not at you, Selena," he said calmly. "I apologize for not listening to your warning against an immediate announcement of our engagement. I admit I was wrong not to foresee this." He paused. "Anyway, thank you for not saying, 'I told you so,'" he added.

She had reluctantly agreed when he wanted to make the announcement before he left the United States. She had joined him at the embassy the last day before he returned to Karastonia. There had been a small engagement party. No press. It had been very pleasant.

She was slightly mollified by his apology. "That would serve no purpose."

"You are being very generous. This must be a difficult predicament. Especially when you have to deal with it all alone." He stopped for a moment. "I'll wind up a few things here and be there tomorrow or the next day. Thursday at the latest."

Had he missed her? His voice had certainly grown low and intimate with the last few words, sending shivers down her spine, setting up tiny explosions of warmth at her nape. It was a lover's voice, and she was as stunned by her own reaction as she was by the offer.

She had missed him more than she'd expected during the past few weeks. Or was she only impatient to get this thing done, now that it had been decided?

"That isn't necessary," she said quickly. "I just wanted you to know that I'll be at my parents' house. I'm leaving as soon as I can arrange an appointment with the movers." With regret, she looked around her apartment, at all the things she'd collected over the past ten years.

"Leave it all, Selena. You needn't be bothered with such details. I'll take care of everything."

It was a tempting offer. Leave everything to him, let him hire the movers, deal with the lease. She could make one more trip—this one to her car, suitcase in hand—and drive away from the problem.

She collected her thoughts, overcoming the temptation. "Saber, the reason you hired me for this job—"

"Hired?" He erupted in anger. "Selena, you are going to be my wife!"

"Will you be quiet and listen?" she demanded, not unkindly, but firmly.

Deathly silence followed her words. She sensed his struggle with himself over the thousands of miles that separated them. His irritation seemed to bounce off the telephone satellite and into her living room. She would be willing to bet that no woman had ever spoken to him like that. She could speak firmly now because she wasn't tied to him. The idea of what his reaction would be when she was, brought on a moment's trepidation.

"Saber, you want me to set an example for the women of Karastonia. You selected me because I'm able to function independently, because I don't have to depend on anyone to solve all my problems. Now, if you won't let me handle this situation on my own, I'll have to presume you didn't mean any of it. And in that case we may as well call this off right now."

"Blackmail, Selena?"

"No," she said immediately. "Not at all. Just a reminder of the reasons for this marriage."

Another pause, which may or may not have been a satellite time delay, he said, "How long will you need? Surely you agree that there is no further need to postpone your coming to Karastonia."

"Yes," she said slowly. "I do agree, but perhaps we should stick to our timetable. It will take me a month or six weeks, at least, to wind things up here. Besides packing and moving, I want to go to New York to do some shopping."

"I'll give you a week to pack. We can stop in Paris for you to shop."

Good Lord, didn't the man hear a word she said? "Saber, I don't *want* to shop in Paris. I want to shop in New York. Three weeks."

"Ten days."

She sighed and held the telephone away from her ear to glare at it. Then she sighed again. "Ten days," she said finally.

The ten-day deadline stretched to two unbelievably hectic weeks. Even so, if it hadn't been for her mother's help, she would never have accomplished everything even then. Now they were all packed, the bags were loaded into the limousine, which had arrived a short time ago bearing her fiancé.

Selena was waiting with Jayne in the drawing room when Saber and her father came out of the study.

Turnus wore a beaming smile. He looked better than he had looked in some time. His color was good and his step had more spring in it. "Ready to leave?" he asked Selena unnecessarily.

She had no idea what had caused the last-minute delay but she smiled back and said, "Yes." If her smile was a little uneven around the edges, no one seemed to notice.

The chauffeur waited. Turnus and Jayne entered the car first. As Selena started to join them, she looked back one last time at her childhood home. She'd agreed to this undertaking, this venture into the unknown, but the actual leave-taking was more than a bit daunting.

It was silly of her, she knew, but Selena was hit with the sudden and unexpected temptation to run upstairs and hide in her room.

As though he could read her thoughts, Saber put a supportive hand at her back, surprising her. She met his dark, unsmiling gaze for a moment.

Suddenly his expression softened. His smile was warm and self-confident, making her feel slightly better. "I almost forgot something." He leaned into the open door. "One minute," he said to her parents and took her arm. He turned her away from the car. "Come with me."

They reached the dappled shade of a willow tree a few yards from the drive. Saber reached into his pocket and withdrew a small velvet-covered box.

Selena gaped when he withdrew a ring, dropped the box back in his pocket and reached for her left hand. "Good heavens, Saber."

The flawless diamond was blue-white, and as big as a cherry from George Washington's renowned tree—if there was such a tree. Historically speaking, there had always been some question about the legend. Surrounding the large stone were rubies the size of cherry pits. "Good heavens," she repeated weakly as he slid the thing onto her finger.

She had tried to convince Saver that it wasn't necessary for him to fly all the way to the United States to accompany her and her parents to Karastonia. But he'd insisted, determination hardening his voice each time she protested. It was almost as though he read hesitation in their telephone conversations and expected her to change her mind. Now he placed the ring on her finger with the same determination. It was a perfect fit.

"Thank you. It's beautiful." She forced a sincere smile. "Truly breathtaking." For someone who rarely wore jewelry, except for a utilitarian watch and her grandmother's pearls, the ring would take some getting used to. Luckily she was tall and her fingers were long, so the proportion wasn't *too* unfortunate.

"It was my mother's," he said as he looked down into her face. He hesitated, as though he wanted to say something more. But he simply gripped her fingers, and when he did speak she had an idea that the words weren't what he'd planned to say.

"I'm honored that you've agreed to marry me, Selena."

She searched his features, hoping for more. They hadn't had a moment alone since he'd arrived early this morning, looking extremely weary after flying all night. But after a brief hesitation, he simply smiled, touched her back lightly and gestured toward the waiting car.

The drive was over too quickly, the airport red tape eliminated too easily, and all at once it was time to board the huge private jet that would take her to live in a foreign land.

It didn't matter that she held dual citizenship; she still considered herself an American. And she was leaving her country to marry a foreigner. She was going to spend the rest of her life somewhere else.

Saber watched Selena climb on board the plane. Her carriage was exquisitely straight. He noticed that the heels she wore caused her hips to move with fluid grace under the smooth fabric of her skirt. She carried the jacket of her royal blue suit over her arm and her soft blouse, an almost colorless cream, draped enticingly over her breasts. Her raven-black hair was twisted neatly into a chignon. He wondered if she'd packed the tiny butterfly clip.

Her expression was serene, but he hadn't missed the panic in her eyes when she'd turned for a last look at her parents' home. He felt a certain sympathy, but he couldn't help her with this. Leaving home was an emotional experience that she'd have to handle on her own.

He wouldn't be of much help to her, period, over the next couple of weeks. His own schedule, in preparation for a honeymoon trip—which wouldn't be a honeymoon at all, he thought wryly—was filled to capacity except for the formal festivities surrounding the wedding.

He was half expecting her to change her mind, which she could do. In spite of the engagement ring she wore, until he put the official wedding ring on her finger, she wasn't his.

Even afterward, she wouldn't really be his for another year. He'd given her a promise of freedom and that was the time they'd agreed on. He had a year to convince her that this marriage could work, that what she could offer her Karastonian counterparts was worth the sacrifice of the life she was leaving behind.

The plane was cleared for takeoff and, as the engines revved noisily to achieve maximum power, Saber thought about the change his own feelings had undergone in regard to his intended bride. Now that the decision had been made, he was surprised at his impatience to get this done and to make her his wife, to settle into, if not a conventional marriage, at least a certain domestic routine. The prospect filled him with the first contented pleasure he'd felt in a long, long time.

He was as sick as she was of the publicity, the notoriety surrounding this marriage. When she'd called from the school two weeks ago, he hadn't exactly been surprised. In fact, he'd been expecting a call every day, expecting her to inform him that she had changed her mind, so it was with some relief that he listened to her story of being asked to leave.

He had read the papers and watched television, and he had seen the pictures. Selena entering the stone buildings on the campus where she taught. Selena thrusting her way through the crowd of reporters at her condominium complex. Selena, looking unhappy but indomitable. She was getting a firsthand view of his onstage life-style. He'd been expecting her to back out. He'd wondered if he could blame her. Several times he'd also wondered if he didn't want her to do just that.

Gradually, as he'd watched her or read about her movements, he'd begun to realize that this woman was not one to walk away because of pressure. Slowly his admiration grew for her poise, her tact, her equilibrium. She was really an exceptional woman; he had chosen well.

But the very fact made him pause, made him wonder about his own ability to resist an emotional involvement.

He was proud of her for showing such spirit. She would have to draw on that strength often over the next days because the situation wouldn't soon get any better. The interest in this wedding among Karastonians—indeed among all Europeans—was, if anything, more intense.

Before they arrived in his country he should try to prepare her for what would happen.

Her picture was splashed on shop fronts and in windows. The wedding was the biggest event in the small country since the monarchy had been abolished and they'd held their first elections. The people were elated that their president had chosen a wife—a second wife.

The romantics among them were demanding to know the intimate details of Selena's life. What she would wear when she arrived, what her life in the United States had been like, what she would wear at the state dinner, who styled her hair, what her students thought of her, what she would wear to be married, who her lovers had been. The last had given Saber pause. He wondered about that himself.

The skeptics of Karastonia, on the other hand, had speculated as to her role as their first lady and questioned her allegiance to her father's land.

The media had demanded interviews, background material, an official portrait. The last had caused a few problems, but finally her father had convinced her to sit for a well-known photographer while she was shopping in New York. That was the picture that now graced the streets and byways of his country.

In Saber's mind the formal portrait wasn't Selena. It displayed her likeness, but it didn't reflect the energy or the intelligence within her.

When they reached cruising altitude, he unfastened his seat belt and got to his feet. "Would you like to look around?" he asked.

She searched his features, her eyes wide with an elusive emotion, and then glanced across the aisle toward her parents. "Yes, I would."

Turnus and Jayne seemed to understand his need to be alone with Selena for a few minutes because they didn't follow. Their comments on the engagement ring had been restrained, if slightly awed.

He showed her the office space behind the cockpit, where his secretary was at work, and the cockpit itself. He introduced her to the crew. Finally he led her to the rear of the aircraft where there was a private stateroom and bath.

"It's very luxurious, isn't it?" Selena said in response to Saber's explanation of the plush facilities.

"The government inherited the plane from my cousin. Along with his yacht and the palace, of course."

She knew the palace from the days of the king, and she didn't relish the idea of living there at all. After the monarchy was abolished, the building had been quickly remodeled. Saber had described the changes; but, even refurbished inside, the exterior was certain to be the formal place she remembered. The office of the president and other administrative offices had been incorporated into the design, as well as the elaborate facilities for formal entertaining, and the living quarters for the president. So she would be compelled to live in the huge forbidding edifice, for now at least. "I see."

Her voice sounded wooden even to herself. Couldn't he understand how unsettled she was feeling? She needed more than a tour of the plane, more than a recitation of the luxuries that would accompany her position; she needed reassurance. She needed personal conversation; she needed a sense of connection and cohesion and contact of some kind. Maybe then this wouldn't all seem so artificial and awkward. She turned to face him.

"Where is the king living now?" she asked. Anything to start a conversation.

"He has a lodge in the mountains and a house in the city and he travels."

"Do you think he's happy with his decision?"

Saber looked off into the middle distance for a minute, thoughtfully. "You know, Selena, he's seventy years old. Before the change in government he looked frail and tired. Now he looks ten years younger. He has more time for reading. He even plays cards with old friends." He smiled absently. "He has begun using a health club...and he's more content than I've ever seen him."

"I'm glad," said Selena softly. "He's a wonderful man." She hesitated. "Saber, I—"

"Selena—" They spoke simultaneously. His smile was rueful. "You first."

Whatever she'd been planning to say went out of her head as she looked into his dark eyes. She'd never noticed the golden glints in their depths. She was mesmerized into silence.

Saber couldn't have missed her reaction. He smiled and touched her cheek.

The contact was electric. It brought her to her senses. Well, she'd wanted contact, hadn't she? "I'm not exactly sure what I want to say or how to say it. It's very difficult."

He took her hand. "Then let me say it for you. You've had a glimpse of what being married to me will be like and you don't relish the experience."

She smiled. "That's part of it," she admitted. She sat on the edge of the bed and traced the design of the spread with a fingernail. "How in the world do you abide all the media attention?"

He joined her on the bed, sitting sideways with his back to the cabin door. "I'm hoping marriage will temper their enthusiasm," he said, smiling.

She frowned.

"Selena." His voice was very low, but unemotional.

She met his gaze questioningly.

"Are you having second thoughts? Are you going to back out?"

For the first time, she saw the anxiety in his expression. The consummate diplomat, the gallant leader, was apprehensive. This courageous man, who had been called the Thomas Jefferson of his country and helped to lead Karastonia into the democratic age, was uncertain.

"Yes, I'm having second thoughts, but no, I have no intention of backing out." Her answer lit a flare behind his eyes; her own dropped under the force of his gaze.

"I'm relieved," he said quietly.

"But, Saber, we must reach some kind of accommodation. Aside from the obvious hassle, I can't be comfortable in this situation unless I have your support."

Her words obviously surprised him. "Whatever I can do, Selena. Surely you know that you have my support."

"I know that you are a very busy man, Saber, but do you realize that we've barely spoken to each other? I don't intend to be a distraction..."

He caught her arm and turned her to face him. "Good God, Selena, you're going to be my wife."

"I know. I just wish," she said almost wistfully, "that we knew each other better."

Saber thought he'd never heard such melancholy in a human being's voice before. But he could change her attitude. Once they were married, once they were settled, he'd see that all her qualms were wiped away.

He opened his mouth to assure her that she had no need for regrets, that he wanted—*needed*—for her to be a distraction, that he, too, wanted them to know each other better. But his secretary appeared in the doorway at that moment to tell him there was a call.

"You go on," she urged, resigned. "I think I'll freshen up." She indicated the bath.

His fingers tightened on her elbow and he smiled impatiently, conveying his apology without words.

The guests had begun arriving several days ago. The hotels were filled to overflowing. Karastonia's beautiful coastal resorts rivaled the Riviera and had always been favorite retreats of the jet set and European royalty. Now it seemed that half the continent had flocked to the tiny country on the Aegean. Liners that regularly cruised the Mediterranean added a stop to this summer's itinerary so that the tourists would have a glimpse of the glitterati at play.

The week preceding the wedding seemed to be a nonstop party. Selena and her parents had a large suite in Karastonia's leading hotel. Saber had offered them the hospitality of the palace but she had agreed with her parents that it wouldn't be appropriate until after the wedding.

She had also agreed with her mother, who hadn't wanted to stay with any of her father's numerous relatives. "This is our last chance to be together, just the three of us," Jayne had argued. "Let's spend the time alone with our daughter."

Turnus had finally relented. He'd been somewhat placated that Selena had chosen to have his niece, Alia, as her maid of honor.

For the past two weeks, they had danced and dined and supped and breakfasted. On stage every minute, as she had put it to her cousin. Alia only laughed. She was enjoying herself thoroughly.

Selena always loved visiting her aunts and uncles and cousins on her trips to Karastonia. But this time she also met people who were familiar only from the pages of magazines, newspapers, or on television. And then there were the elaborate wedding gifts—goblets and urns in gold plate, Chinese export porcelain, ancient French tapestries, English antiques—works of art, all of them.

She often asked herself what she was doing here, amidst all this elegant opulence. She was a college instructor, small-town, U.S.A. She couldn't help but speculate about what kinds of things she would have received if she'd been married in Virginia, to, say, another college professor. They would have been inundated by blenders, toasters, sheets, china and crystal, things they would have used every day. But now, nine-tenths of the gifts she and Saber received would surely end up in a museum somewhere.

And the press, the media—always the media—were ever present. After almost two weeks of the nonstop activity, Selena was tired. Turnus was tired. Only Jayne was in her element. And Alia, of course.

On the day before she was to be married, Selena rose early and sought out her father. She stuck her head around the edge of her bedroom door.

He was seated before a tray table, loaded with food. She eyed the abundance. "Good morning. Have you a date for breakfast?" she asked.

"No, thank God," he answered around a bit of kippers. "At least they leave me at peace in the morning."

"Mother?"

"Is still sleeping," he told her. "She needs her rest, although I don't see how she keeps going even with it. Come in, sweetheart."

She took the chair across the table from him, poured herself a cup of coffee and refilled his cup. He thanked her and raised the cup to his lips.

"Daddy, I'm scared."

"Scared, sweetheart?" he asked. "I've never known you to be scared of anything."

She shrugged. "Maybe I shouldn't have said scared. It's really more of a feeling of apprehension over what my life is going to be like."

"This—" He waved a hand to indicate the folderol surrounding the wedding, and Selena had no trouble understanding what he meant. "This is an aberration and will be over as soon as you're safely married. Unfortunately in this day and time, happily married people hold no allure to the press."

"I know," she answered, dismissing that as the problem. "And it's not as though I didn't understand what I was getting into. I could have said no."

At that, her father shifted in his chair and she gave him a questioning look.

"Go on," he said.

Restlessly Selena rose and went to the window. She folded her arms and stood silently, staring at the incredible blue of the sea for several moments. "This is not a romantic relationship. I think you know that. And I don't pretend to believe that romance is necessary for a happy marriage. I had no immediate plans to marry, but I suppose I thought that someday I would find someone I cared about, probably someone in the academic world who shared my interests, someone I wanted to spend the rest of my life with. Then when Saber came... He is so—" she groped for a word "—dynamic. He *handles* things. I'm afraid I won't be able to keep up with him."

"I have no doubt that you will handle things equally well, sweetheart."

She turned back to look at her father. "And then there's the matter of his first wife," she added quietly.

Turnus's reaction was predictable. His face softened into a daydream expression, with a faraway look in his eyes, a small smile on his lips. It was the general effect of her name on everyone who remembered Lisha.

Selena supposed it was natural for people to think of Lisha at a time like this. Selena wasn't sure she remembered the woman at all. She certainly never remembered her having come to the United States with Saber when he was foreign minister. And though Selena had visited often in Karastonia when she was a youngster, she wasn't sure she'd met Saber's first wife on any of those visits. "From what I understand, she was a paragon. I'm not sure I can live up to that, Daddy."

Turnus turned to her in surprise. "No one expects you to live up to Lisha."

"I'm not sure of that."

"That was a different time, a different world. There was a king on the throne."

"Yes, I know. And I'm not complaining." She smiled. "At least, not much."

She indicated last night's newspaper that was lying on the table in front of the sofa. The editor of the paper had again raised questions about the suitability of an American woman to be the wife of the president. Saber had been furious when he'd seen it.

"You saw the editorial. Saber wants me here to set an example for the women, to encourage them to accept responsibility by taking part in the democratic process. And I can do it, Daddy. I have something to contribute. But I'm afraid that people like that columnist aren't going to take too kindly to my example. He—" again she waved at the paper "—would have preferred Saber marry someone more like his first wife."

"What the editor wants is irrelevant, Selena. It is what Saber wants that is important," her father answered sternly.

"Yes, but it seems I am going to have to walk on eggshells. And you know how good I am at that," she added with a touch of irony. "I tend to say just what I mean."

Turnus laughed. "My dear, you are the daughter of a diplomat. I've been walking on eggshells all my adult life. Besides, you underestimate yourself. I've seen you be charming and gracious to imbeciles on more than one occasion." He grinned.

She came up behind him and wrapped her arms around his neck. Her chuckle joined his laughter. "I love you, you know. I'm going to miss you and Mother."

Turnus patted her arm and they were silent for a minute. Then she leaned around to meet his grin. "And I never appreciated your chutzpah, Daddy. I hope I inherited a bit of that, too. It looks as though I might need it."

"Not at all. Saber will take care of you," said Turnus.

Her father would never understand if she tried to correct his impression so she let the statement lie.

Selena reminded herself of the arrangement with Saber. A year. She would spend a year in Karastonia and if she wasn't content, he would let her go. But that worked both ways.

A year was all he'd promised. If she found that she was indeed happy, it would be up to her to make it more.

Chapter Five

The music from the giant pipe organ—something ponderous by Bach, Selena noticed—was muted by the thick stone walls. She grasped her father's left wrist and looked at his watch. The hands were creeping toward high noon. She gave a nervous smile to her cousin, Alia, her maid of honor and the last of the twelve bridesmaids remaining in the room.

They were all dressed in the same soft shade of pink that lines a conch shell. The flower girls wore ruffled organdy in a deeper shade.

The dark-haired young woman seemed very much at ease.

I wish I were, thought Selena. Numb with apprehension, she waited in the small anteroom near the entrance to the great cathedral and thought of her husband-to-be. Was Nicholas as apprehensive as she was? Was he realizing that now, under the glaring light of all the publicity, it was too late to back out? Was he having regrets?

She looked with distaste at the elaborate bouquet which had just been delivered, and she realized that her hand was hot and clammy.

The bouquet was the one aspect of the wedding that her mother hadn't seen to, and it was much too large even for her fairly tall figure. Perhaps the flowers would have been appropriate if she'd worn the traditional cathedral train.

But, she had decided, and Jayne had concurred, that her life, her duties here, were not to be traditional. And though it was June, and this elaborate wedding would satisfy the most demanding romantic, she was not the traditional twenty-something bride.

So Selena and her mother had decided that sophistication would be more becoming. She had chosen a classic-cut gown of creamy *peau de soie* which was tea length in front and barely brushed the floor in back. The neckline, defined by Brussels lace, was modestly chic. The veil, sewn with tiny stitches to a beaded Juliet cap, would cover her face and shoulders.

"That will not do," said Jayne, tilting her head sideways to study the effect of the bouquet. "Give it to me." Selena surrendered the unwieldy flowers without a word.

A knock on the door signaled the time.

"For God's sake, Jayne," said Turnus, who was visibly nervous. He mopped his brow. "Don't go fooling with that now. We don't have time."

Jayne's clever fingers worked on the flowers but even she was defeated. "This is awful," she moaned.

Suddenly Selena came back to life. She crossed to her mother's side. "Let me." She reached into the center of the bouquet and extracted one distinctive blossom. Called "Path to Heaven," the beautiful flower was to Karastonia what the tulip was to The Netherlands. Similar to the Bird of Paradise, the colors in the stylized flower ranged from azure to indigo and the throat was the same cream as her dress and the small prayerbook she carried. "This will be fine."

She took a deep breath and read her mother's approval in her eyes. "Perfect," said Jayne.

"Well, I guess it's time."

"Be happy, my darling." Her mother kissed her, arranged Selena's veil across her face, nodded satisfaction and disappeared on the arm of an escort.

Alia was next. She gave Selena a hug and left. A moment passed and Selena smiled at her father and tucked her hand into the crook of his elbow. "Shall we go?"

Her father's arm was like steel beneath her fingers. She tried to tell herself that he would support her if she stumbled.

They stepped out of the anteroom. The temperature was several degrees cooler in the cathedral and Selena shivered as she took her first step down that endless aisle. Saber, tall and noteworthy as his build was, seemed a small spot at its end, a small, unfamiliar spot. Her legs would never carry her that far. It was certainly too late for second thoughts, but she had them, anyway.

Oh God, what in the world had she done? She was supposedly an intelligent woman. She must have been insane to agree to such a complicated alliance. She was grateful for the sheer veil that hid her expression from the waiting crowd. A grimace wouldn't be becoming to a bride.

As they approached the halfway point, Nicholas Theodor Saber's form began to increase in size. And continued to grow beyond proportion to their progress, until it filled her vision. His shoulders were impossibly broad. She couldn't see anything else but him.

He was somber in his formal morning coat, his dark eyes unreadable as they met hers. Was he thinking of another woman, another wedding, another day, one swollen with the happy anticipation of young love?

Selena spared only a moment's regret for herself as an adult woman. She had put her romantic fantasies in the drawer with her doctorate years ago. But she was shaken for a brief second, by the loss of the dreams she'd had as an adolescent, dreams she hadn't thought of in years, dreams of everlasting love and happy ever after.

She supposed she should be grateful for the one fairytale element in this marriage. There was no question that Saber would have qualified for the handsome prince in anyone's book.

Saber took her hand; her fingers were like ice. Would he notice? Her father stepped back.

The solemn ceremony began. As Saber repeated the vows, his voice was strong and his words, distinct. She mumbled her way through the first passage. Until she realized that to these people, she probably sounded becomingly obsequious. Then she lifted her chin and spoke clearly.

And it was over. Done. She was married—and in the most blatant glare of publicity since the last royal wedding.

Saber raised her veil. He lightly touched his warm lips to hers. The collective gasp that went through the congregation echoed her own. Kissing in public wasn't the norm in Karastonia.

They turned from the altar, the object of all eyes. Her fingers shook as she took his arm.

Saber paused. He covered her shaky fingers with his big hand and looked down at her with a small smile. A flash winked from off to her left. Later, when she saw the photograph of that moment, she would think that they seemed like any couple, dressed in their finery, newly married and deeply in love. The only thing disturbing about the picture was the unexpected possessiveness in Saber's expression.

The day became a tension-filled blur—a formal luncheon followed the ceremony, a public appearance on the balcony of the palace, dancing, champagne toasts, more dancing, a formal dinner. Finally Selena was allowed to escape to change her clothes for the short trip to the yacht.

They were to cruise the Karastonian coast for a ten-day honeymoon.

It was well past midnight when the limousine neared the harbor. Selena noted with some trepidation that the ship was lit up like a Christmas tree. She glanced at her new husband, hoping there were no further formalities to be endured.

Saber had changed into a dark suit and she was wearing a dress that would have been appropriate for another formal party. However, she could see no press, no cameras, and she gave a sigh of relief.

Saber heard. He smiled. "Tired?"

"A little bit," she admitted. "You, on the other hand, look as fresh as a daisy."

"Appearances are deceiving, but I'm all right." He scraped his hand down his face and she could see that he was indeed weary.

"I don't suppose it was easy for you to clear your calendar for ten days."

He didn't deny it; he simply shrugged.

She looked down at her lap. "Now, you make me feel a bit guilty."

He was surprised. "Why should you feel guilty?"

"Because all I've had to do is attend parties. You've had to attend the parties and do double work, as well. When did you sleep, Saber?"

He gave a dry laugh. "I'm fortunate to be one of those people who doesn't require a lot of sleep."

The captain was waiting to greet them at the quay. She acknowledged the man's good wishes as he gave them both a smart salute and helped her aboard the tender. "Welcome, sir, ma'am."

"Thank you." Selena smiled as enthusiastically as possible under the circumstances. She was almost asleep on her feet. She swallowed a yawn as she followed the captain's directions to a cushioned seat under a small awning.

Saber sat very close to her; she had to fight the temptation to rest her tired head on his shoulder. He seemed to sense her need and laid a strong, supportive arm across her shoulders and pulled her close.

Selena tilted her head back to give him a grateful smile. She wondered immediately if his show of affection was for the benefit of the captain.

She chided herself. She knew she shouldn't look for a hidden motive behind every move he made, but she couldn't help it.

From the first, the media had played up their wedding as a romantic union of two people in love. Once, Saber had talked to her about the portrayal.

"I hope showing a small amount of public affection doesn't make you uncomfortable, Selena," he'd said as they were leaving a party hand in hand.

"Of course not," she had responded without perceptible hesitation. Not *un*comfortable, exactly. But not yet comfortable, either, she had told herself honestly.

Still, she relaxed under the weight of Saber's arm. It was a short, quiet trip out to the yacht. As soon as they reached the vessel, however, the tension returned.

Saber took her hand as they mounted the ladder to the deck. He seemed to sense her exhaustion, though she was sure she'd managed to hide the worst of it, because he cut short the crew's greetings and, still holding her hand, escorted her down a short flight of steps and forward. He opened the door to the salon of the master suite and indicated one of the bedrooms opening off from it.

"That is your stateroom," he said, leading her toward the open door. He released her hand, tugged at his tie and opened the top button of his shirt.

She looked through the door into the spacious cabin, where someone obviously had unpacked her things. Her silver-backed brush and comb were on the dressing table. The bed had been turned back and the sheer white gown and peignoir her mother had selected in New York were arranged across it. New York seemed like another lifetime, on another planet. She realized that Saber was staring at the flimsy lingerie. Her color rose.

"I'm right over there," he added, gesturing toward a door on the opposite side of the salon. His smile was slightly twisted. "I'll leave you now, Selena. Get a good night's sleep. Call if you need anything." She felt his lips on her forehead.

Though she was exhausted, she was also oddly, unexplainably disappointed by his hurried, almost hasty, goodnight. This was, after all, the first night of their marriage. It would seem more fitting to relax together in the salon for a minute's conversation. She opened her mouth to suggest something of the kind.

Saber waited politely.

Finally, however, she simply nodded. "You're right. We probably both need rest. Good night, Saber."

The door closed behind him. She looked at the gown, made a face and stripped off her dress. In the drawer she found a few things that must have raised the eyebrows of whomever unpacked her clothes. She dragged her favorite old Redskins football jersey over her head and crawled beneath the covers.

Married. She reached for a pillow and brought it to her chest. She looked down at her hand, at the shining gold band that proclaimed the actuality.

The diamond-and-ruby engagement ring had been shifted to her right hand for the ceremony. Now she pulled it off and placed it in a dish on the bedside table. But she left the wedding ring in place.

Married . . . to a man she barely knew.

Saber peeled off his jacket and tossed it on his own bed. He rolled his sleeves back, whipped off his tie and slung it away with an impatient gesture. He opened another button of his shirt. Then he returned to the sitting room and collapsed into a chair.

Hell! What had he done?

As he had stood at the altar this morning, waiting for his bride, he had suddenly been hit with the strangest feeling. He'd let his eyes roam over the congregation, looking around at his friends, personal, political and professional. He'd been shocked as he realized the power represented by many of the people in the cathedral, powerful people assembled from all over the world.

And, suddenly, Saber had longed to be anywhere but where he was.

Later, at the reception, as he'd shaken hands, smiled and introduced Selena, he'd tried, on another level of his mind, to make excuses for the urge, to tell himself that he was simply tired. All the worn-out clichés had come too easily to mind. The excitement of having been in on the birth of a nation was waning. The burdens of his position were heavy. The rewards were no longer enough; the pressure of his job was finally reaching him.

But Saber had known this morning that this time it was more than a clichéd reaction to pressure. He had recognized, for the first time, that he had never had a life of his own.

He'd been groomed for important work from the time he was a child. His parents, although not warm people, had been considerate enough and not overtly demanding. They had merely assumed that he would do what was expected of him. And he had never disappointed them. But now, suddenly, he wished his existence were easier, tamer, more normal.

The entire concept of wanting more time for a personal life for himself had jolted him anew as he'd stood in the receiving line at the reception, but he'd realized it was true. Now, here in the salon of the master's cabin, he finally located the privacy, quiet and solitude he needed to reexamine the prospect and his attitude toward it.

He, Nicholas Saber, fancied the opportunity for leisure. Now that the situation in the country had begun to stabilize, he could delegate more authority. He mulled over ways that could be accomplished. Not right away, of course. He'd been elected; he had to serve out his term.

As he stared out over the sea he laughed aloud, the sound emerging as a dry and disillusioned bark. Here he sat, thinking he'd like to simplify his life, and he had just landed himself with another complication, perhaps the most complex, the largest complication of all.

A wife... a wife whom he barely knew.

* * *

As is often the case when exhaustion sets in, Selena's mind refused to release its grip on consciousness. She lay there wide-eyed for half an hour, listening to the motors, feeling the gentle rocking motion of the ship become level as it found the sea and increased power.

Though the numbness she'd felt since she entered the cathedral that morning had slackened somewhat, it had not disappeared completely. She was grateful for that, afraid that if it did, she would really be depressed.

Finally she got out of bed and went to the door. She opened it a crack. There was one lamp burning.

She'd barely noticed their surroundings when Saber had shown her to the bedroom. Now she looked around the salon, furnished in shades of aquamarine and white with splashes of lemon yellow. Comfortable overstuffed chairs were strategically placed to enjoy the view of the sea. Saber was sprawled in one, jacket off, tie discarded and shirt unbuttoned at the collar. He hadn't seen or heard her enter. He sat with his chin on his fist, staring blindly out through the large plate-glass window. Beyond the window, an undulating path was painted by moonlight across the dark water. Off to the right the lights of the capital city defined the horizon. She was surprised to see how far they'd travelled.

As she watched, he scratched his beard with a knuckle and laid his head against the back of the chair. He looked so very lonely. His features were heavy with doubt and his dark eyes held a strange sadness. His expression set off a corresponding sadness in her.

She took a step back, meaning to withdraw. He raised his head with a jerk. "I thought you would be asleep." He erased all traces of emotion from his features and got to his feet.

She made an ineffectual motion with her hand and stepped into the room. "I couldn't sleep. Too keyed up, I expect."

"Would you like something? A brandy?" He held up his glass, the bowl resting in his large palm.

His gaze had drifted to her bare legs. She should go back into the bedroom and close the door. She hesitated, thinking of the expression of loneliness and regret that she'd caught on his face.

Was he thinking of his dead wife? Was he remembering the love they'd shared, the marriage that was so very different from this one?

Suddenly Selena decided to set aside her own misgivings and try to do something for this man who was her husband. She'd figuratively made her bed. Mistake or not, it was up to her to find a way to be comfortable in it. And she certainly wouldn't find comfort if he didn't find it, as well.

A tiny smile played at one corner of her mouth. "What I'd really like is something to eat."

He laughed as he got to his feet. "I can take care of that easily enough." He went to the desk and picked up the telephone.

"Saber, no. It's too late," she protested, coming farther into the room.

"If my bride is hungry, it is never too late. How about a cheeseburger and a soda?"

He'd obviously been talking to her mother. She loved junk food. "A cheeseburger sounds wonderful, but I'll soon be spoiled by such indulgence."

He looked at her for a minute, seemingly trying to decide something. She stood still under his examination. At last he smiled. "I doubt seriously that a little indulgence would spoil you."

She studied him, puzzled by the remark. "What do you mean by that?"

He shrugged and sipped from his brandy. "I was sitting here feeling guilty."

"Why on earth would you feel guilty?"

"I've asked a lot of you. I suppose I've just now stopped to think how much. I feel guilty about what you've given up."

So that was the reason for his expression—or at least a partial reason. She thought for a minute. What could she say?

"You're giving up a lot, too, Saber," she said lightly. "I intend to be a very demanding wife."

He lifted a dark brow. A corner of his mouth twitched. "Do you now?"

Selena relaxed. "I want mustard, catsup *and* mayonnaise on my cheeseburger. I like it rare, with tomato on the side."

Saber laughed as he went to the telephone and ordered for both of them. Burgers, fries, soft drinks.

"I'll get some clothes on," she said.

He started to say something, then changed his mind and nodded.

Back in the bedroom Selena looked at the lovely silk lingerie set that she'd tossed over a chair. She dismissed it as too suggestive. She pulled on a pair of white pants and socks and caught her hair back in a clasp.

"It will be here soon," he told her when she returned to the sitting room. "With tomato on the side. Our wedding supper was wasted on us both, it seems."

She knew he was teasing. "Wedding supper" was a misnomer, to say the least. The guests had been served from an elaborate banquet table that groaned under the weight of the food. Still, she answered seriously. "I was too nervous to eat anything."

"Right now a cheeseburger is probably more appropriate fare to accompany the sort of talk we need to have, anyway."

The comment drew her eyes to his face. He wasn't looking at her.

"Talk?" she asked mildly. She wanted to comfort him, she wanted to feel relaxed in his company, but she wasn't sure she was up to a serious talk. Not tonight.

"I know you're troubled, Selena. About your changed status, about what your life will be like. God, after the past few weeks, I am a bit uneasy, myself."

"You are?" Even having witnessed his sad expression, his choice of words surprised her.

"Certainly. Everything has happened too rapidly for either of us to have adjusted. We knew it will take some time. That's why I promised you that we wouldn't share a bedroom until you decided the time was right."

If she ever did, thought Selena. Still, it was kind of him to restate the conditions of their marriage. Reassuring, somehow. Especially in light of the way he'd looked at her legs when she entered the room.

She began to relax. The numbness faded and was replaced, not by depression as she'd feared, but by a growing curiosity about this man she'd married. Her thoughts were interrupted by a knock on the door.

A young man in uniform came in bearing a huge tray, which he set on the table in front of Selena. If he was surprised by her casual attire he was much too well-trained to let on.

Her eyes widened at the amount of food. "Good grief, Saber. Are we supposed to eat all this?"

The young man blushed and cleared his throat. "The chef thought you might like a choice of his desserts. Something sweet to finish with. Er..." His voice trailed off and the color in his face turned a screaming red. "He's famous for his sweets."

Selena caught her breath.

Saber nodded, unsmiling. "Thank you. That will be all."

The young man beat a hasty retreat.

The door had barely closed behind him when Saber burst out laughing. It was a relaxed, happy sound.

Selena tried to hide her surprise. Was this the same man whose loneliness was etched on his face a few minutes ago? The mask of dignity he habitually wore seemed to have been cast aside. He looked years younger.

His laughter died, but a smile lingered around the curve of his mouth. "I think he was baffled by your football shirt. He's probably never seen one before. I wonder what he thinks the number designates."

She looked down at her chest. The numerals 20 were painted there. "My age?" A grin began to grow as other possibilities occurred to her.

His mind must have been running along the same lines because he grinned, too. "Do you think the chef wanted to provide us with something to keep our energy level high?" he asked, chuckling as he eyed the elaborate selection.

Her gaze followed his. "If so, he certainly is optimistic," she said.

There was what her mother would have called a "pregnant pause," followed by a moment of silence, but then Saber laughed again.

She joined in his laughter, grateful that the atmosphere between them was the easiest it had ever been. Perhaps . . .

Selena wondered if the reporters, who wrote so romantically of their marriage, would have believed that they spent their wedding night, what was left of it, munching on cheeseburgers, French fries and Grand Marnier soufflé, and talking about American football.

Chapter Six

Selena woke on the softest, smoothest sheets she'd ever slept upon. She stretched, paused and looked around in confusion. Yes, this was her bedroom; there was her purse on the dressing table.

But she was unable to remember how she got here. She remembered yawning a lot; she remembered her eyelids growing heavy. The last thing she remembered was asking Saber to pour her a cup of coffee. She needed a jolt of caffeine to keep herself awake.

She turned her head warily and then closed her eyes with a soft sigh. She was sure that she still wore her slacks at that point, but this morning they were folded neatly on the same chair where she'd discarded the sheer gown and peignoir. Warmth crept into her cheeks. Well, they *were* married.

She bathed and pulled on her swimsuit, a new one selected by her mother. She observed herself dubiously in the floor-length mirror of the bathroom, then rolled her eyes. It was midnight blue, a sleek wet-look fabric, and it zipped up the front. At the top of the zipper there was a large ring. The legs of the suit were cut very high on her thighs. Too high, in her opinion.

Why had she ever let Jayne take care of this purchase alone? Or any other, for that matter, she thought, her eyes sliding to the extravagant lingerie that she'd passed up last night.

She turned her body to look at herself, this time from the rear. The sight caused a soft moan to escape from her lips. Her mother had obviously decided that a certificate of marriage and a ring upon one's finger necessitated a bathing garment that was blatantly seductive. She picked up a knee-length robe and hurriedly slipped her arms into the sleeves.

Heaven knows what else I'll find when I finish unpacking, she thought as she left the suite and went looking for Saber.

He was in the main salon immersed in reports. But as soon as she entered, he dropped what he was doing and rose.

Her heart took a plunge when she saw that his mask of dignity was once again firmly in place. But he smiled as he came to her side and took her in his arms. His lips were cool and he seemed to be holding himself in check. She reminded herself, as he kissed her, that the affection was for the benefit of the crew.

However, a moment later she wondered if the kiss needed to be quite so thorough. His cool lips were suddenly warm and hungry and firm against hers. When he finally raised his head she was slightly breathless. While he appeared to be totally in control of himself she did notice a muscle contract in his strong jaw.

"Did you sleep well?" he asked, still holding her. His breath caressed her cheek as he studied her face.

Her voice was calm but her eyes flickered as she answered, "What little sleep I had was very restful, thank you."

That appealing masculine slash appeared in his cheek, but it was gone in a fleeting moment. "Would you like some breakfast?"

She pulled out of his arms. "Surely you're kidding, Saber. After last night I may not eat again for a week." Despite their amusement at the chef's selection of sweets, they had managed to put quite a dent in the assortment.

"If you are going to be busy," she went on, noticing the scattered papers, "I might work on my tan."

"I do have a few things that have to be attended to. All the problems don't stop when the president takes a honeymoon. I'll join you as soon as I can."

"Don't rush. I understand."

She left him there and made her way to the forward sun deck that she'd seen from their quarters. It was guaranteed privacy from the rest of the ship by a screen. She took off her robe and lay down on a padded chaise lounge. In moments she was asleep again.

Saber found her there half an hour later. He looked at her for a full minute, letting his unguarded gaze roam over her long, smooth legs, her small waist and full breasts. The ring at the top of her suit was a formidable temptation. He never would have believed that this woman he'd married could be so sensuous, so unconsciously seductive. But the last weeks had been arduous and trying, and not because of all the work he had to do. He shook his head. She was completely unaware of how quickly his desire for her was growing.

Last night he'd been surprised by something he'd not thought likely—that he could relax with her, that they would converse as friends and companions. Later, though, when he'd carried her to bed, when he'd unsnapped and unzipped her white slacks and peeled them off her, he'd been hard-pressed—he laughed at the very appropriate expression—not to kiss and caress her into arousal.

He'd known she was lovely. He'd known that, eventually, making love to her would be a pleasure. But he'd not expected any difficulty about waiting until they had learned some things about each other. He'd not expected to be in this uncomfortable and constant state of near-arousal when he was near her.

It was a dilemma, one that she'd soon notice since they were going to be together in close quarters for ten days. His new wife wasn't blind.

This morning he found half of himself wishing for a state emergency that would necessitate their returning to the capital. But the other half wanted to take her to his bed and sail on endlessly while he lost himself in her sensuality.

Suddenly annoyed, Saber spun away from the sight. He returned to the main salon and picked up the papers he'd been working on earlier. Luckily for his peace of mind, there was always business to be taken care of.

Selena heard her stomach growl before she realized she was hungry. She picked up her watch from the table beside the lounge. She'd been here for over an hour. This early in the season, she had very little tan and had to be careful not to burn. She got to her feet and put on her robe. Then she went looking for Saber.

She found him conferring with the captain in the main salon. He turned when she entered. "I thought we might have dinner tonight in Entchulla. What do you think?" he asked her.

She recognized the name of the small harbor town fifty or sixty miles down the coast from the capital.

"Sure." She smiled and drew closer. He held out his arm in invitation and she had no hesitation about moving easily into the embrace. "I think that sounds wonderful. I haven't been there in years but I seem to remember a little Italian restaurant near the harbor."

"Indeed, it is still there." He seemed pleased that she was familiar with the town. "That's where I planned for us to eat tonight."

The captain spoke again. "Very well, sir. We should dock about seven o'clock," he said. Then he left them alone.

Saber instantly and abruptly dropped his arm.

Before he could go back to his papers, Selena made some offhand remark to cover her shock—she wasn't sure afterward what she'd said.

Saber's response was unexpectedly stilted and withdrawn. To say his attitude surprised her would be an understatement. Last night they had talked easily and openly, as though they were friends—or at least, headed in that direction.

She looked up at her husband with clouded eyes but he didn't meet her gaze. She wondered what had happened between last night and today. She had never been one to skip around an issue so she asked, "Saber, is something wrong?"

"What do you think is wrong?" he asked, now introducing a strong cord of irony into the conversation. He sighed heavily—as though she were a pesky problem he had to deal with before he could get on with more important things—and touched her arm in apparent apology. "Nothing's wrong, Selena. We both knew the first few weeks were going to be difficult," he added with more sincerity. "We just have to wade through them. Besides, the business of state never really stops." He indicated the papers on his desk with a wave of his arm. "I have to finish these before the day is over."

She withdrew a step, provoking a narrowed look. "I'll leave you to it, then," she said stiffly. Then she announced, "I'm going to find some lunch. Will you join me or shall I have the chef send you a tray?"

"A tray, please," he answered absently, returning his attention to the papers in front of him.

Selena had to make a real effort not to stomp out. She couldn't believe it. The kiss he'd given her this morning had left her shaken. The first full day of their marriage and her new husband could kiss her eagerly in front of others; but when they didn't have an audience, he became so engrossed in his work that he couldn't spare the time to have lunch alone with her.

For a long minute, Saber watched the doorway through which she had disappeared, a guarded expression in his black eyes.

They met for drinks together that evening before the trip to Entchulla. Saber served Selena, then sat down beside her on the plush sofa.

After only a few minutes, however, even that brief interlude of privacy was interrupted by a call.

When Saber came back from the radio room he was all business again. "Do you have any objections if one of the appointments secretaries begins to set up a schedule for you?" he asked. "There have been quite a few requests coming in to the office for you to appear at various functions."

"I don't mind. Will I have to give a speech? I would need time to prepare for that."

He shook his head. "You could get by with saying a few words of thanks or encouragement, depending on the circumstances. I'll tell the secretary to limit the appearances to ceremonial occasions for now, until they can consult with you."

"Fine," she said, and he left her to return to the radio room.

She sensed that she was being handled like a commodity, but then scolded herself for the feeling. She'd known she would be expected to do this sort of thing. What Saber hadn't told her before their marriage about her duties as wife of the president, her father had filled in.

The villagers had seen the yacht offshore and were waiting when the tender docked. The newlyweds were welcomed warmly and briefly, and then left to enjoy their meal. Again, Selena was aware of Saber's withdrawal once they were alone.

Determined to discuss the situation between them, which could easily take on a nightmarish quality, Selena rose early on the second full day of the trip—she refused to call it a honeymoon, even to herself—and donned a floor-length terry-cloth robe she'd gotten last Christmas. She didn't want to take the time to dress because she might miss Saber when he left his room.

She was waiting in the salon that separated their bedrooms. "Good morning, Saber," she said, turning from the window when he entered.

"Good morning," he answered, a surprised smile smoothing out his features.

"I would like to talk to you," she said, her tone businesslike. She thought he took an instinctive step in her direction, but only one. When she looked at him expectantly, he halted.

"Certainly," he answered, recovering quickly. "Shall we go out on deck for breakfast? We can talk there."

"No." She spread her arms. "As you can see I'm not dressed yet."

"We were out late. I thought you would still be in bed."

She dropped her arms and pushed her hands into the pockets of the robe. "I wanted to catch you before you went to work." She hesitated. "You were going to work, weren't you?"

He nodded shortly.

"I thought this was to be a time for us to get to know each other, Saber."

"And I thought you realized—"

"I do," she interrupted. "I do realize that the government doesn't ever stop. I am not going to be a demanding wife, or a complaining one. But yesterday's off-again, on-again show of affection made me edgy." Irritated was what it made her, but she chose the other word as more diplomatic.

He gave her a long, hard look. She knew she'd surprised him again; she just wasn't sure whether the surprise was because she dared to speak honestly or because she dared to criticize him.

"I apologize if I made you uncomfortable," he said with no expression in his voice.

"I think you should tone down the public display. I know a certain amount of affection between us is expected, and I'm willing to go along, but you aren't being consistent. You give me a rather enthusiastic kiss one minute, and the next you're poring over papers as though I don't even exist."

When he didn't answer immediately, she went on, "We promised to be honest with each other, Saber, and that's what I'm trying to do."

"Very well," he answered simply. "I'll see you on deck for breakfast?" He waited for her nod of agreement before leaving.

After he'd gone, Selena stood staring at the door. How could the man maintain such control?

The initial result of Selena's straightforward discussion with Saber was that the relationship between them now became like a silly children's game. She became the one to withdraw and was particularly adept at avoiding his displays of affection. She didn't think she was making an issue of her withdrawal—the first time it happened, he looked at her with a brow lifted in question. She simply smiled. But after one or two more foiled attempts, he clearly realized what she was doing.

He didn't press her. However, he did begin to spend more time with her. They swam and fished from the stern. Selena caught a large albacore, albeit with Saber's help. They dined on deck under the stars, or on shore in one of the many quaint villages that dotted the coast. They danced to the stereo on board and to the music of either a concertina or a guitar in the villages. But they didn't dance too closely.

She beat him at Scrabble; he beat her at chess.

And there was no way to completely avoid the accidental physical contact, which was beginning to affect her profoundly despite her misgivings.

With each touch, no matter how casual, she felt her desire grow. She often caught his dark gaze upon her, and it had its result, sparking a surprising need. She felt the warm surge of desire more than once under the force of that gaze.

They also argued, sometimes with amusement, sometimes with annoyance. Many of their problems were the result of cultural differences; there was no getting around that. No matter how broad-minded he professed to be, he occasionally lapsed into the dominating male role that was so common to his countrymen.

Underneath it all, under the casual laughter and occasional discord, it was obvious to Selena, and, she thought, to Saber, that the tension between them was building relentlessly. Their efforts at control were eroding, slowly but invariably, like layer after layer of sand washed from the beach by a gentle tide.

Whether the situation would either explode into full-blown anger or flaming passion was a question yet to be decided. . . .

Selena rose early, determined to maintain a positive mood today. They were leaving the ship to visit the ruin of a remote hilltop temple constructed centuries ago by their Greek ancestors.

It was a short climb to the site, so she dressed appropriately in dark blue shorts and a cool cotton shirt in a lighter shade of the same color. She twisted her hair into one long braid, picked up a canvas tote and left the stateroom to join Saber on deck for a hasty breakfast.

When she appeared, he stood politely and she took her seat opposite him. He remained standing for a minute looking down at her, his napkin dangling from his hand. He was different today, somehow, she thought as she observed the play of muscle across his broad shoulders. More relaxed.

He was dressed as casually as she. His shorts and shirt were khaki. His long muscular legs and forearms were tanned a beautiful bronze color and lightly dusted with hair. He looked very...macho.

And there was an odd light in his eye. She laughed uncomfortably under the intensity of his stare. "Something wrong?" She touched her nose, her hair, raised her brows inquiringly.

"No, of course not," he said quickly.

The sun was blindingly bright in the cloudless sky. She squinted in the harsh light, fitted a white tennis visor on her head and reached for a glass of juice.

When they had finished eating, Saber went to have a final word with the captain.

Selena watched him go. The sun's effect was responsible for the warmth she was feeling, for her accelerated pulse rate. At least, that's what she told herself.

She wandered over to rest her forearms on the rail and looked out at the beach that was their destination. From here it looked beautiful, but desolate. A few gulls, some breeze-swept grasses and the flow of gentle waves as they greeted the shore, contributed the only motion in the scene. The mountain looked larger than she'd expected; she had a clear view of the ruined temple at the top and it seemed very far away.

"The tender is waiting," Saber said from behind her, startling her.

"I'm ready," she answered with a smile, holding up her tote bag. He led the way down the ladder to the smaller boat and turned back to give her a hand. She hopped in and headed for the cushioned seat in the bow.

When Saber joined her a moment later, he was barefoot and carrying a pair of low-topped hiking boots with socks stuffed down inside. "I hope my sneakers will be okay, Saber. I don't have any boots."

He nodded, his gaze moving leisurely down her bare legs to her feet. "Sneakers are fine. It's not much of a climb. But you'd better take them off for now, if you don't want to get them wet. We'll have to wade ashore."

Selena nodded and removed the sneakers and her socks and stuffed them into the tote bag. The sailor maneuvered the tender as close to the beach as possible.

Saber balanced on one hand and jumped with effortless grace over the gunwale, barely creating a splash. Before Selena could join him in the water, she felt his hands firmly about her waist.

To her surprise he lifted her easily. Her hands went to his shoulders for balance, to the steel-hard muscles under his shirt, while her eyes sought his questioningly. It was such a playfully intimate thing to do, to lift her like this. And so unlike the Nicholas Saber she was learning to know.

His face was in shadow but his beautiful dark eyes met hers, met and held. He set her on her feet in water that was knee-deep, and held her until she steadied. He removed his hands slowly, almost—it seemed—reluctantly. "Go on in. I'll get our things."

What was going on here? She finally dragged her gaze from his and waded up the slight slope toward the deserted beach.

Saber reached back in the boat. He grabbed his own boots and gathered up a couple of towels and the picnic lunch, which had been prepared by the chef and packed in a knapsack. "Come back for us late this afternoon," he called out to the young man.

"Yes, sir." He saluted and revved the engine. The tender swung about in a long, smooth arc while Saber joined Selena on the beach.

Side by side, they stood watching the wake of the small boat until it disappeared.

When the sound of the motor had faded away, Selena turned to look around the area. "This is nice," she said softly. "Peaceful."

Saber had been here before so he watched her instead. He smiled to himself; her delight was unmistakable.

On the crest of the hill high above them was the outline of the ruins they would explore. But there were no other houses or buildings of any kind, no power lines, no other evidence that man had ever left a footprint on this spot.

He moved toward her until he could smell her scent, that fresh clean smell that was so much a part of her. The breeze from the sea lifted strands of hair off her neck. "Do you realize that this is the first time we've ever been completely alone?" he asked in a husky voice.

Selena had not been unaware of Saber's nearness. Slowly she turned to him. Now the wind and sun were at her back. His expression was the one that was exposed and the open desire she saw in his eyes sent her heart up to lodge in her throat.

Not that she hadn't been expecting something of the sort, a heated look here, a touch there—the warnings were evident. But now, today, it seemed the tension had clearly reached the unbearable point.

"I hadn't thought about it." She lied, trying to ignore the effect of their isolation and the sight of his powerful body.

The khaki shirt was buttoned carelessly, and the thick, dark hair curling damply on his chest, as well as an irregular pulsebeat under the skin of his throat, were a temp-

tation to her fingers. She wanted to touch him intimately
and the fact swooped down on her so unexpectedly that
she caught her breath at its force. She raised her eyes to
his.

Suddenly Saber dropped the things he was carrying and
reached out for her. He didn't ask permission, didn't stop
to think that this might be a foolish move, didn't think he
might regret the action. He simply surrendered to an urge
that was so strong, so primitive, that it would no longer
be denied. He'd barely slept since they left the capital,
knowing that a few feet away his wife lay in a large bed
clad only in a football jersey, her long legs bare.

He hadn't made love to a woman since the night he had
proposed to Selena.

With his big capable hands he brought her soft curves
into alignment with the sharper planes of his body. God—
he almost groaned aloud—she felt good against him.
And, bless the powers above, she tilted her head back, laid
her hands on his chest and rose up on tiptoe.

The glorious sun rode the clear blue sky above their
heads. He looked down into her face. The crystal radi-
ance clarified each of her fine features and painted the
flawless purity of her skin a golden color. He could feel
the heat on his shoulders, smell its warmth in her hair and
on her skin. "You are so beautiful," he murmured.

A sigh escaped; his mouth sought hers hungrily, and he
could taste the simmering flavor of sunlight on her soft
lips. He flicked her lips with his tongue and she opened
her mouth to his exploration. Her teeth were slick; she
tasted early morning fresh and minty and sweet, so sweet.

When he finally lifted his head they were both breathing rapidly. Deliberately, holding her dreamy gaze with
his, he slid his hands down her back to her hips and held

her close, trying to ease the ache in him. "I want you, Selena."

Her eyes widened as she felt the evidence of his arousal. "Saber—" she said hesitantly.

"I know, I'm out of line," he declared harshly. A muscle in his jaw convulsed. "But, you wanted honesty. Dear God, I didn't realize that I would want to make love to you quite so quickly, and so desperately. I won't force you, but I'm hurting, Selena. And we are married."

She let her head fall forward until her forehead rested on his chest. "Oh, Saber." She shook her head. When she raised her eyes to his again, she wore a small smile. "I won't pretend I haven't felt this coming on. You could probably convince me."

She saw the satisfaction flare in his eyes.

"But I'm not certain this would not be wise. Not yet."

The satisfaction didn't fade as she'd expected it to. "Why would it not be wise?" he asked with an indulgent smile that was hard to resist.

She touched his cheek; the muscle jerked again. She pulled free, surprised at how agonizing the action was. "For a lot of reasons," she answered evenly. "We promised ourselves we would get to know each other. You just said it yourself, Saber. This is the first time we've even been completely alone. What if we make a mistake?"

Saber shoved his hands into his pockets and nodded shortly. His eyes were black and hot as they roamed over her. "And you are nervous. Why, Selena?"

She hesitated, wondering about the best way to tell him. It was something he would discover eventually. It was better for him to know what to expect, and they had pledged to be honest. "I haven't had a lot of experience at this kind of thing."

The silence with which he greeted her words was deafening. But the rhythmic pounding of the ocean rushed in to fill the void. She risked a look.

Saber was clearly stunned by her revelation. When he finally spoke, the words were delivered as an accusation. "Are you trying to tell me that you're a virgin?" he demanded, his voice rising on the last word.

"I'm not *trying* to tell you anything. I *am* telling you— I am not sexually experienced." She couldn't imagine why he should be angry about such a thing. What difference could it make to him? It was her business. "I'm sorry if it bothers you."

But he was angry. His brows met above his eyes, his lips thinned, his fingers curved into his palms. He was very angry.

As though she had betrayed him.

"I suppose now you'll expect me to set a romantic scene when we do go to bed together."

She paused; the moment stretched into eternity. "You?" she responded finally with a smile saturated in disdain. "Certainly not." Her anger rose to meet his. She lifted her chin to a "go-to-hell" angle. She spun on her heel and started to walk away from him. "But the choices I've made about my life have not really been your concern, have they?" She tossed the parting shot over her shoulder.

"Until now," he returned sharply. Hands thrust into his pockets, he followed her. "Why the devil didn't you tell me?"

"I didn't realize that such experience was part of your job description," she answered without turning.

The sandy white beach blurred before her eyes, but she kept her head up and kept on walking. She had gone a hundred feet or more before he spoke again from behind her.

"Selena—" From his tone of voice he appeared to have gained control of himself.

But Selena was not appeased. How dare he take that insulting, accusatory tone with her? As though what she had were contagious.

Determinedly, she continued her chosen path parallel to the waterline. A random breeze pulled at the tennis visor she wore and she tugged it back down into place.

"Selena," he persisted. "Where are you going?"

"Anywhere, nowhere," she snapped. "Away from you." She tossed her braid over her shoulder and lengthened her stride.

At last, with a firm hand on her arm, he brought her to a halt.

She gave his hand a pointed look.

He dropped it immediately. "Stop it. You can't run away forever. I'm sorry I overreacted, but it was a shock. You'll have to admit that finding out that you are a virgin—"

"Because I'm over thirty? Or maybe because I'm an American?"

"Neither. That wasn't what I meant at all." He plunged the fingers of one hand through his hair in a gesture of frustration. Or was it exasperation? "I really do apologize, Selena. I didn't mean to insult you," he assured her quietly.

"You didn't," she retorted promptly and with determination. When he looked disbelieving, she went on, "But you have disappointed me, Saber. The first night of our marriage I thought that perhaps we would be able to come to terms with each other fairly quickly."

Back in Virginia, she had allowed that passion-heady love wasn't the best basis for marriage because it seldom lasted. On the other hand, she did want them to feel *something* for each other. "I didn't expect romance, but I guess I did expect consistency. Instead, the next morning you were like a different man completely. It was as though the man who had eaten cheeseburgers with me had never existed."

Saber took a deep breath, stretching the cotton shirt across his broad chest. He planted his hands on his hips and glared down at her. "Do you want to know what happened?" he snapped.

His height, his broad shoulders made her feel diminutive in comparison, and she was far from being either dainty or petite. She realized that, despite his stance, his anger was no longer directed at her, but directed inwardly toward himself. "Yes."

"Because, the next morning I came to the pool and watched while you sunbathed. You remember that bathing suit—ah, yes, I can see from your expression that you do. The wet-suit look, I think they call it, complete with a zipper down the front. I realized then that it was going to be difficult—in fact, it was going to be damned near impossible—to keep my hands off of you when we were alone."

He ignored her gasp of astonishment. "No comment?" he asked after a minute. "Oh, hell, Selena, come on. Let's climb a mountain. Maybe if we work off some of this energy it will be easier."

They didn't speak while they sat in the sand and donned their shoes and socks. Saber slung the knapsack on his back and they set off.

The mountain wasn't brutal, but it wasn't easy, either. Saber led the way but kept an eye on her until he was satisfied that she wasn't a bumblefoot. They stopped to rest once on an outcropping of rock that was about two-thirds of the way to the summit.

Saber leaned down to give her a hand. He grasped her forearm and effortlessly boosted her up beside him. "Ah, thanks," she said, taking a moment to catch her breath. "I must be out of shape."

"I wouldn't say that," he murmured, his gaze lingering on her damp shirt.

She let the provocative remark pass. She did feel calmer for the exercise. She hadn't really done anything strenuous, hadn't played tennis or swum, since—good heavens—since the weekend Saber had proposed. No wonder she was keyed up.

They climbed until they had nearly reached the summit. "Look," said Saber, dropping their equipment and turning her until her back was to him. His hands remained on her shoulders. "It will rain later."

She felt the warm weight of his fingers as she looked toward the water. Except for the sound of the wind, it was quiet. A few dark clouds, touched at the edges with silver, had moved out over the blue waters. Through gaps in the clouds, sunbeams radiated down like dozens of golden pillars holding up the sky.

"Oh, Saber," she murmured. "I've never seen anything so beautiful and dramatic." She looked over her shoulder to meet his smiling eyes.

And could not look away.

Suddenly the tension was back, vibrating between their locked gazes like a strummed wire. The resonance reached all the way to her toes. He moved his hands down her arms to her hands. Linking their fingers, he wrapped both of their arms across her stomach and pulled her against his broad chest. She saw his eyes darken, became aware of the acceleration of his heartbeat against her back. She felt her knees weaken and was sublimely grateful for the support of his body.

Saber dipped his head with the obvious intention of kissing her. But, at the last second, when their lips were only millimeters apart, he stopped. His mouth curved in a small smile that unnerved her. "Ah, Selena. What am I going to do with you?"

His tone was low and seemed to have grown dangerously mellow, but she had no trouble understanding him. However, she couldn't have spoken if her life had depended on it. She shook her head.

"Shall we see if we can reach the top?" He grinned wryly. "Of the mountain," he added smoothly.

She nodded.

"The rest of the climb isn't as difficult as it has been so far."

Clearly he was speaking metaphorically and she felt her pulse accelerate. She finally found her voice. "Yes, I understand."

He hugged her quickly and let her go. "Come on. I'm hungry."

Half an hour later they unfolded the cloth on the steps of the ruined temple and unpacked the food. "This looks delicious," said Selena, spreading a napkin across her lap. She filled a plate for each of them with fresh crudités, dried fruits, bits of smoked meat and sharp cheeses and fresh-baked bread.

Saber poured a rich red wine into two plastic cups and handed one to her. He touched his cup to hers. "To a beautiful day spent with a beautiful woman," he said, his voice dropping to a low, intimate level.

"Thank you," she responded.

Most of the clouds had moved out to sea and the temple ruins were once again splotched with sunlight. Saber smiled at her, and after a moment they both turned their attention to the food. A tenuous peace hung between them as the afternoon melted away. That, for the time being, was enough.

* * *

The same smile was in place on Saber's face early that evening while he waited for Selena to join him in the main salon. The promise of the afternoon clouds had been fulfilled and a cool rain was falling, streaking the windows. The stereo played softly in the background and candlelight cast deep, curious shadows into the corners of the room.

A small table had been set for two before the window. He looked around, wondering if she would be uncomfortable in the blatantly seductive scene.

He shrugged as he checked his formal bow tie in the reflection from the silver ice cooler. After today, surely they were past that. His wife wanted him. And he sure as hell wanted her. They'd both recognized and admitted the sensual attraction. Now, the decision made, he was merely trying to speed up the timetable.

As surprised as he'd been when she made her announcement this morning, he found that he was beginning to get used to the idea of an inexperienced wife. His initial shock had been for her sake, because she deserved more than this "arranged" marriage he'd foisted on her...and for his sake, because he had expected a worldly sophisticate to whom the physical aspects of marriage would be no more, or less, meaningful than any other love affair—and then he'd discovered she'd had no other love affair.

He was to be the first, and that fact added a dimension of solemnity, that he hadn't intended, to their marriage as well as a sense of responsibility that he wasn't sure he wanted.

But, after considering the situation, he'd seen that this was just one more reason why she was so right for him—and he for her. He would like for this experience to be perfect for her and he felt confident that he could make it so.

He rubbed his palms together in anticipation. This was going to work out after all. And without any careless emotional entanglements. Just the way they'd agreed.

The moment she walked through the door, he knew that at the end of this evening he would not recall what they ate, what they talked about, what music was on the stereo.

Her formfitting gown was the green-gray color of the sea beneath the rain clouds. It was cut low across her breasts and clung precariously to her shoulders. The fabric shimmered as she moved, accentuating her small waist and feminine hips. The hem stopped at her knees. The shape of her calves, clad in pink silk stockings, was redesigned by the high heels she wore.

Like a man in a trance he approached her. "Selena," he murmured. "Words escape me."

She laughed—the soft, husky sound enchanted him—and shook her head. He could smell the familiar scent of her shampoo. Her hair spilled across her shoulders and was held away from her face on one side by the tiny butterfly clasp.

"Thank you, Nicholas."

Saber realized that was the perfect response. She didn't demur, she didn't deny, she didn't dismiss the compliment. Though his wife lacked vanity, she did have a healthy self-confidence, and tonight she knew she was beautiful.

She'd called him Nicholas. How odd, he thought.

She looked around at the candlelit scene. "The table looks lovely."

He shook himself mentally and dragged his eyes away from her. "Shall we?" He held her chair and she sat down.

Before he took his own seat he touched a bell, and the steward appeared immediately with the first course.

The evening had been wonderful. From the moment Selena had entered the salon and witnessed Saber's dumbfounded response to her appearance, she'd been overjoyed that she'd managed to engage his attention so completely. She had wondered if she would ever be able to accomplish such a thing.

And now they walked along the corridor toward their private quarters. Selena realized that her footsteps had begun to drag, so she deliberately quickened her pace. She was ready to cast aside the vague and silly timetable they'd set for themselves. Since Nicholas's admission of desire and clear demonstration of frustration this afternoon, she was eager.

Saber opened the door and stepped back for her to precede him. She took two steps inside and stopped. He came up behind her, standing close, but not touching her.

Selena took in a deep breath and held it.

He grinned at her back. "You look like you're being led to the guillotine."

He teased rather than reproached, but she was quick to deny his words. "No, I'm just wondering about the etiquette for this."

"Why don't you just relax and let me show you," he murmured softly from behind her.

Her bare shoulders had driven him crazy all night. They gleamed with alabaster perfection and he wondered if they could possibly be as smooth as they looked.

They were. He caressed her from her delicate collarbone to her upper arms. He bent his head to touch his lips to that delightful place where shoulder and throat and jaw met, and felt her shiver. He sensed correctly that she would feel more comfortable in familiar surroundings.

"Come," he said gently, leading her into her own bedroom rather than taking her to his. "We're going to take this very slowly."

In the pale light of dawn, Saber looked down at his wife. Her tousled hair was spread across his shoulder, her cheek rested against his chest. Under his arm he could feel her rhythmic breathing. To look at her she seemed relaxed. But there was something slightly off kilter, a remaining thread of anxiety that revealed itself in the angle of her shoulder, the position of her leg. Even in her sleep, she seemed to cling to a certain independence, as though she couldn't completely let go.

He sighed. Once more he found himself in the position of watching Selena without her being aware of it. The resulting disquiet was far greater than the last time. Before, when he'd watched her sunbathe on the day after their wedding, he'd been assaulted by physical desire. Today he was struck with a more dangerous and emotional reaction that was difficult to deny. That day his body had been moved; now, his heart was moved, and he could not afford that.

He eased himself away from the sleeping woman and got out of bed. He reached for his robe and left the room.

Pull yourself together, he cautioned. Coffee, he needed coffee, hot and strong and black. He went in search of some.

For years he had buried himself in his work. He couldn't afford the distraction of love; he would not live with the vulnerability that intimacy demanded.

These days were like a block out of time; they would soon pass and he had to be ready to reassume his duties.

Later. Later, when he was back at work, when his hours were filled, he'd be able to handle the emotions Selena had begun to provoke in him. Later, when he knew her better, he wouldn't be so fascinated.

When Selena awoke, the bed beside her was empty.

Her emotions were in a turmoil. Their lovemaking had been exquisite. Everything that should have happened did. But the experience also had been somehow oddly unfulfilling and she would have felt better about herself if he were here beside her.

She dragged herself into the shower. When she came out of the bathroom ten minutes later, toweling her hair dry, she felt marginally better.

Saber was waiting for her. "I brought us some coffee."

"Thank you." She wrapped her wet hair turban-style and took the cup he offered. He relaxed in a chair, his long legs stretched out in front of him, crossed at the ankle; his expression was closed and tight. But he was studying her very closely.

"You're not very happy this morning, are you?" he asked quietly.

"No, not very happy," she answered after a pause.

He sipped his coffee. "You were right when you wondered if we might be making a mistake. We should have waited," he said finally.

"Probably." Selena flashed him a glance, remembering the moment on the beach yesterday when she'd uttered those words. She wandered to the window and stood staring out at the overcast day. The color of the clouds matched her mood. Gray.

She noticed that he hadn't apologized for making love to her. Thank God for that, at least.

She eliminated all emotion from her features before she turned to look at him. His own expression was laced now with self-reproach as he met her steady gaze.

"Well, we were swept up in the moment, but it was a mistake we don't have to make again. There isn't a lot we can do about it now, is there?" she asked.

She thought she saw a smile—no, surely not. When he spoke she knew she'd been wrong. "No, there isn't a lot we can do about it," he agreed gruffly.

The cruise continued as before, except Saber was even more detached, more deeply engrossed in affairs of state. She saw him only at mealtimes. She wondered if he had given the captain an explanation for the tension and withdrawal, because surely the crew had noticed that the honeymoon couple were less than devoted.

But then she dismissed the idea. First, Saber wasn't the kind of man to explain himself. And second, the crew members were much too well disciplined to talk about their president's personal life. They probably felt sympathy for the poor man who had to work even on his honeymoon. And finally—there wasn't the media pressure here to know every detail of a dignitary's life. Thank goodness.

At least on the yacht they were isolated, protected from the real world and its very real pressures. Soon they would have to forfeit that luxury for the jobs each of them had to do, jobs that would complicate their already complicated lives and push them even further apart.

Neither of them was ready yet to reenter that real world. But both of them knew it couldn't be avoided.

Chapter Seven

When the yacht docked at midnight, ten days from the day Saber and Selena had set sail, there were a few journalists hanging around the gate to the harbor. But they were stringers, sent there to wait, since the time of arrival hadn't been announced. Their presence was not a nuisance; a few pictures of the smiling couple and they were satisfied.

One of the photographers remarked on Selena's newly acquired tan, and a reporter questioned Saber about the fine-arts exchange program with Italy. Incidental matters, Selena was relieved to note, as they got into the waiting car.

The drive to the palace was completed in silence. Selena was apprehensive about settling into a new routine, and she wondered what would be expected of her.

Saber showed her to her quarters and when their luggage had been delivered, he dismissed both the driver and the housekeeper who had been there to greet them. "I'll show my wife around," he told her. "Thank you."

Selena had barely had time to respond to the introduction, but she didn't miss the sharp, unsmiling look the woman gave her. She wondered about that.

At one time, Saber explained, these had been the queen's rooms and the floor plan was identical to his apartment. But there hadn't been a queen in the palace for over thirty years. This space was usually reserved for visiting guests.

Except for the sound of his voice and their footsteps, Selena hadn't, until this moment, thought about the fact that she was to be left, more or less, on her own. True, Saber had told her that she would have her own apartment for the first few weeks. But for some reason the idea of such seclusion hadn't registered. At least on the yacht there had been people close by; here she felt totally isolated. "Is there going to be speculation about our living apart?" she asked.

He was silent for a minute. "No. The housekeeper sees to this area of the palace. She wouldn't allow anyone to work here who was a gossip."

Selena listened and observed as Saber showed her through the apartment. Decorated in shades of burgundy and garnet, and tones of gold, the rooms were sumptuous and ornate. The fabrics were heavy—damasks, velvets and thick-weaved silk tapestries. The woods—mahogany, teak and ebony—were dark. She found the rooms very formal and cold—and depressing.

"The O'Haras stayed here during the wedding," Saber told her as he prepared to leave.

"I'll bet Bree and Ryan loved this," she muttered.

To her surprise, he chuckled and let his gaze roam over the room. "Bree said the place reminded her of a dungeon. You're welcome to make changes. I'm nearby, right down the hall, if you need me." He hesitated. "Actually there used to be a door between our apartments but it was closed off when the remodeling was done and these became guests' quarters. I hope you'll be comfortable here, Selena."

"I'm sure I will be."

They were standing beside a dining table with seating for six. He looked around for a minute, as though he were at a loss. "I have a breakfast meeting scheduled for tomorrow morning. One of the appointment secretaries will come by to talk to you and I'll try to see you at lunch." He snapped his fingers. "No, I forgot. I'll be tied up then, too."

She was suddenly very tired. She wished for a woman friend, for her mother, or even for Bree O'Hara, someone who might understand her feelings of abandonment.

At last she spoke, not caring whether or not he sensed her discouragement. "Don't worry about it, Saber. I'll look for you when I see you. Good night." She turned her back on him.

Saber studied her back for a minute. Her shoulders were unnaturally straight, her body too still. Why did he have this feeling of guilt, this feeling that he was deserting her? This was what she wanted, what they both needed—space and time. Wasn't it?

"Good night, Selena," he said finally. "I'll see you sometime tomorrow."

The rooms that Selena occupied weren't far from Saber's apartment but they might as well have been at the other end of the country, thought Selena, as she stood staring out over the courtyard.

For the past two weeks she had only the most cursory contact with her husband. Sometimes he seemed to regret not being able to spend more time with her; other times he seemed grateful to escape. What contact they did have was usually in the company of others, or was rushed and hurried because Saber was on his way somewhere else. He spent several nights out of town.

He was working to catch up on all the meetings he'd postponed during their wedding and honeymoon. With the exception of that one fatal day, he'd worked steadily during the cruise. However, she had no illusions, not since the diplomatic dinner in Washington—the night she'd decided to accept his proposal—that his duties ever slackened.

She had gotten her first look at her own schedule on the morning after their return from the cruise, when a secretary appointed by the council of ministers entered her sitting room.

It had been early, barely seven o'clock. She was glad she'd dressed before sitting down to breakfast because the man just barged right in without knocking.

"Madam Saber?"

His voice had startled her into spilling her coffee. "Yes, and who do you think you are?" she snapped, using her napkin to blot the brew off the table.

He had been unperturbed. "I am Charles Tyron, secretary to the council of ministers. I have here—"

"Mr. Tyron, it is quite early," Selena had interrupted sharply, ignoring the papers he was waving in her face. "I don't know what it is you want but I have not yet had my coffee, and I do not appreciate your barging into my quarters without knocking."

"I do apologize," he had said stiffly, not looking the least bit sorry. "I assumed you would be ready to receive. Karastonian women—"

"I am an American." She realized immediately that she had said the wrong thing. He straightened his shoulders and peered down his nose at her.

She, in turn, looked him over carefully. He was tall, as thin as a reed and pitifully humorless. He reminded her of Ichabod Crane. Wire-rimmed glasses sat on the end of his nose. He peered over the rims instead of through the glass and she wondered why he bothered to wear them in the first place.

That morning, they had met for fifteen minutes. During that time, Charles Tyron had also taken her downstairs to show her the space that had been set aside for her temporary use until a proper office could be prepared. It was a tiny little cubical—two desks, two chairs, one filing cabinet. She hoped they didn't have to spend much time together there.

The schedule, which he presented to her, was already set in concrete, it seemed. She asked once, when he was telling her about a ribbon cutting at the new wing of the hospital to be followed by a luncheon with the nursing staff, if she would have time to visit some of the patients. He was horrified that she would even *think* about meddling with his precious schedule.

She found, as the days passed, that the events he scheduled for her were entirely ceremonial, nothing of substance, nothing she could get her teeth into.

On another occasion, she inquired about possibly speaking to the government classes at the university. That was when she learned that the ratio of women to men in the College of History and Political Science was somewhere around one to fifty. Tyron told her this grudgingly in order to explain why she might lack credibility in speaking to a class comprised of men.

Selena kept her temper with the greatest resolve.

It took only a few days, also, for Selena to discover that Charles Tyron didn't like to have to explain himself. He always listened to her questions with minimal tolerance and a hint of boredom. If she offered an idea, he promised to bring it to the attention of his superiors. If she followed up, he evaded the topic.

Perhaps he didn't like his job any more than she liked him.

She decided that if Saber wanted her to contribute, he was going to have to let her have some leeway in planning her own schedule. She had always handled her own correspondence, but she could see from the number of letters that had been handed to her that she needed her own secretary, someone she could actually talk to in a conversational exchange, not a barrage of words from one side that barely pierced the surface of the mind of the other.

She had mentioned the idea of a personal secretary to Saber during lunch yesterday. He'd agreed readily to her idea of offering the job to her cousin, Alia.

As soon as they finished lunch she had telephoned Alia's home, only to be told that Alia was in the United States, visiting Selena's parents for a few days. That news caused a wave of homesickness to wash over her. She left a message.

She was also thrust quickly into another dilemma, this one on an entirely different level. The housekeeper who took care of their apartments had been the maid to Saber's first wife.

Selena was treated constantly to long, evaluating looks from the woman, to heavy sighs and oblique remarks about Lisha's youth and beauty and sweetness.

After one of those experiences, Selena found that she was unusually grouchy for the rest of the day. She realized that the emotion which prompted her crankiness was jealousy. She had never been jealous before and the feeling unsettled her.

After two weeks of the stifled atmosphere, she steeled herself to confront Saber at the first opportunity. She discovered that opportunity was as elusive as a hummingbird. But she had to do something.

Saber seemed to be treating her as the men of Karastonia had treated their women for centuries—protectively, like chattel, like possessions—and she would not stand for it.

Saber wanted her to be a new role model, he'd said, for the new Karastonian woman. How could she be one, when he seemed content to leave her in the archaic past?

At last a day arrived when she thought she might have a chance to be alone with him. She rechecked the schedule and dressed carefully for a dinner with the Italian ambassador. But rather than present herself at the reception room at the proper time, she left her apartments early and went the short distance down the hall to Saber's rooms. She knocked on his door.

He opened it himself. His hair was damp from the shower and she could smell the scent of something fresh and outdoorsy. Onyx studs were in place in his shirt but the ends of his black tie dangled loosely and one of his cuffs was open.

"Selena." He was clearly surprised. He fumbled with his cuff, trying to insert the cuff link. "Come in. Is something wrong?"

"Yes, Nicholas. Something is definitely wrong. You're avoiding me."

"Don't be silly, Selena. You haven't mentioned a problem. Damn." The last was directed to his cuff, which he was struggling to fasten.

Without thinking, she took the cuff link from him and tended to the task. "No, because I didn't want to bother you." Drat, why should she apologize? "That is, you didn't seem to have the time to listen."

Saber's eyes narrowed as he stared down at the shining head. She had pulled her hair back into an intimidating bun. He liked it loose. She wore a subdued black dinner dress; he preferred her in colors.

He realized suddenly that he was looking for things to criticize, for his own self-protection. The brush of her fingers against the skin of his wrist was soft and warm. Her scent was floral and spicy, very appealing. He could feel the awakening of his desire.

He shook himself mentally. "I'm sorry if you had that impression. I'll always have time to help you with a problem." She had finished fixing his cuff. He put a hand to her chin to make her look at him. He heard the huskiness in his voice when he continued, "But you have to mention it first. I am not a mind reader, Selena."

Their gazes locked but whatever might have been said was interrupted by a knock at the door.

With a sigh, Saber left her and went to answer. He talked for a moment and then closed the door again. "The ambassador is not feeling well tonight and asks to be excused."

"Oh, I'm sorry." The man had served with her father years ago in Washington, when they were both young embassy clerks. "I'll call on him tomorrow, if you'd like."

"That would be kind of you." He hesitated. "I've asked the staff to serve dinner up here. Do you mind?"

"No," she said quietly. But her surprise was tempered with glee. Maybe now she could straighten out a few matters.

An hour later, Selena threw her napkin down on the table in disgust. "Don't be sarcastic with me, Saber. I don't need this. I may have to put up with that Ichabod Crane of a secretary, but I don't—" At his warning glance, she broke off. The butler removed her plate and set a compote of sherbet before her.

When he had gone she continued, "I don't feel that I'm contributing to the women of Karastonia. All I've done is cut ribbons. Anyone can cut ribbons."

Was that a hint of a smile at the corner of his mouth? "And what is the solution?"

"Well, you're the president and I don't want to go on with any plans without consulting you, but you're never around when there's a decision to be made."

He sighed tiredly. "Selena, I can't help that."

"I know. I'm not asking that you be at my beck and call. But how can I do the things that you seemed to want me to do..." She let her voice trail off. When she spoke again it was stronger. "You do still have a use for me, don't you? You didn't get me here under false pretenses?"

"Don't be silly. Of course I didn't. I have just been unusually busy since our return...."

"The year is going to end eventually, Nicholas."

His gaze was instantly drawn to her but she didn't notice. An idea had suddenly occurred to her. "I may have a solution," she said thoughtfully. "What I propose is this—" She linked her fingers together and propped her chin on them. "It's an idea I borrowed from my parents. You know, Nicholas, it wasn't easy on them when they were first married. Daddy was gone a lot and so was Mother. You may not know that they separated once.''

He raised a brow. ''No, I didn't know that.''

''Yes, despite the fact that *they* were in love, their marriage was in trouble.'' She let her lids fall slightly to hide her response to the flare in his eyes. ''The point is, marriage isn't easy under the most ideal conditions.''

He did smile then and she realized how ridiculous that sounded. She had never been married; he had. He spoke before she could continue.

''I agree that it is very difficult for two people, two independent people,'' he amended, ''to join their lives. I'd be interested to know how Turnus and Jayne handled the conflict.''

''They allowed at least one hour a day for each other. They set the time for eight o'clock in the evening, or thereabouts. Sometimes it was the hour before and sometimes the hour after. If they were in the same city, of course they were together alone and face-to-face.''

Selena paused and smiled, then continued, ''Many times, though, their date had to be over the telephone. But they set aside that hour for themselves, and they vowed that nothing would interfere with it. If Father had a diplomatic function to attend or if Mother had a booking, they worked it out. If we were all at home, I knew that their hour together was inviolate. I have an idea they didn't always talk.''

Saber eyed her speculatively. ''How interesting,'' he said.

''Saber, I know that we're not even sure that our marriage will last. But, even if it doesn't, I don't want my time here to be useless. I love this country. Maybe if we can talk together regularly...''

''All right.''

She was just getting wound up to argue in favor of her suggestion. His statement took the wind out of her sails. "What?"

"I said all right. We'll make a date for every night at eight o'clock."

"And no matter what—"

"No matter what. We'll meet together if at all possible. If not, we'll speak on the telephone, and we'll talk about whatever we want or need to discuss. It's a good idea, Selena."

He was really pleased, she thought with some surprise. She smiled with satisfaction. "Thank you, Nicholas."

"Is there anything else bothering you?"

She was hesitant at first but, at his urging, she finally told him about the situation at the university. "One thing... from something you said when you asked me to marry you. I think we should have a major push for registering women to vote. That would generate some interest in the subject. I could arrange for you to do some public-service announcements that would appeal especially to women."

He seemed to pick up on her enthusiasm. "That is a very good idea. You must appear in it with me."

Time passed quickly and, for the time they spent together, they returned to the easy camaraderie they'd shared the first night of their marriage.

There was one other item she wanted to talk about, but she hesitated. The hour was late; she would have to go soon. Finally, she decided to take the chance. "Nicholas," she ventured, "how important is Mr. Tyron to you?"

The question surprised him. "He's been with me for a number of years. Why?"

"If Alia decides to go to work for me, I don't think I'll need anyone else. You probably depend on him for more important duties."

Saber's eyes narrowed. "The truth, Selena. What's happened?"

She sighed heavily. "The truth is I'm having trouble working with a man who doesn't give me credit for having a feasible idea of my own. I've mentioned the voter registration campaign and a number of other issues to him, areas where I might be of help. He always comes up with a reason why they won't do. And then he sends me off to another ribbon cutting."

Saber's eyes narrowed as she spoke; she saw a spark of anger there and hoped it wasn't directed at her. "I'm sorry, Selena. Charles hasn't brought any of your ideas to me for consideration."

She wasn't really surprised to hear that. "Then I'll make a list for you."

He nodded. "Good."

She glanced at her watch, though she knew exactly how late it was. "Well, I guess I'll be going."

His mouth lifted at one corner. "I'll walk with you."

Selena's first instinct was to decline his company, but she decided that would sound foolish. She tried for lightness in her voice. "Thank you. I wouldn't want to be mugged on the way home." She preceded him out the door. The hall, as usual, was chilly and damp.

"Saber, have you ever thought of moving out of here? Of living in a real house?" she said as they walked slowly along. She didn't know why she asked the question—she supposed as a conversational gambit—but she was surprised by his answer.

"I've never thought about it," he said evenly. "I've lived in one part of the palace or another since the king gave me my first appointment when I was twenty-eight. It was convenient for him to have his people nearby. Now it's close to the governmental offices and convenient to the legislature, so I guess I'm confined here for now." When they reached her door, he turned to look down at her. A strand of hair had escaped her chignon. He tucked it behind her ear.

She caught her breath when his warm fingers lingered on her neck. "You couldn't drive back and forth to work from another place?" she asked, hoping the effect of his touch was reflected in her voice.

"It's something to consider," he replied thoughtfully. "Why do you ask, Selena? Are you unhappy living here?"

She answered before she thought. "No more than any other place, I guess."

His face became closed to her, suddenly and completely.

"I'm sorry, Saber. I didn't mean that like it sounded," she said quickly. "I just—"

"Of course not," he said, cutting her off.

Before she could speak again he gave her a formal half bow. "I'll see you tomorrow night at eight, then. You'll have a list of other suggestions?"

"Yes, yes, of course," she said distractedly. "Saber, please . . ."

But he'd turned and walked away, leaving her standing there alone, staring at his back. Damn.

The courtyard was stark and deserted. Moonlight painted the paths silver, the grassy verge black, the marble stones white. Saber, still dressed in his formal clothes, harmonized with his setting. He strode determinedly along the perimeter next to the castle wall, like a man with a place to go. In reality he was trying to work off some of his frustration.

Selena's innocent question about leaving the palace had taken him by surprise. If he'd ever thought about a home of his own, it was an idea for the distant future. He would not want anything like the cold, formal house he'd grown up in or the palace where he'd spent most of his adult life, but a real home, comfortable, bright with light, on a bluff, overlooking the sea. With a garden.

Maybe someday, when his responsibilities were ended, he'd have such a place.

He thought about Selena's proposal that they spend a certain time together every day. It wouldn't be easy to arrange, not at first, not until he made it clear to his staff that he meant what he said when he told them he was not to be disturbed. They would eventually get the message, however.

Every night at eight. A smile spread over his features. This might work out well. He'd been reluctant to admit to himself that he was dissatisfied with their infrequent meetings. No matter that they were safer, he'd missed having her to talk to. Her intelligence was often a challenge, but she certainly never bored him.

He veered off the main path and onto a narrower one that led to a small cemetery, and without realizing it he came to a stop before his first wife's grave. He stood there for a long minute.

Lisha had been a sweet, lovely child and he had grieved over her death. He wondered what would have happened if she had lived. They would have grown apart; he was sure of it. She had been a clinger and he would have eventually disliked that. She had no concerns other than him, his home, their hope for a family. She had never taken an interest in his work, had seemed bored on the rare times when he'd mentioned it.

He would always have loved her, but one thing he knew—Lisha paled beside the image that rose to his mind now when he thought of Selena.

Lisha would not have understood his deep concern for his work, his occasional preoccupation, as Selena did—most of the time. Selena. He was married to a woman who was as different from Lisha as the sun is from the stars. Could he make her happy enough to stay here permanently? Or at least content enough?

Saber ran a tired hand around the back of his neck and plunged his hands in the pockets of his trousers. He let his back curve, his shoulders slump, his head drop forward in a posture of exhaustion and lassitude.

Selena looked out the windows of her apartment. Below, Saber was the picture of despair as he stood staring at the grave of his wife. Selena squeezed her hands together tightly until her fingers grew numb and she blinked in an attempt to clear her eyes of the tears that had sprung up without warning.

With a heart that felt like a lump of clay and a burning in the back of her throat, she turned away, unable to bear the sight of his grief any longer. She had been concerned about this and now she knew it was true—he would never get over Lisha.

And how did she feel about that, Selena asked herself. She'd come here with her eyes wide open. She knew their relationship was to be based on companionship, need, friendship. She'd never been deceived into thinking that he would love her.

But now she'd begun to suspect that she needed more, that marriage was a bad bargain without love or, at the very least, something that closely resembled that emotion.

Had she, deep down, wanted his love, subconsciously yearned for it? Had she foolishly pictured herself as the unawakened princess, to be roused with a kiss from the handsome prince? Admittedly, she'd had a crush on this man when she was very young. But a teenage crush rarely blossomed into a mature relationship.

She crossed the room with restless strides, stripping off her dress as she headed for the shower. She would make a place for herself in Karastonia or she would leave. It was that simple.

Saber had agreed to the daily contact, a good first step. Maybe some of the feelings she needed would result from that. She vowed to herself to make the most of those meetings. Then she would see what happened.

The interview with Alia went well. Selena had known her all her life but only as a much younger cousin with whom she shared family events.

Alia was as intelligent and ambitious as Selena had thought she might be. When Selena explained what she hoped to accomplish, the young woman responded with enthusiastic support and some ideas of her own. It was agreed that she would come to work at nine o'clock the following morning.

That evening, Selena was able to report to Saber that she was happy with her choice.

Saber had some news of his own, which he imparted with a slight grin. Charles Tyron had been reassigned and her liaison with the council of ministers, from now on, would be David Leandos, a man of her generation, whom she knew and liked.

She wondered if the man she thought of as Ichabod had requested the change or if Saber had ordered it. Nonetheless, she had a sneaky feeling that Charles Tyron was as happy as she was.

Chapter Eight

The dinner with the Italian ambassador, postponed for a week when he had come down with a virus, was rescheduled for tonight. Selena was looking forward to spending a quiet evening with her father's friend and his wife—and her own husband.

She wore a stylish gown of black lace with a modified heart-shaped neckline and long, tightly fitted sleeves, and she'd swept her hair into a chignon and misted herself with her favorite fragrance. She met her own gaze in the mirror. Would Saber like the way she looked tonight?

While she was dressing, she had slowly become aware of a disturbing feeling inside her, a strange, odd feeling, and one which put her on an emotional edge. She put her hand over her stomach to quiet the flutter there.

Occasionally their nightly meetings were in his apartments, occasionally in hers, which were more formally decorated. Tonight they were dining here; the ambassador and his wife would arrive later, but, for now, Saber was waiting in her living room.

One night earlier in the week, he'd had to be out of town and they'd talked on the telephone. True to his word, he'd called at exactly eight o'clock. But the instrument was oddly inhibiting and a poor substitute for a face-to-face meeting. They talked more freely and easily, and for a longer period of time when they were together.

The last few evenings spent with him had been—*productive,* her mind told her as she clasped her grandmother's pearl choker around her throat. *Enchanting,* said her heart. He was thoughtful, complimentary and—*reachable.*

She sensed that Saber was benefiting from their meetings, too. His schedule was as horrendous as ever; its effects were often visible in the lines of strain in his face, the shadows around his eyes. Most evenings he left her to return to his office—but he left more relaxed and refreshed than when he'd arrived.

As she was doing tonight, she'd dressed carefully each evening and, judging from Saber's reaction, he'd approved of her efforts. Of course, she had never gotten the stunned reaction of that unforgettable night on the yacht, but his appreciation was unmistakable.

She had also tried to prepare herself with something of importance to discuss with him. She still dreaded conversational lags. When she had no subject to focus on, she suspected that she might be revealing more about her personal feelings than she intended. Fortunately such lags were rare.

A few seconds later, she paused at the door to the sitting room and observed that Saber was more relaxed than she'd seen him. He had put some music on the stereo—cleverly hidden in an antique armoire—mixed himself a drink and now sat with his feet propped comfortably on an ottoman. She was heartened by his apparent relaxed mood as he waited for her.

This was what she'd hoped for, that he would begin to anticipate their meetings as something to look forward to. She watched him from the door. Then her eyes were drawn to the window. Her heart felt heavy as she recalled the scene beside his wife's grave.

He was about to drink from his glass when she moved into his line of vision. Her appearance halted his hand in midair. The relaxation that had stamped his features eased suddenly to an expression she couldn't read.

"Selena," he said softly, rising and coming toward her. He lifted a hand as though to touch her, and then let it drop back to his side.

He continued to stare at her until finally she tilted her head, looking at him quizzically. "May I get you a drink?" he asked.

She barely wavered. "Yes, please. I'll have a dry sherry."

He smiled and he did touch her then, just a fleeting brush of his fingers against her forearm, but she felt a tingle all the way to her toes. "You father would be pleased with your choice."

"You're right. Maybe I'm finished with rebelling." She smiled. "Don't ever tell him this, but I happen to like sherry." Her voice trailed off when she noticed that he was preoccupied. "Saber, is something wrong?"

He recovered quickly. "Nothing more than the usual. Difficult day." He turned away to get her drink. "How are things working out with your cousin?" he asked as he handed her the glass.

"Alia has quite a creative mind. I'm pleased with her."

"And the plans for your classes at the university? Are the officials still giving you difficulty?"

He was clearly filling time. Selena's curiosity was aroused. Still she hesitated, remembering the scene they'd had the last time this subject was discussed. Saber had been angered by the obstacles placed in her way when she went to the university with her proposal. She wanted to teach an adult-education course on government, specifically aimed toward women.

The structure of her curriculum had to be approved, however, by the university officials and, while they acknowledged her doctorate in world history, they had questioned her expertise on the structure of the new Karastonian government.

Saber had wanted to call up the president of the university, order the man to give her a position. After all, he'd made her a promise. "You might as well be back in that college in Virginia," he snapped as he'd paced the floor of her office.

Selena had understood the school's wariness, however, and she'd tried to make him understand, too.

With some effort and a bit of amusement, she had managed to calm him down. "The king could have delivered such an order, Saber, but not you. This is what happens in a democracy," she had reminded him, provoking a wry grin. She'd gone on to explain, "Besides, they didn't turn me down. I'm going to take a competency test after the Independence Day observances are over. I have too much to do between now and then to spend all my time studying."

Saber had grumbled, but, since then, had helped her enormously by making sure she had easy access to all the information she needed. For the most part, the governmental structure of Karastonia was similar to that of the

United States, but there were disparities. She would have to be letter-perfect if she wanted to satisfy the officials.

Now she answered his question carefully. "The university officials have been cautious, as they should be. I'll be ready for the test, Saber. I'm not worried." She lifted her eyes to meet his gaze. Her mouth tilted wryly. "But I am apprehensive about the class offering in the fall. It would be embarrassing if no one wants to take my course."

He chuckled. "You underestimate yourself, Selena."

"I hope you're right." She shrugged. "I'd hate to be faced with an empty classroom."

He raised one brow; a corner of his mouth lifted. "You could insist that Alia take your course. That's one. I may not be king, but if I put my mind to it I could probably come up with several more names."

"That's an idea," said Selena. Encouraged by his humor, she laughed suddenly. "In fact, now that you mention it, I could fill the class with my relatives," she teased. "Why didn't I think of that?"

Saber turned his glass slightly for a minute, held it to the light. The amusement, what there was of it, had disappeared from his expression and he cleared his throat. "Speaking of our Independence Day observances, I have something to ask of you. A favor," he said without meeting her eyes.

"Certainly, Saber."

"We are going to be rather crowded around here during the festivities. Our first guests will begin arriving soon. I wonder if you would mind moving in with me so we can use these apartments for some of the visitors."

His expression, when he finally looked at her, was inscrutable. She had no idea how he really felt—whether he wanted her there or was expecting her to offer another solution. Of course, there were other bedrooms in his apartment. She could have all the privacy she needed or wanted.

She tried to keep a lighter, casual tone to her voice. "No, I wouldn't mind." Tomorrow would be a good day, she decided, running over her schedule in her mind. "I'll start packing in the morning." She watched him over the rim of her glass.

An expression she couldn't interpret flared briefly in his gaze. "Fine." He smiled quietly.

The ambassador was charming, his wife was witty and the dinner went well. At the end of the evening, Saber's mood was mellow as he stood by Selena's side. They had bid good-night to their guests and now Saber was preparing to leave. They were laughing easily over an anecdote the ambassador's wife had told at dinner.

Saber opened the door to the hall, paused, folded his arms across his chest and leaned a shoulder against the jamb. "I enjoyed this evening, Selena. I've enjoyed all the evenings we've spent together."

"I've enjoyed them, too." Silence fell between them as her smile diminished, but it was not an uncomfortable silence. The easy ambience of the evening remained for a few moments. But then it began to fade, to be replaced by a developing sense of anticipation.

They both became aware of it at the same time. As Saber straightened from his relaxed posture, Selena smoothed her skirt. She met his gaze, then looked away. "Well, I suppose I'd..."

The words stuck in her throat when he laughed aloud, an odd laugh, one with no humor. He reached out to slide his hand around her waist. "One of the first things I observed about you was that, when you are nervous, you begin your sentences with *well*." His voice was low, very low, and husky as he pulled her forward and into his arms. "Are you nervous about something, Selena?"

"Nervous?" she murmured. She could have objected to the embrace, but she didn't. She let herself be molded against his hard body.

His fingers splayed over her lower back. He didn't hold her tightly but the restraint seemed to cost him some effort. His head dipped; his warm lips brushed hers briefly. He tasted of rich, dark wine.

She knew suddenly that she wanted this, wanted it with surprising intensity. Her eyes drifted shut; she waited, expecting him to deepen the kiss. Instead he muttered, "It's been too long since I've kissed you."

His breath was warm against her lips. She opened her eyes. "Ah-h. Yes, it has," she answered softly. His gaze was dark and unfathomable. She realized that her arms were around his neck, her fingers in his hair.

Then he kissed her again. And again it was brief and light.

She really longed for a kiss that sparked the sensation she'd felt on the yacht, a take-charge, lusty, authoritative kind of kiss. She could feel the tension in him and she waited, her anticipation underscored by the heat radiating from his body, by his purely masculine scent.

At last she could bear it no longer. "You can do better than that," she said huskily. She tightened her arms around his neck and pulled his head down.

And then his mouth covered hers, hard and hungry, and totally satisfying. Their surroundings faded away; it seemed as though they were encapsulated in a world all their own.

When, at last, he raised his head to look at her, that dark gaze was slightly unfocused and his breathing was ragged and unsteady. He searched her expression as though for an omen, a sign of some kind.

She felt as though she might drown in those shadowy eyes. The silence between them was thick and heavy and she felt compelled to break it. "Nicholas." That was all she said—just his name, softly.

But the word had a strange effect; she could see him reestablish command of himself. The metamorphosis was swift. In seconds he was in complete control again. He smiled a suitable smile, said a conventional good-night and left rather abruptly.

She stood in the door watching him go, her eyes stinging for some reason. She wished she hadn't been so impatient, hadn't broken the silence.

The next morning Selena asked Alia and the housekeeper to help her pack and move her things into Saber's apartment. The housekeeper spent the morning in grudging assistance. There seemed to be approval in her attitude, though, something Selena hadn't seen before.

Alia, on the other hand, was helpful but preoccupied.

"Is something bothering you, Alia?" Selena finally asked when they were alone.

Alia looked at her, then away. "No, nothing," she said quickly.

Too quickly. "If you need to talk I hope you'll consider me a willing listener and a friend."

"Yes, I will," said the young woman quietly. "But, I'm fine. Really."

Well, that's all I can do, Selena thought, studying the girl. She couldn't force Alia to share what was obviously a personal problem.

"There is something I would like to ask you," Alia blurted out fifteen minutes later, taking Selena by surprise.

Selena paused, a sweater in her hand. "Yes?"

"I've learned much from you about American women..." Her voice trailed off. "How would you, uh, do you think—" Her voice rose on a note of panic and she turned away again. "What do you think about the practice of arranged marriages?" she finally asked.

Oh, dear, thought Selena. Her cousin was definitely of marriageable age. She was hit suddenly with the suspicion that Alia's parents were pressuring her to marry someone she didn't like. Perhaps for a dowry—she knew that they lived very simply. "Are you speaking generally or from special interest?" she asked gently.

Alia shrugged. "I suppose I mean generally." She seemed to be holding her breath as she waited for Selena to answer.

Which really meant that Selena's suspicions were correct. "I wouldn't accept it for myself, of course," said Selena. "The idea of someone else making a lifetime commitment in my name, maybe to someone I couldn't like—" she shook her head "—I couldn't do it."

Alia turned back and for the first time Selena saw the tears. "It isn't that I don't like him. I haven't met him yet."

Selena's jaw dropped. "Your parents are arranging a marriage with a total stranger?" she demanded, aghast at the idea.

All at once Alia's chin lifted. "He's from a fine family. I am very lucky. And I am going to meet him tonight. He is coming to our house for dinner."

Now the girl seemed to be defending the practice. The unexpected turnaround surprised Selena even more. She searched her mind for the right thing to say. But before she could speak at all, the housekeeper reentered the room.

Alia shot her a warning, pleading glance that she could easily understand. The subject would have to be dropped for now.

Selena was grateful for the interruption; she had no idea what her response would have been.

By six-thirty that evening, Selena had moved everything into Saber's apartment and was settled. More or less. Living in such close quarters was going to be a challenge.

Selena and Saber met in the sitting room at seven-thirty. She was wary; he seemed distracted; neither of them referred to the parting kiss last night.

Selena accepted a drink and sat down, but he prowled the room like a restless lion. Perhaps this was not the time... they made small talk for a moment. Finally Selena could contain herself no longer. "Saber, something came up today. I want to talk to you about it." She set her glass aside.

"Certainly," he answered, giving her his attention.

She described her conversation with Alia. There was a determined gleam in her eye as she concluded, "I didn't realize that such an antiquated custom was still widely practiced. It's a good thing we were interrupted because I probably would have given advice that my uncle wouldn't appreciate one bit." Restlessly she stood and walked away from him. Then she spun back and settled her hands on her hips. "Saber, how am I to encourage women to take responsibility for their lives, or to participate in the election process, if they are denied participation in a basic decision like whom to marry?"

Selena didn't notice that Saber's expression had clouded at her words. He went to the window to cover his inner predicament. "I doubt that Alia would be denied participation, Selena," he said carefully. "Her father wouldn't make her marry someone she didn't care for."

Again Selena began to pace. "She doesn't even *know* the man, Saber. How can she care for a total stranger?"

He watched her move with the grace that was so much a part of her. "And if she did know him?" he asked quietly. "Would that make a difference?"

"Not really. Most young people are a lot smarter than their parents give them credit for being. They should be able to choose their lifetime partners, don't you think?"

"I think that arranged marriages are often very, very happy," he said.

She glanced up to see that his expression had taken on that somber look she hated. It suddenly dawned on her— Saber's first marriage was arranged. "I'm sorry, Saber. Forgive me, I shouldn't have raised the subject."

The seriousness changed to puzzlement. "Nonsense. Why shouldn't you? No subject is taboo."

"Your first marriage. I know how much you loved Lisha—" Still did, if the demeanor she'd witnessed when he stood at Lisha's grave was any indication.

"Yes, I loved her," said Saber, fighting off his own feelings of guilt. "But, Selena, I was twenty, Lisha was eighteen. We certainly weren't mature enough to make that kind of decision for ourselves."

Selena cursed herself for bringing up the subject, now, just as they were beginning to make some progress in their own relationship. "Well, I'm sure there must be exceptions to every rule," she told him, hoping to ameliorate her earlier harshness. She laughed softly and shrugged.

"But I would never forgive my father if he tried that on me again. Never."

A heavy silence descended on the room, a silence so profound that she could hear her own heartbeat. She realized that she'd made another mistake, but she couldn't, for the life of her, figure out what it was.

"Would you forgive the man?"

"Of course not, but the father is the major villain. A father should encourage his child to make the important decisions."

At last Saber gave a tired sigh. "Ah, Selena, I knew it would come to this someday." He looked at her, then raked his fingers through his hair and sighed again. "What if I told you, Selena, that Turnus and I did just that? Arranged this marriage?"

She swung to face him and stared, just stared, for a minute. Then she gave a nervous laugh. "I'd say you were teasing. Daddy wouldn't. Besides, you asked me yourself."

"Of course I did. But it's time you knew the truth, Selena. We promised each other honesty. I had worked out the details of our marriage with your father before I proposed to you. He knew I was thinking of marriage and he contacted me."

What was he saying? After last night...Selena had just begun to hope, to believe that he had some feelings for her... "No," she breathed. No, it couldn't be possible. Her father wouldn't have contacted Saber and offered her like a pig on a plate. Would he?

She searched Saber's features for a smile, a glimmer of amusement in his eyes, anything that would indicate he was not serious, that would refute his statement. But his expression was unreadable.

"You are serious, aren't you?" she whispered. God, she'd never known mere words could hurt so much. She put her fingers to her mouth; she felt tears gathering in her eyes and fought them back. "You lied to me."

"I am serious and, no, I haven't lied to you. I just didn't tell you all of the truth. My reasons for asking you to marry me were genuine. The only thing that you didn't know was that I had first arranged it with your father."

"And my conditions—you let me believe I was in charge of my destiny. While all the time it was a done deal. Tell me, Saber, was I one of a list of women you were considering?"

Saber winced. He couldn't let this go further. He caught her by the shoulders. "No, Selena. You're getting this all wrong. It was clear from the first that you were—*are*—the perfect wife for me. But if you had refused my proposal, neither your father nor I would have tried to push you. You made the decision yourself."

She could recall the scene clearly. He had made it all sound so appealing, the opportunity to help the women of Karastonia, the escape from an uncomfortable professional situation. Most appealing of all—she made herself face her true feelings, her real motives—was the chance to be married to a man she'd always been half in love with.

For when it came right down to it, she could have found another job, she could have helped the women, without resorting to marriage. She wanted to marry this man because she was in love with him. Maybe her feelings had all been subconscious, but they were finding the light of day now and she refused to deceive herself any longer.

So, what should she do about it? Could she compete with a dead woman for his affection? Would his feelings ever be as deep as hers? And could she live with him always knowing that she would never have his whole heart?

That a part of his love would always be held in reserve for someone else?

"So," said Saber tightly, thrusting his hands into the pockets of his trousers and rocking slightly on his heels. "Now that you know the truth, do you want to be released from your commitment?"

"Released? You mean divorce?" She was horrified.

Instead of answering her question, he eyed her strangely and said, "I can understand your frustration. I shouldn't have kept this from you."

"Would you have told me?" she asked. Curiously, her initial anger had faded but she was still confused and stung. And hurt, so hurt. Why?

He looked at her, his expression ambiguous, his gaze intense with some emotion she couldn't identify. "I just did," he answered.

"I mean—" She waved her hand helplessly through the air. She didn't know *what* she meant and she refused to be provoked into making a decision while she was in such an emotional turmoil. She forced laughter into her voice to hide the hurt there. "I can't believe this." Maybe later when she was calmer she could think the situation through more clearly.

He took a step toward her. "Selena—"

She stood her ground and lifted her chin. "Well, at least you didn't lie about your feelings, Saber. I accepted from the first that this wasn't to be a romantic relationship."

Instantly, she wished she could have called back the words. They sounded too much like a challenge. When he spoke again she realized that he had taken them as one.

"If you got that impression, I must not have made myself clear," he said with a dangerous glint in his eyes. "Perhaps I should demonstrate again." He didn't give her time to protest; he pulled her into his arms. His hands spread suggestively over the curve of her hips. "I want you, Selena. I've wanted you since the day I flew to Virginia."

She tried to hold herself aloof but the moment he touched her she felt the warmth begin to spread along her spine. Deliberately, he moved her against him and she felt him, hard and demanding. Already her body was betraying her, relaxing in places where it shouldn't. She caught her breath. "That isn't romance," she murmured, mesmerized by his dark gaze.

He gave a deep chuckle, a satisfied, purely masculine sound that competed with the heavy drumbeat of her pulse. "It isn't?" he asked softly, nipping at her ear. "Then why do you feel so right against me? Why does the sight of you make my heart pound?" His breath was hot against her throat. "Don't you feel it, too?"

As though in a dream, she was floating and the only thing to cling to was Nicholas. Her fingers tightened on his broad shoulders; she turned her face, unconsciously searching for his mouth. But her self-protective instincts weren't completely lost. "It's only sexual," she whispered to herself.

He went completely still; she could feel the sudden tension that knotted his muscles into immobility. Then something seemed to snap in him like a tightly strung wire. For a heart-stopping moment, she thought he would move away.

Instead, keeping one arm around her, he swept the other beneath her knees and picked her up as though she were a cloud of down. "Then we might as well enjoy the sex," he growled. He crossed the lighted area, proceeded down the hallway and stepped into the obsidian blackness of her bedroom. The heavy door, propelled by his kick, settled into its frame with a thump.

He set her on her feet and his voice came out of the dark. Not softly romantic, no, definitely not. But thick with passion and desire. "If you don't want this, Selena, you'd better stop me now."

She hadn't realized how shallow her breath had become until she tried to garner enough for speech. She couldn't manage the words to tell him that she had no intention of stopping him, that she wanted him as much as he wanted her.

So, instead, she reached out for him through the darkness. Her fingers encountered the fabric of his shirt. Speech wasn't necessary, she discovered, as she found the buttons and began to free them.

Long before they reached the big bed, their clothes had—somehow—melted away. In the darkness, with the softness of satin-covered down beneath them, his touch was sure. He knew exactly where to kiss her, where to tease her lightly with a stroke of his clever fingers, where and when to caress more firmly.

In minutes her body was damp and singing, ready for him. He filled her smoothly, his breath escaping on a soft moan of satisfaction as she lifted toward him, accepting, eager. The tension built, gathering excitement from their rhythmic movements, perfectly in tune. Selena held her breath, feeling the anticipation grow, expand, increase to the level of infinite pleasure.

And suddenly spill over into ecstasy.

He called her name, a hoarse cry, and joined her in paradise.

Selena sighed softly when he rolled to his side, taking her with him, his strong arms wrapped tightly around her, his lips against her temple. Beneath her cheek she could hear his powerful heartbeat. She didn't think she had ever felt so secure, so protected, so...loved.

Slowly their bodies cooled; slowly their breathing returned to normal. She didn't know how much time had passed, but she was taken by surprise when Saber reached out and touched the switch beside the bed. She blinked at the sudden brightness.

Saber swung his legs to the floor, stood and reached for his clothes.

"Saber...?" Surely he wasn't leaving.

He smiled slightly but he didn't meet her questioning gaze. He checked his watch. "I have to make a run out to the airport. There's another problem on the border and the security chief is flying in from the north for a quick meeting."

Was it just her imagination or did he seem glad for the excuse?

Damon, the security chief that Saber had gone to meet, had to speak to him twice.

Saber was recalled to the present. Damn. He couldn't seem to concentrate, couldn't get his mind off Selena. Beautiful, sensuous, passionate Selena. His wife. God, he'd never felt like this.

He shook himself mentally and focused his attention on the man who stood at his side. They had been talking for over an hour. The man was ready to leave; the plane was waiting. And nothing had been resolved. "Try to keep Bafla calm for another few days, Damon," he said finally, speaking of the man who owned the large area near the border. "He sincerely believes that the monarchy should have been retained. But he isn't a difficult man at heart or a troublemaker."

"I know, Saber. He just wants personal appeasement from the president himself."

"And I don't have time for that right now. As soon as the formal celebration is over I'll come north and talk to him again."

Damon nodded. "I'll tell him that. Goodbye, Saber." He boarded the waiting plane.

Saber was chauffeured back to the palace, his mind still more on his wife and their relationship than on the problems of the country. This was why he hadn't wanted anything to do with emotional bonds. He didn't *want* to fall in love.

He entered his quarters—*their* quarters now—and halted to look at the door leading to his wife's room. He'd learned quite a lesson earlier. His desire for her had become impossible to control. The memory of their lovemaking haunted him as he headed for his own room.

Chapter Nine

The guests began to arrive; the palace was crowded. With the Independence Day celebration bearing down on them, Saber had given Selena—at her request—a list of extra tasks she could help with. During the days they saw each other only in passing. They did talk each night, but there was so much to be done that their meetings were abbreviated. They spoke mostly of business matters.

Selena told herself she was relieved; she had followed his lead—to steer clear of personal matters for now. She would rather keep things on a casual level until after the pressures of the holiday celebrations had eased. Then she was going to insist that they settle things between them. And she had a lot to say.

At first she had been hurt and confused. Why had he left so abruptly? She wasn't normally a weepy person, but tears often threatened to spill. She made sure they did so out of sight of anyone. When her confusion had cleared a bit, she realized that he'd been as overwhelmed as she by the force of their lovemaking. Her hurt turned to perplexity. She stopped crying and started thinking.

The formal schedule for the capital city was spread across her desk. She and Alia had been working since early morning.

The schedule had been approved months ago, but there were a number of regional committees that had decided to organize local celebrations, as well. They wanted guidelines to insure that their festivities would be in keeping with the rest of the country. What they really wanted was reassurance, thought Selena, and that was easy enough to provide. With each letter, she intended to enclose a copy of her own ideas for encouraging women to register to vote.

At eleven-thirty she yawned and told Alia that she thought she'd leave for an early lunch. "These letters are ready to be typed. I'll be back in time to sign them so we can get them in the afternoon's mail."

Saber was in their apartment, packing hurriedly. He called out to her to come and help.

"Thank you," he said when she took the shirt he'd been folding and made a neat package out of it. While they worked he explained that he had been called to the border on a mission that couldn't be postponed.

She knew that Saber had planned to visit there after the holiday. The same large landholder on the northern border who had given him trouble in the past had been stirring again, he explained. "Bafla is threatening voluntary annexation to a neighboring country. He's been a problem since the democratization process began. If I allow him to, he will lead others in the move. I realize it's the worst possible time, but I have to go. Do you think you can—"

She interrupted. "Don't worry about things here. I'll manage."

Saber stopped what he was doing and took her by the shoulders. "Thank you," he said again. He smiled, a tender smile. The last time she'd seen him smile that way was the night... She took a step into his arms. He bent his head but before his lips reached hers there was a discreet cough from the doorway.

The housekeeper apologized and grinned—the woman actually grinned. "Excuse me. Your driver is here. He says the car is ready, sir," she said.

Saber tightened his arms about Selena. "I'll be gone for one, possibly two nights. I'll call you." He kissed her then, but the kiss ended too quickly. Selena watched him go. When he was away the time passed slowly.

After a solitary lunch, she went into the bedroom to rest for a few minutes. She was so tired lately, she thought, with some surprise. She was rarely tired. "I hope I'm not coming down with something," she murmured to herself as she drifted off to sleep.

When the telephone rang three hours later she awoke disoriented and groggy. It was Alia, calling from her office downstairs to ask if Selena wanted her to bring the letters to her to be signed.

"No, no." She scraped her hair away from her face and looked at the clock in astonishment. She couldn't believe she'd slept so long. "I'll be down in a few minutes."

The deep sleep in the middle of the day scared her a bit. It was so unlike her. Again she wondered if there was flu going around.

Saber hadn't called; it was nearly nine. When the phone finally rang, Selena snatched up the receiver. "Hi," she said breathlessly.

There was a brief pause, and then amusement in his voice when he spoke. "Hi, yourself. You must have been sitting right beside the telephone."

She didn't want to give the impression she'd been living to hear the sound of his voice, but she had. It was difficult to sound blasé when her heart was spinning in her chest.

"I'm sorry to be late calling. Hold on a minute." He put his hand over the receiver. She could hear his muffled tones but not what he was saying. When he came back on the line he sounded impatient. "Selena?"

"I'm still here. How are things going?" she asked.

"Bafla, the man I came to see, has gone out of town." She could hear the anger in his voice.

"After you traveled all that way?" Selena said, her voice rising. She was angry, too, on his behalf. "That's rude."

He chuckled again. "You're damned right. The explanation is that he was called away to deal with an emergency, but clearly he's decided to avoid a face-to-face meeting. I should be home tomorrow but I'll have to come back here next week."

"So it was a wasted trip. I'm sorry."

"I am, too. Anyway, I'll see you tomorrow. Good night, Selena."

Selena's parents had called that morning to congratulate Saber. They were unable to get to Karastonia for the celebrations. Selena would have been more disappointed if she hadn't hoped to see them soon.

She had a few things to say to Turnus, not that it would do any good.

"Saber, as soon as the holiday is over, I would like to go home for a visit. I'll probably leave day after tomorrow. Do you mind?" she asked.

They were having breakfast together. The ceremonies commemorating the Independence Day festivities were to be held this afternoon.

He had been out late last night again, meeting with a trade representative from the United States. She didn't know what time he'd returned last night, but this morning she was foolishly glad to be able to have breakfast with him.

Slowly he set down his coffee cup and looked at her. There was an odd expression on his face. He stared fixedly, until she squirmed slightly.

"If the timing isn't convenient for you, Saber, I can wait a week or so."

"But you will go?"

"Yes, of course," she said, surprised. She couldn't imagine what his problem was. She smiled, deciding that this was an appropriate time to share her suspicion. "I need to—"

"And do you plan to return?" he questioned bluntly.

She hesitated. The harshness of the interruption saddened her, especially in light of what she'd been about to tell him. Her feelings were hurt, but she'd be damned if she let him see. "I thought I would," she said coolly. Distress was churning inside. "Why? Would you rather I didn't?"

He tossed his napkin down and stood. "Don't be ridiculous, Selena."

"Ridiculous? Thanks a lot, Saber." She would have said more but he turned on his way out the door to glare at her.

"I'll see you at the parade," he said, and left.

These little episodes were growing more and more frequent. She was still muttering to herself when she entered her office a few minutes later. The first thing she noticed was a huge bouquet of flowers on Alia's desk. The second was the dreamy look in the young woman's eyes.

Selena shook her head, smiling at the fickle heart. Antonio must be something indeed. She and Alia had been too busy in the office for the past few days to talk much about the man Alia's parents had selected for their daughter. But she'd heard enough to realize that Antonio was the kindest, most handsome, intelligent man in the land. Clearly theirs was one arranged marriage that might work out.

Absently, Saber answered the woman on his left, but seconds later he couldn't have repeated her question. Selena, at his right, totally occupied his mind.

She wanted to go home, she'd said. *Home.* He'd hoped that by now she could have begun to think of Karastonia as her home. Clearly she didn't.

When she'd introduced the subject this morning, the room had tilted on its axis, the atmosphere had become charged—from his point of view, at least. But his wife was blithely unaware that his whole world had changed in the blink of an eye. He loved her. And the thought of her leaving was like a stone in his chest.

God, what a fool he'd been! He'd assumed he could bring this strong, vital woman here and *not* fall in love with her—no matter how hard he fought it.

It had been extremely difficult for him to hide his reaction to her request. He didn't want her to go. It was as simple as that. Only his pride had kept him from begging her not to.

Once she said that she would return, he was appeased, but only slightly. She could very well get back to the States and decide to stay. And there wouldn't be a damned thing he could do about it.

He'd forced an indifferent smile as he'd agreed to her trip. But she would never know what the detachment had cost him. Her request—hell, it wasn't a request, it was an announcement—had festered inside of him all morning long like a sore place that refused to heal.

He realized unexpectedly that he was tired. He accepted the salutes, returned the smiles, tried to muster enthusiasm for the celebrations, but he found it difficult.

A place of his own, an uncomplicated, settled—but still productive—life-style. He'd never had such things. Never thought he needed them. Until Selena.

He was not going to run for president again. He'd made that decision a few days ago. He'd do what was expected of him for the time left in his term, and, if they wanted him, he would stay active in a consulting capacity. But that was it.

His parents would be horrified if they had lived to see this. But he knew now that he didn't want the cool, respectful kind of relationship they'd had. He wanted to be able to talk to his wife when he felt the urge, not just for one hour every night. He wanted a real marriage and he intended to have it.

If she came back, reminded a small voice in the back of his mind. The subconscious suggestion annoyed him.

As she looked out over the crowd, Selena smiled to herself. Except for the colors and design of the flag, she might have been attending a Fourth of July celebration in small-town America, complete with bands and banners, songs and sunshine, food and frolic.

Of course, in small-town America she would not be sitting beside her husband in the reviewing stand, watching the parade as first lady of the land. She would be happy to be just where she was if Saber's disposition weren't so mercurial. She had suddenly thought. Maybe he didn't *want* her to come back.

An aide approached her husband and whispered in his ear. She saw a dark expression cloud his features, and she wondered what had happened now. In a low voice he gave instructions to the man, who then nodded and disappeared into the crowd.

Daylight was fading when the last band marched past. Saber escorted her from the box toward the limousine for the short ride back to the palace. They moved unhurriedly through the crowd, speaking to various people.

To look at Saber, none of the people around would know that anything was wrong. But Selena realized that he'd had bad news.

The tension was palpable in the limousine, especially when she noticed his suitcase on the seat beside the driver. "You're leaving right now?"

He nodded. "As soon as I drop you off, I have to go back to the border. I'm sorry I'll have to skip our talk tonight, Selena."

"We have guests coming for dinner, Saber," she said, unable to believe that whatever it was couldn't wait until the morning. Or…maybe he wanted to go, maybe this was an excuse to get away from her. How much business could you accomplish at night, she wondered bitterly.

"Damn it, Selena, I thought you'd understand. You'll have to handle this on your own. I can't socialize when a corner of the country may be breaking off."

She was being unreasonable, she knew, but her disappointment was great. She'd wanted to tell him then, on that important day, on the first anniversary of the birth of the country's democracy, that she thought she was pregnant with their child.

After the chilly conversation at breakfast, she'd steeled herself to wait until evening. And now he was telling her that he had to leave. "How long will you be gone?" she asked stiffly.

"I don't know. I'll call you tomorrow night at the same time."

The limousine came to a smooth halt at the door to the palace. "If I'm still here," she said as the chauffeur opened the door and helped her out.

Like a shot, Saber was out of the car after her. He grabbed her arm and spun her to face him. "It isn't my choice to leave tonight, Selena," he said through gritted teeth.

The driver stood at attention holding the door. Selena felt sorry for the poor man, obviously trying very hard to be invisible.

"I thought you'd be more understanding," he accused, straining to keep his voice low.

"I do understand," she answered woodenly. Then she relented slightly. "I'll be here tomorrow night. Have a safe trip."

He dropped her arm and she started up the steps. She didn't watch the limousine pull away.

The next night at nine o'clock Selena sat beside the telephone, waiting for it, willing it, to ring. She could not believe that Saber was doing this to her.

She glanced at the clock again an hour later and wondered desperately if this marriage had a chance. Was he really that angry? She'd simply said she wanted to go to

Virginia for a few day. How could he accuse her of not planning to come back?

And the progress she'd made here. Did he think that was unimportant to her?

They had a lot to talk about. Damn it, why didn't he call?

Nicholas raked his fingers through his hair, which was already standing on end. He hadn't slept in forty-four hours. His eyes were red-rimmed and swollen.

"What the hell is the matter with them?" he demanded, indicating the bank of telephones on the desk. "I *have* to get through. I have an extremely important call to make." He glanced at his watch, though he knew exactly what it read. He was four and a half hours late in calling Selena. She'd said she would be there tonight, but he'd be willing to wager that if he didn't call, she'd be on the first plane out tomorrow morning.

He was beginning to know his wife, to sense her vulnerabilities; she would think he didn't want to say goodbye and that would hurt her. "Right now."

"But, sir, the telephone lines are down because of the mud slide. There is no other way to call."

He looked at his watch again. Twelve-thirty. If he got through right now, she would be asleep, but he'd damn well have someone wake her up.

She would think he'd done this deliberately. After their argument, the things they'd said to each other, she couldn't believe otherwise.

And the first plane left at dawn. He looked at his watch for the third time. "Let's go," he said to his aide. "If we can't get the damned phones to work, I've got to get back to the capital."

"But, sir, the airports are closed because of the weather."

The weather. *Will you understand, Selena? Will you realize that the "every night at eight" pact is at the mercy of the elements?*

"We'll drive," he told his aide.

"But, sir—"

Saber whirled on the man and froze him with a steely eye. "Look, Marcus, lay out all your objections at once. Spit them out. Because if you say 'but, sir' to me one more time, I am going to fire you. Do you understand?"

The man gulped and nodded.

"Now, get me a car. One with four-wheeled drive. We may have to work our way around some mud, but we're going home. Tonight."

Selena folded her jacket away in the overhead compartment and smoothed her skirt as she sat down in the first-class section of the airplane. She smiled at the flight attendant, who, with some surprise, had welcomed her aboard.

The reporter waiting at the entrance to the airport hadn't been surprised, she thought as she fastened her seat belt. She'd wondered who had informed him about her departure. She'd also had to deal with the man's questions—where was she going, why was she flying commercial, when would she be back—before she could make her way to the plane.

The hatch was sealed; the attendants took seats and buckled themselves in.

Selena laid her head against the seatback and waited for the sound of the engines to rev up in preparation for takeoff. Her eyes closed and immediately an image of Saber appeared behind her lids. The resolute decision she'd made last night to take the first flight out this morning didn't seem like such a good idea at the moment.

He'd known she was leaving. If he'd only called to say goodbye. She didn't want to tell him about the baby over the telephone, but she might have done so, anyway. Would it have made a difference? She would like to think so. She would like to think he'd be thrilled. As thrilled as she was.

Suddenly she sat up, filled with anxiety. What if something had happened to him? Oh, God.

The noise of the engines swelled to fill the cabin. She fumbled with her seat belt. She had to get back to the palace. Now.

The attendant noticed what Selena was doing and shook her head frantically.

"I have to get off," Selena mouthed over the cabin noise. The woman's jaw dropped, but she recovered quickly and reached for the telephone on the wall beside her.

In minutes the roar subsided. Selena felt a surge of relief as the buckle finally popped open. The other passengers were looking at each other. She grabbed her carryon bag and stood.

The flight attendant spoke into her phone again, glanced at Selena, said something else and hung up. She met Selena at the hatch.

"I'm awfully sorry to inconvenience you. Please..." She gestured helplessly to the other people. "I apologize, but it's very important."

The woman looked puzzled but she didn't hesitate. "Yes, ma'am," she said. "You forgot your jacket."

The copilot had come from the flight deck to open the hatch. The other passengers watched with curious interest.

Selena could see the stairs being rolled forward as she took her jacket from the young woman. "Thank you." She looked out into the sunshine, anxiously impatient.

And then all words were stolen from her.

Saber looked grim. His hair was disheveled, his shirt and trousers were rumpled and his tie askew. He took the rolling stairs two at a time; before they even reached the plane he was at the top. She stepped out to join him. "Saber, what on earth—"

He gripped her arm. She could feel the tension in his fingers. "Selena—" He broke off and looked around in frustration. The flight crew stood a scant three feet away. At the bottom of the steps she could see two airport guards, and more reporters. A mud-splattered Range Rover was parked at an angle to the tarmac and Saber's aide waited by the open door.

A strong gust of wind picked up his tie and flung it over his shoulder. "Selena—" he said again.

One of the reporters put his foot on the first step and the move set off a strong resolve in Selena. She shook off the air of bewilderment that had slowed her reflexes.

She put a smile on her lips and turned to the flight crew. "Something has come up that necessitates my postponing my trip." She held out her hand to the pilot. He took it. Without haste she shook hands with the rest of the crew, calling them by name. "Thank you very much for your kindness," she said and smiled at Saber. "Shall we go?"

The reckless gleam in Saber's eye sent her heart up into her throat and almost brought her to a halt, but she met it with a warm smile. He smiled, too. His smile didn't, however, quiet the mounting dread that her husband might deck one of the reporters if any one of them tried to interfere. She disengaged her arm from Saber's grip and switched positions so that her hand was now in the crook of his arm. From there, if he needed it, she could give him a warning pinch.

But they managed to get past the reporters with a non-committal word or two. At last they reached the Rover. She wondered where the vehicle had come from. It certainly wasn't Saber's normal mode of transportation. It didn't have the tinted windows of his limousine, either, so she and Saber had to maintain polite expressions until they reached the outer perimeter of the airport. But, on the seat between them, he held her hand in a tight grip.

She started to speak, but he stopped her with a warning glance at his aide. She settled back in the seat. It wasn't a long drive to the palace, but they sailed right past the gates.

She turned her head to look back. "Where are we going?" she asked, worried now.

He squeezed her fingers. His smile was strained. "It's a surprise."

A surprise? She lifted a brow. Surprises weren't Saber's forte. What was going on?

At last they pulled off the highway and began to climb a hill. The car stopped in the courtyard of what appeared to be a private residence. He helped her out of the car and took a key from his pocket. "Come back in an hour," he told the aide, and didn't wait for an answer.

He opened the door and turned to look at her. "Come in," he invited.

The entrance hall was dim. Saber flipped on a light and led the way into a living room.

Suddenly she was overwhelmed. The house was completely empty. She swung to face him, a dawning smile illuminating her face. "Saber, is this what I think it is?"

At the sight of her smile, he relaxed a fraction. He draped an arm over her shoulders and guided her to the wall of glass overlooking the sea. "And what are you thinking, wife?"

Her voice dropped to a hopeful whisper. "Is this ours?" she asked, expectant, but unable to believe in the dream until he actually said it was so.

He framed her face with his large hands. "It is ours if you agree. Selena, I've never felt so frustrated in my life as I did last night at eight o'clock. The telephone lines were knocked down by the same mud slide that blocked the main road. And the airport was closed in by fog."

She listened openmouthed, watched his face—so open to her now—with growing wonder, able to feel the frustration he'd felt, able to experience his anxiety. She started to speak.

"No, let me finish. I couldn't talk with you. I had no way to reach you or communicate with you. Or touch you." He did that now, his fingers moving a strand of her hair aside, lingering to caress her cheek. He looked at her, not making any effort to hide his love, to control the emotion or the moisture in his eyes. "I thought it would kill me," he murmured. "I love you, Selena.

"I know that I've seemed detached but I no longer want to be that way. I cannot stand the physical isolation from you, either. I love you more than I thought it was possible to love anyone. I want you, not only in my apartment, or a house, but in my bedroom. And if you don't want that, too, I'll have the driver turn right around and take you back to the airport. I don't mean I'll let you go, because I'll never do that. But you can go to your parents' home. I'll continue to call every night at eight but I'm warning you the first time I hear any weakening in your voice, I'll come to get you immediately.''

She raised her hand to his face and let all the love she felt for this difficult man shine through her eyes. ''Saber, I love you, too. Our pact to be together every night at eight was symbolic, don't you see? I'm sorry you couldn't get through last night, but I wasn't testing your commitment.''

''Then why are you going home? Why are you leaving me?'' he demanded harshly.

The harshness was born of grief, she saw. ''Because I have an appointment, a special appointment.'' She smiled so he wouldn't misunderstand. ''With a man who specializes in taking care of older pregnant women. But I can wait to leave until tomorrow.''

''You're going to have a baby?'' he said softly. His eyes narrowed as the knowledge made its impact. He looked suddenly as though he found it hard to breathe.

''Not just me. Us.'' She grinned. ''And I hope you're happy, Nicholas. Because I'm ecstatic.''

He began to smile, the worry and the tension melting from his face. The expression of relief brought tears to her own eyes. Finally he folded her in his arms against his broad chest. She could hear his heart racing. He stroked her hair and murmured her name. She snuggled closer and was just getting comfortable, when he raised his head.

He was frowning. ''You are going to see a specialist? What's wrong? Are you having problems? Because I'd love a child, Selena, but I won't take a chance with your health.''

She spent the next hour reassuring him as they toured their new home. They paused at the front door on their way out.

"I'm not jealous anymore."

What an odd thing to say, thought Nicholas. "Jealous? Of who or what?"

"Of Lisha," Selena admitted. She'd never told him this before. "I was horribly jealous of her at first. Everyone adored her."

He caught her close to his side. "Ah, Selena. You never had a reason to be jealous. Lisha was my wife and I loved her," he said. "But you are my wife now and I love you, because you will always walk beside me, not behind me."

When they finally returned to the palace, Saber was immediately swamped by members of his staff. The questions began as soon as they entered the building.

He gave her an apologetic smile. She stood on tiptoe and kissed his cheek. "See you at eight," she whispered and disentangled her fingers from his grip. Her smile held the promise that tonight, during their private hour, they would not do a lot of talking.

As she mounted the stairs to their apartment, she felt his eyes on her back. She heard him say that the situation at the border had been resolved.

The situation between them had been resolved, as well.

She would be waiting for him tonight at eight o'clock and every night for the rest of their lives.

Epilogue

Saber collapsed into a chair that someone had thoughtfully pushed behind him. "A girl," he said weakly.

"A girl," the beaming nurse confirmed as she lifted his daughter up for his inspection. He held Selena's hand as he'd been holding it for the past six hours. In reality, though, she had sailed through labor with very little help from anyone.

"She's beautiful, isn't she?" said his wife a short while later, her eyes drooping slightly with weariness.

"She's perfect."

A girl, he thought in growing wonder. Like her mother—only beautiful, independent, intelligent. Everything a woman should be.

Saber leaned down to kiss his wife with all the tenderness and love he'd learned from her over the past seven months.

Selena had passed the competency test insisted on by the university, with flying colors. And when classes began last fall, her course in government, focused toward women, had begun, too.

She had been nervous, afraid that no one would sign up. Ever concerned, she'd wanted reassurance that she was, indeed, making a difference in the young democracy. After that week of registration, she never asked for reassurance again.

Her class was mobbed, and the university asked if she would consider teaching full-time. She was still thinking that over. With a new baby and a new house, her days would be full. And her nights were reserved for Saber.

"I'm very proud of both of you," he murmured.

"Saber? I asked you if you still like the idea of naming her for my mother."

He smiled. Turnus would be thrilled. "Yes, I like Janie."

She laughed softly. "You were a million miles away."

"No, just twenty years or so," he mused.

"What were you thinking?"

"What a fine marriage we'll arrange for this one." His grin was devilish. "I already have someone in mind."

He ducked to avoid the flying pillow.

* * * * *

FAST CASH 4031 DRAW RULES
NO PURCHASE OR OBLIGATION NECESSARY

Fifty prizes of $50 each will be awarded in random drawings to be conducted no later than 3/28/97 from amongst all eligible responses to this prize offer received as of 2/14/97. To enter, follow directions, affix 1st-class postage and mail OR write Fast Cash 4031 on a 3" x 5" card along with your name and address and mail that card to: Harlequin's Fast Cash 4031 Draw, P.O. Box 1395, Buffalo, NY 14240-1395 OR P.O. Box 618, Fort Erie, Ontario L2A 5X3. (Limit: one entry per outer envelope; all entries must be sent via 1st-class mail.) Limit: one prize per household. Odds of winning are determined by the number of eligible responses received. Offer is open only to residents of the U.S. (except Puerto Rico) and Canada and is void wherever prohibited by law. All applicable laws and regulations apply. Any litigation within the province of Quebec respecting the conduct and awarding of a prize in this sweepstakes maybe submitted to the Régie des alcools, des courses et des jeux. In order for a Canadian resident to win a prize, that person will be required to correctly answer a time-limited arithmetical skill-testing question to be administered by mail. Names of winners available after 4/28/97 by sending a self-addressed, stamped envelope to: Fast Cash 4031 Draw Winners, P.O. Box 4200, Blair, NE 68009-4200.

OFFICIAL RULES
MILLION DOLLAR SWEEPSTAKES
NO PURCHASE NECESSARY TO ENTER

1. To enter, follow the directions published. Method of entry may vary. For eligibility, entries must be received no later than March 31, 1998. No liability is assumed for printing errors, lost, late, non-delivered or misdirected entries.
    To determine winners, the sweepstakes numbers assigned to submitted entries will be compared against a list of randomly pre-selected prize winning numbers. In the event all prizes are not claimed via the return of prize winning numbers, random drawings will be held from among all other entries received to award unclaimed prizes.

2. Prize winners will be determined no later than June 30, 1998. Selection of winning numbers and random drawings are under the supervision of D. L. Blair, Inc., an independent judging organization whose decisions are final. Limit: one prize to a family or organization. No substitution will be made for any prize, except as offered. Taxes and duties on all prizes are the sole responsibility of winners. Winners will be notified by mail. Odds of winning are determined by the number of eligible entries distributed and received.

3. Sweepstakes open to residents of the U.S. (except Puerto Rico), Canada and Europe who are 18 years of age or older, except employees and immediate family members of Torstar Corp., D. L. Blair, Inc., their affiliates, subsidiaries, and all other agencies, entities, and persons connected with the use, marketing or conduct of this sweepstakes. All applicable laws and regulations apply. Sweepstakes offer void wherever prohibited by law. Any litigation within the province of Quebec respecting the conduct and awarding of a prize in this sweepstakes must be submitted to the Régie des alcools, des courses et des jeux. In order to win a prize, residents of Canada will be required to correctly answer a time-limited arithmetical skill-testing question to be administered by mail.

4. Winners of major prizes (Grand through Fourth) will be obligated to sign and return an Affidavit of Eligibility and Release of Liability within 30 days of notification. In the event of non-compliance within this time period or if a prize is returned as undeliverable, D. L. Blair, Inc. may at its sole discretion award that prize to an alternate winner. By acceptance of their prize, winners consent to use of their names, photographs or other likeness for purposes of advertising, trade and promotion on behalf of Torstar Corp., its affiliates and subsidiaries, without further compensation unless prohibited by law. Torstar Corp. and D. L. Blair, Inc., their affiliates and subsidiaries are not responsible for errors in printing of sweepstakes and prizewinning numbers. In the event a duplication of a prizewinning number occurs, a random drawing will be held from among all entries received with that prizewinning number to award that prize.

SWP-S12ZD1

5. This sweepstakes is presented by Torstar Corp., its subsidiaries and affiliates in conjunction with book, merchandise and/or product offerings. The number of prizes to be awarded and their value are as follows: Grand Prize — $1,000,000 (payable at $33,333.33 a year for 30 years); First Prize — $50,000; Second Prize — $10,000; Third Prize — $5,000; 3 Fourth Prizes — $1,000 each; 10 Fifth Prizes — $250 each; 1,000 Sixth Prizes — $10 each. Values of all prizes are in U.S. currency. Prizes in each level will be presented in different creative executions, including various currencies, vehicles, merchandise and travel. Any presentation of a prize level in a currency other than U.S. currency represents an approximate equivalent to the U.S. currency prize for that level, at that time. Prize winners will have the opportunity of selecting any prize offered for that level; however, the actual non U.S. currency equivalent prize, if offered and selected, shall be awarded at the exchange rate existing at 3:00 P.M. New York time on March 31, 1998. A travel prize option, if offered and selected by winner, must be completed within 12 months of selection and is subject to: traveling companion(s) completing and returning a Release of Liability prior to travel; and hotel and flight accommodations availability. For a current list of all prize options offered within prize levels, send a self-addressed, stamped envelope (WA residents need not affix postage) to: MILLION DOLLAR SWEEPSTAKES Prize Options, P.O. Box 4456, Blair, NE 68009-4456, USA.

6. For a list of prize winners (available after July 31, 1998) send a separate, stamped, self-addressed envelope to: MILLION DOLLAR SWEEPSTAKES Winners, P.O. Box 4459, Blair, NE 68009-4459, USA.

EXTRA BONUS PRIZE DRAWING
NO PURCHASE OR OBLIGATION NECESSARY TO ENTER

7. The Extra Bonus Prize will be awarded in a random drawing to be conducted no later than 5/30/98 from among all entries received. To qualify, entries must be received by 3/31/98 and comply with published directions. Prize ($50,000) is valued in U.S. currency. Prize will be presented in different creative expressions, including various currencies, vehicles, merchandise and travel. Any presentation in a currency other than U.S. currency represents an approximate equivalent to the U.S. currency value at that time. Prize winner will have the opportunity of selecting any prize offered in any presentation of the Extra Bonus Prize Drawing; however, the actual non U.S. currency equivalent prize, if offered and selected by winner, shall be awarded at the exchange rate existing at 3:00 P.M. New York time on March 31, 1998. For a current list of prize options offered, send a self-addressed, stamped envelope (WA residents need not affix postage) to: Extra Bonus Prize Options, P.O. Box 4462, Blair, NE 68009-4462, USA. All eligibility requirements and restrictions of the MILLION DOLLAR SWEEPSTAKES apply. Odds of winning are dependent upon number of eligible entries received. No substitution for prize except as offered. For the name of winner (available after 7/31/98), send a self-addressed, stamped envelope to: Extra Bonus Prize Winner, P.O. Box 4463, Blair, NE 68009-4463, USA.

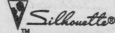

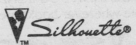